CHASING EVE

A Novel

by

Sharon Heath

Author Photograph by Marcella Kerwin
Cover Art by Holly Heath
"Amazing Grace," John Newton, 1779 (Public Domain)
"Love Lifted Me," James Rowe and Howard E. Smith, 1912 (Public Domain)
"That's All Right Mama" by Arthur "Big Boy" Crudup, 1946 (Public Domain)
Walt Whitman, To You, 1856 (Public Domain)

Library of Congress Control Number: 2019919143
1. Contemporary fiction 2. Literary fiction
ISBN 10: 1-950750-28-0
ISBN 13: 978-1-950750-28-3
Thomas-Jacob Publishing, LLC, Deltona, Florida USA

Contact the publisher at TJPub@thomas-jacobpublishing.com.

You have not known what you are, you have slumber'd upon yourself all your life,
Your eyelids have been the same as closed...
Walt Whitman, *To You*

Love lifted me, love lifted me
When nothing else could help, love lifted me...
James Rowe and Howard E. Smith, *Love Lifted Me*

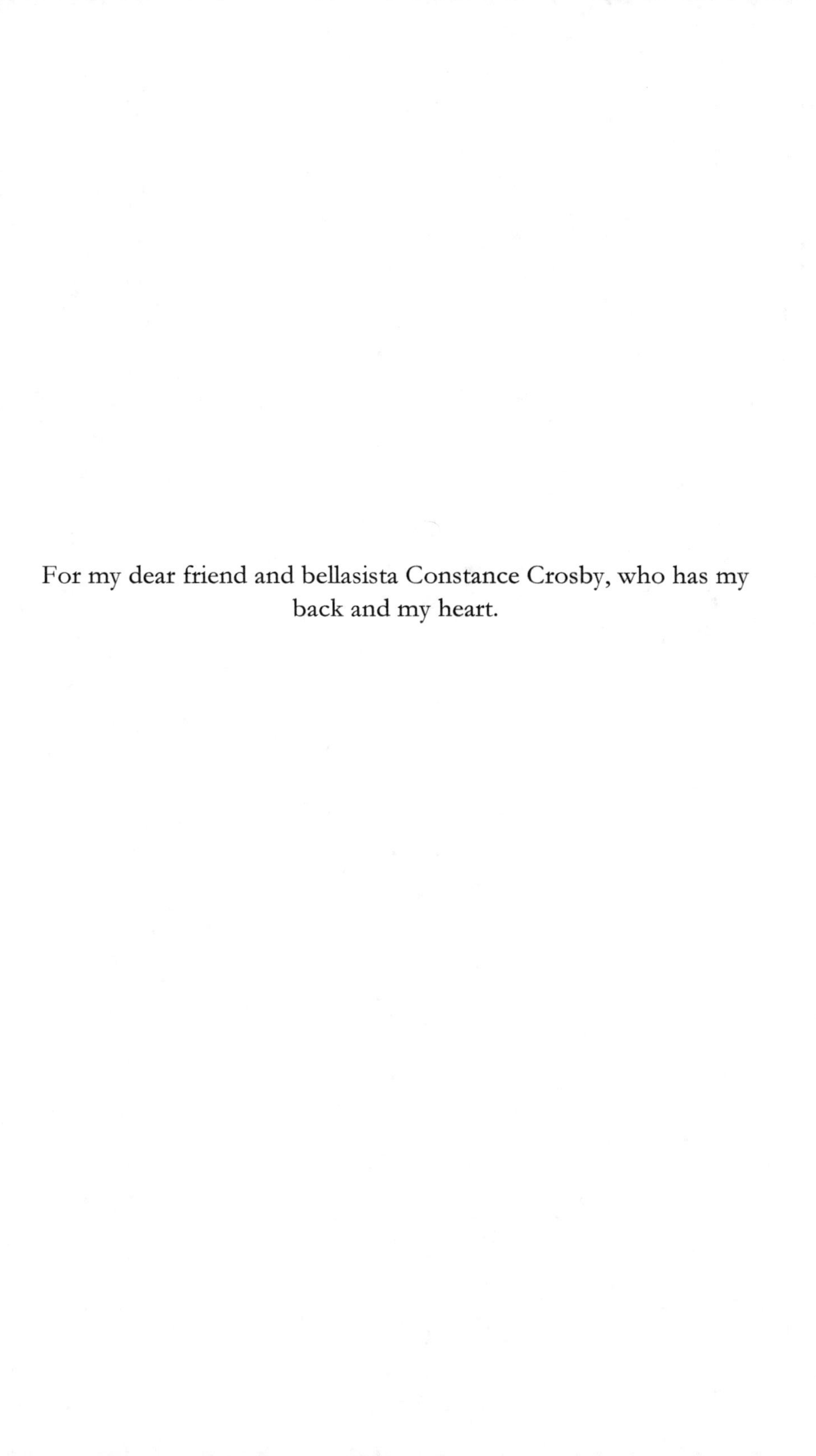

For my dear friend and bellasista Constance Crosby, who has my back and my heart.

Prologue

THE DREAM WAS always the same, announcing itself first only with sound. Crushing, nerve-stripping sound. The blast and roar of it was all the more terrifying since it was accompanied by a darkness so absolute that she felt blinder than her cat Jezebel, trapped in a world absent the dimension of vision, absent of light.

Inevitably, the blackness yielded to patches of misty irradiation, like the pale tinting of lacework that announces the end of a migraine. These mysterious visual hintings resolved themselves into streaky clouds whose ephemeral forms whooshed from front to periphery, suggesting she was in motion, propelled at great speed.

Fight or flight, a voice seemed to say. Her eyes traveled from her bare lap to her fingers, white and nervous, frantically twisting the knobs of an instrument panel. The unbearably meaningless wall of sound resolved itself into the strivings of an engine, and comprehension dawned suddenly as she felt her head craning, her eyes squinting at the panoramic window of the plane she was flying, unable to penetrate past the clouds that would not get out of her way.

Her terror was absolute. This plane would crash, or something would crash into her, if she could not manage to see.

One

ARIEL THOMPKINS WAS dying for a change. She just hadn't gotten around to admitting it yet. At seven a.m. that particular spring morning, she was aware only of emerging from one nightmare into another as she took a flying dive off her bed onto her dust-bunny-carpeted floor. Her hasty descent was unintentional. Slamming her hand against her retro clock radio wasn't. Anything to silence some troglodyte shock jock's self-congratulatory laughter at a crude play on words involving a particular part of the female anatomy.

From her undignified pose, cheek to floor, she eyed the evidence of last night's lapse of judgment. Just inches from her nose, an almost-empty bottle of Merlot stared back at her. An anarchy of dripped burgundy swirls and greasy smudges from a Grubhub-delivered Fatburger blurred the wine label into the shape of a giant winking eye. She looked away, but took its insinuation to heart as her chest burned with acid.

Last night had been a mistake. The Fatburger was an all-too-frequent indulgence, but she hardly ever drank. Certainly not this much. And never alone. Not a good sign, she knew. But she'd been unusually bored last evening, nothing worth watching on TV, wary of web-generated ennui, and too wiped out to venture into the night to Starbucks or Book Soup. The word she was avoiding threatened to burst in on her, but she held the door fast. A single young woman who allowed herself to acknowledge the depth of her loneliness might just as well put out a welcome mat for its inevitable hangers on: self-pity and despair.

Pivoting her head to the right, she met Jezebel's cataract-clouded eyes. Her own wild lunge at the radio had obviously catapulted the cat out of bed. Ariel had a vague recollection of her twitching fingers tapping Jezzie's silky white belly—as if the otherwise pitch-black cat were the instrument panel in her recurring airplane nightmare—until that crude voice had broken in like the hijacker from hell.

She sat up, gingerly exploring what felt like a bruise on her cheek, and put her face right up to Jezebel's nose. "You little stinker. I'll bet it was you brushing against the radio last night that changed the station. Honestly, some of these creeps are even worse than Howard Stern." The cat blinked back at her.

Ariel lifted Jezebel to her shoulder and scrambled back into bed with her, reclaiming the still-warm spot bearing the impression of their two bodies. "I forgive you," she whispered, planting a delicate kiss on the cat's nose. She slipped in and out of a delicious half-sleep until the insult of someone's car alarm broke through.

Half an hour later, she was altogether unaware of the intriguing picture she presented, her elbow resting on her small kitchen table, her chin propped up by her palm as she leaned intently over a spread-eagled copy of the *Los Angeles Times*. Her loose, light brown ringlets cascaded across the page, while her still unshaven, strong and shapely legs pretzeled themselves into a nearly perfect figure eight. A small article captioned "'First Eve Bones Discovered in Africa?" caught her attention. As the smoky halo of the day's first cigarette lofted over her head, she unhooked her left foot and excitedly wiggled her toes within their cozy white gym socks as a child might do while Jezebel crunched away at her dried Friskies with the gusto of a much younger cat.

"You know, I almost named *you* Eve."

No response, not even a slight twitch of her ears. Ariel laughed ruefully. "You're right. That did *not* dignify a response. Only crazy people talk to their animals."

She picked up the newspaper again. Jezebel took a moment to stretch her ebony limbs before launching into a full-out self-cleaning campaign. The kitchen faucet offered its own punctuation to the cat's wet licking sounds in the form of a steady drip into the bottom-burned pot that had recently simmered up Ariel's soft-boiled eggs. Ariel glanced at the counter, where haphazard piles of dishes and a tower of opened cartons of frozen dinners offered evidence of a week's worth of solitary meals. She averted her eyes and returned to the article.

> "New genetic evidence supports the claim that all modern humans are descended from a single woman who lived in southern Africa 140,000 years ago, a woman who has become known as the Mitochondrial Eve or 'the mother of us all.' That finding does not mean that only one woman was alive then, but that all other women's lineages eventually died out. Descendants of that woman began migrating out of Africa 75,000 years ago.
>
> A UCLA researcher announced today that the anthropology department has taken particular interest in the recent discovery in Ethiopia of a 140,000-year-old, nearly intact human skeleton, dubbed 'Eve' by her finders since her age approximates that of the Mitochondrial Eve. 'The fossil is of a young woman, but the teeth are worn right down to the gums,' said the researcher. 'This appears to be the oldest human specimen yet found.'"

Ariel laid the newspaper down over her dish, now garnished with dried egg and marmalade-smeared toast crumbs. As she lifted her coffee cup to her lips, the smell of sour milk assailed her nostrils. Grumbling, she shuffled to her ancient refrigerator and peered inside. Its minimalist stock included a couple of eggs, the offending pint of non-fat milk, and a suspicious-looking container of what just might be months-old tuna salad.

She nearly jumped as a series of loud crashes sounded from somewhere in the apartment. Trembling, she rushed into the living room. "Are you okay?" Jezebel crouched tensely beside a shabby, floral upholstered chair in the corner, her rump raised as Ariel stooped to stroke her until the cat calmed down. "My poor darling. Getting blind as a bat, aren't you?" She flicked her eyes up to the ceiling. "Lord, let me win the lottery so I can pay for your operation."

She bent to pick up the books Jezebel had knocked off her bookshelf, a makeshift affair of boards and bricks left over from college. What was she supposed to do with this mess? It was a precarious set-up.

The shelves were filled to overflowing, most of the books stacked on their sides in piles two or three deep. Many of them had hastily torn slivers of paper nosing out of them as bookmarks.

Ariel sneezed three times in quick succession as the accumulated dust of over half a decade got up her nose. She tried wedging a handful of books back onto one of the shelves, but the space was too narrow. She was left with one paperback still in her hand. Turning it over, she saw it was Colin Turnbull's *The Forest People*. It had been assigned reading in the one anthropology class she'd taken. She smoothed her hand over its green and black cover. This one had been too good to dump with her college textbooks into one of the giant trash bins behind her apartment building the day after she graduated. It had been a miracle she'd been able to even approach those hulking steel containers. She'd been wary of them ever since the night she'd crammed for her Art History exam. High as a kite on a manic mix of caffeine and Adderall from a friend with actual ADD, she'd convinced herself they were part of some dark cosmic design—malevolently lurking behind apartment buildings, rolling into the middle of alleys while the city slept, so that when you were already late for school the next morning, you'd be trapped in Alley Hell.

Shaking her head at her lunacy, she plopped down cross-legged onto her living room's threadbare carpet. Jezzie cautiously ventured out from under the chair and settled beside her. Ariel pushed the book's spine along the cat's silky back, reassured to hear the deep, steady motor of her purr.

It was all coming back to her. Turnbull had caught her imagination back then. Hooking her on the lives of his beloved Congo pygmies, despite the fact that they were completely primitive, or as her classmate Ryan Bell had put it at the time, "too fuckin' weird, man." To be fair, at first they'd struck her as weird, too. She couldn't imagine how anyone could walk around stark naked in the forest, bugs and snakes everywhere, and not have the constant heebie-jeebs.

Stroking Jezzie hand over hand, pulling her fur sleek from head to tail, Ariel recalled that the BaMbuti pygmies had a sacred song for everything—waking, eating, watching the sun go down. She felt a heaviness descend on her. Here in the so-called civilized world you couldn't write songs sweet enough to make people drop to their knees in gratitude without somebody cannibalizing them in commercials to sell cars and junk food.

Jezzie moved away in a huff, her tail aloft like a black mast, and it occurred to Ariel that she'd probably gotten a little intense with her petting. She riffled through the pages of the dog-eared paperback, and then paused at its mid-section. She hadn't remembered these photographs, reproduced in grainy black and white, capturing Turnbull's forest people in the midst of their daily lives. Men with arrows, men playing music, a group of men setting off for the hunt.

She resumed flipping through the pages, then stopped and went back, catching the tip of her tongue in the slight gap between her teeth. A mahogany-skinned woman was crouched on her haunches, her hands clasped together with her elbows resting loosely on her muscular thighs. Her shoulders rolled forward ever so slightly, and she held her head a little bowed, her expression solemn. An older woman, standing at her side, was smearing something on her forehead that Ariel suspected just might be blood.

It was the younger woman's breasts, though, that really got her attention, hanging down her chest like two widened brown bananas, pointy-nippled with the points aiming in opposite directions. And the large handful of flesh on her otherwise taut body, the roll of fat at her midriff supporting two unbearably alive-looking breasts.

Ariel's thoughts turned to her mother Emily, gone so many years now that few actual memories of her survived. Not that her living presence had made that much of a dent. "Died of insignificance," Ariel had said at the time to her best friends Terry and Jasmine, taking a perverse pride in their shock at her cavalier attitude at being orphaned just a few days before her eighteenth birthday.

Of course, that had been sheer bravado. She never told them how haunted she'd been by her last image of her mother, breathing laboriously in her hospital bed while *Wheel of Fortune* droned from a television suspended overhead. Ariel had kept her eyes glued on the long thread of spittle that dangled from her mother's chapped lips to her grayish-white sickroom pillow. Anything to distract her from her mother's diminutive breasts, laid bare from her body's twistings inside the faded pink and blue flowered hospital nightie tied skimpily at her navel.

Ariel wondered if there had ever been a fullness to those embarrassingly bared breasts, their nakedness all the more shameful as their wearer had no knowledge of her exposure. Barely more than nubs—Ariel had clearly inherited her own more generous versions from her father's side of the family—they'd never had anything as substantial as milk in them. Her mother had once confessed apologetically that a post-natal infection had prevented "all that."

Compared to Emily Thompkins, Turnbull's bushwoman had breasts full of presence— breasts with personality. Ariel snorted. Brushing past the sagging arm of the easy chair whose shredded upholstery bore witness to the chronic application of Jezebel's claws, she burst into singing what she remembered of Lloyd Price's "Personality" on her way to the shower. She and Terry had first heard the song on oldies station K-Earth 101 when they were thirteen or fourteen, and they'd fallen for its unabashed enthusiasm.

"Charm!" Breaking into a bouncy dance step, she grabbed a towel from her hall closet. "Love!" She flung her coffee-stained robe from her body as she approached the bathroom mirror, glancing momentarily down at her own breasts, palely pendulous, with their large and darkly stained nipples. Her grin was wide and her brown eyes shone as she brought her face close to the glass, burbling the substitute lyrics she and Terry had made up, both of them sprouting tits and rear ends in adolescence like ripening fruits on summer trees. "And, plus you've got a great big aa-aa-as!" She soaped her glistening skin with delight at the memory of how bawdy and bad they'd been.

Less than twenty minutes later Ariel caught sight of her new neighbor Benjamin Doyle, looking intimidatingly attractive in his sockless black penny loafers, skinny jeans, and white T-shirt as he trudged up from the laundry room just as she was preparing to exit her apartment. She hastily tucked the gray shirt of the U.S. Postal Service into her matching shorts and shoved the door closed with her hip. As they passed each other on the staircase, Benjamin opened his mouth as if to say, "Good morning," then closed it when Ariel shyly averted her eyes and slipped past him on her way down the stairs. Which was why she missed seeing his eyes gleam with interest as he took in the loose curls that bounced with her every step; the pink flush spreading across her broad cheekbones and nearly perfect Grecian nose; the turquoise butterfly tattoo on her left wrist; her generous curves defying the anonymity of her uniform. He reluctantly tugged his eyes away as his overflowing laundry bundle claimed his full attention. He struggled to fish his key out of his pocket and open his front door, socks dropping right and left at his feet.

Nearing the sidewalk, Ariel flicked her eyes upwards just once as she heard Benjamin swear. She knew his name; she'd seen it when she'd looked for the new name for unit 312 in the West Hollywood building's communal mailbox. No second, female name: just Benjamin Doyle. But who was she kidding? With his trim build, perfectly sculpted biceps, and those brooding blue eyes under a slicked-back head of dark hair, he was way out of her league. She banished him from her mind with a fatalistic shrug.

Opening the dented door of her Toyota Corolla, she prepared to apply her best efforts to getting the car started. For the first time in ages, the motor turned over on her first try. As soon as she turned on her car radio, the sultry sounds of Kehlani's "Butterfly" snaked into the car. She sang along to the suggestive lyrics; they almost made *her* feel "brand new."

She opened all the windows. It was going to be one of those perfect L.A. days. Not too hot or smoggy, with the wispiest of clouds flirting with the sun. This was the kind of weather that made delivering mail feel less like a dead end than a way to fully enjoy the perks of living in southern California.

I'm a lucky woman, Ariel thought, signaling to make an illegal left turn into the post office parking lot. Not like all those lemmings in suits, cooped up in dead-air offices. They call them sick buildings. And no wonder. They make you sick.

Just as she began to make her turn, another driver—her silver head barely visible over the wheel of a much newer, undented Toyota—approached from the opposite direction. The old woman frowned anxiously at Ariel's car and slowed to a crawl, as if unsure whether to continue to drive forward or let Ariel complete her turn. Darting a glance in her rearview mirror, Ariel decided she could spare a few seconds and, with an air of largesse, waved her through first.

As Ariel's front wheels hit the driveway, the sound of a siren blasted her serenity, then just as quickly whined itself into an ominous I-know-it's-close-by dead silence. She stiffened, preparing herself for the certain ticket. Instead, her head whipping first to her rear left, then right, to locate from which side the policeman was approaching, she spotted him. Oblivious to her, he was stepping out of his vehicle on the other side of Beverly Boulevard. His hand resting on his still-holstered nightstick, he walked toward a weathered-looking black man who'd just jaywalked his shopping cart across the street.

She let out a guilty but relieved breath that the cop wasn't coming after *her*. She hurriedly parked and—darting a quick glance back at the two of them to reassure herself that no gun was pointed at the homeless man—locked her car before heading into the Bicentennial Post Office to sort her day's worth of mail.

Two

THE HOMELESS MAN wasn't so lucky. The cop had threatened him with arrest if he didn't keep moving. By the time Ariel had finally lugged her overflowing mail pouch out of the low-slung brick building and into her delivery van, an exhausted Theosophus Kelly was pushing his shopping cart to the rear of the entry to the now-abandoned Beverly Hills branch of Golden State Bank a mile away. The cart was overflowing with stuff, one of its front wheels was gimpy, and the damned thing kept getting stuck. A corner of the wine-stained blanket he'd thrown on the top dragged down to the ground. He was counting on the untended ficus trees that shaded the concrete path from street to front door to shield his presence from the vigilant eyes of the Beverly Hills P.D. One rousting by the fuzz was about all he could handle in one morning. Sure enough, just as he settled his behind down onto the low wall bordering a disused flowerbed—for the first time this day taking a load off his swollen feet—a squad car cruised by. His shoulders relaxed as soon as he determined they hadn't seen him.

He lit up his last remaining cigarette butt, inhaled deeply, and coughed, his bloodshot eyes tearing as the pain cracked across his chest. "Damn Pall Malls," he muttered. He preferred a filtered cigarette, but he had to make do with whatever he found. He clenched the butt with his teeth, and his right eye winked shut at the assault of undulating smoke as he reached down and loosened his shoelaces. He stopped short of giving his feet the full relief they craved, muttering apologetically to his toes, "Can't do it too much or I'll never get these laces tied up again." Once upon a time, his gravelly voice might have sounded sexy to the right woman, but those days were long gone.

Hard living had aged Theosophus way beyond his thirty-five years. The lines that creased his kind, once-handsome face etched a tale of too much disappointment, too much pain. His forehead was furrowed into a quizzical triangle that reinforced the hangdog sag of his eyes, and wide grooves fanned the drop from nose to mouth to chin like two snakes of sadness.

As the minutes passed, Theosophus watched the urban parade. Cars whizzed by in regulated spurts, punctuated by annoyed blasts of horns as wayward drivers dared to break the furious flow by attempting to park or turn. This being Southern California, the number of pedestrians on the sidewalk was minimal. And this being Beverly Hills, a fair number of Mercedes and BMWs swept past Theosophus' tired eyes. But Wilshire Boulevard was a major thoroughfare, linking the breezy beach community of Santa Monica with the third world grime of downtown L.A., so that Theosophus saw a lot of beat-up old clunkers, economical Nissans and Hondas, and plain old American Fords and Chevies, too. The inhabitants of all these various smog-churners checked their cell phones, smoked their cigarettes, chewed their gum, sang to their radios, applied their make-up, and picked their noses, with no seeming awareness that they could be seen.

Theosophus liked to look. Even though a lifetime's worth of bad luck had squeezed the will right out of him, confining him in a prison of enervated and often drunken passivity, his curiosity was still alive.

"No accident they called me Nosy," he'd tell his whiskey buddies. "Hell, for a long time I thought that was my real name. The way Mama told it, when I was just a baby in my crib, right there in their bedroom, she and my daddy would see me standing up in that little bed, holding on to the rails like my life depended on it. Squinting to see them better when the two of them were getting it on."

No matter how many times he told the story, he'd be tickled into laughter, imagining being in his father's place, uncomfortable at being observed in the sex act by a baby, but also getting off a little that the product of his own seed wanted to see his moves. And just as predictably, his laughter would grow hollow-sounding inside his ears as he recalled his father's desertion of the family when he was only four, leaving the barest of memories of the man who everyone said was so proud when he was born. Theosophus was never sure whether even those recollections were his own or merely a composite of the few blurry black and whites he had of his daddy and himself, embellished by Mama and Granny's reminiscences.

For sure, there were a lot of memories of his younger days that he knew were his very own, like his terror of the cockroaches that scuttled across the bathroom floor when he had to pee in the middle of the night. Granny called them *cock-a-roaches* in her high-pitched Alabama voice, and those horrifying creatures with their creepy-crawly, wiggling feelers caused more whuppings than anything else in his childhood.

For years, he'd hold onto his urine every night so he didn't have to navigate that bug-filled bathroom, pressing his two hands frantically against his dick in a vain effort to hold back the tide, until his bladder burst into the dreaded warm soaking of his bedsheets.

Mama never seemed to care why he peed himself so often. She only resented peeling the stained sheets off the bed each morning, their now-cold dampness infecting the bedroom and her hands with the smell of a neglected urinal. She'd look her rage at him as she marched those bedclothes out of the room he shared with his half-brother and sisters to stuff into the plastic garbage bag that soon smelled like a urinal itself. She'd take the bag with her to the Beverly Hills house she cleaned every day, washing its coarse contents right along with the unsuspecting rich old white lady's eyelet-bordered bedclothes. Mama would always whup him good after lecturing him. Didn't he have any consideration for her, having to sneak his smelly sheets into Mrs. Levitt's house? Going on about how she and Granny couldn't afford their own machine and all, didn't he know, and how she had a mind anyway to never wash his sheets again, see how he'd like the fusty feel of them night after night, if it weren't for the fact that his brother and sisters would complain about the smell. And then she'd bring out the awful hairbrush that never touched a hair, tattooing its harsh design onto his butt. Or, if she was late for work, she'd just yank down his pants, having to make do with using her bare hand to slap her frustration at him.

Somewhere inside his resentment of Mama lurked a knowledge that she didn't want to hurt him. She was just tired out from taking care of two families and two houses with nobody to help her out, except sometimes some dog of a man would do her the favor of sleeping in her bed for a few weeks or months and get her pregnant again.

It was only when he went swimming one summer with his best new school buddy Antwan—at the public pool adjacent to the projects where Antwan and his mama lived—that he gave up the bed-wetting for good. The steamy, smelly men's locker-room was the site of his conversion into a non-bed wetter. Changing into the dazzling aquamarine swim trunks Granny had taken the bus all the way to a downtown L.A. discount store to buy, he was confronted by a group of strange boys who gathered around to look at his chafed and inflamed buttocks, a perennial source of pain resulting from a devilish combination of Mama's hair-brush beatings and urine-soaking. The rest of them had picked up the taunt of one particularly nasty bully, chanting "Red butt, red butt."

Antwan had pulled him outdoors to the pool area, where a tanned and toned lifeguard patrolled the decking, his TV commercial looks stunning the black and Mexican kids into an intimidated obedience.

"Won't nobody bother you when Matt's looking. He watches out for us younger kids," Antwan had whispered knowingly, socking Theosophus on the arm to show he didn't care if his friend's butt was red.

He would learn years later how pissed-off Matt Hayes of Malibu was that a nasty, hide-the-assets-and-cry-poor divorce tactic by his gynecologist father had necessitated his mom's move into a modest apartment—leaving his falling-apart mother muttering embarrassingly, "You'd think a man who spent half of his waking hours looking up women's vaginas would have more respect for his own wife!" Especially since it required that Matt sacrifice his passion for surfing to get a summer job to pay for college the next year. Every bully from the projects was a welcome target for a piece of Matt's anger at his dad.

Matt was a good kid, though. He'd become a friend to Theosophus and Antwan, showing them strokes that would move their bodies more smoothly through the water and filling them with fantasies of white boy life as he described the high of riding the waves. Theosophus could see young Matt now, laying down his Day-Glo orange bullhorn to show how his body swayed on his board for balance, his lean limbs graceful, his blue eyes seeing an approaching white beach as far away from this dark-body-dotted, heavily-chlorinated pool as anything could be.

It was an older Matt who'd helped an older Theosophus get his custodial job at UCLA. Theosophus winced. He didn't want to think about that. It was worse than the cockroaches—which he'd won the battle over in the end. Once he made up his mind to venture into that terrifying bathroom at night, he'd perfected the art of the tip-toe, figuring that the less of his foot that made contact with the tiles, the less the chance of it touching a dreaded roach. "Like one of them ballet dancers," chuckled Theosophus, pirouetting around his shopping cart before reaching deep inside for the bottle he'd hidden for just such a moment. He didn't want to think, or the losing of his job would come back to him. No, he didn't want to think about that at all.

Three

ARIEL WAS IMAGINING herself treading hesitantly on the soft-needled earth of an African forest, inching toward the crouched figure of a toothless old woman, when the reverberations of an over-amped bass blasted into her fantasy, announcing that something was coming at her.

"Jesus!" Jumping out of the way of a speeding black Trans Am, she knocked her mail bag hard against her right leg, a couple of sharp-edged catalogues slicing her knee. Half of her wanted to jump into her delivery van and take off after the son of a bitch, but she knew it was futile. How fast did she think she could go in her U.S. Post Office utility vehicle? "No better than a golf cart," she muttered, hobbling across the sidewalk to lower her pouch onto old Mrs. Goldberg's lawn and sitting down to resentfully rub her knee. The pasty flesh covering it was already turning into a Rorschach of ugly bruising and scraped skin.

These bastards treat Martel like a freeway, she reflected, not for the first time since taking over this route from Denise, a dedicated Catholic who was on leave after delivering her fifth child. Denise was a slow-walker. Ariel figured it came from not wanting to get home any sooner than she had to, only to be met by the noisy demands of all those kids.

As far as this neighborhood was concerned, Denise's absence had been Ariel's gain, for these folks were volubly grateful to her for getting them their mail earlier rather than later, most of them being old and retired, time weighing on them like drying concrete. Even bills and circulars advertising cut-rate carpet cleaning were a welcome relief from the ticking of the clock, the endless drone of leaf-blowers, and televisions turned up loud to give the illusion of company.

Come to think of it, it was a miracle Denise's slow trot hadn't gotten her run down years ago. Ariel laughed out loud, ruefully acknowledging that she'd probably been dawdling herself as she'd crossed Martel. As she hefted her bag onto her shoulder, she wondered what she'd been so lost-in-space about. And then she remembered. It was those Eve bones.

She limped up the slightly inclined, Saltillo tiled walk leading to Mrs. Goldberg's front door. Roses, yellow and pink, their petals layered like peonies, bordered the pathway. They smelled like heaven. She wished Denise would just give in and stay home forever with all those babies, leaving this route permanently to her.

———————————

Even though Ariel was spot-on about the loneliness of the old, she'd have been surprised to learn that Selma Goldberg had been standing at her living room window for a good fifteen minutes, anticipating the arrival of the new mail lady. Selma muttered to herself, "What was her name? Alice? Abigail?" What did it matter? So she'd ask her again, trusting she wouldn't hold her rotten memory against her. She was nice, so much nicer than that lazy Denise who couldn't budge herself to get here until the last minute and yet couldn't be bothered to utter a few courteous words. It dawned on Selma that this one might be a *shikseh*, too, but who cared? The girl looked happier to see her than her own daughter Edith, who came over once a week, her smile stiff and her conversation unimaginative. And all those repetitious questions about her health, like she was going to maybe die tomorrow? Selma sometimes wondered if that was what Edith was secretly wishing, so that she could be relieved of her daughterly duties.

Anticipating Ariel's appearance, she'd been watching from her front room window when the reckless driver nearly ran the girl down. Letting out a little gasp, she'd nearly dropped the still-warm packet of chocolate chip cookies she'd baked for her. A nice round sponge cake would have been her preference, but she'd been concerned that the girl wouldn't be able to find room for it in her bag. A smashed sponge cake wasn't worth thinking about. Instead, she'd wrapped a bunch of cookies in a couple of paper napkins.

She didn't think Abi ... whatshername would mind. She'd put the cookies into a Macy's bag with a couple of handles so she could hang it over her wrist and take a nibble any time she wished as she walked her route.

Rushing to the door to see if the girl was all right, Selma flung it open and cried, "He nearly killed you," only to be greeted by Ariel's startled gaze as she looked up from the mail slot. Ariel quickly rearranged her features into a reassuring smile.

"Hey, Mrs. G, don't look so upset, it really doesn't hurt much at all."

Selma was only momentarily taken aback by the casual appellation. She reasoned silently with herself that if she couldn't even remember such a nice girl's name, she could certainly put with her calling her "Mrs. G."

Coming from a long line of repressed Methodists, Ariel couldn't help but respond to the warmth of these elderly Jews on her route, but she found their intensity a little melodramatic.

Try as she might, though, she couldn't stop Mrs. Goldberg from hauling her into her dining room—with its unfamiliar, tapestry-upholstered dining room chairs and its conflicting smells of chocolate chip cookies and pot roast—to inspect her knee, on which the eagle eyes of Selma Goldberg had detected what Ariel had to admit were an *I Ching* hexagram's worth of scrapes. Ariel rolled her eyes as the insistent Selma went to fetch some iodine, chanting "Bastard!" several times as if wrapping the word around Ariel and herself in a sacred ritual.

While Selma banged around in her medicine cabinet, Ariel took a deep breath and let her mail pouch down onto the thick Persian carpet, wondering at its pristine cleanliness. Does she really eat here? she wondered, thinking of the greasy spills and crumbs that littered the linoleum under her own kitchen table. Jezebel would have a field day with this rug, she realized, imagining the animal digging her claws into its rich pile.

Ariel complained to herself half-heartedly that she was running late, then took a bite out of one of Mrs. Goldberg's cookies, which was still warm enough to spurt melty chocolate across her tongue.

Humming a little as she chewed, she let her eyes travel to a gallery of photographs, clearly hung with great care on Selma Goldberg's dining room wall. Most of their burnished frames looked as old as the sepia-toned photographs they enclosed. The largest was of a man and woman, neither of them young, though he was clearly the older of the two, his hair considerably thinned out at the crown and whitish at the sides. The couple posed with an air of formal dignity, dressed up and somber for the camera in front of a heavily draped window.

The man stood behind the woman, their bodies lightly touching. His erect bearing was turn-of-the-century Prussian military, as was his walrus mustache. Something about his eyes commanded Ariel to come closer. She stood abruptly, banging her sore knee and silently swearing as she approached the photograph. She tiptoed, wary of having Mrs. Goldberg catching her nose to nose with one of her ancestors. The shape of the man's face was a ringer for Mrs. Goldberg's, as were his beautiful dark eyes and wide forehead. Only, his left eye sagged down just perceptibly at its outer corner, giving his whole expression a saddened cast.

The woman by his side didn't so much look sad as mysterious. She wore a dark dress with white lace at the collar and cuffs, and her ornate black slippers had cutouts across her slightly age-thickened ankles. Her smile enigmatic and her eyes luminous, the woman rested one arm across an ample and surprisingly sensual lap that looked like it could have produced scores of descendants. She was resting her left hand so lightly on the bench where she sat that Ariel imagined it moving, lifting up to twine its fingers with those of her masculine partner and flying off with him out the window into the darkest night.

Ariel dashed back to her chair, banging her knee yet a third time, as she heard Selma Goldberg's feet shuffle down the hall.

"Here," Selma said authoritatively, entering the room. She reached down to swab Ariel's scraped skin with scarlet liquid that ran like blood down her shin.

Before she could stop herself, Ariel heard an unwelcome "Ow!" escape her throat and watched alarm rise up in Selma's eyes.

"Not to worry, Mrs. G. I just forgot how much this fucking stuff burns." Her hand flew up to cover her mouth.

Selma's eyes twinkled. She lowered her body with a relieved "oomph" onto the chair next to Ariel. "You think I'm going to wash out your mouth with soap, or something?" She leaned forward confidingly. "My Edith, you'd never know she was brought up in a good home the way she'd yell I was the meanest mother in the neighborhood. You'd think maybe I was a monster for putting a little iodine on her." Then suddenly, Mrs. Goldberg fell silent.

"What is it, Mrs. G?"

Selma shrugged. "Children. One day you're wiping a scraped knee, the next thing you know they're ready to put you into a home." She snorted derisively. "Home! More like a concentration camp for the drooling relatives nobody wants." Ariel shifted uncomfortably in her chair. Selma put up a hand. "Oh, I know what kind of pressure Edith is under, but who told her to have so many children?" Ariel, who was having a hard time following her, tried nodding sympathetically. "Four already, and now, God forbid, one more in her belly. It's what she gets for marrying that Max. It isn't enough he makes her keep kosher?" Selma shot her a sharp look. "Those Orthodox, you know, they're like rabbits. As if the strength of our people comes from sheer numbers. I told her, 'You think maybe the birth of enough Deborahs and Rebekkas and Jacobs will compensate for the obliteration of my Uncle Morris and Auntie Miriam? You think you can wipe away God's darkness in abandoning us so easily? You think maybe God was taking a little nap while that madman Hitler'—and here, to Ariel's horror, the old woman actually spat onto the carpet—'and his thugs were piling up mountains of Jewish bones?'"

Ariel gasped.

Selma glanced up, startled, as if she'd forgotten where she was. "*Oy,*" she said, rubbing the heel of her shoe over the damp spot on the carpet, "what's the matter with me? I invite you into my house and right away it's me and my troubles." Noticing a gratifying smear of chocolate on Ariel's cheek, she shifted gears with astonishing agility. "So what do you think? The cookies, they taste all right? Not too soft? Maybe a little too sweet?"

Ariel had to go to some pains to assure the woman that the cookies tasted just right, that, in fact, she'd never eaten such delicious cookies in her life. "Not ever," she found herself repeating, seeing the doubt still written on Selma's wrinkled forehead.

Seemingly still not satisfied, the old woman worried at it. "A sponge cake, it would have been better?"

Ariel laughed. She got the game. "Well, a sponge cake now. Let's see—that'll have to wait till I actually do get run over. You can bring it to me in the hospital."

Selma snorted. "You're having a joke with me, eh?" She smoothed the folds at her lap contentedly.

As she hefted her bag up onto her shoulder, Ariel swung her head back toward the gallery of photographs. "Maybe you'll tell me about those pictures on your wall sometime." She thumped her pouch apologetically. "But I gotta go now or Uncle Sam will have my, er ... I'll never get this mail delivered today."

"Watch out for yourself!" Selma called out to her retreating back. "Maybe I'll make you a little *homentaschen* tomorrow. Just keep an eye out for those hooligans in their cars!"

<h1 style="text-align:center">Four</h1>

IT DIDN'T TAKE a hooligan to make Ariel miss delivering Selma's mail the following day. The Union 76 Station at Third and Robertson wasn't her favorite place to get gas—she swore they charged you double for the thrill of filling your tank within walking distance of the pricey little boutiques and antique shops hugging Robertson all the way to Melrose. But the Corolla had called her unhappy attention to her fuel indicator by a fit of coughing spurts and drags, just as she was gloating that she was going to make it to Miller-Robertson Animal Hospital early enough to be on time for work. Jezzie had struggled all night to bring up what was obviously one exceedingly recalcitrant hair ball, and Ariel knew she would die of guilt if she didn't pick up some Laxatone this morning to help ease the damned stuff out.

Which was why she nearly had a nervous breakdown when the gasoline hose at pump number three refused to honor the deal she and her credit card had made with it, adding injury to insult by wildly spewing its foul-smelling contents the moment she removed the hose to inspect it. Which, in turn, was why she hadn't even bothered to object when a capable masculine hand carefully took the hose from her and actually managed to stick it back into her tank, where it obediently began to do what it'd been supposed to do in the first place.

She glanced down in disgust at her splattered Nikes, then looked up to offer her thanks.

"Oh."

He laughed and extended his hand. "I know what it's like. Done it myself. I'm Ben Doyle." He flushed. "Benjamin, actually. You live a floor below me, don't you?"

Reaching out her own hand, she realized it was covered with gasoline. "Oh, hell." She quickly drew her hand away, then left it mid-air, as if she couldn't figure out where to put it.

"Oh, for God's sake, you're covered in it, aren't you?" He sped away to get some windshield towels and, returning, took her hand in his and gently wiped it.

She couldn't move. He laughed. She looked up sharply. "What?"

"I don't know—it's just that I've been wanting to introduce myself to you for weeks. You a native?" She looked confused, until he added, "Angelino, I mean." She nodded. "Just moved out here myself. From Iowa, actually. Anyway, it's funny, isn't it? Bumping into each other at some random gas station?"

Ariel's stomach lurched. Those serious blue eyes of his were crinkled warmly at the corners now. He wasn't one-dimensional after all, but she wasn't sure if he was being genuinely kind or just polite. But he was saying something. "Do you … Is your route around here?"

"Hmm?" She looked down at her uniform, catching her scraped knee as she did. "Oh." Flushing, she quickly explained about Jezebel. He actually seemed interested. Then he said, "Hey, you wouldn't want to have a beer with me after work tonight, would you?"

She blinked. Twice. Guys like Benjamin Doyle usually treated her as if she were invisible. But he'd said he was new in town. He was probably lonely. Well, she knew about lonely, didn't she? With an unvoiced *what the hell?* she replied, "Sure. I mean, I don't think I have anything planned for tonight."

She had to pretend to have the stomach flu to call in sick for the rest of the day and get home to do some reasonable facsimile of housekeeping before he showed up. She needn't have bothered. He didn't even glance inside her apartment when he arrived. She nearly laughed at her craziness before reluctantly shutting the door behind her, her just-washed hair cascading damp ringlets around her face. Benjamin actually took her elbow as they descended the stairs, and she barely knew what to do with herself when he held open the door of his Jeep Cherokee for her. She felt more than a little clumsy as she maneuvered her body into the passenger seat.

Fortunately, as soon as he started up the motor Benjamin proved to have a talent for conversation, so they didn't have to suffer through too many long pauses. But once they ended up at Jameson's, they had to compete with Monday Night Football to hear each other. She found herself shouting, "No, my mother's dead," after being asked, "So, does your family live close by?"

Benjamin startled her by standing abruptly. He slid his tall frame beside her on the booth just before their waitress arrived to take their order. Their arms were touching. "That's better," he pronounced. "I'm so sorry about your mother." She didn't know what to say, so she pretended to study the menu. There was a moment's pause and then he asked, "Do you know what you want?" She stiffened, then gave an embarrassed little laugh.

Once they'd ordered, he leaned back and massaged his left shoulder. She struggled to take her eyes away from the coiled brown hairs on the back of his hand. "Man," he said, "I've got the trainer from hell. He's determined to get this Iowa boy in shape, even if he has to kill me in the process." She tried smiling. A trainer. Of course. She became distinctly aware of the fullness of her own thighs.

But between Benjamin's affable manner and a pint of one of Ireland's finest, she broke free from self-flagellation long enough to begin regaling him with stories of growing up in L.A., throwing in the obligatory celebrity sightings that non-locals loved to hear about. She even allowed herself to ask a few of the million questions she had about him, starting with, "So how does an Iowa boy decide he wants to be an actor?"

Benjamin responded surprisingly non-defensively. If anything, he looked pleased by her interest. "It's all down to the University of Iowa Cinema program. Not that I was in it. I was actually on track to becoming a biomedical engineer. But my roommates were in film, and they needed someone to lead in their senior project, and I used to goof around with my sister when I was a kid, doing scenes from our favorite movies, and … well, I got hooked. Crazy, huh? Nearly gave my parents a heart attack."

She laughed. "I get that. Not exactly a secure career path." She made a face. "I should talk. Miss English Major has stretched her horizons by delivering mail."

He studied her. She wasn't sure whether his expression was sympathetic or merely appraising. More to get out of the spotlight than anything else, she said, "You introduced yourself as Ben, then switched it to Benjamin. What do you like to go by?"

He made a face. "You've got me there. At home everyone calls me Ben Junior. And I mean everyone. Friends, teachers—certainly family; my dad's Ben Senior." He flushed. "I guess you realized that." She gave him an encouraging smile, and he continued. "But when I came out here, I got lucky enough to land an agent pretty quickly. It was actually thanks to one of those Cinema program pals. Anyway, he told me that 'Benjamin' was going to work better for lead roles." He laughed. "The poor fool sees me as a hot property."

Ariel didn't doubt it for a second. "So what do you prefer to be called?"

With warmth filling his eyes, he said, "Hadn't thought about it until now, but I think I'd like you to call me Ben."

"Hi, Ben," she said softly, liking the sound of it on her lips and sensing that something had just shifted between them.

Somehow they got to the fact that they'd both been born in 1992, actually within a month of each other. Their waitress, overhearing, asked for each of their birthdays, informed them with an air of dead seriousness that his was on the cusp of Taurus and Gemini, while hers made her pure Aries. Since neither one of them knew what that meant, they decided it was more significant that their shared musical tastes ranged from the golden oldies to Lana del Rey, Francis and the Lights, and Kehlani; that they'd both binge-watched *The Night Manager* and *Fleabag*; and that they preferred Harp Lager to Guinness. The latter so much so that she got home in rather worse shape than when she'd left.

But she didn't care. She'd spent her first evening since college with a man she liked, one who could actually hold a decent conversation and who didn't try to push his luck when he walked her to her apartment. She didn't even care that she stepped into a curdle of cat puke as soon as she shut the front door.

Five

AS SHE TURNED the corner from Third Street onto Martel a few weeks later, Ariel realized she was hefting enough extra weight to add an extra ounce of perspiration to her upper lip. In a lethal series of Tuesday and Thursday night dinners, she'd been *strudelled* and *homentaschened* into an extra five pounds—all of them seeming to have a particular affection for her thighs and buttocks—by the relentless Selma Goldberg. Selma's winning way with pastry dough was undeniable, but worse, she'd turned out to be an all-around genie in the kitchen, her delectable recipes for roast chicken and *knishes* and aromatic matzo ball soups a testimony to the fine-tuning of generations of Jewish matriarchs.

Ariel, who'd been wooed into an improbable friendship with Selma by the older woman's genuine interest in her and by her fascinating stories of *shtetl* life, had to admit that the dinners were a welcome bonus. Selma's lovingly wrought, unfamiliar concoctions were a far cry from the macaroni and cheese and tuna casseroles that her mother had disinterestedly dished up when she was a kid. Even farther from the microwaved TV dinners she made for herself these days, their lack of taste and texture obliterated from awareness by the books that she inevitably propped next to her plate as she shoveled in the calories. She'd started to think that the talent for good cooking (or the lack thereof) must be in the genes.

Ariel mused that Mrs. G had really outdone herself last night, spooning an intoxicating dish called noodle *kugel* onto her plate beside a generous hill of wafer-thin-sliced brisket. She unconsciously licked her lips as she raised the lion's head knocker on the woman's front door.

"Selma," she called out. "It's me. I've got your mail."

No answer. Where was she? Disappointed and vaguely worried, she shoved Mrs. Goldberg's daily ration of circulars into the mail slot. The next-door neighbor's mean old cat Nicholas nearly tripped her as she turned back down the walkway. She was convinced that the ancient, bitten-eared tabby lay in wait for her with the express intention of bringing her down.

"Someday I'm gonna bring Jezzie out here and sic her on you," she swore, reluctant to admit that her own half-blind cat wouldn't stand a chance against this battle-scarred veteran. The tom licked his hind leg with a "Who cares what you think?" air as she marched toward his owner's house.

Ariel's bag was nearly empty when she sensed a strong wind kicking up. She looked up at the cloudless sky. The Santa Anas had arrived, and it was only Monday. She made a face. The hot, seasonal Southern California winds were great if you were at the beach or drinking beer in an air-conditioned condo, but they were hell when you earned your living lugging mail out-of-doors and slept on the second floor in a poorly ventilated apartment building. Ariel dreaded the sweat-drenched tossing and turning in her sheets that was sure to come that night. She wondered if she should finally bite the bullet and spring for one of those lightweight portable air coolers they sold at Sears. Sure, the Santa Anas would probably last for a week at the most, but wasn't it worth the expense to be spared the torture of insomnia? And what about Jezzie? Was it fair to subject her to days' worth of panting and lying flattened under the bed just because her human was such a cheapskate?

It was earthquake weather, too, she reminded herself grimly, charily sliding her clammy shorts-exposed thighs onto the burning seat of her delivery van. She'd left the towel that she used to cover the seat in the still-unsorted bundle of clean laundry in her basket at home. And now it occurred to her that she'd forgotten to stow the basket in her bedroom closet. Jezebel's hairs would be all over her clean linens. Disgusted with herself, she aimed her vehicle for the Bicentennial Post Office.

Depositing her mail truck behind the building, she headed back toward her sunbaked Corolla. Behind her, someone called out. "Hey, Ariel!"

Turning, Ariel saw her co-worker Kineesha Washington, whose symmetrical cornrows glistened over her forehead with little pearls of perspiration as she moved toward her with gazelle-like grace. She felt a particular bond with Kineesha, the two of them being the only mail carriers working out of this particular postal branch who'd been to college. But the reason for Kineesha's underachieving was more valid in Ariel's eyes. Graduating with a major in sociology, Kineesha was just about to go on for her Master's when her older sister had been killed in a shocking three-vehicle car wreck on the 405. Now she had a quartet of nieces and nephews to feed.

But at this moment Kineesha was grinning impishly. "Want to get in on the raffle, hon?" she said. "We all know it's earthquake weather, right? Henry's taking bets on when it's going to hit. And if it doesn't, we'll use the takings for a group breakfast this Sunday at Du-par's to celebrate that we're still alive!"

Ariel shuddered. In the past, she'd tried making a joke to her co-workers of the last big quake, centered in Northridge in 1994. None of them believed she could have remembered anything, since she was less than three at the time, but she did. Hiding under the skimpy kitchen table with her mother, who nearly pinched her to death as the cabinets emptied themselves onto the suddenly unstable floor. She'd off-handedly described it as "the dance of the dishes," but she could tell that her forced, jittery laughter had betrayed her very real terror.

She didn't like the idea, betting on disaster, but she liked it less that Kineesha would know she was still a chicken, so she grinned a lie. "Sure," she said, forking over a five-dollar bill.

"Damned stupid thing to bet on," she muttered twenty minutes later, certain she was going to broil to death in Sears' jam-packed parking lot. She watched helplessly as scores of customers entered the store. She was convinced they were buying up the last of the air coolers before she could even find a parking space. Her hair plastered to her cheeks with sweat, she hurried toward the entrance, but just then a gust of hot wind propelled an errant newspaper page up from the grimy pavement. The paper tackled her ankles and flapped right around her calf. She looked around in embarrassment at being singled out by this piece of flying trash.

When she reached down to extricate herself, one of the smaller headlines caught her eye. "Eve Bones to UCLA," it announced tantalizingly, and, with only a moment's hesitation and one more quick glance to see if anyone was looking, Ariel scrunched up the page and shoved it into her battered handbag before entering the store.

Buying the air cooler turned out to be the easy part. Ariel assumed that lugging mail around for years had given her some pretty decent arm muscles, but trying to maneuver the boxed cooler up the stairs of her apartment building was killing her. Actually, it wasn't that heavy, but the damned thing was cumbersome. She'd tried knocking on Ben's door to ask him to help her, but he wasn't home. She wondered if he was out on an audition. In his four months in L.A., he'd landed only one bit part on *Brooklyn Nine-Nine*—totally psyched that he'd actually had a scene with Andy Samberg—and a non-speaking (and therefore poorly paid) role in a Bud Light commercial. She couldn't believe he hadn't been gobbled up yet for something better. He looked younger than his twenty-seven years and, as far as she was concerned, he way out-classed most of the current crop of working actors in the looks department. It was probably because he was a million times smarter than anyone in the position of casting him.

She couldn't believe she was actually kind of seeing someone, not that either one of them had mentioned exclusivity. But still. Her delight that they shared a taste for old movies and old music (even down to the two great Otises, Johnny Otis and Otis Redding) and her surprise at the number of challenging books on his shelves had landed her right where she never wanted to be. Stevie Nicks had gotten that one wrong, hadn't she? Drowning in the sea of love was decidedly not where she wanted to drown.

But she'd been about as good at saying no to Ben's invitations for dinner and movies and walks as she was to a piece of Selma's *kugel*. She'd even submitted to fooling around a little with him on his double bed last weekend, though she'd tried to protect her vulnerable feelings by stopping things before they got out of hand. She knew that as soon as Ben got his big break, she'd be history.

Ariel cried out as the air cooler box slid away from her grasp and dropped heavily onto her living room floor. She knelt down, on the brink of tears. If she'd broken the damned thing, she was going to kill herself. It had to be at least a hundred degrees in her apartment. She wiped the perspiration from her forehead and invoked God's name a couple of times as a pungent smell invaded her nostrils, reminding her that she'd failed to empty Jezzie's litter box that morning. Gritting her teeth, she fled to her bedroom. As she tossed her sweaty shirt onto the bed, she noticed that Jezebel had puked all over the laundry basket in the corner.

"Oh, for Christ's sake." She wished that somebody were there to set up the air cooler, pour her a beer, and massage her swollen feet. Instead, she yanked on her refrigerator door, leaving it open to cool the kitchen while she poured herself a glass of beer and turned on the radio. She settled herself at the table with her legs stretched out on a second chair and took a long draft of the ice-cold liquid. She leaned her head back and was just beginning to feel like a halfway normal human when Jezebel bounded into the room.

A foam mustache cresting her upper lip, Ariel burst into laughter. "You've been hiding, you naughty girl. Should've known all I had to do was open that fridge and you'd come running."

Only after feeding the cat, cleaning up her feces and vomit, taking a shower, and consuming a Lean Cuisine Bow Tie Pasta and Chicken, did Ariel—her naked body spread lazily across her sofa beside a sleeping Jezebel—allow herself to indulge in thoughts about Ben. She wondered how long it would be before he found some luscious, long-legged actress to replace her. He could be out with one at that very moment. God only knew how many he had to choose from at Gracias Madre.

She hadn't been surprised to learn that Ben, like hordes of other aspiring actors, earned his living waiting on tables at one of West Hollywood's innumerable trendy restaurants. While she'd never frequented such places herself, she'd read about Gracias Madre in *Los Angeles* magazine, where the reviewer had made the offhand comment that, while the organic Mexican dishes made with locally sourced ingredients were unusually delicious, so was the male and female wait staff.

Ariel had no idea what a beguiling picture she presented, her full breasts and gently rounded belly a soft ivory cushion to the contrasting ebony of Jezebel's fur, her hands graceful as she tenderly stroked the animal, her sweat-dampened hair curling delicately around a face whose big brown eyes were luminous with melancholy.

A door banged shut somewhere in the building, and Ariel wondered if it was Ben returning home. For the next fifteen minutes she nearly held her breath, hoping he might call or text. *No way I'm going to call him*, she promised herself, visions of some blond babe in his bed. She summoned her will to banish the image and heaved a protesting Jezebel onto the threadbare carpet before heading to her bedroom to don a sleep T-shirt. She'd suddenly felt too exposed in her bare skin.

Ariel nervously paced from room to room and only stopped when she tripped on her splayed-open purse in the living room. "Oh, I forgot," she muttered to Jezebel, who'd been shadowing her footsteps. She fished out the crumpled-up newspaper from her bag and flung it over a litter of unopened bills on the coffee table. Jezebel immediately jumped onto it, and Ariel nudged the cat off. "Do you have to treat any available piece of paper like your own personal throne?" She smoothed the paper out the best she could, wrinkling her nose just thinking about where she'd found it. "No better than a bag lady," she grumbled. But she was too curious to stop now.

Piecing together a few rips, she was able to discern the text well enough to read that the UCLA anthropology department was slated later that week to receive the bones of the recently discovered "Eve" for a series of complex measurements and dating tests. The article went on to describe the special arrangements that were being made to protect the fossilized remains of this putative human ancestress in their flight to L.A. from Ethiopia.

Scratching a flea bite on her calf that was only partly scabbed up, Ariel wondered what kind of plane was bringing Eve to L.A.

Her father had flown special missions just like this one. As her mother told it, the more exotic a flight's origins or purpose, the more he liked it. Invariably, her mother would tack on at the end, "Anything to get him as far away as possible from me."

Ariel had hardly known the man and, Lord knew, he hadn't seemed to be particularly interested in *her*. He'd scarcely acknowledged her when he breezed home for a meal and a snooze and some freshly laundered clothes before his next flight. It hadn't been too many years later, just before her twelfth birthday, that he'd breezed himself right out of their lives forever. A terse letter of notification from a two-bit private airline, accompanied by a paltry life insurance settlement for his survivors, informed them he was gone for good. Though she didn't dare voice it to her mother, whose bitter "Well, that's that" was the last comment she would ever make about her husband, Ariel hadn't believed it for a moment. She just knew that he'd been captured on some secret spy mission and was craftily biding his time till making a daring escape.

Ariel's eyes traveled to his framed picture up on her bookshelf, where the uncanny Jezebel now leapt with astonishingly good aim for a half-blind cat. His youth captured forever, her father looked particularly handsome in his Air Force uniform, his cocky grin revealing his youthful confidence that he owned the world.

Well, she thought, he'd owned her, hadn't he? While twelve-year-old Terry and Jasmine's bedroom walls had been papered with scissored-out magazine photos of Luke Perry and John Legend, she'd adorned her own cork bulletin board with romanticized sketches of her father—posed masterfully at the cockpit, alighting victoriously from a 727 with a suitcase in each hand.

At night, she lit candles under the drawings and mesmerized herself with fantasies of a father who couldn't drop those suitcases fast enough to embrace the beloved daughter to whom he'd come home for good.

It occurred to her that Terry and Jasmine had been realists in those early days, cleverly willing the images of their cherished teen idols onto the features of the pimply-faced boys of Webster Middle School at the weekly make-out parties they all attended in the seventh grade. But at least for a while none of the boys at school could compete in her imagination with her idealized ghostly phantom. Freud might have *tisk tisked* a bit, but a pre-teen boy was barely a blip on the radar to the father-starved girl. So, when the lights would darken and the orgy of slow dancing and kissing and even a little feeling up would commence to the strains of "You're Beautiful," and "Yellow," she volunteered to serve as sentry—prepared to warn her friends if a parent, somehow smelling what was going on, threatened to enter the vicinity of those tentative tryings-on of the sexual mystery. Her own private anthem was from an old 45 rpm her mom used to play sometimes when Ariel was a little kid, a melancholic, echo-chambered number called "The Big Hurt," with sounds of an airplane taking off in the background.

And while her friends squandered their babysitting money with religious regularity on hair styles and clothes that aped Gwen Stefani's silver-blond glam or visible thongs and spaghetti strap tank tops that failed to cover their bra straps, she saved her dollars, hiding them under her mattress, for the day she'd be old enough to take flying lessons, convinced that she'd meet up with her dad on some secret mission. They'd soar the skies together someday.

Ariel shuddered as she recalled her youthful dream. "Well, it didn't work out like that, did it, Jezzie?" she reminded the cat, who rubbed her tail saucily against the edge of the picture frame. "I didn't exactly take to flying, did I, girl? Pissed away whatever chances I had with those boys, whatever youthful charms I had, only to freeze up at the controls."

She picked up the protesting animal and took her into the bathroom, where she posed the two of them in front of the mirror.

"Youthful charms, what a joke! It's a good thing he never did come back, never saw what I'd become," she laughed falsely, dragging her fingers through her now dry and somewhat limp curls. Jezzie stared sightlessly at the mirror, purring with pleasure at the strength of Ariel's desperate embrace.

Ariel shuffled back into the living room and turned on the TV, but as soon as the titles for "Catastrophe" came on, she felt the drowsiness of a day's worth of heat and humidity overtake her. It was only as she was succumbing to sleep that she realized she'd never called Selma to make sure she was okay. "Great friend *you* are," she muttered to herself before dropping off.

———————

Ariel would never have dreamed of the red-hot rage that—at that very moment—was consuming her elderly friend. Impatient, frustrated, Selma cursed her daughter Edith for bringing her to the hospital against all her imprecations. What—did Edith think she was maybe doing her a favor, persuading malpractice-suit-dreading Dr. Samovitz to have her admitted because of her own guilty overreaction?

"I'm all right, I tell you," she'd insisted over and over again to her disbelieving daughter, whose already overworked forehead wrinkled even more deeply with anxiety; to Edith's husband Max, with his usual I-know-better-than-you air; to the emergency room male nurse, a *fagela* if she ever saw one, whose impassive face announced that he'd seen it all a thousand times before; to Dr. Samovitz, who'd made his token appearance at Cedars-Sinai emergency room only to ignore what she had to say—"as if I'm invisible, maybe?" she'd berated him. Samovitz had checked her into the hospital for observation before waltzing out of there as fast as he could with a promise to return the next day. "What a cowardly *putz*," she'd complained to Edith, insisting for the hundredth time that it was no big deal, she'd only felt a little dizzy.

"Never again will I call her if I don't feel so good," she vowed to herself as she attempted to turn her body under the too tightly tucked hospital sheets. "Thanks be to you, Lenny Glabman, for selling me that tainted fish." She swore aloud, for she was convinced that it was her purchase from Glabman's Deli that had made her tummy go all queasy, causing her to lose her balance and scaring her just enough to phone her daughter.

"I only buy from him because he delivers," she'd shouted to Edith, as the exhausted woman had finally bid her angry mother goodnight. "Next time I won't worry about spending my money; I'll take a cab to Canter's. The more I spend now, the less for you later," she'd whispered to Edith's departing back.

As the sedative she'd been given coursed through her bloodstream, a thought broke through. "Ariel," she moaned. "I wanted to show her that picture of Chaim I found. I forgot that I asked her to stop in today." Before dropping into dreamless sleep, Selma cursed her rotten memory.

Six

WHILE SELMA GOLDBERG slept the sleep of the drugged, three floors below, a much younger female still languished in Cedars' ER waiting room. She'd arrived several minutes before the old woman had registered at the front desk, but unlike Selma, she'd had no proof of insurance, no well-off relatives, no hospital-affiliated internist to push her to the front of the line. Only a reassuringly sizable but grubby wad of fives and tens begged off of guilty Beverly Hills locals, clutched in her pale and fragile hands, prevented the officious admitting nurse from fobbing her off on County General.

Sixteen-year-old Jane Deare sat with dulled eyes, fingering the bills in the pocket of her torn and faded jeans, her only company the hacking cough that had brought her here to wait for the doctor who would, hopefully, write her a prescription to make the pain in her thin chest go away. The other supplicants in the room had given her a wide berth as soon as she'd given vent to the wetly malevolent cough.

Her friends Sarah and Danny had been urging her to come here for days. They'd taken such pity on her that they'd even vacated their own lucrative customary stations on Little Santa Monica so she could accumulate enough cash to be seen at this hospital. Danny was sick, too—exhausted most of the time and way too skinny—which was how he knew that the Cedars emergency room was the best place to go. "I was too fucked up," he'd told her, "to get help soon enough. You've been a smart girl, staying away from the shit that can give you HIV, but I don't like the sound of that cough. You've got to get some antibiotics or something."

Danny and Sarah's protectiveness didn't extend to accompanying her inside, though; there was a cop stationed at the entrance to the emergency room, and neither one of them was exactly a stranger to the law. Jane was, though, and her fake I.D. pushing her birthday back a few years should get her through. Nobody in L.A. would know that she'd run away several months ago from what was supposedly her home in Ohio.

"Not *my* home," Jane muttered to herself, causing the wrinkle-ridden, dark-skinned man across from her with the bloodstained bandage on his hand to get up and seat himself even farther away.

If it weren't for the cough, and now her muttering, no one would have noticed her at all. Her wraith-like frame and listless posture blended right in with the pale cream, fake-leather institutional seats bolted down to the floor. Jane supposed that was so nobody could pick up one of the chairs and throw it at the smarmy receptionist who kept telling people to sit down and wait their turn. She hated the stranger's condescension. It reminded her of her stepfather telling her to shut up while he stuck his smelly dick into her vagina, her mouth, her anus, even poking it at her ears. Anywhere, she used to think with that sense of separateness from her body that would overtake her with his touch, where he could find a hole. Well, there was a hole now, wasn't there, a great big one, where she used to be? She'd fallen into its bottomlessness and could barely find herself anymore. She hardly knew what it was in her that had gotten her feet moving out of that hell of a house, out of her town, all the way to L.A. She was like a chicken with its head cut off that doesn't even know that it's dead. Only, if she were dead, how come her chest hurt her so?

––––––––––

Around the corner from where Jane Deare sat with scant hope, Theosophus Kelly made an unusually slow passage along the empty sidewalk skirting San Vicente Boulevard. Bewildered visitors to the splayed-out body of this City of Angels often found themselves getting lost due to their ignorance of there being not one, but two separate San Vicente Boulevards serving as major urban arteries. Native drivers made grateful use of both of them, for each pulsed its rhythmically timed spurts of traffic through wide-laned diagonals that cut through the clogged streets of Santa Monica and Brentwood on the west and mid-Wilshire and West Hollywood on the east, which was where Theosophus found himself.

To his left was the amply-funded, ever-growing complex structure of Cedars-Sinai Medical Center; at his right the behemoth Beverly Center shopping mall, looking for all the world as if God had vomited down his disgust at the less than angelic aspects of the city and turned the effluent to stone.

As large as these giant companions loomed on the physical horizon, Theosophus was oblivious to both. He could afford access to the mercies of neither one. What consumed the whole of his current awareness was a tiny point at the bottom of his right foot, where two tormenting hours ago an itch had commenced that just wouldn't go away. For most people, such itches presented, at the most, two challenges: if such an itch occurred in public, there was the potential embarrassment of removing a shoe in full view of strangers; even if it occurred in private, there was always the possibility that the itch would not be relieved when scratched, but merely cloak itself with a secondary pain particularly sensitive to any attempts to snuff out the prickling. For Theosophus— who didn't give much of a damn what he was seen doing in public just so long as folks would leave him alone—such an itch presented a particularly risky dilemma, for in all likelihood, if he removed his right shoe he stood a serious chance of not being able to get it back on again. Living on your feet did that to you.

No one had to tell Theosophus that he was a survivor. He knew it. And he also knew that as much as that itch was screaming for attention, he wasn't about to give in to it. Just like his mama, who'd paid no mind to his tearful entreaties when she took the hairbrush to his butt, he wasn't going to let this itch deter him from his goal, a small neighborhood park on Santa Monica Boulevard where he had a decent chance of resting unmolested till the swelling in his soon-to-be unshod foot went down. Theosophus hardly cared that he would be companioned by the usual group of male and female prostitutes, junkies, and runaways, for the very presence of those others was a kind of guarantee that he wouldn't be rousted by the fuzz, who let that park serve as a kind of run-off valve for the human misery that might otherwise clog up the communities that the two San Vicentes served.

By the time he'd parked his shopping cart under an unclaimed tree, Theosophus was screaming back at his itch, telling the sonofabitch to cut it out or he'd cut the whole damned foot off with the rusty butcher knife he had stored inside his grubby blanket.

Little did he know that it was his yelling that had gained him a vacancy at this night's verdant lodgings. The cluster of homeless teenagers who, just minutes before, had been lounging and scrounging here—Jane Deare's Sarah and Danny among them—had split when they'd heard what they mistakenly figured was one of the street's ubiquitous crazies coming up the block. Schizophrenics were even more unpredictable than their own kind.

Theosophus stopped yelling when he finally got the shoe off. He figured that there must be a God after all, because his itch just lapped up the scratching by his yellowed fingernails, long as a lady's and thick as toenails. Like a cat being caressed, his foot responded by arching itself this way and that to his hand's quick touch. In his ecstasy, he didn't even notice that the threads at the heel of his right sock were beginning to give way, announcing a new upcoming calamity in the form of a raggedy hole.

Seven

AS THEOSOPHUS KELLY rested his head on a pile of newspapers—his hand curled around a near-empty bottle of Old Taylor that he'd rescued from a trash bin—and the runaways of West Hollywood Park spread themselves out along the seediest stretch of Santa Monica Boulevard to sell their bodies for a song, a majority of the denizens of the City of Angels settled into the hard-won sleep of the work week, innocent of their good fortune in having warm beds with clean pillowcases on which to lay their heads. The post-war apartment building a scant few blocks away on Poinsettia was quiet, its residents, including Ben Doyle, all tucked into their beds, safe from the vicissitudes of the urban night. All but Ariel, that is, who'd wakened just before ten p.m. after her unplanned evening nap to the impersonal flashing of her TV screen.

As soon as she came to, she groaned. She knew from past experience that falling asleep before her actual bedtime doomed her to a rotten night's sleep if and when she managed to drop off again. It didn't help that she kept imagining Ben entangled in the arms of a blond beauty. As she began to obsess over the fantasized twists and turns of her rival's long bimbo limbs, Ariel found herself squashing one Marlboro after another into her chipped glass ashtray. When she went to put her tenth butt out, her nicotine-stained fingers could find no free space among the previously gutted cigarettes languishing on the ashtray battlefield. Wrinkling her nose as she jabbed its glowing red tip against one of the butts in the pile and muttering that she really would quit soon, she was only too glad to be distracted by the frenetically paced local news theme music, which some poor TV station technician had inserted right in the middle of the preceding Ford commercial.

Vowing, "No more smokes for tonight," she yanked the laundry basket at her feet up onto the couch and began to fold carelessly, smirking at the smooth banality and sameness of the anchorman look, when tonight's current specimen announced an upcoming news bit about "'First Eve,' after a few words from our sponsor."

"Not *our* sponsor," she objected to Jezebel, who looked up from a serious hind leg licking at her post close to the warmth of the TV screen, as if to agree.

But the words of the guy with the Jack Kennedy haircut had hooked her. She flung the already folded t-shirts away from her lap onto the threadbare rug, not even bothering to yell at Jezebel for immediately climbing onto the pile as if it were her due. Heedless of her previous promise, she got up to fetch a fresh pack of cigarettes. Cursing the remote for losing itself again, she rushed over to the TV to turn up the volume, only to turn it down again in response to her adjoining neighbor banging on his wall in sleepy indignation.

When the anchorman's face came back up on the screen, she could hardly believe the smug substitute for wit with which he described "the return of Eve to our own Garden of Eden," in front of a crude rendering of a flat-nosed, toothless hominid, depicting what the fossil might have looked like when blood coursed around her now denuded bones.

"Let's hope this baby'll get herself some plastic surgery while she's visiting," the jerk yukked to his female co-anchor, who grinned fatuously back at him before moving right on to "the fabulous weather Eve can expect to greet her when she arrives at UCLA."

"That's it?" Ariel shouted at the screen. "Someone who may have actually been the ancestress of us all gets discovered, and all you can say is that she needs a nose job?"

Marching angrily around her apartment, Ariel cursed the newscaster, his female colleague, the station managers, and all of the idiots who kept them and their sponsors in business.

Returning to the couch, she cradled her knees with her arms. She wanted more, wished they'd kept the drawing of Eve up on the screen so she could look into the rendering of those ancient black eyes. She imagined them looking back at her in recognition. Rubbing her hands down her own thighs and shins, Ariel wanted to stroke those old bones back to life again.

A memory came up to her, unbidden. She, a small child, watching her mother in the bath, lifting up a thin, white leg to meet her razor, the curve of her calf gracefully sloping down toward a delicate ankle that Ariel had wanted to touch in the worst way. But instead she'd stood a silent, admiring witness to her mother's rarely displayed femininity.

Come to think of it, her mom had never been one to encourage much of a fuss about the female form—her own or Ariel's. It took her mom's best friend since childhood, Nora, to clue Emily in that the little fried eggs on her thirteen-year-old daughter's chest were well on their way to becoming actual breasts.

Nora was one of the few women Ariel had looked up to as a kid. Her mom was too distant and prudish and embittered to encourage the kind of idealization that her dad inspired. Actually, Nora was perfect for the role. A good eight years younger than her mom and as tall and slim as a model (but with breasts like Dolly Parton's, only the real thing), she had full, naturally-red lips, teasing brown eyes, rich mahogany skin, and an air of casual acceptance of the ungainly child she trusted enough to babysit her own two kids.

The reason the breast thing came up at all was that Ariel had actually managed to get both of Nora's kids to sleep on time one night and was bored shitless, a Dodgers game having preempted her favorite TV shows and both Terry and Jasmine at some make-out party that all three of them had been invited to. Ariel had planned on going to it herself until Nora asked her to babysit, a welcome opportunity to add to her flight lesson fund. There was no zit-faced boy she wanted to be smooching in the dark, but she couldn't stop wondering whom her friends had paired up with and how far they were going.

It wasn't so much that she decided to go through Nora's dresser as that she discovered herself in front of it, standing on Nora and Joseph's plush, nearly-white bedroom carpet, slowly sliding open one wide, antique-white drawer after another, her hand exhibiting a life of its own as it carefully extracted a lacy 38D concoction from one drawer, and a dusty-rose, V-necked, softer-than-paradise sweater from another. Removing her sweatshirt in front of Nora and Joseph's mirror, she'd struggled with the unfamiliar bra hooks. Then, seeing how ridiculously the taboo garment hung on her thin torso, she rifled through the middle drawer for some scarves to fill in the two imperiously large cups.

She must have wanted to get caught, she realized now. How else explain how she'd managed to fall asleep, still wearing the contraband finery, on Nora and Joseph's king-sized bed, with its sumptuous red-velvet bedspread? Well, she'd chosen the right person to discover her. As she opened her eyes to Nora's waking touch, the woman's gaze was as steady and relaxed as if she'd come home to find Ariel doing her homework. Ariel remembered the feel of Nora's hand on her shoulder through the softness of the sweater, as if Nora's fingers were themselves made of cashmere. Nora actually pulled Ariel to her own ample breasts for one brief moment before helping her off with the sweater and bra and scarves without a word and slipping her Webster sweatshirt back over her head like she was a little girl.

It was just a few days later that her mom suggested, with a completely failed attempt at casualness, that it might be time to get "a trainer." It took Ariel a few moments to understand what the hell she was talking about; she arrived at that insight not through the unfamiliar euphemism but the awkwardness of her mother's demeanor. She was in the midst of indignantly declining when her mom added that Nora had offered to come along.

A week or so later, Nora drove them to the mansion-like Saks Fifth Avenue on Wilshire Boulevard to buy two white training bras. With her tact and vivacity, Nora managed to turn it into an Event by insisting they all have lunch afterwards at the restaurant on the top floor, surrounded by other patrons who looked like they had nothing to do but shop all day, a concept entirely new to Ariel at the time. Ariel saw something described on the elegantly calligraphed menu as Croquettes-Monsieur—which she was sure was what Holly Golightly would have ordered in her place—and stumbled over pronouncing it when it was her turn to order. She was ashamed when her mom ordered a plain old grilled cheese sandwich, which she could heat up for herself any time. Nora casually ordered a Waldorf Salad and smoked salmon with *crème fraiche* as if she'd uttered those elegant words a million times before, and she smoked a Virginia Slims cigarette with her coffee afterwards while Emily Thompkins drummed her pale fingers nervously on the table and looked across at her loquacious friend with lips and eyes thinned with envy. Ariel often wondered how the unlikely pair had become friends in the first place, but then she remembered her affection for Terry and Jasmine and recognized that friendships forged in childhood tended to hold fast no matter what.

Pulling Jezzie onto her lap, Ariel was struck by how readily she'd changed her tune about the bra-buying outing once it was clear that Nora was to be part of the plan. She winced as she speculated how hurt her mom must have been by that. It just never went right with the two of them.

Ariel shook her head. *Don't even go there.* She was almost glad when Bill Maher's self-satisfied grin popped up on the TV screen. Jumping up to turn off the television, Ariel wondered idly where on the UCLA campus they were going to be studying Eve's bones.

Later, after scrounging up an Ambien and gratefully letting her head fall into the soft folds of her pillow, she mumbled groggily. "Haines Hall. That's where I took that anthro class. They store artifacts in the basement." She pulled Jezebel even tighter to her body, whispering, "I bet they're keeping her bones in Haines Hall."

Eight

ARIEL'S FIRST INKLING that she was getting a little obsessed with Eve's bones came when she found herself going on and on about them to Selma. It was one of their regular Thursday nights, and the two of them were sitting in Selma's den, eating popcorn and watching a video of *Breakfast at Tiffany's* on Amazon Prime.

"You want maybe a little more butter?" Selma asked, a frown creasing her pliant brow.

Ariel's mouth was too full to speak, so she just shook her head.

"Salt. Maybe it's not enough? I can get some more from the kitchen."

Ariel put up a hand. Swallowing the last of her mouthful, she said, "No, really, Mrs. G, it's perfect." Pointing to her nearly empty bowl, she added, "Can't you tell?"

"Ach, what's the matter with me? You need more!" The older woman hurried off to the kitchen. Ariel could hear the banging of pots and tiny explosions of popping corn. She belched, apologized absentmindedly to the thin air, grinned, and reached for the remote to pause the film.

She leaned back against the velvet throw cushion that Selma had insisted on tucking behind her and sighed contentedly. Everything in this house looked, smelled, and felt good. No doubt about it, Mrs. G's house had style. It was a far cry from her own mismatched thrift store rescues and nothing like the clean but colorless furnishings that Emily Thompkins had seemed to favor.

In every place Ariel had lived as a child, the sofas, chairs, and walls were beige. Shit, she thought wryly, even our skin matched the decor. As if her mom were afraid to let in a little color for fear that a riot of bright reds and blues and yellows would take advantage of the opening and burst through the door. Ariel giggled. Like a gang of primitive squatters, forcing Emily to confront the fact that she couldn't bleach nature out of her life forever, that blood and dirt and sky were going get her in the end.

What would Eve think about a room like this? Really, about any of their rooms? Even the concept of a room. Ariel clapped a hand to her forehead. Jesus, this was starting to remind her of the time she and Terry had taken acid when Terry's parents were out of town one weekend. Terry's trip went sour almost immediately. She'd curled up like a fetus in her bed and couldn't be budged for the next eight hours. But Ariel, filled with a luminous energy, had paced the contours of Terry's parents' living room, tracing her fingertips along the walls as if she were feeling her way along the membranes of a living, breathing creature. All the while mumbling like a zombie, "The living room. The *living room*."

Whoa, baby, Ariel thought. She smothered an incipient laugh by pretending to cough up a popcorn kernel. Selma would probably throw her out of the house if she knew how crazy she was.

She picked up the stainless silver bowl at her feet and swirled designs with her index finger through the buttery detritus at the bottom. She realized that she'd made an "A for Ariel," just as she used to doodle on her class notes in middle school. Sucking her finger and then licking the salt from her lips, she imagined how excited Colin Turnbull must be—if he were still alive, anyway—about the discovery of Eve. As one of the world's greatest anthropologists, he'd probably insist on getting his hands on those bones himself.

Ariel was so consumed with her thoughts that she hadn't noticed that Selma had taken a circuitous route back from the kitchen, her thick-heeled shoes tapping briskly on the wood floor of her spare bedroom before making their more muffled way up the plushly carpeted hall back to the den.

Plopping down with a grunt, she passed Ariel a fresh bowl of popcorn, waving a photograph in her other hand.

"It's Chaim," Selma breathed heavily.

Ariel frowned. "Selma, are you okay?"

"It's nothing. I told you, they didn't find anything wrong with me, except a little something with my inner ear." She hurried on. "But I wanted to show you this before Edith"—she mimed spitting down at the floor—"tries to put me away."

Ariel eyed her doubtfully, then wiped her greasy hands down the sides of her jeans before carefully taking the edge of the yellowed photograph between thumb and forefinger.

Selma brushed popcorn kernels off the couch as Ariel studied the picture. A faraway look came over Selma's face, then she laughed abruptly.

Ariel looked up as Selma reached over and clutched at her elbow.

"Look at this popcorn," she said, her hand sweeping in the direction of the carpet, which was littered with unpopped kernels and spongy popcorn fragments, some of them flattened from having been stepped on. "When Chaim was alive it was sunflower seeds. We called them *semitchkes*. Chaim loved them. We used to joke that he ate them by the truckload. I kept a clean house, but it was okay by me that my Chaim made a mess all the time in this den with the shells. He worked so hard for me, for Edith, it was the least I could do. I'd clean them up in the morning, but every night, after dinner, it was like a ritual—he'd go into his closet, take off his shoes, come into the kitchen in his sock feet, like a little boy, and pretend to sneak a package of them out of the cupboard while my back was turned at the sink. As if I would have begrudged them to him? Then he'd shuffle into this den, put his feet up on the coffee table, and go at the *semitchkes* like a parakeet. He was so fast and good, he could pop a seed into his mouth, crack it open with his teeth, and remove it from the shell with only his tongue, leaving his hands free to turn the pages of the book he was reading. He was a great reader, Chaim, and a fast one. Whatever the book—Sholem Aleichim, Tolstoy, Isaac Bashevis Singer—he'd go through it as quickly as he went through those *semitchkes*."

Selma leaned over to look at the photograph Ariel was holding. "A handsome man, don't you think?"

Before Ariel could agree with her, Selma's body began to shake. Ariel reached toward the old woman to comfort her before she realized that Selma was overcome not with tears of grief, but the beginnings of a belly laugh.

"A handsome man," Selma said, "but I'll tell you something, when he ate his beloved *semitchkes*, he looked just like a lizard, his tongue darting in and out so fast. You should have seen him. My Chaim, a lizard—but a lizard with glasses!"

The image was too much for them. They rolled around in laughter, laughing till the tears streamed down both their faces, holding their sides as they groaned in pain.

Selma got up suddenly and left the room. Ariel wondered where she'd gone, worried that she'd had another attack like last week's. A toilet flushed, and when Selma returned, she muttered apologetically, "When you get as old as me—you know—it leaks a little."

Relieved, Ariel grinned. "That reminds me, Mrs. G. You think you're old. Have you heard about Eve?"

"What's this? Gerontology now?" When Ariel hesitated, she smiled encouragingly. "So *nu*? I'm all ears."

Ariel bit her lip. She wanted to tell it right, so that Selma got it. *Got what?* But she just went on.

"Selma, do you ever wonder where you came from?"

Selma frowned. "I didn't tell you? I was born here, but my family came from Kodnya, not too far from Kiev." Her eyes flashed. "Only, the Nazis leveled it. Not a building left standing, they should all rot in hell."

Ariel tried again. "Well, that's terrible, but it's not exactly what I mean. More like roots. More like what your ancestors were like."

Selma peered at her, then put a hand on Ariel's thigh. "Ariel, dear, for Jewish people not so much really changes over the years." She lowered her voice. "Thousands of years. Oh, maybe the customs have been a little different here and there, cooking with the spices of whatever country we fled to next, speaking languages other than Hebrew, obeying the laws of the land. But there's a flavor in the humor and a respect for life and family and learning that even a faithless Jew feels in the bones."

Ariel rapped the table, babbling excitedly. "Bones! That's just it. Selma, have you heard about Eve's bones?"

Selma pulled back. "You're making a joke with me?"

"No, no." Ariel tried to explain. Except that, somehow, telling Selma how she kept coming across tantalizing tidbits about Eve spilled into an embarrassing regurgitation of her mother's death, her ultimately successful struggle to have herself declared an emancipated minor, how much she still missed her father, and what a waste of time it was to even fantasize a future with Ben.

Selma sat without comment, her posture erect and her eyes half closed, until the thing that had gotten hold of Ariel finally let go. In the silence, the old woman considered her. "So, *nu*," she said finally, "this discovery ... what do you call it? Eve? You think she had something you don't? Some magic clue that your own mother didn't teach you?"

Ariel was too raw; the words just slipped out. "My mother didn't teach me shit."

Selma flicked a glance up at the ceiling. "You shouldn't say it. Your own mother."

Ariel squirmed. "I know it sounds terrible, but she really didn't have much to give. And even if she had ... I mean, it's a different era now. Everything's uniform, homogenized. The Web, the Gap, McDonald's everywhere from Machu Picchu to China. Have you listened to the radio lately? No, I guess not, but—trust me—it's depressing. I was born less than two decades after a major league cultural Renaissance. My mom had R&B; you had swing. But now most hit songs have about as much soul as pieces of Styrofoam shifting around in a cardboard box. And that's just the tip of the iceberg. Politics are a disaster, and not just here. Everywhere. We're all living under the threat of extinction. I know it sounds dumb, but the whole show seems so useless."

Selma fell silent and stared glassily at the photograph in Ariel's lap. She laughed weakly. "Look at us. A young woman like you *shlepping* mail on her hip instead of children, and an *alter cocker* like me spending too much time moping about the past." She spread her hands. "So you think that old African knew something we both don't?"

Nine

WE'RE BORN WITH few instincts, to root and suck and fling out our tiny arms in fear of falling, a holdover from our primate ancestors' risk of spilling from trees as they slept. Naked and vulnerable and nearly blind, we see but hazily the face of the bountiful one—a mere arm's distance away—who holds the power to feed us, to make us feel safe and warm and less alone. But a mother feels her own way in the dark, reliant on resources, inner and outer, that may or may not be there. Will she manage to offer enough to fortify us for the terrors and disappointments to come? Some of us—perhaps most of us—never quite escape our original caul of helplessness. But we try.

Jane Deare shuffled lethargically down Hollywood Boulevard. What little spirit her cough had left her with had been drained out of her by a series of doctors and nurses and lab technicians at Cedars-Sinai.

She'd hated having to undress for them, her white arms goose-fleshed from the icy air-conditioning that some undoubtedly fully clad technician had set on high. She didn't know which was worse—waiting to be seen, scantily covered by the paper nightie that an obese, greasy-haired nurse had disdainfully flung onto the examining table, or the needles that they'd pricked her with, as if she hadn't been penetrated enough in her sixteen years to last a lifetime.

The last of the doctors had insisted she spit into a cup, placed his stethoscope against her chest, then told her he wanted to admit her. At first, she hadn't understood what he meant. Casting an anxious eye up at him for further explanation, she noticed how exhausted he looked. He didn't seem much older than she was. His voice was nearly as high-pitched as her twelve-year-old brother's, and he couldn't be much taller than Bobby, either. But he had dark circles under his sad brown eyes, emphasizing the thickness of his glasses, and deep lines crossed his forehead as he stared at her. His name tag said "Dr. Nussbaum." It was only then that she'd noticed the funny looking, round velvet cap fastened to the top of his curly black hair with a couple of bobby pins. She wondered if he was a Mason or something. Her legs swung nervously back and forth over the edge of the examining table.

He wanted her to stay the night until all the test results could be read. His eyes looked kind and concerned. Jane thought he seemed nice, but who could tell?

Another series of deep, racking coughs had shaken her body, which she'd taken as a sign. Nodding at him as tears blurred her vision, making him look for a moment like a kindly seal, she asked him what she needed to do. He disappointed her by suddenly putting on a more impersonal air.

He'd stuffed his stethoscope back in his lab coat pocket, and waved over at the nurse who was standing in the corner of the room with beefy arms crossed in front of her.

"Nurse Johnson will help you," he'd said, as he went out the door.

Jane had looked up haplessly as the old cow moved toward her, an evil glint in her eye. Putting her fat face right up to Jane's, so close that Jane could see how thick her pores were under her clumsily applied pancake makeup, Nurse Johnson asked her if she was really eighteen, said she looked a whole lot younger than that, and where were her parents, anyway?

Jane excused herself to go to the bathroom. As the nurse turned aside to tend to some paperwork, she surreptitiously grabbed her clothes and bundled them close to her chest, trying to look casual as she headed for the ladies' room with one hand in front and the other trying to hold the paper nightie closed over her butt. She'd slammed the door shut against the stares of two pimply-faced, thuggy-looking guys standing around an injured friend's gurney. Inside, she stuffed her arms and legs back into her shirt and jeans, and still holding her sneakers and socks, fled the ER. Nurse Johnson yelled down the hall that she couldn't do that, she might have a communicable disease, they'd have to report her, it was against the law.

So now she was a fugitive, just like Sarah and Danny. She was desperate to find them. After she'd left the hospital, she'd looked for them in all their regular haunts, scrounging change along the way to buy some over-the-counter cough medicine at Rite-Aid that hadn't helped at all. She didn't even have her socks. She'd dropped them when the hospital security guard had initially looked like he was going to run after her, though he was actually rushing to buzz open the doors for two paramedics, hurriedly propelling some poor soul on a stretcher from an ambulance whose engine they'd left running. It must be a terrible emergency, she'd thought, as she hightailed it toward Santa Monica Boulevard.

Jane's nostrils flared as she passed a McDonald's. The aroma was tantalizing, despite being mixed with car fumes and a faint smell of urine emanating from the grimy, chewing-gum-splotched sidewalk. She couldn't remember when she'd had a real meal. She stopped to count the change left in her jeans pocket. After splurging on bus fare yesterday to make the hunt for Sarah and Danny a little easier, it was just about enough for a bag of potato chips and a Coke. She kept her eyes peeled for a grocery store as she began to walk again. She wished she had the guts to steal something more nutritious, like beef jerky or a small carton of orange juice, and stick it under her shirt the way she'd seen Sarah and Danny do it. But now that she was a fugitive, she couldn't take the chance.

She knew that she could come up with some money real fast if she were only willing to do what most of the runaways did for it. But she'd left her home in Ohio to avoid just that kind of thing, and if it came down to it she was convinced she'd just kill herself instead. She would slit her wrists with a broken soda bottle, just like she'd seen in the movies. She knew she could take the pain. She'd experimented with it in her old bathroom, cutting her index finger with a razor blade, watching the red blood well up from the consecutive lines with satisfaction, smearing it across her cheeks and forehead and looking deeply into her eyes in the bathroom mirror until she didn't know who she was looking at anymore.

Not that anybody had noticed when she started sporting Band-Aids on her fingers all the time—least of all him, when he snuck into her bed in the middle of the night.

As sometimes happened, Jane became so lost in her dark reverie that she wandered blindly, as if in a fugue state, heedless of where she was heading. She "came to" at the corner of Hollywood and Vine amidst a herd of tourists who stood in small groups, the men with cameras slung around their necks and big bellies protruding from hokey Hawaiian shirts, their doughy wives with slack-jawed, bored-out-of-their-minds-looking children in tow.

The first time Sarah and Danny had taken her here to laugh at the fools who thought they'd see movie stars at this running sore of a place, she'd felt only pity for these people who'd saved up their hard-earned vacation money for their big trip to Hollywood, like it was the Promised Land or something. They'd come with their hungry fantasies and bulging wallets, only to crowd, along with scores of other disappointed and confused Midwesterners, looking for celebrities who wouldn't be caught dead these days in this part of town.

Her stomach grumbled, and she felt as hollow as the time she'd let her first dollar bill get away. It was the summer of her seventh year. Uncle Harry had offered to take her and Bobby along with his own kids to the lake. Harry was a plumber, and he piled all six of the kids in the back of his red truck that smelled of pipe grease and other things she didn't want to think about. But before they could climb into the roomy truck bed, he handed each of them a crisp dollar bill, solemnly telling the saucer-eyed children to hold onto their money real tight so that they could spend it on anything they wanted at the snack stand when they got to the lake.

Jane hadn't been too fond of Uncle Harry. He was a short, fat man who had the annoying habit of telling her that he loved her rosy little cheeks, grabbing them with his hammy hands and twisting them and laughing as if he expected her to like being pinched. But when he handed her that dollar bill, she felt like Harry was the most generous man in the world.

He probably wasn't driving that fast, but with the wind whipping her hair out behind her, Jane felt like they were going a hundred miles an hour. As they sped past wide open fields fronted by evenly spaced power poles, she stood up in the truck bed, holding onto the side with one hand and waving her dollar bill at cows and horses who looked up impassively from their grazing at the truckload of shrieking kids. She felt like a millionaire as the money flapped like a flag in her hand.

And then, suddenly, the wind wrested her dollar bill from her. She saw it sail down the road where they'd just come from. She banged on the cab window, shouting to Harry to stop the truck, she'd lost her dollar, they had to go back.

Harry had stopped, all right. Just long enough to tell her how stupid she was to let her dollar go. Refusing to go back for it, he had a malicious gleam in his eyes as he told her she'd have to watch the other kids eat their snacks and go without anything for herself as a punishment for treating her money so carelessly. Her belly rumbled as the vision of the hot dog on a stick she'd planned for herself dissolved. When Harry got back in the driver's seat, none of the other kids would look at her. She tossed her head and announced that she didn't care anyway. But her cheeks felt like they were on fire.

Jane was jogged out of her reverie as a drag queen with heavy mascara and over-drawn orange lips knocked against her as he rushed to make the flashing Walk signal. A sign saying "Grocery" jutted out from a small building over the sidewalk ahead of her, and she picked up her pace. But when she got closer and saw a couple of impassive-faced Koreans in crisp white shirts standing in front with their arms crossed, looking at her like she was dirt, she just kept walking. She didn't feel hungry anymore.

The sun shone brightly a few days later as the doctor who'd seen Jane at Cedars-Sinai ER walked briskly along the well-swept sidewalk of Olympic Boulevard, just inside the Beverly Hills border. David Nussbaum quickened his pace to make the light, unaware of the cursing he'd incited from the driver of a beat-up Ford Mustang who had to stomp both feet on his worn brakes to avoid hitting the diminutive, yarmulke-wearing man who'd suddenly obstructed his right turn.

The driver banged his fist angrily on his dashboard before turning to his passenger, who held a trembling hand to her chest. Kineesha Washington's almond eyes—the ones her co-worker Ariel found so beautiful—were wide with fear. She had to catch her breath before remonstrating with her boyfriend Nat for launching into one of his all-too-familiar diatribes about how the Jew-boys made this part of town such a drag, and why didn't she live closer to her own people, anyway?

David Nussbaum was out of breath himself. He'd woken up late, with barely enough time to wash and dress before rushing out of the house for temple. It seemed like he could never get enough sleep to make up for his exhausting twelve-hour shifts at Cedars' emergency room.

As he passed Noah's Bagels, its small sidewalk tables ringed by clusters of casually attired, secular Jewish men and women his own age, he glanced at his reflection in the shop window. Realizing that his yarmulke was ridiculously askew, he hastily straightened it and fastened it more securely to his curly head with a bobby pin. Looking quickly across the street at a large brick building, he saw men and boys, clad as he was, in suits with *tzitzit* fringes hanging down their legs from beneath their jackets, and elegant looking women and girls dressed with great flair in Old World-style dresses and hats and fashionable shoes with heels suitably low enough for walking distances, for no one drove to temple. It was *Shabbos,* after all.

He was about to dash across Olympic Boulevard when a teenaged girl stepped out in front of him with her delicate palm thrust forward. David, impatient to join the group of people beginning to file into the synagogue, had a momentary confused thought that this painfully thin creature with the scraggly hair overhanging her face wanted him to read her fortune. He passed a hand over his forehead as he heard her faintly mumble, "Spare change?"

David darted a quick glance across the street. They'd all gone in. He shrugged and shook his head.

"I can't. It's *Shab*—" But just then, as she began to turn aside, the wind blew her hair away from her face so that he could make out her features. "Say, wait a minute." He grabbed her hand. Her eyes widened with alarm. "Didn't I examine you at the hospital a few days ago? Aren't you the one who ran off?"

"Let me go." She tried to jerk away from his now determined grasp.

"Don't. Wait," he said gently. But there was urgency in his voice, too. "I won't hurt you. Don't be afraid. I just want to look at your test."

Jane darted a glance over at the curiously staring people lounging at the sidewalk tables, none of whom had been willing to part with a dime so that she, too, could sink her teeth into one of the heavenly smelling bagels. As David repeated that he wouldn't hurt her, something in his voice persuaded her to stop trying to pull away.

He inspected her forearm, then looked up, his face wreathed in a wide smile.

"At least it's not T.B." He tapped the place on her arm where she'd been punctured. "See? No red, raised bumps." She looked at him blankly. "Hey, cheer up. You're not as sick as I thought." He put a hand on her shoulder. "How've you been feeling?"

Jane kept looking uncomfortably at the people seated nearby, so he gently pulled her around the corner.

Although Jane reported that her cough was a little better, he was still concerned about her. But what could he do? He gave her his card and made her promise to phone him on Monday to get the rest of her test results. Made her promise, too, that if she felt any worse, she would call his colleague, Fred Samovitz, whose name and number he wrote onto the back of his card. He told her he'd warn Samovitz that she might need to come in. And then he thought about Samovitz's fee.

Looking over one more time at the synagogue across the street and reassuring himself that no stragglers lingered to see what he was about to do, David reached into his pocket for his billfold and extracted every bit of money inside. He pressed it into the girl's palm.

The synagogue reverberated with the cantor's mournful song when David finally sat down next to Max Schulman. He liked to stay on good terms with Max because of his wife Edith.

Edith had been David's babysitter when he was little, and he'd been smitten with her delicately molded features, her sharp, intelligent black eyes with their long curling lashes, and her slender body that she flirtatiously flounced through his house to "Bennie and the Jets" and "The Loco-Motion" once his parents' car pulled out of the driveway. She wore flared skirts that he used to try to peek up as he played with toy cars on his bedroom floor.

But David wasn't thinking about Edith now. He was thinking about Jane. Worrying about her, whether she was carrying something worse than T.B., whether she'd actually call him on Monday or get herself over to see Samovitz. He felt guilty for letting her go her own way.

He felt guilty, too, that he'd given her money on *Shabbos*. He shouldn't even have been carrying it on him, let alone allow it to pass from his hands into another's. He wondered if giving money to beggars constituted doing business, especially since she'd been a paying patient at the hospital where he worked. No one saw him, he felt sure. No one but God. He could only pray that God was busy elsewhere, with more important matters, that He hadn't noticed David's sin.

Ten

UCLA VICE-CHANCELLOR Matt Hayes wondered what kind of past sin had gone around and come back around to condemn him to pose like this under the blazing sun like some mindless, but well-clothed mannequin. What a waste of a perfect Saturday.

Someone shouted at him. "Hold it! Yes, right there. Now lift your chin up just a little."

His ice-blue eyes flicking over to the *L.A. Times* photographer to make sure he'd got it right, Matt stifled an impulse to scratch the back of his neck, where a drop of perspiration was working a torturous path downward from his still boyishly full head of blond hair. After serving for several years as a university administrator, it was second nature to keep a toothy yet dignified smile plastered onto his face, when all he really wanted to do was shed his Armani suit and dive into the turquoise pool of this official Vice-Chancellor's residence on whose Malibu-tiled decking he and the photographer stood.

The press conference had been called at the last minute, which was why the journalist and his crew had intruded on his all too rare hours of leisure this Saturday morning. His wife Bonnie and their two leggy teenaged daughters had seemed only too pleased at this break in the Hayes family routine of Saturday brunch taken together on the lanai alongside the pool. The girls hated arriving at the valet lot of Barneys upscale department store in their mother's sedate Volvo station wagon, so they'd headed out of the carport in Matt's black BMW convertible like there was no tomorrow, the girls yattering away at each other a mile a minute while their fashionably cut, white-blond hair danced in the wind. Their mother gripped the steering wheel, an intent expression on her still good-looking, if a little hard, face.

"Out for some serious shopping," Matt muttered under his breath, his hand unconsciously reaching toward the roll of fifty-dollar-bills in his pants pocket.

Assuming Matt was scratching his balls, the photographer politely looked away.

Matt wasn't supposed to be doing this interview at all, but the Chancellor had come down with one of those miserable summer colds a few days ago and had called Matt last night, filling him in on the plans for a major interdepartmental research project on the fossil find from Africa that Bernice Behrens from the anthro Department was spearheading.

Bonnie had rolled her round, green eyes and clutched her hand theatrically to her white-nightied breast when she'd handed him the phone. Chancellor Biggs was a notorious hypochondriac who was rumored to frequent with embarrassing regularity the esoteric offices of homeopaths and faith healers, his latest guru supposedly a gold-turbaned Hindu from Punjab who'd taught at the Mayo Clinic and was now known around town as "the Savant to the Stars." But Biggs sounded really sick when Matt got on the phone.

"Matt, I'b gudda owe you wud."

As he heard Biggs out, his heart sank. He'd been working late nights all week, overseeing bargaining talks with the union that represented the university's huge janitorial staff, and was looking forward to two days off to call his own.

On free summer days, Matt Hayes liked to sneak off to a particular stretch of Hermosa Beach, where none of the local boys knew or cared what he did for a living. They merely knew him as "Old Wild Man," which they'd nicknamed him out of respect for how brazenly a man who was as ancient as their fathers handled the waves.

Handling the custodian's union had been another matter. The janitors were a feisty lot. Always wanting more. Matt figured they had a pretty good deal. Decent pay, great benefits, a pleasant working environment. Ever since he was an undergrad here, Matt had found the sprawling, ever-growing campus beautiful, with its rolling lawns and graceful old brick buildings punctuated by sharp statements of architectural modernity.

He hadn't had much direct dealing with the custodial staff before this current crisis. Except, he reminded himself, for that one time he'd finessed Theosophus into a full-time job after bumping into him on Crenshaw Boulevard a decade ago. Matt, a then moderately ambitious Assistant Dean of Student Affairs, was already a regular weed smoker, and the Adams-Crenshaw neighborhood was a great place to score. When Matt ascended the steps of a fifties box of a building, Theo had been coming out of the apartment where Matt's dealer—a beret-sporting skinny guy named Lacey—handed out pungent smelling baggies of the stuff like it was gold. Recognizing Matt instantly, Theo had approached his old idol with a sinuous, cat-like walk, a wide white-toothed smile breaking over his face like a dawning sun.

Diverted from his mission by curiosity about what the sensitive kid he'd been surprisingly fond of had gotten up to in the intervening years, Matt had ended up that night in a smoky bar on Venice Boulevard, downing shots of Old Taylor with Theo like it was Pepsi Cola.

Matt had sure enough gotten high that night, not on weed, nor even Old Taylor, but on the dense and smoky atmosphere of that nightclub, where couples of every race swooned together to the velvety seduction of the Simms Twins' signature song, "Soothe Me."

By the time Etta James was belting out "My Dearest Darling," several of the women in the club had given him the eye. Matt had wanted to dance with them in the worst way, but he was still cautious after the debacle of bumping into Terry with Bonnie and their two daughters the previous year. He'd had to call if off with Terry after that. Too much was at stake. The girl had been heartbroken, and he had to admit it had been harder on him than he'd imagined.

But Theosophus? As Matt described to the assembled reporters the attention that the UCLA faculty would be focusing on the bones of "First Eve," it occurred to him that he hadn't bumped into Theo on campus for some time. Maybe he'd look up his phone number in the employee files and give him a call.

———————————

Across town, Ariel's phone pinged maddeningly as she fumbled with the key to her front door until, swearing like a sailor, she finally managed to get it open. Worried that it might be Selma needing something, she set her leaking bag of groceries down onto the kitchen floor and made a dash back to the living room where she'd dropped her purse, nearly tripping on Jezebel's tail, which the cat flapped defiantly back and forth on the carpet to protest such an unceremonious intrusion into her naptime. Ariel banged her shin on the coffee table as she extracted her cell phone from the purse's side pocket.

"Shit," she said, moaning in pain and rubbing her leg with her free hand as she brought the phone to her ear. Realizing the caller had probably heard her cursing, she tried to make her voice sound extra polite. "Hello?"

The voice on the other end sounded disconcerted and a little husky. "Ariel Thompkins?"

It sure as hell wasn't Mrs. G. Nor did it sound like anyone else she knew.

Oh, great, Ariel thought as she irritably nudged a now curious Jezzie away from her with the toe of her worn sneaker. The use of her last name was a dead giveaway that it was a telemarketer, probably offering her some new credit card service she had absolutely no use for.

"Yeah?" she said accusingly.

The voice surprised her. It giggled and notched a bit higher on the scale. "Ariel, you're not going to believe this. It's Terry."

"Terry?" Ariel's own voice hit soprano. She flopped down on the sofa. "No way. I don't believe it." But she did. The voice was different, but she'd recognize that infectious laugh anywhere. Suddenly she was fifteen again. "Hang on," she said. "This calls for a cigarette." Watching a couple of ragged smoke circles waft into the air, she tried to make her mouth into a more perfect O-shape as she listened to Terry explain why she'd called. Ariel pictured herself and Terry and Jasmine leaning in toward one another beside one of the outdoor lunch benches at Venice High, their heads nearly touching as they tried to hide the forbidden chest-searing Marlboro they were passing back and forth.

Ariel had lost touch with both of her old best friends years ago. Jasmine, having listened to brain-dead white kids call her brother Neal "Buddha Head" too many times to count, had moved to Maui right out of high school to work for an uncle who managed vacation condos.

And Terry, always clever and practical, had shot beyond her humble beginnings by working her way up the ranks of Paramount Studios' publicity department, then used that as a stepping-stone to a big bucks post in marketing at Citibank in Manhattan.

Terry was talking so fast now that Ariel had a hard time keeping up with her. As the gist of it began to seep in, she frowned. Terry had evidently gotten so sick of the stuffiness of the higher financial altitudes—and, p.s., a protracted engagement to an ex-Wharton MBA who bored the hell out of her—that she'd come back home for some soul-searching, taking a temp job at a second-tier publicity firm until she figured out what she wanted to do. Ariel's eyes traveled across her untidy living room and stopped at the scene of Jezebel kneading an already torn-up patch of carpet.

"And listen to this," Terry said, "not only have I moved back to this godforsaken town, but Jasmine called my mom the other day to say she was going to be here for a few days next week. This calls for a serious reunion, don't you think?"

Ariel nervously stabbed out her cigarette and looked down at the dimpled thighs that spread out of her shorts like a couple of uncooked sausages. She tried to keep the self-loathing out of her voice. "Of course." She paused. Did she really want to commit to this? "I can't wait."

From Ariel's perspective, their reunion came much too soon. Before entering Gracias Madre for the first time, she checked out her face in the window of a black Rolls in the valet queue in front. Right behind it was a line of other expensive cars, each of their windows as good as a mirror, for, without exception, their exteriors were polished to a glossy shine. A far cry from her sticky-tree-sap-besmirched Corolla with its pitted paint job that she'd parked around the corner to avoid the seven-dollar valet fee and the obligatory dollar or two tip. She'd had to look over the multitude of street signs several times to figure out if she could park there without getting a ticket. "District 7 parking only." "Two-hour parking between 6 p.m. and midnight." "No parking after 11 p.m." Half of them seemed to contradict the other half, but she decided to take the risk.

She licked her teeth to try to ensure that no lipstick adhered to them. She wasn't used to the coral lip gloss she'd bought at the Beverly Center yesterday after work, along with the long black skirt that a Macy's salesgirl with overdrawn, surprised-looking eyebrows had assured her "flattered her figure." Running her hands down her sides, she mused that she had a figure that definitely could use some flattering. Peering into the Rolls' side window, she wondered if she would have better used her money to get her hair done.

One of the valet guys, wearing ironed-to-a-shine tight black trousers, a red vest, and an apologetic smile on his broad, brown face, came up to her and asked her if she knew her way into the restaurant. She guessed she'd been loitering next to the Rolls too long. But she forgave him. The poor bastard was probably afraid she was going to steal the most expensive car in the queue, misinterpreting her nerves for the shifty-eyed demeanor of a thief.

Her feet felt like lead on the diagonally laid brick floor of the outdoor patio area, littered with trendily coiffed and tatted types lounging on cushily upholstered chairs at marble and wood-topped tables. She clutched her purse tightly to her midriff as she anxiously scanned the space for her friends.

Suddenly, Ben was at her side, whispering in her ear, "You look like Bo Beep minus the sheep." Ariel's cheeks reddened. She noted the red apron tied pertly at the waist over his tight black trousers. His blue shirt was unbuttoned just enough to hint at his lusciously tanned chest.

"You look like a gigolo," she said. As soon as the words escaped her lips, she wanted to kick herself.

He stepped back and squinted at her.

"Wow. Really?" He took a second to regroup and came back with a generous "You that nervous?"

She was mortified, unsure which was harder for her, the prospect of seeing Terry and Jasmine in the flesh after all these years or finally entering the restaurant that she was convinced teemed with competitors for Ben's affections.

It was he who'd suggested she meet her old friends here. She'd been lying next to him in his bed, having finally succumbed to temptation after smoking a spliff with him, something she hadn't done in years.

Her mind conjured up the one-night stand she'd picked up in desperation last year in a local bar. That particular charm school graduate had emptied himself into her like she was a gas tank, then without skipping a beat, had turned away from her and started snoring. Which left her free to interrogate herself. What had she been thinking, asking this guy up to her apartment in the first place? He'd had red hair and sported a feeble attempt at designer stubble that had made a comeback a decade ago and now seemed here to stay. On him, it looked like the traces of a pig-out on spaghetti marinara. After she'd wakened from a few hours' fitful sleep to the sobering presence of his clammy, freckled body in her bed, she'd kicked him out. The jerk had actually had the nerve to ask whether he could ring her up sometime for a booty call.

Ben, she wouldn't kick out, even if his determinedly sensitive lovemaking hadn't been able to bring her to a climax. She should have warned him, she supposed, but how do you say these things? She'd finally managed to assuage his obvious guilt by telling him—with no little embarrassment—that she'd been more than satisfied with what they'd done together.

"Really?" he'd asked dubiously.

"Really," she'd replied, and meant it. She was grateful that he hadn't asked her to amplify, as talking about sex wasn't exactly her métier. It was already a stretch to lie on the bed with him afterwards without pulling the sheet over herself. Instead, she'd tried to concentrate on brainstorming where she might meet up with Terry and Jasmine for their reunion dinner while he leaned his head on one hand and gently stroked her naked thigh with the other.

"Why not Gracias Madre? The food's great, the service sublime." He licked her ear, sending a thrill down to her belly.

"I don't know." She winced at hearing the whine in her voice. She didn't have the guts to confess what she feared lurked at the place where he worked.

"Aw, come on. I'll make sure they treat you like royalty. Throw in a few freebies. Your friends will think you're the coolest thing in town."

Ariel had hesitated, hope and fear competing. He was so sweet. He wouldn't suggest that place if he were banging somebody there. Would he?

So, as Ben's breath quickened and he lowered his body over hers again, Ariel's last thought before oblivion had been, Oh, what the fuck, why not?

This is why, she told herself, as she balefully looked around the room. The female patrons of this restaurant even sat cool, casually displaying long legs and boyish thighs barely covered by expensive short skirts. Many of them wore ridiculously high V-cut heels that seemed designed to show off their small ankles and graceful calves. Wiping perspiration from her upper lip, Ariel doubted that any of these women ever sweated.

Her eyes flicked over the escorts of these prize blooms; to a man, they were expensively, if casually, attired. Many of them sported man buns or goatees, but it did seem that most of them were significantly older (or younger) than their dates. Then she stole a shy look at the man who stood next to her and lit up momentarily with the thought that he was better looking than any of them, and it was his bed she'd slept in last night.

She shot him a look of gratitude. "I'm sorry about what I said. I mean, the gigolo thing. It was bullshit."

He smiled at her complacently. "Of course it was. You think I don't know you?" His eyes swept away from her and focused somewhere over her shoulder. "I'll bet those are your buddies."

Ariel swallowed, her hand creeping to her chest as she turned to see the two women who stood with an air of uncertainty at the entrance. They were both unusual looking. Jasmine, just as petite and flat-chested as ever, wore a floral sundress, her shiny black hair in a long braid trailing halfway down her back, making her look a little like a child with an adult's face pasted onto her. Terry was still stunning, a cloud of chestnut curls surrounding her exotic, heart-shaped face and her breasts so high and full they might have been fake (though Ariel knew they weren't). She was a standout even in this crowd.

Terry burst out in what Ariel tended to think of as a smoker's laugh, halfway to a cough, causing the murmurings at nearby tables to stop for a moment, leaving only Gracias Madre's sound system— broadcasting Fleetwood Mac's warning not to stop thinking about tomorrow—to pierce the silence.

As Ariel wrapped her arms around her two friends, Terry

whispered in her ear, "Do you know him?" All three of them looked over at Ben, who winked jauntily and gave Ariel the thumbs-up sign. Terry shot Ariel the knowing look so familiar from high school days and whispered lasciviously, "What a hunk."

Like teenagers again, they giggled nervously as Ben showed them to their table before hurrying over toward the beckoning hand of another customer.

"God, Ariel, you really struck gold," Terry pronounced. "I've never seen such a good-looking guy."

"What about Matt Hayes?" Jasmine teased. "You used to say he was the most beautiful man in the world."

"Don't even," Terry warned.

Ariel brought out a pack of Marlboros, and three heads bent toward each other to block the wind from the open sky. She shook out her match as Terry and Jasmine blew smoke out of their noses with a studied air. When Ariel took a second match to light her own cigarette, Jasmine nodded with satisfaction and turned to Terry with the air of repeating an old familiar mantra.

They said the words in unison. "Three on a match, bad luck."

As it happened, even on two matches, they were out of luck. A restaurant hostess glided over in haste to inform them that there was no smoking in West Hollywood restaurants, even in outdoor patios, making a pinched face and removing the offending cigarettes in her delicate fingers as if they held rat's tails.

Terry asked the inevitable question, "Why the hell are three supposedly intelligent women smoking in this day and age, anyway?"

Ariel shrugged, offering what she knew was a lame, "Because it's too hard to quit?" But she knew it was because she couldn't stand the thought of putting even more pounds onto her thighs.

Terry rushed to say, "I try to keep myself to two or three a day."

"That's what Ben does."

Terry laughed. "Oh, it's Ben then?"

Ariel flushed, grateful when Jasmine took another tack entirely, "You're right. It's hard to quit, and vaping's not the great alternative it's painted to be. Did you know those things can blow your jaw off?"

"Yes," Terry responded dryly. "There's always that." And the three of them burst into laughter that caught the disapproving attention of the table next to theirs.

Ariel realized with a sense of exhilaration that, with her old friends by her side, she didn't give a damn what anyone else thought.

Eleven

IT WAS 2:30 A.M., and the City of Angels still hummed. Its waves of traffic sounded like the sea. Drunks wove their treacherous way home after the melancholy closing of bars and nightclubs; Adderall-high big rig drivers snapped their gum and crowed to each other on CB radios; coke dealers in shiny Caddies and BMWs schmoozed prospective customers on their cell phones; swing-shift workers fantasized beer and bed and fought the urge to nod off at the wheel.

In the depths of night, though, the sky was still not black, and none but the brightest stars were visible, for a haze of still-lit neon and street and traffic lights lifted up from the sleeping earth like a vast penumbra.

The throb of a police helicopter troubled the air. Its rotating blades and nervous searchlight woke Theosophus, who lay stretched out on the remains of a cardboard box on the edge of West Hollywood Park. He'd been dreaming that he was back in his childhood home, snuggled up with Granny under her old Alabama comforter, the one that her own mama had sewn for her wedding night. The one he and Granny used to cuddle under after he'd peed his bed.

In his dream, full of remorse and fear for the whupping Mama would be giving him in the morning, he'd tiptoed to his granny's bedside and waited till some Southern sixth-sense woke her. In her sleepy voice, thick like honey, she'd murmured, "Come warm your young bones next to my old ones, boy. Set yourself down with me under the sweet comfort of your great-granny's stitches."

His dream had been spoiled by the approaching helicopter.

Shielding his eyes from its blinding light, Theosophus shook his fist at the invasive monster and cursed loudly, causing other bodies dotting the overgrown grasses of West Hollywood Park to yell at him to shut the fuck up. He felt around the pile of belongings beside him for last night's bottle of cheap booze. His throat and belly hot with the last drops, he despaired of getting back to his dream. That damned thing kept circling over his head. To his whiskeyed-up gaze, it looked like a giant roach in the sky.

A mile or two away, another helicopter circled over Poinsettia Avenue, but failed to wake Ariel, huddled on a pile of blankets on her frayed living room rug alongside the snoring bodies of Terry and Jasmine and Jezebel. But it did manage to turn her own dream of doing the Walk It Out with Jasmine into a nightmare. DJ Unk's voice dissolved, and she found herself flying a plane, her father in another one near her, but she couldn't find him, couldn't see.

The helicopter hadn't wakened Ben, either. He was already awake. In fact, he hadn't gone to sleep since returning from his shift at Gracias Madre to an apartment building that reverberated with shrieks emanating from Ariel's impromptu slumber party. As the helicopter aimed its beam at the carport behind the building, Ben grinned. In her regression to high school hysteria, Ariel reminded him of his sister Anna.

He and Anna had a private joke that they were mutants in the family gene pool, resulting from too much exposure to toxic weed-killers by their overzealous gardener of a mother. Anna loved the movies, too, and when they were teenagers the two of them spent endless hours watching their favorite old films on TV and then acting out the key scenes almost verbatim. Anna had her own ritualized way of complimenting him. "Ben," she'd say, "you're so fucking good, you could be a movie star." But she never failed to light up when he'd point out that she herself had a gift for comedy. And it was true, her imitation of Diane Keaton's loopiness in *Annie Hall* was so spot-on it'd make anybody laugh out loud. Anyone, that is, but their parents, who were so caught up in the Christian born-again movement that they panicked over anything the edgy side of *Bambi*.

Anna had been his biggest supporter—hell, his only one—when it came to his plans to move to L.A. He only wished he could have gotten her out of there long ago. His folks treated the news like he was defecting to Sodom and Gomorrah. He grinned. Given the high percentage of gays in West Hollywood, they were closer to the truth than they knew.

But what had he been thinking of, comparing Anna and Ariel? It certainly wasn't that they looked alike. He shook his head, hating to admit that his once boyishly cute sister had gone to seed. Saddled with three kids before she was twenty-five, Anna looked old now and loaded down with the heaviness of Midwesterners who didn't waste much time worrying about fat grams and endorphins. She and her family consumed the products that Hollywood commercials advertised as voraciously as they consumed the TV shows that were the excuse for the commercials' existence.

Oh sure, Ariel was no waif either, unlike this city's anemic ideal, but her body curved in just the right places: her big-nippled breasts a breath-taking cushion, her ass with just enough meat to hold in his hungry hands. No, it wasn't her body that reminded him of Anna. Nor her face, which he had to admit was more beguiling than his sister's, with a kind of light in her eyes—at least when her guard was down—as if she could see something he couldn't.

Maybe it was how she and Anna both laughed hard. Talked hard. Swore like fishwives.

Ben got up to take a leak. Scratching his balls pleasurably as his water arched toward the bowl, he realized that that was it. Ariel and Anna—coarse talkers, both of them, but accepting and big-hearted. They didn't superimpose their own beliefs on you. Wanted for you what you wanted for yourself. Coarse talkers, but refined souls.

As the helicopter finally spun away, Ben muttered. "Thank God." The silence was palpable. He imagined Ariel sleeping nearby and felt his penis grow hard. He thought of the tenderness that wet her lashes as she pretended a sarcastic disparagement of her cat, of the worry lines that etched more deeply across her forehead when speaking about the old Jewish lady on her route, of how expansively she gestured, her eyes like sparklers, whenever she mentioned that African fossil—though she'd gone all shy on him, changing the subject, when he showed her a small *Newsweek* article about it that he'd clipped out for her recently.

He grunted, and his dick went soft again. The thing was: he wasn't sure of her, was he? Like Anna, Ariel was full of encouragement about his acting—helping him memorize his sides before auditions, dropping everything to speed to his door and hug him when he'd phone her that he'd gotten a callback. And he'd gotten the distinct impression she'd enjoyed being with him in his bed the night before, despite that fact that she hadn't come. But she got as squirmy as a cat that wouldn't be held if he tried aiming the conversation toward the subject of the two of them.

He shook his head. The way she talked, you'd think she found more romance in those ancient Eve bones than in any fantasy of a future with him.

Ben, my man, he told himself, *you might just be setting yourself up for some big-time pain*. Stretching his body out fully on sheets that still smelled of her, he fell into a restless sleep.

———————————

Just one floor down and a few hours later, Ariel cracked one eye open, groaned, closed it again, then sneezed as a rough tongue licked the tip of her nose. A strange sound filtered into her groggy consciousness.

"Meese-ke, moose-ke, mouseketeer, mouse cartoon time now is here."

Terry's burst of laughter from another part of the apartment reminded Ariel why she was here, sitting up from a pile of blankets in a living room that smelled too much like beer and cigarettes. Jezebel kneaded her thigh with great intensity at the prospect of breakfast.

"Terry!" she yelled. "It's too early, you rat. You woke me up."

Her two friends, clad in the panties and bras they'd slept in, bounded into the room as if they'd been up for hours, Terry waving two forefingers over her head like a man-eating insect.

"I'm not a rat. I'm a mouse...keteer," Terry said.

Ariel plopped her body back down on the blankets. "Oh God." Her voice was muffled by the pillow she'd shoved over her head. "I forgot how God-damned corny you were. We never should have watched all those old shows on TV-Land last night."

Terry sat down cross-legged beside her, while Jasmine bent to pick up Jezebel, who instantly twisted out of her arms, giving un-subtle, meowing hints as she padded purposefully toward the kitchen.

"All right, I'm coming, I'm coming." Ariel threw down her pillow and followed, turning back toward her friends with a mischievous grin. Tweaking an imaginary moustache and raising her eyebrows, she mimicked Groucho Marx's nasal refrain. "Say the secret word, and you'll get a can of cat food." She disappeared down the hall.

Terry made a face. "And she says I'm corny."

Jasmine grinned and idly gazed at Ariel's bookshelves on the opposite wall. She walked over and yanked a heavy book from the bottom shelf. She and Terry sat cross-legged together, a large photo album spread across both their laps.

When Ariel returned, she grabbed an opened pack of Virginia Slims from the coffee table. She waved it at Jasmine. "Do you mind?" Jasmine shook her head. Ariel lit a cigarette, took a deep drag, then coughed and sputtered. "Jesus! Menthol. How can you smoke these things?"

Jasmine retorted dryly, "Terry says the same thing, but I notice she pops a mint into her mouth every time she lights up. Let's face it, unadulterated cigarettes taste like shit."

Terry laughed, but Ariel merely shrugged. "I wouldn't know; I've been smoking so long I don't think I have any taste buds left."

"Oh, jeeze, look at this." Terry's gravelly laugh made her jump.

Ariel put a hand on each of her friend's shoulders and squinted down at a somewhat overexposed photo of the three of them, posing what might have been sexily if they hadn't been making such goofy faces.

"Oh, my God," Jasmine said. She pointed to the building behind their pubescent figures. "Isn't that the old Sav-on? The one they tore down to build condos after we graduated? Do you remember—" She left the sentence dangling purposefully.

"Larry Cowell!" Ariel and Terry chimed in on cue.

God, Ariel thought, do we ever change? What innocents they'd been, developing a group crush on the older boy who scooped ice cream behind the Sav-on counter. Did they really believe he didn't see what they were up to, giggling so hard they could hardly spit out their orders, returning so many times the summer he worked there that their little teeny-bopper hips and thighs nearly burst the seams of their lace-up jeans?

"You know," Jasmine said wonderingly, "he was good-looking, but why weren't we turned off by all those zits? Remember?"

Terry snickered. "Probably because we had to be just a little blind to our own to survive. God. Adolescence. Forget the boys. I had my most intimate relationship with Clearasil."

"No, you had your most intimate relationship with Matt Hayes," Jasmine insisted.

Terry laughed uncomfortably. "Change the subject, change the subject. That was later, anyway." She shot a sly look at Ariel. "Hey, speaking of Clearasil, do you remember the time you got busted for stealing a tube of the stuff from Sav-on?"

"Please. Don't remind me. The only way I convinced the manager not to call the cops was to use my mom's sickness as an excuse." When Ariel saw their faces fall, she added hastily, "Let's be fair, though. I wasn't the only criminal. How many times did we sneak each other into the Bruin Theatre, one of us paying for a ticket and then opening the door onto the alley for the other two to get in for free? And how about joyriding in Jasmine's uncle's car? Or borrowing her sisters' tennis rackets without permission and leaving them on the bus?" She grinned. "Now that I think of it, Jasmine's poor family were often the victims of our little adventures."

"Yeah," Terry said, "but 'our little adventures' were always your idea." She tilted her head consideringly. "You know, you were one brazen girl. I always thought you'd end up doing something amazing." As she realized what she'd said, she put a hand to her mouth. "Oh, Christ, I didn't mean—"

"Forget about it. I'm just a chronic underachiever, that's all." Ariel noticed that Jasmine had looked away and was nervously twirling a lock of hair around her forefinger. "Hey. Where'd you go?"

Jasmine flushed and shook her head lightly. "Oh, nowhere really. Larry Cowell. He seemed so mysterious. One of those quiet ones. I just remembered somebody told me he died in a motorcycle accident. His poor mom. He was all she had left. His dad got killed in Afghanistan."

Terry's hand flew to her mouth. "Are you serious?"

Jasmine carefully closed the book. They all stared at it as if Larry Cowell's face were reproaching them from its cover.

Terry sprang to her feet. Avoiding eye contact, she announced, "Pee break," then exited the room.

Ariel raised an eyebrow at Jasmine, who merely shrugged and said,

"Who can blame her? Death's awful."

The silence that followed was oppressive. When Terry returned, Ariel tried to relieve the tension. "You know, it made sense to me that they tore that old Sav-on down. It was funky. But of course we had no idea then. We were so blue-collar, so satisfied with our vanilla and chocolate and strawberry triple-cones, when over in Brentwood they were getting thirty-one flavors at Baskin-Robbins."

Terry objected. "No, no. Sav-on had chocolate chip, too. The chips were big and crunchy. And the strawberry had chunks of fresh fruit in it. You still can't beat the old standards."

Ariel directed a cynical look at Jasmine. "Will you listen to her?"

"Jesus, you guys." Jasmine's tone was raw. "Larry Cowell dies in the bloom of youth and you're talking about ice cream?"

Terry scowled. "Oh, come on, Jasmine, can't you lighten up a little? You always *were* the serious one. Larry Cowell. Matt Hayes. Can't you talk about anything but death and loss?"

As quickly as she'd spoken, her face reddened and her hand flew up to her mouth. She rushed over to embrace Jasmine, who sat in sudden stillness, head bowed.

"Oh, my God, sweetie. I'm just a total asshole." She looked over pleadingly at Ariel. Only last night, Jasmine had described her brother Neal's slow decline as his body increasingly failed to respond to his AIDS cocktail. Neither Ariel nor Terry had been aware of such a thing as HIV Drug Resistance and had been horrified. Jasmine had confided that no one knew when he would go, but it would surely be soon. She'd described her time with her friends as her "sanity break."

Terry pounded her forehead repeatedly with the heel of her hand.

"Stop." Jasmine took Terry's hand in hers. Her cheeks were wet with tears. "You're right. I always was the serious one. But that's exactly why you and Ariel were so good for me." She smiled ruefully. "You two? You were my comic relief. Still are. And who am I to act so self-righteous, anyway? Aren't I the one who's avoided L.A. ever since it became clear that it wasn't going to be 'happily ever after' for Neal? I only came back for this visit because Matt called to tell me he'd heard through their old fraternity grapevine that Neal was feeling abandoned by his favorite sister."

Terry's eyes widened and she looked away.

"Oh, come on, Jasmine." The harshness of Ariel's tone made Terry and Jasmine look at her curiously. "It's absolutely horrible about Neal. The worst." Her hands clenched and her throat felt dry. "But give yourself a break. When reality gets too heavy, sometimes you have to block it out. It's natural. A survival mechanism."

Jasmine nodded gratefully, but Ariel noticed that Terry looked a little doubtful.

Jasmine accepted a used-looking tissue that Terry retrieved from her purse, inadvertently smearing the dregs of last night's eye make-up across her face as she blew her nose. She smiled hesitantly.

Terry found another tissue, spat on it, then reached up to wipe Jasmine's face. "Sweetie, I hope you'll forgive me, but you've got snot all over your face, and I think it's time for breakfast."

Jasmine started to giggle.

Ariel whooped. "Now you're talking. I know what I want. No bacon and eggs for me." She stood up, baring her naked breasts and shaking her panty-clad hips from side to side. "Get up, you lazybones. And get dressed. Let's get decadent. Let's go get some Starbucks and then hit Ralph's for ice cream. And none of this Baskin-Robbins bullshit. I want me some Haagen-Dazs."

Following her lead, Terry and Jasmine snaked around the pile of blankets, undulating like tribal dancers.

Terry chimed in. "Too right! Forget Sav-on. It's a whole new millennium. It's Ben and Jerry's Chunky Monkey for me."

Twelve

AS ARIEL AND her friends snatched pints of their favorite ice cream from Ralph's frozen foods shelves, just a few miles away Selma Goldberg was painstakingly counting her bills before handing her fare to a swarthy, pock-marked taxi driver, who responded with a grunt and a grudging nod to her generous tip. Hurrying to the safety of the curb as a Jeep driver leaned on her horn, Selma chastised herself for trying to demonstrate her lack of prejudice against Arabs by over-tipping the man. As she used to do when Chaim was alive, she apologized to her husband for her bigotry. Flicking a glance up at the smoggy sky, she muttered under her breath. "I can't help it, sweetheart, but they're not nice people. Or not to us Jews, anyway. Did you see the expression on his face? As if he was doing me a favor by accepting my tip?"

Moving briskly down Fairfax Avenue, she saw something ahead that made her clasp her black handbag closer to her chest. She wanted to avert her eyes, but couldn't. In fact, she needed to look to avoid stepping on the splayed out legs of a teenaged boy extending an empty Folger's can toward her. The German shepherd at his side looked wretched, its ribs sticking out reproachfully as it panted heavily in the noonday sun. The boy—he couldn't be more than seventeen or eighteen—was even skinnier than the dog. Skeletal. And his skin looked leprous to her, covered in hideous sores. Navigating carefully around his feet before entering Canter's Delicatessen, she realized that his shoes didn't match. One was a yellowed sneaker tied incongruently with brown shoelaces, the other a much whiter one, hanging open with no laces at all.

The area in front of Canter's take-out counter was filled to near capacity. Selma took a number and prepared for a long wait. Wishing she could get close enough to the long, refrigerated case to assess the freshness of the cured meats and smoked fish she'd come here to buy, she inched her way to the big front window and leaned back against it with a sigh. She observed the small crush of humanity heave toward the counter, which was presided over by several jowly, ham-fisted men with New York accents who held court in a hybrid of English and Yiddish, liberally laced with coarse humor.

From where she stood, she could see both the deli patrons and the waves of pedestrians that continually surged outside. They were a motley bunch, and very different from the people who once made this street the center of their communal life and earned it its nickname, *the Borscht Belt.*

Chaim, do you remember my parents' stories about Fairfax? When they first came here, it was just like the shtetl, *only the streets were paved. I know I've got the photos of them somewhere, standing right here in front of Canter's, holding hands like a couple of babies, even though mama was nearly ready to pop with me. Mama told me people treated the street with respect then, shopkeepers swept the sidewalks almost every hour. It was so full of life! Young mothers with their babies.* Bubbes *with their* babushkas *fitted tightly on their heads. Children running up and down the street after school and laughing—the vendors would give them oranges, and the juice would run down their chins as they called out to one another. Everyone tipping their hats to the* rebbes *when they walked back and forth to temple.*

Selma thought she heard Chaim's voice. She looked for his face in the crowd. *Give me your tired,* he said.

Another voice boomed over Chaim's. "Eighty-five," the counterman shouted. She looked down at her ticket and sighed. Still nine more to go.

Selma found herself staring at a trio of women just in front of her. They were young, somewhere in their mid-thirties, and they chattered away to each other in a foreign tongue. Now that she'd noticed them, Selma could hardly take her eyes off of them, fascinated with their gracefully arched, thick black eyebrows, their luminous dark eyes, their sensuously full lips and richly purple-hued hair. They were beautiful women, Selma thought, but their eyes had no shame. How could these Persians be Jews, with no shame, no humility to them? She had heard they were killers in business, always out for themselves. But wasn't that, she thought guiltily, what Hitler said about us, all of us? One of the women turned around and gazed at Selma, as if she could read her mind. Selma smiled apologetically, then realized that the woman hadn't noticed and was looking right through her.

Selma looked out the plate-glass window. She could see those two mismatched shoes way over to the left. Chaim's voice entered her awareness yet again. *Your poor*, he said.

A pain shot up from her right foot and she cried out. "*Oy!* What's that?" For a brief moment, the room went silent while Selma looked down at a small boy who clung to his mother's skirt and stared up at her defiantly. Aware of the attention, Selma murmured to the crowd. "It's all right. It was an accident. Old toes are too sensitive."

As the room returned to its business, she waited for the boy's mother to apologize. The heavily featured woman just glared at her. Her hair was dyed a brassy blonde, her eyelids smeared with turquoise eye shadow. The woman turned deliberately away and muttered something in Russian to a man by her side. Selma could see that he had an inordinate number of gray hairs jutting out from his sneering nostrils.

Selma put her hand up to her chest, then looked around to her neighbors for commiseration over this lapse of courtesy, but everyone seemed intent on jockeying for position.

Ach, Chaim, you see how it is, she thought. This last wave of immigrants, they're a different kind of Jew. Even the Russians are a world apart from those our families came over here with, the ones celebrated by your beloved Sholem Aleichem. They must have intermarried like crazy, more Russian than Jewish by this time. They're cold, that's what they are.

Your huddled masses, Chaim replied.

When Selma's number was finally called, she was fed up enough to elbow her way up to the counter.

"The lox, it's fresh?"

The deli man didn't know her. She'd been ordering from Glabman's for too long. She had to keep on insisting that he let her inspect the food she was ordering up close, so she could smell it before he wrapped it up in white butcher paper. The people behind her vented their impatience in several languages. For a moment, she allowed herself the luxury of hating every one of them.

As the man held her loaf of *challah* out to her, she hesitated. She wanted to make them all wait a little longer, just for spite, but the counterman was getting pushy, shaking the plastic-wrapped bread in front of her nose.

"C'mon lady, I don't have all day."

Someone opened the glass doors and entered the still-packed deli, and the sound of a dog's howl filled the air. It sounded like it was in pain.

Selma hastily took the bread and shoved it alongside the packages of whitefish and kosher beef salami in the big black Bloomingdale's bag she'd brought with her.

She had to get out of here. The other customers were only too glad to make way for her exit.

As she opened the doors, she saw that the young transient was still there, his head drooped forward over his chest. The dog beside him whined, and, without opening his eyes, the boy lifted a weary hand to stroke the animal's head with exquisite tenderness. The dog stared lovingly at the boy's disfigured face.

Selma clamped her lips together, threw back her shoulders, and walked up the street. As she passed the boy, she stooped to deposit her overflowing bag beside his ill-matched shoes. Her load lightened, she straightened, took a deep breath, and resumed walking. She kept her eyes open for a taxi. There were usually a lot of them on this street.

Chaim kept her company. She nodded as he spoke to her. *Yearning to breathe free*, she heard him say.

Not long after Selma settled herself into the back seat of a dusty green taxi—smiling fixedly at the cabby's ID card on the dashboard that told her it was Achmed Fatwar driving her back to Martel—Jane Deare rushed up the littered sidewalk toward Canter's.

Jane had finally gotten word through the grapevine that Sarah and Danny were working Fairfax, having been rousted from Little Santa Monica Boulevard by the Beverly Hills fuzz, who'd responded to a local restaurateur's complaints that Danny's lesions and his mangy-looking dog Sadie were grossing out his customers.

Danny was sleeping when Jane reached the storefront of Canter's, his frail body curled like a fetus, his long, girlish-looking fingers hooked into the handle of a big, black shopping bag. Even though she was sweaty and out of breath from having run nearly all the way there from West Hollywood Park, she hesitated to disturb his slumber. He looked so vulnerable, so small. It was Sadie's joyful bark of recognition that woke him. He sat up with a jerk, his hand still clutching the bag. He spoke so softly that she had to lean forward to catch his words. His breath smelled strongly of fish.

"Hey, girl," Danny drawled sleepily. "Where you been? We've been worrying about you." He reached up to scratch one of his lesions, then remembered himself and stroked Sadie instead.

As Danny squinted up at her, the sores on his face red and angry-looking in the harsh light of the sun, Jane was bowled over yet again at how handsome he must have been. Even in his deathly AIDS skinniness, Danny's full lips still had pouty lines curved at their sides, setting them off like parentheses. His eyes were almost violet, and, framed with black lashes, they had the kind of heavy-lidded, sleepy look that made girls feel wet down below. Jane could understand why Sarah continued to hang out with Danny, even though these days, with those lesions all over his face, he brought very little money in from panhandling, and sex for sale was out of the question. Nobody wanted to go near him, looking like he did.

While most people contented themselves with the knowledge that AIDS was no longer the epidemic it had once been, Sarah had told Jane that thousands were still dying from it each year, some of them due to HIV Drug Resistance, but many more because of the lack of consistent access to medication by the homeless, particularly homeless youths.

Danny never talked about it himself. But Sarah did, usually when she and Jane snuck into the ladies' of some fast food restaurant for a pee and a wash. Jane had heard the real name for Danny's condition plenty of times, but she could never remember it. The way her mind played tricks on her, she wanted to call it "Kaposi's Tacoma," but she knew that wasn't right.

"C'mon, give it up. What you been up to all this time?" Danny lit up a butt. As the smoke coiled around his head, he grabbed her ankle and playfully shook it. "Sit down next to Danny and tell all. Last I heard, you were off to Cedars to see about that cough. What happened? One of the docs fall in love with you and sweep you off to a romantic rendezvous?" The way he pronounced it, dragging the syllables out, *ronnn-day-vuuu*, he made it sound as seductive as his eyes looked.

Jane flushed, looked away, then looked back down at him. She flung her head back and put a hand on her hip. She ignored both the questions and the invitation. "Where's Sarah?" she asked.

Danny scrutinized the cars stopped at a red light at the corner. He spoke like some torturer was dragging the secret out of him. "She went off to that place on La Brea, whatever it's called." He paused so long that Jane wondered if he'd forgotten what he was saying. When he spoke again, she winced at the sharpness in his voice. "APLA. You know, Association for Pussies who Like other men's Asses. She wanted to see if there was any treatment for people who are, you know, like me." This pause was shorter. "Too far along."

That said, Danny seemed to lose interest in their conversation entirely. Ignoring her, he dug both hands into the bag at his side. Sadie inched closer to him, her tail whacking against Jane's jeans as she gobbled down a piece of white fish.

Jane shivered. She knew exactly how Danny had kept himself alive on the streets, ever since he'd become a runaway—he called it a throwaway—at thirteen. This wasn't the first time he'd pretended he had nothing in common with gay people. She had a sense of the shame that ate at him like Tacomas on the inside, but she still wished he didn't feel he had to try so hard to put a distance between himself and other people with AIDS.

It was then that the coughing started up again. Oh, shit, she thought, clutching her hands to her burning chest, just when I thought I was getting better.

Danny stopped his rummaging, sighed, then snuck an oblique look at her.

He waited until the spasms subsided before speaking. Reaching back into the bag, he pulled something out and held it up to her.

"I think you just wore the both of us out with all that noise. Here. Somebody left me a CARE package while I was sleeping. My mama used to say that good food'll cure almost anything. I bet you're hungry."

He smiled his sexy Johnny Depp smile and urged the food at her. "Want a bagel?"

———————————

Waiting for Sarah's return from the offices of AIDS Project Los Angeles, Danny and Jane sat cross-legged on the sidewalk, tension rising up between them like a Santa Ana.

Danny had watched Jane eat three bagels in a row, stuffing them into her mouth like there was no tomorrow. He and Jane had scared up some money for something wet to chase them down—two cups of Canter's coffee, which put to shame the shit from McDonald's they were used to. Danny had played a few riffs on his mouth organ. He wasn't bad at it, and he knew Jane liked the way he could make it cry. For her, the more melancholy the melody, the better. She'd nod her head slowly like she knew just where the music was coming from. She knew too much for her scant years.

Jane's future was on his mind a lot these days. He worried how she'd survive once he was gone. He wasn't as concerned about Sarah. She was a grown woman, already nineteen. She'd been on the streets long enough to know how to get by. She'd find herself some other guy to partner up with, he knew. That was her way. But Jane was just a baby, with something innocent about her in spite of what her stepfather had done, and Danny was determined that she not go down the same path as Sarah.

He grabbed hold of Jane's shirt and pulled her face closely up to his.

She cried out in alarm. "Stop it, Danny, you're hurting me."

"You know I'm not. You're just scared. Well, you need to be. These streets are mean. And the longer you live on them, the more likely somebody's gonna be grabbing more than your shirt."

Her gray eyes widened and gooseflesh sprung up on her arms.

He continued, his voice full of urgency. "Listen, this is important. I want you to promise me you won't get into drugs like I did, and if you get into hooking, just do the old in and out, no blow jobs, no taking it in the back door, and don't get too scared or lazy to let them off of wearing a glove." Her eyes started to go spacey on him, shutting him out, so he gripped her shirt harder and yanked a few times. "No. Better yet, forget what I said. No street sex. None at all. You won't need it. After I die, you take Sadie. Sarah wouldn't take good care of her, anyway. Chances are she'll hook up with some guy who won't want some mangy dog hanging around. If you take Sadie, you won't get rich, but you'll get by. People feel a lot sorrier for the dog than they do for us. Sadie'll get you through."

As if she knew he was talking about her, Sadie uncoiled herself from her nap, stood up, and stretched her legs out in front of her with a pleasurable groan. She nudged Jane's shoulder with her nose. Jane's mouth started to move but no words came out.

Danny couldn't let go of her yet. "Promise. Promise me. Look at my face. I don't want you to end up like this."

Jane's eyes began to stream and, hesitantly clasping the hand that gripped her shirt with her own, she nodded slowly, only to be startled by a sharp voice from behind her.

Sarah's shadow stretched over the two of them and she stood with her arms crossed, glowering. "What do you mean, 'end up like this?' You think I've been standing in line all day, scrounging up some help for you for nothing? It ain't over yet, my man. I haven't heard any fat lady singing yet, have you?"

Thirteen

MATT HAYES SEPARATED the BMW clicker from the rest of his ring to give to the parking lot attendant. It wasn't that he imagined the guy had the inclination or gall to steal something from his trunk, but, realistically, you never could tell.

Entering an ivy-covered brick building, he shook his head at what had brought him to Montana Avenue this morning. What a wuss he was. Just because Chancellor Biggs was too embarrassed to ask his skeptical wife to pick up some Chinese herbs for his latest ailment, did it follow that Matt was the only person Biggs could call on to do his dirty work for him?

As he opened the door to Dr. Baba's waiting room, a gold-turbaned receptionist looked up, smiling beatifically. He answered his own question. *Why not? I'd rather be here than wrangling with the maintenance men over how much of the piping in UCLA's underground tunnels needs to be replaced.*

The current crisis involving UCLA's infrastructure had a long history. The campus had once been powered, heated, and air-conditioned by ducts that laced through an underground tunnel system, hidden beneath the campus' earliest buildings like organs under the skin. Only the colors they were painted distinguished the wide pipes that enclosed a network of steam, sewage, gas, electricity, and phone lines that made the academic animal go.

The university, a small city itself with an enrollment of over 40 thousand and a staff of about 20 thousand, had since ceased its dependence on outside utility companies, and some of the duct systems were outdated and empty, particularly since the campus now had its own state-of-the-art power plant. But others still functioned, enclosed in Pyrex piping, blue and yellow tubes, and pipes shaped like green spider legs. It was these still working systems, pulsing through the hot and dusty archaic tunnels—some of them claustrophobically narrow passageways barely six feet high—that required constant, labor-intensive attention. These were the sorts of no-glory expenses that private benefactors were least inspired by and the miserly state legislature barely interested in. Chancellor Biggs was only too glad to dump the responsibility for negotiating how much work could get done in the tunnels for how little expense onto Matt, whose relaxed affability went a long way with the guys in maintenance.

As Matt pondered the current challenge of redesigning adequate emergency safeguards in the predicted likelihood of the "Big One," he heard his name called. The receptionist invited him through a beaded-curtained doorway and down a wide hall, depositing him at the back of a small line of patients—all of them expensively dressed and most of them extremely attractive. He wondered momentarily what it was like for Biggs to frequent a doctor who ministered mostly to females. Running his fingers through his hair, he grinned at the dark-haired woman in front of him. If they were all this good looking, maybe he should sign up with Dr. Baba himself.

He soon changed his mind. The brunette stepped back, pointing toward the front of the line and saying breathlessly, "Isn't it amazing?" He wondered why this meticulously groomed woman would wear such an offensive perfume. Craning to catch a better glimpse of what she was pointing at, he realized that the assault on his nostrils wasn't coming from her. An exotically-clad quartet of women was busily plucking specimens from row upon row of coarse twigs and malodorous roots, twisting them briskly into plastic packages before handing them over the counter.

It was his turn all too soon. He took pains to make clear that the herbs he was picking up were for Biggs and not himself. One of the efficient Amazons thrust him a bulky, gold-embossed shopping bag that smelled like a men's locker room. After writing a sizable check from his own personal account, he promised himself to remember to get Biggs to reimburse him as soon as he got back to campus. He'd planned to do a few errands on the way back to the Chancellor's office, but there was no way he'd drive around any longer than necessary with this noxious stuff in his car.

Turning around to face the hive of nurses gliding up and down the hallway, he worked to keep his expression neutral. What a racket, he thought dryly. These must be Dr. Baba's forty thieves.

Across town, waves of heat were already shimmering off the pavement, and Ariel felt the perspiration spring from armpits that smelled like a women's locker room as she reluctantly exited the post office on Beverly Boulevard.

She turned in alarm as something bumped against her from behind.

"Oh, shoot, I'm so sorry," Kineesha said. "I really wasn't trying to knock you down." Struggling to shift the load of mail overflowing from her bag, she laughed, her dimples beguiling as she teased, "Thought I was a robber, 'bout to steal all those social security checks?"

"Jesus! Forget robbery. I didn't even hear you coming." Ariel pointed to her own groaning bag. "Too preoccupied with figuring out how long I'd be out in this killer sun with all these end of the month checks to deliver. The only thing that stops me from totally resenting SSA delivery day is knowing how much I'm going to need these checks myself when I reach my golden years."

Kineesha shook her head. "Ain't it the truth?" She elbowed Ariel playfully, inadvertently unsettling the balance of her own bag's contents so that an envelope slipped out and fell to the ground. "That's why we've got to push on up, somehow, you and I."

Ariel had also seen the piece of mail fall, and she and Kineesha touched knees as they knelt simultaneously to retrieve the envelope. Ariel got hold of it first and casually glanced at the address. She did a double take.

Kineesha raised an inquisitive eyebrow.

"That name," Ariel said excitedly. "Miss Ada Munro? Haven't heard it in years. I used to have a middle school teacher named Ada Munro. English and social studies. Everybody loved her. I wonder if it's the same person."

"There's one way to find out." Kineesha squinted at the envelope. "Hayworth's just a half a mile away."

"No, I couldn't."

"You shy?"

"No, no, of course not. It's just that she was already a veteran by the time my class came along. She must've taught thousands of students. She'd never remember me."

"Mm-hmm," Kineesha said. "Shy." She looked at her watch. "Sure you don't want to write the address down before I go?"

"Oh, fuck off." Kineesha put up her hands in mock defense, and Ariel grinned. "Last one back buys the other a beer?"

"Honey, wish I could, but Nat's coming over for dinner tonight. I've arranged for the kids to spend the night with friends." She made a face. "The dog had better appreciate what I go through for the sake of a little romance."

"Tell me about it," Ariel shouted, as Kineesha opened her van door. She stared as the van pulled away from the curb. From what Kineesha had already told her about Nat Jones, she doubted that the dog did.

It was only when she was safely installed in her own mail truck that Ariel allowed her thoughts to return to Ada Munro, arguably the best teacher she'd ever had. She'd first been assigned to Miss Munro for sixth grade English and had her again in the eighth. Entering her brightly decorated classroom for the first time, she'd been horrified by how tall and ugly the woman at the chalkboard was, with her mottled complexion, a nose almost as broad as her cheeks, and big hands and feet that looked like they'd been grafted onto her from a giant. Her glasses were so big and thick that they made her look bug-eyed. But once Ariel got to know her, her odd looks didn't matter at all.

One of the perks of being what they called a "mentally gifted minor" at Webster was being allowed to skip geography in the eighth grade to participate in the journalism class, taught with a liberal hand by Miss Munro. The one area in which Miss Munro claimed her authoritarian prerogative was in the appointment of the editor of the school newspaper that was published weekly by her class. That year, Miss Munro had chosen Ariel.

It was as editor that Ariel had organized flying lessons for all five of her editorial staff at a Santa Monica Airport-based flying school. Little had Miss Munro known it was Ariel's way of inching toward her fantasy of linking up with her missing father in the skies somewhere. Reflecting on that time, Ariel turned the key in the ignition. If only she'd been as cool at the controls up in the air as she'd been in the simulation chamber.

Realizing she was setting herself up for a heavy dose of the blues, she reminded herself that it had taken some moxie to arrange a free day of flight simulation for a bunch of teenagers. And, to be fair, she hadn't been too shabby as editor-in-chief, either—doing an exposé on the amount of hazardous trash on L.A.'s beaches (which begat a subsequent issue devoted to the tide of medical waste, hypodermic syringes, and raw garbage that actually led to the closure of much of the Atlantic coast); spearheading a series on the segregated stand-off between Hispanic, black, white, and Asian students at Webster; and staging, with Jasmine and Terry's help, a Dungeons and Dragons Day for the whole eighth grade as part of an issue devoted to ways kids could entertain themselves besides zoning out on TV.

But at the time, she'd felt like a fraud. Which had only been reinforced during the end-of-the-year parent-teacher conference. Ariel hadn't missed her mother's thinly-veiled disbelief when Miss Munro said that she could imagine Ariel doing anything when she grew up, from becoming an astronaut to climbing Kilimanjaro. In the end, her mother's lack of faith in her daughter had proved to be justified, hadn't it? About the only thing she ever scaled was the wall of Jasmine's backyard when the two of them would sneak out in the middle of the night to smoke Jasmine's dad's Pall Malls.

Ariel parked her Postal Service van at Gardner and Third Street and struggled to retrieve her bag. God, she muttered, no wonder I'm so addicted to cigarettes. Can it really be true that I've been smoking since the eighth grade? She felt a sudden stab of guilt. Before his death from emphysema, Jasmine's dad Hiromasa had to wear one of those awful oxygen hook-ups. He would've been heartbroken to know that Ariel had aided and abetted his thirteen-year-old daughter's flirtation with nicotine. Thank God he never found out. Weird nose plug or not, he was a sweetheart of a man. Actually, the whole family was genial and generous, confounding the dumb Occidental myth of the inscrutability of Asians. How she'd envied Jasmine her closeness to both the L.A. and Hawaiian wings of her family, just as she'd coveted Terry's exuberant Italian-American cousins who visited most summers from the East Coast.

Shuddering, she stuffed a thick wad of catalogues into a cobwebby mailbox. If Miss Munro thought she'd made a dent in parent-child relations by talking up Ariel's merits, she'd been deluding herself. All her mom had to say before her death about her daughter's future prospects was to warn her never to count on a man to be there for her and to make sure she got herself a job that would reliably put food on the table.

Well, she'd come through on both scores, hadn't she? Sensing a hard-core funk coming on, Ariel called Terry on her lunch break and asked if she wanted to meet later at the King's Head pub. Terry was only too glad to join her for some beer and mutual sympathy, having been persuaded by a quickly depleting savings account to deliver her resume to a high-profile publicity firm just that morning.

After a couple of pints of Guinness and several instances of Terry repelling the advances of boozed-up Brits, Ariel mentioned her brush with Miss Munro's mail.

"Oh, Ariel," Terry enthused, "do you really think it was her? I mean, she wasn't exactly a spring chicken even then. Remember how she grabbed hold of me with one of those huge hands of hers when we were touring the zoo for the paper, and I had to literally pull her up the hill? And that was—shit, I can't be too loaded to figure it out—fifteen years ago? Honey, I hate to say it, but we're getting old."

"Cut that out. We're supposed to be cheering each other up. And we're definitely not old."

"I don't know if anything will be able to lift my spirits if I actually get that job. I can't believe I'm meant to spend the rest of my life helping expand corporate coffers. And what about you? Do you see yourself delivering mail for the rest of your life?"

"I don't even think about it. I—"

Terry interrupted excitedly. "You know, what if you got into journalism? Miss Munro was right about you—you were terrific on that Webster paper. And you even had that brief stint on the *Daily Bruin*."

Ariel chuckled. "Come on. You know that I only volunteered for the *Bruin* because I wanted to get together with the editor at the time. Remember Gary Linley?" She shrugged. "I actually did get to sleep with him, but he lost interest fast enough. Threw me over for some size-four sorority girl named Dorothy. But I was stuck working side by side with him for the rest of the semester. Torture."

"Yeah, but he did publish that great article of yours about the underground tunnel system. How cool was that? The whole school was talking about it."

"Christ, I forgot about that. What a trip—can you believe there's a whole city down there? I actually got a tour of the part under the hospital. God, the things we remember. Right before we went down there, the facilities guy told me that when there's a fire in the hospital— actually in any hospital—they avoid panicking the patients by announcing over the public address system, 'Paging Dr. Firestone.'"

"Well, if I'm lying on my deathbed and I hear those words, I'll be sure to run." Terry cocked her head. "But wait, let's give credit where it's due. You might've been the creative genius, but I'm pretty sure I was the one who first told you about the tunnels."

"You know, I do believe you're right. But I don't think you told me how you found out about them. I mean, it's not like most people knew."

Terry put a hand on Ariel's arm. "Didn't I ever tell you?" Ariel shook her head. "It was classic. Remember how I did my work-study hours at the Powell Library?" She grinned slyly. "Well, for some reason, most of the students who worked in the library were big dopers. There was a big storage closet we used to sneak into on our breaks to get high. One night, somebody accidentally opened the door right next to the closet and we could see some old stairs leading down to God knew what. Well, of course we just had to check it out. We piled down the stairs and followed this weird maze all the way to Haines Hall. After that, we'd go down there to get loaded when there were too many of us to fit in the closet." She giggled. "We weren't the only ones. We found a pack of Zig-Zags next to some fraternity graffiti right under Royce Hall."

"God, to be young again. Go anywhere, do anything, just for the hell of it."

"Oh, come on. Think of old Miss Munroe. You just know that old woman was getting off on her work." Terry grabbed Ariel's hand. "Why not you and me, too?"

Ariel shook her off. "Forget it. You're probably right about yourself. I mean, look at you. You could do anything you want, with all your skills and a great resume to push off from. But me? About all I've developed over the past five years are a set of callouses on my heels it'd take a butcher knife to cut through. So let's get real." She waved at the bartender. "Or really drunk, anyway. Can I buy you another beer?"

Fourteen

JANE DEARE HAD more reality than she could handle. She kept losing track of Sarah and Danny, and it was getting harder to avoid the more predatory homeless kids, who'd started to grumble that she thought she was above them. All because she refused to let a series of dirty old strangers do disgusting things to her in the backseats of their cars.

More and more these days, she found herself walking L.A.'s deserted sidewalks until it was really late, ducking into storefronts whenever she saw a black and white cruise by, just so she could show up at West Hollywood Park after the other runaways had finally passed out on the grass.

On this particular night, she felt like she was just about at the end of her rope. She'd been walking until her back and feet hurt, there was a slight tickling at the back of her throat that scared her that she might be getting another cold when she still had the awful cough from the last one, and she'd been holding her pee till she thought she'd burst. Turning onto Santa Monica Boulevard, she realized that West Hollywood Park had never looked so good. Breaking into a frantic run, she dashed past scattered sleeping forms. But she turned on her heels as soon as she entered the ladies' room, holding onto her crotch like a two-year-old.

The man she'd glimpsed, zipping up his pants as he emerged from one of the stalls, called after her. "Wait a minute. I swear on my granny, I won't hurt you."

Something about his tone made her take the risk of turning around.

But she stood tensed on the balls of her feet, ready to flee if necessary. Under the dim light of one naked bulb, she could make out a crooked smile and a pair of bloodshot eyes. Still facing him, she began to slowly back away.

He raised his dark hand and stepped back. "Naw, naw, you don't have nothin' to be afraid of from me."

Her eyes narrowed, but she hesitated.

His slurring seemed to improve as he sought to convince her, gesturing at the graffiti-covered walls. "It's just ... you should see what those kids have done to the men's room. So many needles around the toilet, I was afraid I'd get stuck before I knew it." He spread his hands helplessly. "Hate needles almost as much as roaches."

Jane found herself confessing to him in a whisper, "I hate needles, too."

"Well, then we've found our first thing in common." His face opened into a sweet grin, and she decided that, in spite of his drunkenness, he looked like a nice man. But her body was just about beyond caring whether she was right or not. She was nervously dancing around and had to restrain herself from putting her hands back between her thighs.

He seemed to sense her anguish. "How 'bout I give you some privacy?"

Thank God, he was gone. As she said a silent thanks that the cubicle had a lock on it, she noticed that there was no toilet paper on the cardboard roll. She looked around helplessly, then jumped as she heard the man's voice again.

"Thought you might need this." His big hand was waving a couple of paper towels at her from under the stall door.

He was leaning against the side of the building when she came out. He laughed. "You look like you just took the weight of the world off your shoulders." As a flush spread from her neck to her ears, he hastened to add, "How's about we have a little something to eat together before settling down for the night?"

Jane was about to refuse when her belly gave a few little lurches. She hunched her shoulders, whispering, "I don't have any food."

"I do." He studied her. "Tell the truth, with the drink and all, I have to remind myself to eat sometimes. But your skinny little arms tell me you're running on empty yourself. And I'm pleased to say I've been saving a couple of oranges and a whole box of Ritz crackers for just such an occasion."

He motioned her to follow him toward the rear of the park's storage shed, speaking softly as they tiptoed around a teenager smelling of pungent B.O. passed out on a sleeping bag "I've seen you here before, haven't I?"

She nodded. She waited nervously at the edge of the shed while he fished around a piled-up shopping cart. As nice as he seemed, she wasn't about to follow him behind the building. When he emerged, he handed her a broken-down cardboard box to carry.

He led her to a spot some distance from the park's other inhabitants and gestured for her to set down the cardboard for them to sit on. He dumped the oranges and the box of crackers onto the grass before he sat a polite few inches away.

The oranges were so sweet and so ripe that juice ran down both their chins. They laughed and pointed at each other, and he pulled a handful of napkins from his pile.

He licked his sticky fingers and reached around for a bottle of whiskey. He held it out to her. She shook her head. "Smart girl," he said. He gestured with the bottle. "Do you mind if I ...?"

Jane couldn't get over his good manners. He was what her grandma would have called a gentleman.

He took a big slug and made a face. "You from around here?"

She froze.

He didn't seem to notice. He leaned forward confidingly. "I grew up not so far away myself. The city's changed a lot." He shook his head. "Didn't used to be so many of us out of work and out of luck. Leastways, not on this side of town."

As he talked, Jane found herself finishing off the box of crackers. She yawned, then quickly put a hand over her mouth.

"Tired?" Theosophus pointed to her goose fleshed arms. "Not so easy to fall asleep when you're cold. Now that's the one thing Mister Old Taylor's good for. Keeps me warm on chilly nights." He stood up, brushing blades of grass from his trousers. "Guess I got lucky to have a little company before going to sleep tonight." His eyes raked several sleeping bodies close by. "You have any particular place you like to lay down?"

Jane had begun piling up the orange peels and sweeping crumbs off the cardboard. Still looking down, she whispered, "Not really."

"Got a blanket somewhere?" he asked. She shook her head. "I guess we got to do something 'bout that."

Before Jane knew it, he'd wandered off. She was afraid he'd just run out on her. But now she saw him approaching with an army surplus blanket in his arms. He handed it to her and gestured with his head. "I'm gonna go over there. If you wake up before me, I'd surely appreciate it if you would leave the blanket next to me, or just stick it on top of the shopping cart back there. I'd kinda like to hang onto it if I can."

He looked up at the sky. "It's a pretty night. Summer's good for sky watching." He shook his head. "Can't believe it's already July."

Jane stared at him. She didn't even know what day it was, let alone what month. "Well," she said shyly, "they say time flies when you're having fun."

In no time at all, he was snoring. But still, she felt safer having him nearby. It reminded her of the days before her daddy moved out and Mister Creepo Vern moved in. Her ma had seemed happier then. Well, at least sometimes she did. Actually, Ma's moods had always been a little like the weather. When she was in her sunshine phase, nobody could beat her for cheerfulness. She'd put her own peroxide-streaked hair in high pigtails and fix Jane's hair up the same way, both of them with the hair pulled so tight in their rubber bands that their eyes looked almost Chinese. Then she'd put a little of her palest pink lipstick on Jane's delicate, cupid's bow lips and pose the two of them in front of the tall mirror on the back of the bathroom door, and they'd make silly faces at each other, giggling like crazy.

One of the street kids nearby cried out in his sleep. Jane tensed and found herself thinking about how it had been when Ma's mood went cloudy.

She'd take to her bed for days, leaving Jane and her brother Bobby to fend for themselves with endless bowls of Sugar Pops and non-stop TV watching. The two of them would sit cross-legged on the sickly-green den carpet, so close to the television that, had their ma seen them in one of her medium sunshine moods—when she acted like other kids' mothers (which was actually pretty comforting)—she would have yelled at them not to sit so close to it or they'd go blind. But they couldn't really enjoy either the belly-bloating binge of Sugar Pops or going nose to nose with the Teenage Mutant Ninja Turtles, with the awareness taking up all the space in their heads that Ma had locked herself into her darkened upstairs bedroom again. Maybe she was dying up there. All they knew for sure was she wouldn't open that door no matter how hard they knocked and how loudly they screamed that they needed her, especially with their daddy away on one of his increasingly frequent sales trips.

After a while, though, instead of taking to her bed in one of her gloomies, Ma'd go out on the town, dressed a little too cheap, with her hair frizzed up like that yellow-colored Easter basket grass. And from one of those forays, she'd brought back Vern. Jane could tell that Bobby liked him, his freckled face lighting up to have a man in the house when his daddy was away so much, she guessed. But something about Vern's red face and black, beady eyes and the way he looked at her, all intense-like, made young Jane's tummy clench up. She shook her head, wishing she'd said something to Ma back then, but how could she have known that her tummy was giving her a warning?

Her face went slack. It wouldn't have mattered anyway, she reminded herself. Look what happened the last time she tried to talk to Ma about Vern.

That had been just after she'd arrived in L.A. The bus had let her off at a station on Vine Street, just below Hollywood Boulevard. She was scared to death, with only a little more than ten dollars in her pocket left over from her saved-up allowance money, all by herself, and with no place to go. But the sun was shining so brightly and, even on that tatty street, the air smelled good with some unfamiliar scent that she imagined was orange blossoms, and she suddenly felt sure that if she could get up the guts to call her ma, she'd catch her in one of her sunny moods from the olden days and Ma would listen to her. The fact that she'd tried to do it before she left and Ma wouldn't hear anything bad about Vern—instead, insisting Jane ought to go to church and pray to be released from the devil that had gotten hold of her—Jane brushed aside as she punched in the comfortingly familiar numbers of her home phone. She didn't even mind that the phone booth stunk powerfully of stale pee.

When Ma answered, Jane felt suddenly very heavy, and for a while, no words would come out. She could tell from her ma's tight voice that she had a black storm going on inside her. And indeed, when she'd managed to squeak out a faint, "Ma, it's me," the line had gone dead.

Jane wished she hadn't eaten all of those Ritz crackers. She felt sick. She got up, dragging the blanket behind her. Only when she'd curled right next to Theosophus was she able to fall asleep.

Fifteen

THE NIGHT BEFORE the holiday weekend Ariel had decided to treat herself to a binge on some of her favorite old movies, including two of her all-time favorites, the *Aristocats* and the Clark Gable/Claudette Colbert version (the only one, as far as she was concerned) of *It Happened One Night*. Both Ben and Selma had other commitments—Ben rehearsing for his first theatrical lead, Captain Cat, in a local equity waver production of *Under Milk Wood* and Selma off to Edith's house for a rare *Shabbos* dinner together.

Terry had called earlier to invite her to a girls' night out with a couple of publicity cohorts, and Ariel had been tempted to join them until she found out they were planning to go to the trendy Tower Bar on Sunset. She figured she'd fit in at a place like that about as well as a goldfish in an expensive aquarium. Besides, it was one evening she didn't mind spending alone. She needed to get a grip on herself for tomorrow's drive to San Diego with Ben. It was increasingly difficult to stay cool about her feelings about him, and she needed to find some way not to go over the deep end.

Which was why she was pissed off at herself for springing so enthusiastically out of bed the following morning when Jezzie started licking her nose with her exfoliating version of an alarm clock. Ariel muttered, "Alright, all right, give me a minute to take care of my business." She snuck a peek out the bedroom curtain on her way to the bathroom. How fucking predictable. Even if there'd been a heat wave the week before, L.A. had suffered a regression to low cloudiness or downright fog nearly every Fourth of July she could remember, and today promised to be no exception. She opened a can of tuna and shrimp for Jezebel. "It's so typical. Yesterday was gorgeous. Tomorrow will probably be a scorcher, but on the Fourth of July we get a reprise of June gloom."

Ariel continued to grumble as she stuck her head in her closet and tackled the problem of what to wear. She noticed that her fingers were a little shaky when she pulled her blouse off its hanger. She couldn't help but feel nervous about going on something resembling a date with Ben. She was all too aware that she consistently violated every radio shrink's admonition to hold your sexual horses until dating led to commitment, but if she'd been guided by that piece of conventional wisdom she'd still be *vagina intacta*, wouldn't she? She nearly burst into tears when she saw that the blouse she'd hoped to wear had a stain on it. "We are a little sensitive today," she murmured.

She'd always rationalized that if the sex was good, she and her partner would have a great motivation to get to know each other. But somehow, it never seemed to work out that way. Which, she guessed, was why she'd been so taken aback when Ben had suggested driving down to San Diego for a tour of the town and dinner at the landmark Hotel del Coronado. Especially since she'd heard that no place was more beautiful, or more romantic, than that Mission-style hotel—especially on the Fourth of July when they set off their famous fireworks display. She just hoped that the skies would clear enough for her to actually see it.

She held her breath as she tugged a pair of stretchy black pants over her hips, praying that the tight fit would visually girdle her butt down a size, rather than emphasize its current more-than-generous proportions.

As she inspected herself in the mirror, her case of nerves threatened to degenerate into a hard-core bad mood. It wasn't just because of her fat ass—or even her date with Ben. Something Terry had said on the phone last night kept re-playing in her head. When Ariel had passed on the Tower Bar plan, claiming terminal insecurity, Terry had acted as if she was personally letting her down. What she actually said was, "What the hell has happened to you? Of the three of us, you were always up for anything. A risk-taker. Now it's like pulling teeth trying to get you off your couch."

Well, screw her. Ariel marched back into her closet and searched for the sexiest top she could find. She struggled into a fitted pullover patterned with red and white flowers. When she saw herself in the mirror, she thought, Jesus, why not eighty-six the black pants for a pair of blue jeans, and have everybody salute you? She shrugged out of the blouse and flung it across the room. Entering the closet for the third time, she recalled that it had been on a Fourth of July ages ago that she'd talked Terry and Jasmine into a joyride in Jasmine's uncle's car. Little punks, they were barely tall enough to see over the steering wheel and kept getting confused between which pedal was the accelerator and which the brake. But that had been part of the thrill—Terry laughing like a maniac, Jasmine screaming like a banshee, adrenaline shooting through her own system like speed. No, better than speed. Less teeth-grindingly uptight. More like an orgasm of the spirit. Okay, that was a pretty weird thought, but they were pretty crazy. Didn't they realize what could've happened to them? Shit, they were only fourteen. She could just imagine the LAPD calling her home in the middle of the night with the news she'd been busted for grand theft auto. Her mom would've died.

She did anyway.

Well, they hadn't gotten caught, had they? But they sort of did the time they cut class to smoke dope at the Griffith Park Observatory. That one had been her idea, too. Finding the observatory closed, they'd sneaked into nearby Ferndell, instead. Following its meandering path through tropical vegetation and passing a joint back and forth, they'd tripped out on the shared delusion that they were tracking Alice's white rabbit. Until some creepy ten-ton guy in military camouflage jumped out of the bushes and exposed himself, jacking off like crazy. They'd fallen all over themselves, screaming back to the car.

As she raised a pale green sweater over her head, Ariel had an unsettling thought. If all those pranks she got up to were so stupid, how come she was grinning from ear to ear just thinking about them?

The phone pinged and she ran awkwardly to it, struggling to get the sweater down over her head so she could see. She caught it on the third ring. "Yeah?"

"Hey, baby, what's wrong?" Ben sounded nervous. Before she

could respond, he went on. "I hope it's nothing bad. Actually, I've got a little bad news myself. Fucking assistant manager's covering for David while he's on vacation. Three guys are out sick with that shitty summer cold that's going around, and he's getting heavy with me, saying if I don't come in to work today to cover for them, I'm out of a job."

Ariel licked her lips and forced the words out. "Oh, don't sweat it. I woke up feeling kinda funky today, anyway. I was thinking of giving it a pass myself."

"Shit, I hope you're not getting sick. If you want, I'll spin down before I go in with some of those Dr. Baba herbs I've been telling you about. I'm sure they're the reason I'm the only one on my shift to fight off the bug." He laughed faintly. "Also why I'm so close to the wire with my checkbook balance." Silence on her end. "But, with the play coming up, I figure it's worth the expense. I've definitely got enough for both of us."

"No, no, I'm sure I'll be fine. I just need to get some rest."

"Listen, will you give me a rain check?" He gave a laugh. "Actually, right now it'd be more like a fog check. We'd probably have a better time on a sunnier day anyway. How about next Saturday?"

"Sure."

"You know I wouldn't do this if I didn't need the money." His voice grew silky. "I'm going to miss you."

Her voice was strained. "Me, too."

It was only ten minutes later that Ben banged futilely on Ariel's door, a bag of Dr. Baba's herbs in hand. Unbeknownst to him, and contrary to her claim that she was headed for bed, she'd taken off in her Toyota for an undoubtedly overcast Venice Beach as fast as the aging Corolla would go.

A heavy mist swirled around her head as Ariel bent down to pick up a shell. She studied its lustrous underside. It was perfect. If anything, the ocean's rough churning had buffed its rainbow-hued patina. "Mother-of-pearl," she murmured. What a sweet name for its glossy surface. Turning the shell over, she rubbed her thumb over the coarse ridges of its exterior, telling herself what a weirdo she was for wondering if anyone had ever thought of calling such crustiness "Pearl's Father."

There was hardly anyone else on this stretch of Venice Beach, just her and a few winos. One really great thing about an overcast Fourth of July was everyone knowing that the beach, foggier than inland areas on the best of days, would be a shitty place to spend the holiday. Which made it a perfect match for her mood today. Besides, she'd always loved looking for shells. It was an excuse to slosh bare-footed along the shore, sliding her toes across smooth fingers of sand sculpted by the tide.

Venice was like home to her. Had actually *been* her home. When she was a toddler, she and her mom (and her dad, when he was in town) had lived just a few blocks east of here in a cozy little Spanish-tiled cottage near Rose Avenue, a hop and a skip from where the old Pioneer Bakery sent tantalizing whiffs of sourdough into the air every Saturday morning. The area had managed to elude the first wave of beach property gentrification (until finally succumbing to the juggernaut of Google offices in 2011), and she recalled with gratitude spending her elementary school years in such a cozy enclave, where college students and undiscovered artists coexisted peacefully with Mexican-American couples popping out scads of broad-faced children, who almost never seemed to cry and half of whom seemed to be nicknamed Gordo or Gorda. In those simpler days, the local corner store, manned by multiple generations of the Escalera family, sold plastic packages of fried pork rinds along with the ubiquitous potato chips and Fritos. She was particularly partial to their powdered-sugar-dusted *Pane Dulce*—so much bigger than her hand that she had to use both of them to hold one—and the deliciously fresh ham, sliced to just the right thinness by the ever-smiling, but sad-eyed Señor Escalera.

But the beach itself was different, a larger home away from home to people who lived far from its damp air. And even after her mom moved them into an apartment on National Boulevard near Webster Middle School, she'd been coming here for more years than she cared to remember. She and Terry and Jasmine would take the number seven, baby-blue City of Santa Monica bus, noisily crowded with scores of bare-chested teenaged boys with boogie boards tucked under their arms and gaggles of giggling girls in florescent pink lipstick and scanty one and two-piece swimsuits they kept tugging down over their fannies. Ariel remembered how relieved the bus driver would look when he deposited the lot of them at the end of the line, close enough to the

Santa Monica Pier that she could pretend its carousel's old-timey organ music was heralding their arrival.

When they weren't spending the day on that pier, with its cheap arcades and fortune teller booths and a Ferris wheel offering a view all the way to Catalina, they would take the ritual walk out onto the long stretch of nearly white sand beside it. If it was toward the end of summer, when the sand had had all of June and July to heat up, the walk toward the water was accompanied by dramatic screams as she and Jasmine hopped from foot to foot across the burning ground. The more organized Terry would smile at them with a wise-ass grin for being the one to remember her flip-flops. She'd trail behind them at a leisurely pace, her hips swaying provocatively as she swung her big straw bag containing everything from Coppertone to the requisite pack of contraband Marlboros to dog-eared copies of such classics as the *Sweet Valley High* series when they were younger and *The Catcher in the Rye* when they'd moved on to Venice High.

Ariel recalled that it was when they were in line at the pier's celebrated homemade potato chip stand that Terry and Matt had connected in the summer after tenth grade. It would have to be there, because Matt and his rich Palisades surfing buddies wouldn't be caught dead laying out on that particular stretch of sand. No, in those days— and for all she knew, still—the class structure of the western part of Los Angeles County was delineated by which beach you and your friends frequented.

Venice Beach, littered with empty bags of Laura Scudder's, mangled beer cans, and cigarette butts, welcomed students and alumni from Venice High (and all the middle schools that fed into it) like a frowsy hostess in a pick-up bar. Small tribes of white kids from blue-collar homes tried for tans on extra-long beach towels. The boys raced into the water with their boogie boards as soon as they'd marked off their turf with their towels, while the girls settled in with MP3 players and gossip. And in the shade of the pier, Chicano boys, wearing low-slung Chinos and sexily unbuttoned-to-the-waist Pendleton shirts, smoked roll-your-owns on wool blankets, pretending disinterest in their sexy girlfriends with their black hair teased up to the sky. Those super-cool S.A.'s—it took Ariel ages to figure out the initials stood for South American—only deigned to relieve themselves from the heat by rolling up their pant legs and slowly walking to the water's edge like they didn't give a shit.

Harder to reach from city bus lines, State Beach farther up the coast was frequented by the kids from Westwood's Uni High and Beverly Hills High and their feeder schools. They were joined by students from the privates: Harvard, Westlake, Marlborough, Windward, and Crossroads, attended by the sons and daughters of doctors and lawyers and entertainment industry executives.

The perfect white sands of Malibu were reserved for mostly-blond-haired, athletically-toned gods like Matt Hayes from the Palisades, who wore zinc oxide on their perennially sun-burnt ski-jump noses like primitive war paint and whose girlfriends wore the skimpiest bikinis of all.

The thing they failed to recognize at the time was that Mother Nature is a great equalizer. In her broad book, the sand was the same, the ocean was the same, and the longings and personal insecurities of the kids up and down the coast were very much the same. But the exigencies of social class had implacable laws of its own that defied the inclusiveness of the natural world. Ariel wished she'd known that then. It would have spared her and her friends, especially Terry, no end of suffering.

As Ariel sat back on her haunches facing the awesome expanse of gray water, she recalled the moment they'd all met Matt. He was shockingly older than they were, twice their age and already an Assistant Dean at UCLA, and only Terry, with her well-deserved self-confidence, had felt free enough to respond to his flirting. Ariel and Jasmine were both titillated and daunted by the way Terry held her own with him. They both thought he was insanely good looking, though neither of them had to say so. Ariel could tell by the way Jasmine kept looking down at the ground, by her own sudden desire to be anywhere but where she was, watching the lean, but well-muscled older guy with the best tan she'd ever seen make a move on her best friend.

She remembered spending hours on the phone with Jasmine that night. They kept assuring each other over and over again how they weren't jealous and that Matt was ridiculously old—how old, at that point, none of them knew. The assurances got tired after a while, as Terry and Matt became an item that ended up lasting nearly until graduation, when Terry found out he was married to a woman he'd knocked up in his first year of college. Terry had actually bumped into them and their two girls on her way to a dental appointment in the Palisades. Needless to say, Terry had been devastated and never quite recovered the confidence in herself that Ariel had so admired.

Of course, it had felt wrong all along. Matt was old enough to be Terry's father and, besides being an adulterer, could have been prosecuted for statutory rape if Terry's parents had known. Matt had actually used that as a reason to keep their love affair secret, the dog. But Ariel could understand how it was hard for Terry, for any of them, to hate him. Matt Hayes was a serious charmer, and it was nearly impossible to believe he'd intentionally caused anyone harm; he made a fairly convincing case, if you were inclined to believe him, that he'd been torn all along, trying to please the two females—four, if you counted his kids—in his life.

Despite her envy (and yes, she had to admit it did amount to envy) of Terry's ability to inspire such drama, even of the ultimately sorrowful kind, Ariel's crushes had tended to be of the humbler variety, on guys their own age. Long before Matt had entered the picture, and as her idealization of her father began to yield to actual grief, boys on the beach had begun to register on Ariel's radar. Here, on this very stretch of sand, she'd stared at scores of delectable males through the big tortoise-shell sunglasses Jasmine had given her for her fourteenth birthday. What could have been sexier than a fourteen-year-old boy on the beach, with all the energy of childhood finding its flower in a newly husky voice, in hair just beginning to sprout on a sun-kissed, lean chest, in wet hair flung away from an earnest forehead and slicked back with the flourish of a short black comb? And in his offers to smear the intoxicatingly perfumed Coppertone over your own hot back, which seemed to have grown a million new sensuous nerve-ends.

As the cry of a gull superimposed itself over the crazy laughter of the winos, Ariel wished with all her might that she could steal just one of those summer days back from time, exchange her shell for it, take the hand of one of those sweet-faced boys and re-do her life with him.

Suddenly something flashed through the air to her left. She turned her head just in time to see a seagull land on a pile of seaweed that hosted a swarm of tiny beach flies. It stood still for a minute, looking straight out to the sea. Ariel tried to discern what it might be looking at so intently, but nothing moved on the water. The sound of a plane hummed overhead. Her head fell back and she squinted up at the sky, shielding her eyes with the hand that held the shell. The plane emitted white smoke in long puffs, and she waited patiently—while the seagull bit at pests under its wing—to make out its message. It was a long one, long enough for the gull to get bored and fly away.

Ariel scratched her ankles as she waited. Shit. Sand fleas, she thought. They'd follow her home for sure.

The plane, its tidings conveyed, disappeared from view as Ariel made the long walk back to her car. The white letters drooped hazily in the air, and Ariel wondered if the one who it had been intended for had seen it before its current state of decomposition.

As "Laila, will you marry me?" melted in the sky, she speculated how long it would be before she'd have to flea bomb her apartment, unconsciously tucking the shell into the pocket of her faded, blue-and-gold UCLA sweatpants.

Opening the door to her Toyota, she stepped back when confronted with the stale heat trapped inside despite the mist outside. She pulled off her sweatshirt, rolled down her window, and gingerly slid in. It took several frustrating tries for the engine to turn over.

Foregoing her usual impulse to turn on the radio, she buckled her seat belt and began driving aimlessly. She couldn't go home yet; she didn't even want to think about you-know-who. Someone behind her honked, and finding a pair of angry eyes nearly boring holes in her rearview window, she picked up speed. After her hours on the beach, she was jarred by the pressured density of the traffic, which even on this holiday seemed to want to insist that she know her direction. But she found herself letting her hands, rather than her mind, lead the way, as if the steering wheel were the marker on a Ouija board. Before she knew it, she was driving up Westwood Boulevard toward the entrance to UCLA.

Well, this was certainly interesting. She hadn't visited her alma mater in ages. *Is that what you're telling me?* she wondered. "Come to mama?" she cried out loud, laughing wildly.

The driver of the car next to her—a handsome young Asian guy with silky black hair tied at the nape of his neck and a birthmark the size of a grape on his sculpted cheekbone—gave her a strange look.

Suddenly, her skin prickled. Eve was on this campus, somewhere in the anthro department in Haines Hall. But the first building she approached after parking her car was the Student Union. Memories flooded back of going crazy with Jasmine and Terry when they learned that Jimi Hendrix had once played there. It was in the Grand Ballroom that she had held hands with Jasmine, tears streaming down both their faces as Maya Angelou snapped her fingers and swayed her hips, reciting in that deep, sassy, carefully enunciating voice of hers "Still I Rise."

Ariel recalled, too, how formidable the grounds had looked from this vantage point on her first day as a freshman. The orientation map in her hand revealing her greenness as surely as a camera strung around a tourist's neck, she'd pushed herself up the athletically-pitched incline at breakneck speed for fear of being late to her first class, a highly-touted lit course taught by supposedly the coolest professor in the English Department. Jake Rosenberg was his name. She'd been in a terrible hurry because she'd only managed to get herself wait-listed for the class and needed to get Rosenberg's signature on an admittance slip to enroll.

She'd rushed into a standing-room-only lecture hall in Royce with sweat pouring down her forehead and a disheartened realization that she'd never be admitted with so many people already ahead of her.

But then she'd noticed that, late as she was, the room was heavy with silence, the hawk-faced man standing beside the podium in a rumpled tweed suit looking back at his students as if he were waiting for *them* to begin. Jake Rosenberg's eyes were bloodshot and his body looked like it was positively vibrating. Most of the other students gazed at the podium as if they were witnessing the second coming of Christ. When Rosenberg finally spoke, the terrific acoustics in the room reinforced the impression; his words came out like they were issuing from all four walls.

"People," he said. He actually started to cry then, with raw convulsive sobs, but his next words were clear enough. "Love one another."

Without a moment's hesitation, he stepped down from the raised platform and slipped out through a side door. For a few surreal seconds, the room went dead silent again and Ariel wondered whether she'd imagined the whole thing. Then a collective sigh rippled through the lecture hall like the first stirrings of a Santa Ana. Eager students in the front rows, obviously Rosenberg fans—girls with box braids or blond, beachy waves; boys sporting longish hair or buzz cuts —began reaching toward each other and hugging. She wished she could believe that their show of feeling was sincere.

Ariel had glanced at the guy next to her. His handsome, Nordic-featured face was lightly-pocked with old acne scars that gave him a little character, and he wore John Lennon-type granny glasses. It took her a moment to register that he was staring back at her. Before she could flick her eyes away in embarrassment, she noticed that he, too, held one of those hopeful class admittance slips. She looked up at him.

"Your guess is as good as mine," he said. "But it's hard to imagine a guy like that not letting us into his class because it's against the Fire Department rules." And then, with a wry grin that haunted her bedtimes for weeks, he said, "See ya," and slipped away. For weeks after that, she kept looking for him, but she never saw him again.

She did get admitted to the course, but Jake Rosenberg didn't end up teaching it. He was fired without objection for showing up that day on acid. The associate prof. who took over for him was adequate, but she'd always wondered what her life would have been like if Rosenberg had stuck around. Maybe she and the pock-marked guy would be an old married couple by now. And then again, maybe not.

Reaching Haines Hall, Ariel was surprised to find that the doors were locked. Yes, it was a holiday, but she'd seen plenty of students going in and out of the Powell Library on her way up here. But then she recalled that when she was an undergrad, about the only campus buildings open beyond normal class hours were the two libraries. She wondered idly if the library staff were paid overtime for the shitty hours they were required to work.

She leaned against a pale-barked tree in front of Haines Hall and sniffed the air. She didn't know what kind of tree this was, but it smelled just like semen. She shook her head. Christ, next to Jake Rosenberg, she had to be the weirdest person on the planet. While other people were having barbecues and preparing to set off fireworks, she was daydreaming about semen trees and Eve bones.

She studied the building's august facade. She could almost see herself, five years ago, flying down the steps from one of Professor

Edgerton's lectures, fired up over the pygmies' notion that, when the forest died, they would die, too.

She had no idea why she'd come here. What did she think, that they'd let a nobody like her get near a world-shaking research subject? Sure, anthropologists as a group tended to be nice enough. She remembered that much about Edgerton and his guest speakers. They would probably put up with talking to an alumna about what they were up to. But what would she ask, anyway? Outside of what she remembered about the BaMbuti, she didn't know her ass from a hole in the ground about anthropology. All she needed was for somebody to think she was some crazy postal worker with an obsession with the dead.

But still, it was tantalizing to be this close to what might actually be the bones of the shared ancestress of our species.

Sixteen

SIX MILES AWAY from where Ariel stood in rapt reflection on her proximity to Eve, Theosophus Kelly washed himself as best he could in the dank and dirty men's room of West Hollywood Park. Surprisingly, given the circumstances, it wasn't that hard to get clean. He'd found himself an almost unused bar of Dial soap in somebody's trash a few weeks ago. He kept it secreted like gold inside the folds of his best blanket, wrapped up in some nearly pristine tin foil he'd rescued from the back of Ralph's Market on Third Street, along with a precious roll of paper towels he'd bought with cash at the 99 Cents Only Store on Fairfax. But the powers-that-be disdained spending city money on heating the water at a park used mostly by transients, and the icy water that issued from the grimy tap shocked his underarms, his inner thighs, and his privates the way no cold temperature of a lonesome night could. That's why he waited until the afternoon to do his washing up whenever possible. At least he could get some sun on his back afterwards and feel for a few fleeting moments like a member of the human race again.

Theosophus wasn't so far gone in his drinking and roaming to forget what it was to live like other people, with a roof over his head and a little bit of earth to call his own. The funny thing was, the streets were his home now, but he felt like an intruder wherever he went. Some of the old guys he drank with, they claimed that they felt like they owned the city once they started sleeping rough. But Theosophus only felt that way when he had a buzz on. He might not give a shit what anybody else thought, but he didn't feel good inside about how he was living. The thing was, he hadn't felt so good about his life before he'd hit the streets, either.

Oh yeah, there were times, especially in his twenties, when he felt the power of his youth and good health. He was smooth, he was cool. He'd known what was happening, known he was handsome, and he could enter any bar from South Central to Mid-Wilshire and expect to score some honey for himself, no problem.

He hadn't been rich then either, but he got by well enough, supplementing his fry cook job, which paid poorly but assured him of a couple of free meals a day, with a little profit on the side for obtaining weed, and sometimes even a little coke, for his co-workers and friends. Nothing big, nothing likely to get him busted. He'd never wanted to risk that after Granny had filled him up with enough spooky stories about jailbirds turning good-looking guys into their surrogate women to keep him staying as close to the straight and narrow as was realistically possible in the parts of this City of Angels where the dark people lived.

Stretching out supine on the prickly grass of West Hollywood Park, Theosophus shielded his eyes from the sun's glare. Ever since he was a young boy, when his third grade teacher had shown his class a book full of maps that used different colors to differentiate mountains, plateaus, forests, and bodies of water, Theosophus could never imagine his own city without picturing its sectors as black and brown, yellow and white, depending on what kinds of people lived there. In this inner landscape, the parts that he frequented—the largest part of the city by far—were so black that you would have to have the eyes of a cat to see the street signs, while the much smaller area around UCLA, where he later ended up working, was so white it nearly blinded you. And while the darker sector was home, the other was where most people he knew wanted to be. He didn't like to think it was like that, but how many of his classmates who'd done well at school had stayed in the ghetto? It wasn't a mystery why the dark part of town erupted after the cops who'd beaten the shit out of Rodney King were acquitted. White people called it a riot, community activists called it an insurrection, but even at ten-years-old Theosophus knew what it really was. Unbearable heartache.

A memory came to him of watching the Miss America pageant on TV with his brother Gwayne and their two sisters when they were all kids. Flopped comfortably on the floor, their young bodies radiating out from that flickering box like the legs of a big brown spider, he and Gwayne had pushed Matchbox cars around and pretended not to look at the television, while Joylene and Araytha, each cradling a lily-white Barbie bought by Mama the previous Christmas, fussed over one white contestant after another as they paraded across the screen, commenting, "Ooh, she pretty!" and, "Girl, I like her hair. It's so yellow it's almost white."

And then Miss Louisiana or something had come along, a Creole beauty with her exotic milk-chocolate face fit to be split wide open with the size of her grin. His sisters had erupted in disgust. "Why'd they let that one in?" Araytha said, while Joylene shouted, "Girl, how'd she get in that contest? She so ugly!" He'd found himself ruthlessly running his Matchbox Camaro right over his brother's Mustang, and the next thing he knew Mama was taking the hairbrush after the two of them for fighting again.

Theosophus rolled over and, propping up on his elbows, rested his chin in his hands and let the sun beat down on his back. He became aware of horns honking, sirens blaring, drivers cursing out their windows. Traffic on Santa Monica Boulevard was hell at this hour.

Mama. He used to think she was good looking, but she lost her glow as the years wore on. The first time he noticed the depth of the bags under her eyes was when he watched her cry after her old white lady boss died without writing her a reference letter. Nobody wanted to hire her to clean their house because they could get some immigrant from El Salvador who was scared to ask for more than a few dollars an hour.

She started working as what they called a home helper after that, taking care of old and cranky sick people, working night shifts most of the time. He and his brother and sisters could never play in the house in the daytime for fear of waking her. And then Granny died, right in her old bed that she used to sneak him into after he'd peed himself, and Mama broke his heart by insisting on burying Granny's old Alabama comforter with her. Mama just seemed to fall apart then. He remembered the refrigerator gone bare, and he and Gwayne trying to get up the nerve to steal some food, their bellies all hollow with an unfamiliar aching, and Mama just letting the housekeeping go, with no Granny to spell her. And he remembered how he couldn't catch his breath when he heard Mama tell her cousin Veneta she was too afraid to go to the bank to see she'd overdrawn her account because what could she do about it anyways? And later, when Mama had the Alzheimer's, she didn't even know him. She looked right around the room, calling, "Theosophus? Theosophus?" Even though he was standing right there in front of her. It liked to break his heart how much he was still on her mind, though she couldn't see it was he who was holding her hand.

Theosophus' achy bones were warmed up enough now to get moving. He had somewhere he wanted to go. He went around behind the shed where he stored his shopping cart. He re-inserted his washing-up supplies, careful not to disturb the neat piles the little white girl Jane had made of his things when she'd returned his blanket.

Now there was a girl who didn't value herself. She barely raised up her head when he talked to her, like she was scared that by talking she'd be taking up too much room, and she hardly ever smiled. He remembered how her grin looked like it cost her something when he'd teased her, "Cat got your tongue?" Pretty little thing, but faded, skinny, almost see-through, as if the few years she'd been alive had bleached the spirit right out of her. He felt the same kind of discomfort for her as he'd had for his sisters, though she couldn't look more different from his sisters if she'd tried. Yes, he chuckled, she definitely looked like she belonged on the white part of the map. He stopped. But did she? She lacked the assurance, even the appearance, that she belonged in this world. In that, she had more in common with the people of South Central and East L.A.

———————

Three miles and a world away, Matt Hayes groaned and kicked away the opulently patterned Ralph Lauren duvet entangling his legs. He hated the damned thing, anyway, preferring cleaner lines and more muted colors to this riotous blanket that looked like it belonged in some pasha's boudoir. The duvet, along with the canopied four-poster it covered, the mad assortment of differently shaped throw pillows that took up most of the bed when it was made, and the heavy, antique furniture that filled the rest of the room were the price he paid for his frequent insomnia.

Bonnie, who hated sleeping alone but hated even worse his restless tossing and turning, had allowed him to make one of their spare bedrooms into a refuge on those nights when nothing but reading some predictable spy thriller could get him back to sleep again. But the deal she'd extracted from him for this abandonment had been his permission for her to decorate the room as she liked. It was a vision informed more by the femininely-inclined decorators who manned the showrooms of the pricey Pacific Design Center than by the tastes of the sort of man Matt was. The sort of man he was preferred function over form and took deep satisfaction in flinging the gold and burgundy-fringed throw pillows off the bed at two or three in the morning with vengeance. The sort of man he was liked to munch Mrs. Fields chocolate chip cookies as he read himself back to sleep without worrying about the chips staining the ridiculously expensive mauve satin bed sheets. Which was why he'd tiptoed so furtively downstairs and into the kitchen last night that he'd nearly scared his daughter Holly to death as she stood on tiptoe, trying to pull something down from the highest pantry shelf. That was the shelf where Bonnie stored the cookies and candies that she kept on hand for visiting UCLA donors' wives. She made sure they were as difficult to reach as possible for the family she worked so assiduously to keep fashionably thin.

He winced and lifted a warning finger to his lips when he saw Holly open her mouth to scream.

The hand that she clapped against her face failed to hide the familiar expression— twinkling eyes, wrinkled up nose, and guilty grin—that Matt was always a sucker for. Except this time, his own expression mirroring hers, they both knew it wasn't one of *his* rules she was breaking.

She whispered the question that she didn't really need to ask. "Daddy, what are you doing down here?"

For a moment he just stood there. She nearly took his breath away. Clad in a pink flannel nightie dotted improbably with a gray and brown, kitschy pattern of steaming cups of coffee, she moved away from the cupboard guiltily, sliding across the shiny tiled floor in her rumpled, thick gym socks. Her sophistication-striving, seventeen-year-old self would hate knowing how he saw her. With no make-up to cover the fine dusting of freckles on her face, and her shiny blond hair mussed by sleep, she looked all of eight or nine years old.

Matt grabbed a kitchen towel from its hook, and wrapping it over the lower part of his face, mugged like an old-fashioned bank robber. He poked a finger into her ribs and began tickling her, his muffled voice demanding, "Don't anybody move, just gimme the cookies."

Stifling giggles of delight, she was able to get out enough words to warn him that if he kept it up, she'd wake Bonnie for sure.

She was his girl, all right. Her older sister Jenna was a sweetie, but she was Bonnie's favorite. There'd always been a special, if unspoken, connection between Holly and him.

He poured them both tall glasses of milk and they sat at the table awhile, downing their cookies greedily. She set down her glass, wiped her hand across her milk-mustached upper lip, and looked at him from under shyly lowered lashes.

"Daddy, you know how I said I was never going to get serious about anybody till college?"

Matt's heart dropped. So that was what had gotten her up in the middle of the night.

She paused uncertainly, stammering a little as she went on. "Well, there's this boy I've been seeing. I mean, he's really cute and everything, but that's not the most important thing. It's that he likes me—I mean, who I am inside. I think he really gets who I am."

Matt felt a weight inside his stomach; it quickly condensed into a sour, knotted-up ball. Maybe Bonnie was right; it was bad for your digestion to eat in the middle of the night.

But now that she'd taken the plunge, Holly pressed forward at full speed, the words riding a wave of emotion right into him like he was her shore.

"Greg's not like the other guys. I mean, some of them think I'm great, I can tell by how they look at me, like they're holding me up on a pedestal, if you know what I mean." She blushed. "But he really listens, takes in what I say, asks me questions." She stopped, closed her eyes for so long that he wondered if she'd forgotten he was there.

Matt's knotted up ball was turning into hard-core heartburn. He bit his lip as he was seized by a particularly sharp pain, wondered if he was having a heart attack, then brushed the thought aside. He wanted to get up and take some Mylanta but didn't have the heart to break the intimate connection. Sweat broke out on his upper lip as she opened her eyes, but he managed to smile at her encouragingly.

"I mean, he takes me seriously. I showed him my horse drawings last week. You know, the ones I did a couple of years ago before I quit riding? Well, he said he thinks there's a really creative person in me that just needs some encouragement to come out. He's amazingly creative himself. He's written some really cool poetry."

Matt became aware for the first time of the ticking of the hall clock. He felt slightly flatulent. Thank God, the pains were easing up a little. Now all he had to contend with was the gas.

"But, Daddy, it's like, how do you know when you've found something special that will really last, like your soul-mate? What do the Jewish people call it—your *beshert*? I mean, whether it's Greg or somebody else later, I'd hate to think it's like that and then down the road it's more like you and mom."

As his eyes flicked up at her in surprise, she hastened to correct herself. She grabbed his hand and started anxiously petting it. "Oh, my God, Daddy, I didn't mean it. I really am a dummy, will you forgive me? I don't even know why I said that, that's not even what I think. I know how much you and Mommy are in love."

That was last night. After Holly's outburst, it had taken hours to get back to sleep, and that only after he'd grabbed her to him in a bear hug, told her repeatedly that he knew she hadn't meant it, tiptoed upstairs with her, and literally tucked her into bed.

Sliding out of the four-poster to turn up the thermostat, Matt felt confused. Poor Holly. He hated seeing her in such distress. But he was agitated in his own mind. He wasn't a fool. She damn well had meant what she'd said.

He shuffled into the bathroom, its apricot-hued marble floor like ice to his bare feet. He looked into the mirror and tried to get an honest read from his eyes, whose bags this morning made him look closer to his forty-two years than usual.

Things had never been particularly romantic between him and Bonnie. Getting her knocked up wasn't exactly the best beginning. But they'd ended up being a pretty good match, laughed and screwed well together, wanted more or less the same things. She even tolerated his occasional brief affairs with an almost blind eye, though he often found unusually expensive purchases itemized on their joint American Express bill in the month following one of his peccadilloes. He smiled at himself, intending to look rakish, but—in this lighting anyway—he looked more like a self-satisfied asshole.

"What can you expect from a marriage?" he whispered to the man in the mirror. His shoulders hunched. Now he looked like a wimp.

He knew he had something going with Bonnie that was a damn sight better than his own dad and mom. And, unlike his father, he respected his wife. Sure, he made fun of Bonnie sometimes, got irritated as hell by her addiction to shopping, even by her earnest intentness to be a good wife, good mother, good political partner in his upward climb at UCLA. But he also acknowledged that he'd benefited from those qualities in her. He had a well-run house to return to each night, daughters whose teeth were straight and who didn't do drugs, fuck up in school, or treat either of their parents with too much disrespect. He had a woman to have sex with who kept her body looking young and appetizing, someone who could even laugh it off tolerantly, without rubbing it in, when, in spite of her obvious attractions, he couldn't always get it up.

He brought his face up so close to the mirror that the two of him almost touched. So why wasn't he able to brush off Holly's words as adolescent idealism? The face in the mirror furrowed its brow at him. As for answers, it seemed it had nothing to say.

Seventeen

THE CITY OF ANGELS was pulsing. It was burning. It seemed as if everybody had places to go, deals to cut, a reason to be.

The earth underneath the freeways didn't need a reason. It throbbed and pulsed to its own larger rhythms, luxuriated sensuously under hot, nearly cloudless skies, bathed lazily in irrigation fed to it by humans eager to cultivate agriculture and commerce and planned residential communities that multiplied toward each other like the baubles of an over-dressed woman. Undaunted by its heavy blanket of concrete and asphalt and steel, it generously spun out ample vegetation—California fan palms, spiky yucca, the pungent and mighty eucalyptus, hardy avocado and aromatic citrus trees, bougainvillea and firecracker plant and milkweed. Through all its cycles of drought and flood and fire, it still nourished an abundant wildlife—darting squirrels, shuffling rat-tailed opossums, yellow-eyed coyotes that descended from the foothills to carry off small domestic animals, iridescent green hummingbirds up from South America, taunting crows, garrulous flocks of escapee parrots, melancholy seagulls, and ubiquitous slow-moving pigeons too often fallen to the traffic wars. And, from time to time, it made itself more comfortable by re-settling its layered girth along fault lines that trembling humans called by names like San Andreas and Sylmar and Northridge.

People worried about the Big One, but in fact the Big One was happening all the time, that eternal crackling fiesta of change invisible to all but a few meditative types, psychotics, and acid takers who snuck a tantalizing glimpse of the bigger picture.

Few knew the bones of what supported them, or recognized them as such. But some were looking.

Her lips salivating at the yeasty aroma of the pizza she was carrying back to the new spot Sarah and Danny were trying out in Westwood Village, Jane Deare snuck a quick look at herself in the glossy storefront window of Victoria's Secret. Its red-and-white striped canopy reminded her of the tall hats worn by the men who used to march in her hometown's Fourth of July parade. Except those were red, white, and blue. She remembered standing on tippy toe at the edge of the sidewalk, as far away from her stepfather as possible, anxiously scanning the parading rows of preening men in the absurd hope that she'd find her own daddy among them. She was prepared to forgive his donning of such a silly looking costume if only he would take her away from her ma and the creep she'd made a second marriage to. What a ninny she'd been. Her daddy wouldn't show his face around there anymore, not after Ma got the judgment against him for an alimony that he didn't want to pay. Jane had it all figured out by now. Daddy would have wanted to pay for her and Bobby's upkeep for sure, even have them over to his house on weekends and summers like her friends' divorced fathers, but her ma had gotten greedy, demanding alimony and all. Imagine the nerve of it, when her ma's sneaking around with that Vern surely had to have been the reason her folks had divorced in the first place.

Jane shifted the plastic bag holding the pizza box to her left hand while she ran her fingers through her stringy, blond hair. She'd always been skinnier than she wanted, but she sure looked bony now. The copper-colored mannequin that posed sexily next to Jane's own reflection had wide hips, big tits, and a tiny waist, all of it visible through the see-through nightie it was wearing. Whoever had dressed it up like that hadn't bothered to put a bra and panties on it underneath the pink lingerie. It wasn't decent, even if its titties had no nipples and its crotch no pubic hair.

She wondered why they called the store Victoria's Secret. She'd known a Victoria in elementary school, a plain-looking, unsmiling, brown-haired girl the kids called Vicky, but the teachers insisted on calling by her full name. Jane wondered now why Vicky hardly smiled and chose to hunch over a book on a bench at the corner of the playground when the rest of them played hopscotch and jump rope. Maybe she had a secret that nobody knew about. Those were the days before Ma took up with Vern. Could Vicky have had a secret like the one that Vern discovered about Jane? She'd looked so clean and all, could she have been a dirty girl, too?

Jane squinted at the mannequin, parading in front of the whole world with her no-nipple titties and that wide red grin on her face. She backed away from it hastily, and raced across Westwood Boulevard in the middle of the block, heedless of the yellow Porsche that nearly skidded into a black BMW to avoid hitting her.

───────────────

Less than ten miles to the northeast, a humbler vehicle made its way toward an area awkwardly dubbed "Beverly Hills P.O." Ariel's eyes widened as Ben turned left off of Coldwater onto a street that, within seconds, seemed to leave civilization behind. She was embarrassed that she'd lived in this city all her life and had to have a newcomer show her a part of it she'd never suspected existed. Passing through one more outcrop of homes before committing to a rustic road that made breathtaking, hairpin turns up the mountain, Ben's dusty Jeep Cherokee nosed through a gate with a sign pointing toward the William O. Douglas Wildlife Reserve.

Ben had been touting the beauties of Franklin Canyon to Ariel for weeks. Since the Fourth of July fiasco—which she promised him she'd gotten over—they couldn't seem to get their schedules to sync up for another try at the Coronado Hotel. She'd finally agreed to indulge him by coming here instead, recalling the dry disappointment of Griffith Park when she and Terry and Jasmine had cut classes to goof around there in their senior year.

As they crested a hill, Ariel glimpsed what looked like a vast lake through the trees. Ben navigated around groups of slow hikers, twosomes engaged in relaxed conversation, dog walkers, and young mothers pushing strollers, to pull into an unpaved clearing where a few other cars were parked. As she and Ben emerged from the Jeep to a temperature surely ten degrees higher than where they'd been just five minutes before, Ariel tore off her gray sweatshirt and looked around excitedly. This was a far cry from the urban landscape, a far cry from Griffith Park with its noisy soccer teams, pungent family barbecues, and depressingly sullen and raving homeless. This was nature. This was the country. No sounds of traffic, no leaf blowers, nothing to disturb the feeling that they'd gone back a century or so in time.

She noticed Ben sneak her a triumphant glance, and she laughed, grabbing his hand.

"Okay, I've got to give you this one. It's beautiful."

The wind that whispered around them was alive with the buzzing of insects, and there were mysterious rustlings in the chaparral. Ariel breathed deeply.

Without a word, Ben pulled her closer and led her across the narrow paved road to a low wall encircling the water. Nodding toward the other side, he began to help her over, but Ariel let go of him and awkwardly scrambled over on her own.

"Sorry." She laughed. "But I'm a bit of a hiking klutz. I've got to do it my own way."

"Baby," Ben said, "any way you do it is all right by me. I'm just glad I finally got you here."

Ariel grinned. "Okay, okay, so I'm stubborn." She rubbed her fingers together ruefully. "I've also gotten something sticky on my hands."

He lifted her left hand and put it to his face, sniffing curiously. "No biggie. Tree sap. You can wash your hands off when we get to the reservoir. It's right over here."

The part of the water they came to was murky and shallow and studded with reeds. Ben beckoned her closer. The squishy ground made sucking noises as she tiptoed toward him to peer in. Hundreds of tiny fish swirled noiselessly through the cloudy water. The call of a duck punctured the air. Wide-eyed, she looked up at Ben, and he led her a few feet around to a spot from which she could observe a trio of ducks sedately gliding across the water, their sleek, iridescent turquoise and brown backs glistening in the sun. One dove down suddenly and the other two took off and settled down again, ruffling their feathers.

Ariel laughed, then looked down, where the shallows swirled a few inches from her toes. "It's all well and good, great for ducks," she said, "but there's no way I'm going to stick my hands in that water to get the sap off."

Ben gave her a playful push and she clutched onto his shoulders, screaming. "You bastard, don't you dare."

He grabbed her by the waist. "Ah, got our sticky mitts on my best T-shirt, did we? Now let's see what punishment fits the crime. Maybe a kiss?"

Before she knew it, his warm lips were on hers. She felt herself yield, then, faking a giggle, pushed him away. "Can you circle the whole lake?" she asked hastily.

He gave her a rueful look. "It's called a reservoir, but yes, you can go all the way around, and there are lots of paths up the surrounding mountains, too, that give you a better view." He stepped back a few paces, stared at her quizzically, then shrugged. "Shall we go up or around?"

Ariel pursed her lips and looked out to where the two ducks still kept each other company. "Up first, please." She paused, and a grin swept across her face as she made a swivel motion with her hips. "And then all around."

Ben looked at her in confusion, and then, shaking his head, he laughed. "Oh, you dirty, dirty girl."

———————————

As he led Ariel up his favorite mountain path, Ben could hear her labored breathing. Even though she walked miles every day with a heavy mail pouch slung over her shoulder, she wasn't much of an athlete, and he could tell that she was having a hard time with the incline of their ascent. He stifled an impulse to slow down to let her catch her breath, recognizing that he wanted to punish her.

It wasn't the first time he'd felt frustrated with Ariel. She sure blew hot and cold on him. Sometimes he wondered whether she even noticed his deep feelings for her, or whether she was consciously trying to discourage him. Maybe it was no accident that she'd never had a serious relationship. Or climaxed when they made love. She was so frigging self-sufficient, maybe she didn't want anything more than a little company and some casual sex. Wasn't that what he'd thought he wanted, too, back at the beginning? That and a few cuddles when he got lonely or discouraged? But she'd grown on him, and—as Anna used to like to point out—he was basically a hopeless romantic. With an emphasis on the "hopeless." He just wished he could jolt Ariel out of that miasma of resignation and cynicism that she wrapped around herself.

Suddenly, a shriek rent the air and he was yanked backwards so strongly that he had to fight to keep his balance. With one hand grasping a bush that overhung the path—where pebbles now cascaded from his frantic efforts to stop himself from falling—he thrust his other out to grab Ariel, whose fingers were tightly fastened around his belt. He looked down toward the bottom of the rise and felt momentarily dizzy.

"Jesus," he said, "what happened? You nearly took the two of us down."

Ariel struggled to keep her balance as the pebbles continued to slide past her dusty sneakers. He hastened to instruct her to wedge her feet sideways as they inched up the pathway, secured against clumps of hardy greenery that sprouted from the dry ground.

She stuttered. "I'm sorry, but didn't you feel it? It was an earthquake." Looking searchingly at him, she hesitated. "Oh, shit, you didn't. I thought I could feel the earth move."

As he coaxed her toward the summit, where the earth suddenly flattened enough to allow the two of them to stand together before a panoramic view, he gave vent to a relieved belly laugh.

"What?" Her voice was laced with paranoia. "You think I'm a wuss." She paused. Her words were faint. "It's just that I've got a thing about earthquakes."

He barely registered her. "You felt the earth move." He was laughing so hard now that tears were pouring from his eyes. "I had to get you to the side of a mountain to hear you say that."

Clutching his belly, he looked over at her helplessly, only now seeing that her brown eyes were angry slits.

"What?" he croaked defensively.

"You shit. You bastard. It's not funny. What do you know about earthquakes, anyway? You've never felt one in your life. They're terrifying. They're violent. People do die in them, you know."

Oh, Jesus, he thought.

"Ariel." He tried to stroke her hair, but she batted his hand away. "Baby."

She stepped away as he continued to reach toward her, then quickly glanced backwards to make sure she wasn't backing right off the cliff. Holding two hands up to block him, she snarled. "Don't 'baby' me."

He put his own hands up in the air, then crossed them behind his back. "Okay, okay. I won't touch you. But will you just listen to me?"

Her lips were compressed tightly. He'd never seen her this mad.

"I wasn't laughing at you," he said. "Not at your fear of earthquakes, anyway. Hell, one of the reasons I took so long to move out here is that I was scared of them myself." He sensed the disbelief in her; the dark cloak of cynicism was wrapped tight. "I'll never forget watching scenes on TV of some of the worst ones, with freeways buckled up and apartment buildings collapsing like pancakes on people sleeping inside them. Everybody back home says you'd have to be crazy to live out here." He paused, cocking his head at her. Her eyes were shiny. "The only way I could get off my butt and come out here was to not think about it."

She nodded slightly, as if she knew what that was like.

He took a step toward her, then stopped as she looked as if she would back up again. "I would never laugh at you for being afraid of anything, anyway. What kind of a jerk do you take me for?"

She frowned, then spat out a question. "So what the hell were you laughing at, then?"

His face stretched in an apish grin. "I guess ... it was just ..."

She tapped her feet impatiently and brushed some dirt off her jeans.

"Oh, shit, I guess I was pissed off that you wouldn't give me a real kiss. Before."

"Before when?"

"You know." She obviously didn't. "When we were down by the reservoir."

"What the hell are you talking about?"

His words rang across the mountains ranged opposite them. "You're scared of earthquakes ... I'm scared I'll lose you."

Her mouth hung open. He had the irrelevant thought that he'd never seen somebody's jaw literally drop before. He didn't dare touch her, but he could almost feel the softness of her soul as he watched her startled eyes spill over with tears.

They both heard the sound at the same time, as something whizzed past their heads so quickly that they missed seeing it. Only when it made a second pass, this time right between them, did they make out the sleek contours of an electric-blue dragonfly.

He reached for Ariel. She let him wrap his arms around her and curled her hand inside his like a child. He liked tasting the salt of her tears on her cushiony lips. He tenderly drew her hand down to touch his hardness. She smiled hesitantly up at him, for once letting her shyness show.

He experienced a cessation of time as they sat together awhile on the crest of the mountain, watching a lone hawk circle the big sky. More dragonflies whirred around them. Most of them were blue, like the first one, but a few were the color of fire.

A lizard darted nervously toward a bush, but Ben was quicker. He felt its rapid heartbeat as he clasped it gently, but securely, in the palm of his hand.

Ariel whispered so softly that he barely heard her. "You know, I've never touched one."

He held it up to her. She wrinkled her nose but reached out and stroked the still creature with one finger. She smiled up at him. "Now I think we should let it go." The lizard slid hastily away as soon as he put it down.

A wind had risen, and it whipped Ariel's hair over her face. She giggled as he pulled a few strands out of her mouth.

They looked out together at the rising and falling of the land, ranged against a sky that suddenly hosted a stream of wispy clouds, and they played at descrying animal shapes and human faces in the variegated browns and greens of the mountainside.

"You know," Ben said, "I wonder how much the shapes we're looking at now were changed and formed over time by earthquakes."

Ariel looked at him. "What a comforting thought. I've never thought of them as anything but destructive." She laughed, dug her tousled head into his belly and wrapped her arms around him, her voice muffled. "Like a giant mean bogeyman shaking the world." Peering up at him, she cried out in a shrill, little girl's voice. "Save me, Daddy! Save me!"

Ben ruffled her hair. Then, as if embarrassed, she suddenly sat up, brushing the hair out of her face.

"It's funny," Ben said, "you thinking of earthquakes as the bogeyman. When I was a kid, I saw some documentary on TV about the sixties, and they showed an old commercial, for margarine or something. They had a woman wearing one of those long hippy-dippy dresses, a garland of flowers in her hair, dancing around in a meadow. And then, all of a sudden, they shook the camera around like it was an earthquake and a deep-voiced announcer said, 'It's not nice to fool Mother Nature.' My parents looked at each other and laughed, but it scared the shit out of me, thinking about something under the ground making the earth move like that."

She shook her head. "God, we're such media victims. You get your picture of Mother Nature from a TV commercial." She paused. "It's pretty funny that I think of the earth being shaken by some mean God who has it in for us, rather than it shaking itself to make change." She began to scrape at the dirt with the side of her hand, patting it into a smooth mound that she studded with small pebbles. She studied her creation, then looked up at him. "Do you think of God as male or female? Or I guess I should ask, do you believe in God at all?"

Startled, he laughed. "This reminds me of what happens when you get a group of people together smoking dope. By the end of the evening, you inevitably end up talking about God. Sitting out here is a lot like getting high, only better." Softly stroking her cheek, he added, "Especially with you."

It wasn't until they'd descended the hill, propelled by a sudden ravenous hunger that overtook them both, that Ariel realized Ben hadn't answered her question. But the moment had passed, and she didn't feel moved to ask it again, content, instead, to walk silently by his side, with an occasional hello to passing hikers on the path. She couldn't get over how everybody they met here seemed so friendly, as if they all lived together in a small town. Hardly anybody on the street acknowledged her when she walked her mail route.

A couple approached them, their unleashed German Shepherd puppy rushing ahead to extend greetings and stick a wet nose up at Ariel's crotch. The dog's owners apologized profusely as they called their dog back to them. It obeyed enough to pull its face away from her pants, but couldn't resist making a full nasal exploration of her sneakers as Ariel knelt down to pet it.

"It must be my cat he smells."

The dog's owners nodded with the sort of pleasantly indulgent interest Ariel was familiar with from visits to the vet, where fussing over other people's pets and inquiring after their ages and ailments were like the rituals of admission to a secret brotherhood of animal lovers. If she weren't so hungry she would have liked to talk to the friendly couple a lot longer, but she still managed to throw in a few more descriptions of Jezzie before Ben and her rumbling belly got her moving again.

When Ben opened the car door for her, he leaned in to plant a wet kiss on her cheek.

"What's that for?" she said.

"For your love of animals."

Her eyes twinkled and she meowed. "Yeah, that must be why I like *you*, too."

When they got back down to Sunset, Ben stopped at the light, offered her a cigarette, and said, "Where to?"

It was then that she saw a familiar figure at the corner across from them. He was skating flashily to music from a boom box, which he held to his shoulder as if it were a baby. As usual, he wore the kind of big sunglasses that people wore when they wanted to travel incognito, and his head covering suggested he was reluctant to be recognized. But the bizarre figure he struck and his equally strange routine betrayed his hunger to be seen.

"Oh, look," she said. "There's that guy. Have you ever seen him? I call him the Mad Skater."

Ben snorted. "Jesus, yes. Saw him the first week I got here, I think it was on Beverly Boulevard, across from Erewhon. I couldn't figure out which was more 'L.A.,' a guy in black leotards and a black veil over his head like some old woman in an Italian movie, or a health food store whose name is a play on the word 'nowhere.' Your Mad Skater sure gets around." He made a face, stubbing his cigarette in the car's overflowing ashtray. "Gotta quit, gotta quit." He said the words as if he'd said them a million times before. "Now where ... I know." He sounded excited. "Ever been to Il Fornaio? It's just down the street."

She looked down at her dirt-streaked sweatshirt. "Oh, Jeeze, isn't that in Beverly Hills? I don't know …"

He patted her shoulder. "Oh, come on, who cares? It's Saturday," he said, pretending to hold a pince-nez up to his eyes and speaking archly, in the manner of a runway commentator. "A perfect day for casual wear." He switched back to his normal voice after she raised one eyebrow. "Come on. It's a great place for breakfast. They bake their own breads. And they make the meanest *ciabatta* in town."

She laughed, throwing up her hands. "Okay, okay. How can I say 'no' to you? Besides, you're the actor, you're the one who'll have to live down escorting such a funky woman to a classy joint. But what's a *ciabatta* when it's at home?"

Ben was still extolling the merits of the over-sized loaves of crusty Italian bread when they neared the stylishly rustic entry to the restaurant at the corner of Beverly Drive and Dayton Way. Ariel barely noticed the two homeless kids close to the entrance, smelling pungently of sweat and cigarettes, but she did stop short at the sight of the scrawny dog by their side. This dog looked far too shy to go after her crotch like his healthier looking compatriot in Franklin Canyon. He looked so sad that Ariel was tempted to try to pet him, but then out of the corner of her eye she noticed Ben lean forward to drop some change into a Styrofoam cup on the sidewalk. She saw the young beggar, his open-sored face as skinny as a death's head, look searingly up at Ben.

"Hey, man, how you doin'?" Ben said.

For a moment, the skinny guy just stared at him. Then, as Ben continued to stand there, a smile crinkling his blue eyes, the guy shrugged and mumbled. "Been worse."

Once inside, a pencil-thin hostess led them to their table, which was surrounded on every side by patrons who, Ariel just knew, were celebrities. They had the telltale self-possessed look. She immediately excused herself to the ladies' room, where she stared balefully at her grimy face. Reminding herself of how attentive Ben had been all morning, she washed her hands and face and used a paper towel to rub a rosy glow onto her pallid skin. She really did need to trust him more. She'd been told more than once over the years by Terry how cold-hearted she could come across when she was scared.

Reminding herself of her mother's mantra for when she felt

insecure—"Just imagine the people who intimidate you in their underwear"—she squared her shoulders and opened the bathroom door to the noisy dining room.

Sliding in next to Ben, rather than opposite him, she remembered their earlier conversation. She leaned her head toward his and whispered. "Yes, but the real question is, does the Mad Skater believe in God?"

Eighteen

SELMA NERVOUSLY PLEATED her sweater as she spoke into the phone. "Hello, Ariel?" she said. "So, you're having a nice evening?"

"What's wrong, Mrs. G?"

"What could be the matter? I just wondered how you were."

Ariel answered gently. "Selma, I saw you this morning. I'm still fine." She paused. "Hang on a second, will you?" Selma could hear her whispering to someone in the room with her before resuming the conversation. "What's up?"

Selma clapped a hand to her forehead. "Of course. My rotten memory. You told me your friend was coming over tonight, the one who just moved back. Forgive me, I'm intruding." Her voice began to fade out.

"Selma, don't you dare hang up. What's going on? What are you doing?"

"Not much, really. I was watching that crazy chef on television. You know, the one with the face so red he looks like he could have a heart attack any minute?" Beads of sweat had broken out on her brow.

"What else, Mrs. G? C'mon, I can tell something's wrong. Are you feeling okay?"

"It's just a little dizziness," Selma said defensively.

"Do you want me to call an ambulance?"

"No, please, it's nothing like that. One more unnecessary trip to the hospital and that *momser* Max will have me in a home before you can count to three. Besides, Dr. Samovitz told me it might happen again before it went away completely."

"I'll be right over," Ariel said.

Selma began to say, "Oh, don't—" but Ariel had hung up.

When Ariel arrived, she insisted that Selma spend the night with her.

Selma stooped to pick up a clump of damp leaves Ariel had dragged in on her shoe. "See?" she said, as she pivoted to throw them into a wastepaper basket. "Perfect balance. I'm fine now. It was just a little ..." She looked up suddenly. "And what about your friend? She's at your house still?" Ariel nodded. "I'm spoiling your party. Besides, if you give me your bed, where will you sleep?"

Ariel shook her head. "Selma, you're too much. It's not a party, it's a visit from an old friend who's been dying to meet you, anyway." She patted Selma's arm. "As for sleeping arrangements, my couch and I are the best of friends, since it's in the same room as the TV. I fall asleep there about half the time anyway. So you see, it's not a problem." She paused. "There is one thing though. You're not allergic to cats, are you?"

Selma, secretly relieved, left Ariel waiting patiently in the dining room, munching on some *kugel*. Stuffing a few things into the overnight bag that she'd last used when Chaim was in the hospital, her eyes filled. How many slices of *kugel* had she carefully wrapped in tinfoil, how many loaves of *challah* and jars of kosher pickles had she *shlepped* to Cedars-Sinai in this bag? She'd clung as long as she could to the forlorn hope that she could put flesh back on those sweet bones of his—those sturdy, thick, man's bones, eaten away by cancer. She shuddered with the memory.

When they arrived at the apartment building on Poinsettia, Ariel's friend was waiting for them out in front. Selma could barely make out her features under the diffuse glow of the street lamp, but she could hear her throaty laugh as Ariel pulled up to the curb and rolled down her window. Selma hoped the girl wasn't laughing at *her*.

Ariel called out to her friend, "I can't find a damned parking spot. Why don't you help Mrs. Goldberg up to the apartment while I park?"

Before Selma knew it, a hand reached in to take her suitcase from her and another supported her as she pushed herself out of the car with a groan and negotiated the curb. Ariel's friend said, "Easy does it, let's go nice and slowly." Selma squinted up at her. A pretty girl, she thought, taking pleasure in her shiny curls and her delicately molded features, which broke so easily into laughter. But, Selma argued with herself, what am I thinking? A girl, she isn't. At my age, everybody starts to look like a baby.

Selma put her hand to her chest, not noticing the sudden look of concern on her escort's face. She'd had a sudden memory of her own daughter at the moment she stopped being a baby and became a woman. It had happened at the end of a classmate's *bar mitzvah* party. Selma had pulled up to the synagogue in the family Buick, looking in vain for young Edith's lithe frame amid the groups of giggling teenagers moving restlessly in front. With her fingers plugging her ears, she'd hurried through a maze of unfamiliar hallways toward the rock-and-roll music blasting from the reception hall.

It was lucky that she was there when Edith emerged nervously from the ladies' room, her hands grasping at the back of her new pink dress. Edith had grabbed her arm and said in a strangled whisper, "I got my period, Mama!" Not just any period, but her first period. Selma moved quickly behind her to shield her blood-stained dress from view and steer her out to the car.

"*Momme sheyna*," she'd said. "Don't feel bad. So you got a little blood on a dress. Nobody saw. Another dress we can always buy. What's important is that now you are a woman."

The sound of footsteps broke into Selma's reverie. As Ariel approached, Selma wanted to explain that, if it weren't for Max, she wouldn't have bothered her like this.

But Ariel touched her lightly on the arm and said brightly, "Have you introduced yourselves? Selma Goldberg, Maria Theresa Marella." She leaned closer and whispered, "But for God's sake, don't call her that. To friends and family, she's Terry." Then Ariel nodded to Terry. "Terry, the famous Mrs. G. She makes the meanest pot roast in town. If you're lucky, maybe she'll make you dinner some time."

Selma rushed to assure Terry that she could come over tomorrow night if she wanted, or maybe the night after, which would give her time to do a little shopping.

Terry giggled. "Please, Mrs. Goldberg, there's no hurry. I'm just happy to be meeting you at last. Ariel's been telling me such wonderful things about you."

Selma assumed that Ariel's mention of pot roast was a hint that the *kugel* hadn't been enough. Depositing her things in the corner of Ariel's bedroom, she rolled up her sleeves and turned to the young women. "You're hungry?" she said, but it was more a statement than a question. "Now, don't let me cramp your style, you two. If you show me the kitchen, maybe I'll make a little something while you sit down, relax, do what you were going to do before you had to deal with Mrs. Buttinsky."

Ariel and Terry exchanged a delighted glance. "Well, if you're sure ..." Ariel said. "C'mon then, Mrs. G, let me show you the lay of the land."

Humming happily, Selma padded around Ariel's kitchen in the stretchy socks Ariel had insisted on loaning her. The refrigerator was shockingly bare, but there were just enough eggs to drench the slices of *challah* she'd had the foresight to bring with her for breakfast tomorrow morning, along with a nice new box of powdered sugar and a half-full bottle of maple syrup.

As the first pieces of bread grilled slowly in the frying pan, she reflexively began to wipe what looked like years-worth of accumulated grease from the knobs of Ariel's 1960s-style, turquoise kitchen cabinets. She nervously glanced at the doorway from time to time—after all, she didn't want to shame Ariel, who was a modern working woman with so little time for housework.

When the French toast was ready, she called out to Ariel and Terry, but no one responded. She looked down at Jezebel, who stared back greedily. She shrugged and said, "So, nu? When they're ready, they'll come." She stooped to offer the cat a piece of French toast. Jezebel nearly bit Selma's finger off to get it. Selma, shocked, chided her. "*Oy*, you're not a cat, you're a pig. A greedy, little pig." She set the oven on warm.

By now Jezebel had leapt onto the kitchen counter, where she found her way to the chipped beige bowl that was slimed with leftover raw egg.

"Enough with you, already. You think she wants your germs in her dishes?" Carrying the cat into the living room, Selma heard giggles coming from the bathroom. Jezebel jumped down from her arms and brushed familiarly against a plastic laundry basket full of wrinkled clothes. Selma absent-mindedly began to fold Ariel's T-shirts when she heard a beeping sound. She followed it to a tiny hallway, where a landline was off the hook. Replacing it in its cradle, she wondered if the nearly-blind cat had knocked it off.

A few minutes later, as Selma sat on the sofa petting the cat, Ariel and Terry—mugging maniacally—pranced into the living room. They wore terry cloth bathrobes. Their previously pale faces were as dark as the earth. Cigarettes protruded from their lips, and they'd twisted white towels atop their heads.

Ariel sat down next to Selma and gave her a ferocious grin. Selma smiled back uncertainly. Jezebel leapt over Ariel's lap, then arched her back and spat when she went to lick the now-hardening goo on her face. Selma couldn't help but laugh. Ariel pointed at Terry. "Mrs. G, you should approve of this. It's an Israeli product. They claim it's made of mud from the bottom of the Dead Sea."

Selma wrinkled her nose, noticing for the first time the distinctly fishy smell wafting through the room.

Ariel noticed the folded clothes that were now neatly piled inside the laundry basket. "Oh, Mrs. G, you shouldn't have."

Just then, the doorbell rang. They all looked up in surprise. Ariel muttered, "Who can that be?" Terry lifted an eyebrow at her, and Ariel answered the unspoken question. "Not Ben. He's working tonight."

The bell pealed again, several times. Terry muttered, "Oh, for God's sake, aren't you going to answer the bloody door?" But before Ariel could respond, Terry got up herself and hurried across the room to yank the door open.

Selma saw the girl step back as the man at the door stared in horror at her mud-caked features. He put up his hands as if he were warding off evil spirits.

Matt nearly fled when the ghoul who opened the door said "Matt? Matt Hayes? Is it really you?"

He squinted at her, incredulous. The voice was right, but what was with the weird face? "Terry?" he said.

Matt couldn't believe it. He'd come to Ariel's hoping to get Terry's number. Jasmine had called that afternoon from Hawaii to report on her visit with her brother Neal, but he'd heard nothing after she mentioned her reunion with Terry and Ariel. Jasmine had sounded a little dubious when he asked for Terry's number, then claimed she'd misplaced it. But when he'd pressed her for Ariel's address and phone number, she'd had no choice but to give her landline number to him. He suspected she'd withheld the cell so he couldn't immediately text Ariel and parlay that into a text to Terry. He assumed she wanted to warn her friends first that Matt was trying to track Terry down. Which was all well and good, but when he finally got up the nerve to call Ariel, he got nothing but a busy signal. He'd finally dialed the operator, who told him it must have been left off the hook.

He didn't know why he was doing this. What had started as wanting to make a simple phone call for old times' sake had ended with him actually driving over to West Hollywood like some loser in search of a life.

And now he was standing here staring at the woman who'd inspired all this, her face smeared in what looked like baby shit.

From somewhere behind Terry a thickly-accented voice piped up. "Do you know him? Is he a friend?" As Ariel and Terry nodded like a couple of bobble-heads, the voice continued. "Aren't you going to ask the gentleman in?"

An old lady, short and wide, her eyes curious, came to the door. "How do you do? I'm Selma Goldberg. Why don't you sit down while your friends make themselves more presentable?"

Her words seemed to break the spell. Ariel hastily introduced Matt to Selma, then she and Terry fled to the bathroom.

Matt sat next to a laundry basket piled high with clothes and lorded over by a black cat with cloudy, whitish-blue eyes. The place reeked of cigarette smoke. He had the idle thought that Bonnie wouldn't permit smoking in his own house.

"So," Selma said. "I take it you haven't seen your friends for a while."

He ran a hand through his hair and looked around wildly. God, it was funky here. He wondered if Ariel—and maybe Terry, too—had never grown up. He found himself making a confession. "All the way over here I kept asking myself why I was doing this." He flushed and spread his hands. "But whatever made me do it isn't talking."

She looked at him searchingly. "Me, also, I don't know what I'm doing here." She shrugged, then smiled apologetically. "You want maybe some coffee? I'm sure she's got some; it would go well with the ..." She clapped her hand to her forehead. "Me and my rotten memory! The French toast, it's still in the oven. It must be like rocks by now."

He had no idea what she was talking about, and she couldn't even see him now, having fled to what he presumed was the kitchen, but he nodded. What had he said to her about something inside him doing the talking? It had seemed as if something inside him hadn't shut up since his conversation with Jasmine. And most of what it said seemed to boil down to was Terry. He'd tried arguing with it, telling it that it didn't really mean Terry, but probably something about his lost youth. He must be going through some kind of midlife crisis. But the unwelcome urge had kept after him like a dog at a bone. Terry was back in town, it reiterated. Didn't he want to see how she turned out? Wouldn't it be great to show her how far he'd come?

Terry came back into the living room and curled up against the opposite end of the sofa, her hands clasped around her knees. Her scrubbed and un-made-up face was radiant, and she wore her hair in a ponytail, some of it escaping its band to curl in soft tendrils at her cheekbones. She smelled like the sea. She reached toward a pack of cigarettes on the coffee table and then pulled back. She giggled. "I forgot, besides marijuana, you never smoked." She looked him up and down with unabashed curiosity. "You look so healthy, you probably still don't."

His smile was pained. "Go ahead, I don't mind."

He usually did mind. Cigarettes smelled acrid and shitty to him. But this one couldn't compete with the beachy smell of her. If anything, it actually seemed to go with it. A memory of meeting the young temptress on Santa Monica pier, how irresistibly he'd felt drawn to her, despite the disparity in their ages. He watched the smoke waft out of Terry's mouth and nostrils and stifled an impulse to lean forward and open his own mouth to let it seep in.

He felt the need to explain himself. "I was talking to Jasmine. About Neal." She winced. "I know. It's terrible, the worst." He flushed and cleared his throat. "But anyway, when Jasmine said she'd seen you, I just had to ... I thought it might ... God, listen to me, I sound like I'm sixteen. I guess I just wanted to say 'hi.'"

She took a long time to respond. "Hi." Her voice was soft.

His was, too. "How've you been?"

"Fine."

They both laughed, and he found himself taking the cigarette from her lips and puffing on it, inhaling it like a spliff. He coughed so hard that Selma came running into the room, only leaving again once he'd assured her that he was okay.

By now, Terry was grabbing her belly with laughter. The sound of it was so familiar.

"God, I've missed you," he said.

Terry couldn't believe that she was sitting next to Matt Hayes. She'd thought she'd never see him again. Until this moment, she hadn't let herself know how much she'd wanted to.

But he was saying something to her. She asked him to repeat it.

"So, you and Ariel kept in touch all this time?"

"Actually, no. I mean, it's been awhile. I was in New York and had a job that ate up every waking hour."

"Doing?"

"Nothing important."

"Nothing important!" Terry looked up. Ariel and Selma had entered the room, carrying trays with plates of delicious-smelling French toast and coffee. Terry leapt up to take Selma's tray as Ariel continued. "It might not have been your dream job, but don't minimize your achievements." She smiled at Matt. "This beautiful babe was one of the top dogs at Citibank. At their main corporate offices."

Terry flushed. She scooted closer to Matt to make room for Selma. "Bo-ring." She glanced at Matt. "But what about you?"

Matt smiled. "Well, I obviously didn't get so far. Actually, I never got away from UCLA." He paused. "I'm Vice-Chancellor there."

Before Terry could respond, Ariel blurted out, "No way! Why, I was just there, right outside Haines Hall. You must be thrilled to actually have the bones of Eve right there in the anthropology department basement. I've been closely following the news about her."

Matt looked puzzled. "Well, actually it's not—"

But Selma interrupted. "What, the African?"

Terry nudged Matt in the ribs. "Vice-Chancellor. God, at least somebody's doing something worthwhile. But there's probably a certain amount of BS to it, too. Do you have to entertain big donors?"

"Well, Bonnie ..." Seeing Terry stiffen, he flushed. He pushed ahead. "Well, she takes care of that." He glanced at Terry, then nervously picked at his French toast as he said, "Did you ever meet Bonnie?"

Terry's voice was dry. "Yeah. I'm surprised you don't remember. I bumped into you two—actually you four—in the Palisades. That was why we ..."

Ariel leaned forward. "Anybody want some more coffee?"

"I do." Terry was humiliated at how loud her voice sounded.

Selma inclined her head. "So go on. It's nice to have a wife. And children?"

Matt's face was looking a little green. "Two. Holly's in her senior year at Brentwood and Jenna majors in Communications at UCLA."

Selma nodded approvingly. "Two children. Now that's a nice size for a family." She confided, "My daughter Edith is working on her fifth child." She shook her head. "So much work."

Ariel was back. "Just like the woman who lived in a shoe, eh, Selma?"

The conversation fell around Terry like rain. She wished she could just go invisible.

But when Matt finally got up to leave, he suggested she walk him out to his car. Before sliding into his BMW, he turned to face her and leaned in so close that she could smell the maple syrup on his breath. He grabbed her arm and hissed, "I've got to see you again. Can I call you?"

She shot him a surprised look, then realized he'd already pulled a pen out of his pocket. She hesitated—he'd always been so damned sure of himself. She felt like her body was cut in two: up in her head, alarm bells were going off like crazy, but Matt's piercing blue eyes and crooked grin were setting off the kind of sparks in her belly she hadn't felt for years. She took the pen from his fingers and wrote her number on the back of his hand.

Nineteen

MORNING WAS JUST dawning as a key turned in the lock of Fowler Museum. Matt Hayes reached toward the bank of knobs controlling the building's multiple light fixtures. He marveled at the fund-raising genius of Chancellor Biggs, whose zeal had put UCLA's anthro department on the map by shifting the last of its lab facility and vast collection of artifacts from the damp obscure basement of old Haines Hall to this modernly equipped setting. The state-of-the-art overhead lights in the main viewing room startled him by immediately bursting forth like flash bulbs at a celebrity sighting. In this sudden light, the wood-carved African figurines perched on shelves lining the walls looked for a moment as if they were jumping right out at him.

He smiled sheepishly, then moved toward one of the larger figures, whose reedy skirt stuck out from its hips like a porcupine's quills. Its face disgorged a greenish tongue out of its mouth like a stiff dick. Matt stuck his own tongue back at it before sitting down on an upholstered bench in the middle of the room to review his notes. He was glad he'd come here early, before the staff arrived and before the press conference scheduled to reveal the progress of the anthro department's "first Eve" research. He hadn't had much time to prepare last night, obsessing instead about the date he'd made with Terry for this evening.

What a coup to have tracked her down like that—but how eerie it had been to see her with her face smeared with that goop. Matt reached toward the cell phone in his briefcase. He had to call Terry to reconfirm their date. Would she show up when the time came? He'd felt so sleazy, asking her to meet him at a hotel, but she'd seemed reluctant to let him see her new apartment in Mar Vista after he'd told her about his house in Westwood. Staring sightlessly at a row of very dark, crouched figurines bearing spears, he imagined asking Terry to bring that beauty mask cream with her to the Four Seasons so that she could smear the stuff on her face again. No, better yet, he wanted to apply it himself to her face, her body, put it all over his own body too. He reached down to readjust his jockey shorts as he felt himself get hard.

Scrolling through his cell's address book for her number, he conjured up an image of Terry in bed with him all those years ago, her wild curls spread like snakes across her pillow. Matt was so lost in the past that he didn't hear keys jangling and another person enter the large room.

"Vice-Chancellor Hayes?" the shiny-faced undergrad said timorously. "I'm Shannon Truitt. I was supposed to come early to help set up for the press conference."

He looked into her wide blue eyes that were just as blue and just as innocent as Holly's. He froze. What had he been thinking? This wasn't just any woman. And it wouldn't be some meaningless one-night stand. It was Terry. Making plans with her was dangerous. He had to call it off.

———————

Terry paced back and forth at the entrance to the Four Seasons Hotel, the cigarette smoke that trailed behind her wafting toward a trio of brown-skinned valet guys in bright red vests. For a fleeting moment she registered their curious glances before returning to the brew of hurt and anger that was eating away at her as the minutes ticked away.

She looked down at her watch for what she thought must be the hundredth time that evening. Eight forty-five. *This is ridiculous. What am I doing here, anyway? I was a fool to think that anything could happen between us again. He's married, for fuck's sake.* As he had been the first time around.

A black stretch limo pulled up in front of her, and the parking attendants swung into action. While the shortest of the three went to accept the car key from a goateed chauffeur, the other two flanked the passenger doors. The woman who emerged on the side closest to Terry had the worst adult acne scars she'd ever seen, but the smile that she offered to the young Latino who helped her out of the car was wide and warm, and her black, almond-shaped eyes sparkled. The man who emerged from the other side of the car loomed over the heads of the woman, the chauffeur, and all three attendants.

Terry nearly whistled in appreciation. *Jeeze, he really is gorgeous, but the woman he's with must be his publicist, since she sure ain't his wife.* Flushing, she scolded herself for her cattiness. *Who do I think I am, the Queen of the May?*

As the two of them walked toward her, Terry realized she was blocking the entryway. Moving to one side apologetically, she couldn't help but stare at the man she'd drooled over while downing numerous bags of popcorn. In spite of all her years in the business, there was something about him that made her feel like a star-struck teenager. He flashed a brilliant smile at her, and it was all Terry could do not to break into giggles. She fished hastily into her purse for a cigarette, only to find the actor proffering a gold lighter toward the Benson and Hedges Ultra Light suspended shakily between her fingers. She was vaguely aware of the woman he'd arrived with looking toward her with what looked like commiseration. Before she could finish her embarrassed, "Thank you," the actor was moving away from her like a graceful seal.

Terry stubbed out her cigarette with the heel of the sexy new black boot she'd bought for just this evening and held her parking ticket out toward one of the valets. Fuck Matt, she thought, I'm outta here. Liam Neeson just lit my cigarette. It's got to be a sign.

Terry couldn't help but notice that Ariel was glowing with excitement the following night as the two of them scrambled over the hunched-up knees of a long row of annoyed-looking seated theatergoers. "Excuse me, excuse me," she murmured multiple times, as she and Ariel shuffled awkwardly to their seats in the middle of the row. Ariel jabbed her elbow sharply into her ribs when she sensed her taking the kind of deep breath that usually led to gales of laughter. She hissed at her out of the corner of her mouth. "If you embarrass me tonight, I'll kill you."

As the house lights dimmed and the audience hunkered down for the first act, Terry was uncomfortably aware of the musty smell and creaky, cramped seating of this equity-waver theater on the funky stretch of Santa Monica Boulevard between Cahuenga and Vine. But it was Ariel's first chance to see Ben act in person, and Terry couldn't let her down, no matter how low she herself felt.

She watched Ariel shove her purse farther back under her seat with her feet, her face plastered with a broad grin. Terry hoped that Ben would live up to Ariel's expectations. As the three actors appeared on the tiny stage and began to go through their paces, Ariel was visibly rapt.

Terry, on the other hand, barely kept up with the play. Contrary to her earlier determination to keep Matt Hayes out of her mind, she kept replaying the messages she'd received on her cell phone last night after her fruitless vigil at the Four Seasons. She was damned if she'd pick up his calls.

"Terry," the disembodied, barely recognizable Matt-voice had mumbled into voicemail. Then a long pause. "Terry." Pause again. "I'm sorry. I can't ... make it. I wish ... I'll call ..." After she'd removed her black boots and nylons and stood leaning against her couch, rubbing the bottom of one of her aching feet, she'd checked the next message. This time his voice was sharper. Brusque, really. "This is stupid. You must know it, too. We're not kids anymore, and I'm a married man. I'm sorry if I inconvenienced you." Then, just like that, he'd hung up. She couldn't believe it. His tone so impersonal. As if he were giving some speech at UCLA. She chewed her lip. Bloodless, that's what he'd become.

She was startled by the sound of applause as the lights went on in the theater. Ariel was on her feet, her eyes wide and her voice throbbing with enthusiasm.

"Do you believe it? Isn't he wonderful?"

Terry looked at her blankly, then slowly rose from her seat. Ariel's brown eyes shone. Pink patches dotted her usually pale cheeks. Terry had never seen her look so exposed, so joyous. About to make a cynical remark, she stopped herself just in time. "Mmmm," she agreed. When Ariel wondered aloud if she should go backstage and tell Ben how great he was doing, Terry took pity on her. Oh, baby, she thought, have you got it bad.

"There'll be lots of time after the play to tell him," she assured her, as she steered Ariel through the gushing crowd that lined the aisle for intermission. She had the fleeting thought that only in L.A. was the audience as good-looking as the actors. "Besides, don't you want to have a pee? No? Well, I do. Keep me company."

Once she'd firmly planted Ariel next to the restroom door, reiterating that Ben would need some alone time to compose himself before the final act, Terry escaped into the bathroom, swearing at Matt Hayes into the bathroom mirror. "Fucker. Asshole." Remembering their favorite curse from middle school, she started to laugh. Putting her face up close to the glass, she mouthed the words. *Mother-fucking cocksucker.* "Jesus," she muttered, "you can't get much lower than that."

Matt Hayes momentarily forgotten, she turned to the toilet and pulled down her pants to pee. The seat was covered with drops of urine, and she swore with annoyance at the first poorly-aiming squatter who'd spoiled the pleasure of actually sitting on the toilet seat for those who came afterwards. She hated squatting to pee, always convinced she was going to wet her panties or her shoes.

She was so physically uncomfortable in this posture, with her pulled-down pants straining across her knees and her legs beginning to cramp, that she rolled her eyes heavenward. It was then that she spotted an insect hugging the ceiling. She couldn't believe it. Brown and hard-shelled, it was the biggest roach she'd ever seen. And to make her nightmare complete, the creature had wings. As if to confirm that, it began to flit from one wall to another. The good news was, her urine hadn't yet started to flow, so Terry was able to haul her pants back over her hips and leap out of the bathroom with a yelp and a shudder before the roach had a chance to devour her. Or at least, that was how she told it to Ariel as they filed back to their seats.

The effect of Terry's one exaggeration clearly made Ariel doubt the whole story. To Terry's exasperation, Ariel kept teasing her about "the giant flying roach" as the audience coughed itself into readiness for Act Two. Worse still, Terry realized she still hadn't peed and, reminding herself that she was stuck in the middle of the row, resigned herself to increasing discomfort for the rest of the play. She hoped it would be a brief second act.

––––––––––––––

After returning to the stage, Ben flicked a glance toward the audience. It was too dark to see her, but he had himself convinced that he could sense Ariel's encouraging presence out there, bringing out the best in him. He knew his performance was far more compelling than it had ever been in rehearsal. Something about how real Ariel was, how stubbornly unpretentious and un-showy, made him veer away from anything short of emotional truth tonight. There was just one scene he was worried about, one where he had to kiss his co-lead, Cindy Simmons.

Cindy wasn't an unattractive woman, and she was a decent enough actress. In fact, as if she were responding to the new level of conviction that he brought to his role this evening, she was doing one hell of a job. But he'd never relished kissing her. Something about her was cold. He liked to feel a need, a yearning in a woman. There was a hunger in Cindy, all right, but it sure didn't feel like a hunger for love. Besides, like many of these stylishly skinny Hollywood women, her body was like a young boy's. How in the world was he going to find it in him to put some truth into his kiss?

But when the moment arrived, his answer came so readily that he wondered why it had eluded him. With Ariel in the audience, it was an easy leap to imagine her softly round and welcoming contours as he pulled Cindy's body to him. He put his lips on hers and kept them there for much longer than he'd ever done in rehearsal. They swayed together as one. The memory of Ariel in his bed that morning was so powerful that he actually moaned a little when he finally pulled away from their lingering kiss. Only Cindy's startled eyes woke him from his spell.

The audience was so enthralled with the force of Ben's passion that it had leaned forward during the kiss, as if—as one organism—it wanted to be in on such rapture. And when that little sound came out of him as he stepped away from her, that whimper of feeling so deep and true, it moaned right along with him.

All but Ariel, that is. For her, witnessing that kiss made her own body want to move as far away from the stage as possible. Her shoulders ached with the pressure of pushing herself against the flimsily cushioned back of her seat. Watching Ben lean his body into Cindy's slender frame was the confirmation of her worst fears. She remembered the care with which she'd dressed herself earlier in the size ten DKNY pantsuit Terry had talked her into splurging on, and she cringed. She started to bite her nails, then she realized that she'd actually polished them this afternoon.

She shoved her hands between her thighs, which felt elephantine.

What a jerk she was. Of course. This was why Ben had wanted her to come tonight. He'd fallen for Cindy and hadn't had the nerve to tell her outright, wanting her to get the message this way, instead. She felt the stirrings of rage bubbling up inside. What a coward. A man who checked out of a relationship without being up front about it was nothing more than scum.

Ariel frantically ushered Terry out to the car as the cheering audience was still on its feet. She dropped her friend off with a revealingly throaty "I'll be okay." As soon as she set foot inside her own apartment, she was overtaken by a fit of hyperactivity. Cursing herself for trusting Ben, she paced from one corner of her small apartment to another. Eventually, the phone rang. She froze, saw that it was Ben, then sent the call to voicemail. Ten minutes later, her doorbell rang. As an increasingly frustrated-sounding Ben banged and yelled at her front door, she fled to her bedroom closet and crouched inside, covering her ears. He finally gave up, and she resumed her manic march. Every time she entered her bedroom, Jezebel cocked a sleepy eye in her direction from the unmade bed. As cigarettes were lit, put down into already full ashtrays, and then forgotten, the apartment was enveloped in a haze reminiscent of the San Fernando Valley on a smoggy day.

Though August was just around the corner, and the thermostat in her tiny hallway testified that it was at least seventy-nine degrees, Ariel was freezing. She'd flung her pantsuit onto the bed nearly as soon as she'd gotten home, but now she found herself piling layers of clothes onto her shivering body, starting with some long underwear and ending with the Dead-Sea-face-mask-stained robe she'd bought on sale at Victoria's Secret last year. And still she was cold.

Fuck it, she thought, as she turned up the thermostat to ninety degrees. Her mother would never have approved of the extravagance, but then her mother hadn't lost her man to a little candy corn like Cindy Simmons, had she?

Ariel stopped short in her restless roaming and stared at a crack in her ceiling stenciled into a lightning bolt design by the last earthquake. Stirring again, she moved purposefully now, retrieved a paint-spattered step stool from the space between her refrigerator and the kitchen wall. She dragged the stool to her hall linen closet, and—teetering on the top step—rummaged feverishly through several cardboard boxes on the uppermost shelf. Sneezing several times, she cursed the amount of dust that had accumulated in the unsealed boxes, then grunted with satisfaction at finally finding the one she was looking for. She heaved the heavy box down onto the smoothly sloping handle of the step stool, then dropped it heavily onto the floor. Jezebel flew out of bed like a bat out of hell, her terrified yowl rending the air.

Ariel settled cross-legged on the floor. Wrinkling her nose at the cobwebs that crisscrossed the top of the box, she reached inside and began extracting photo albums. She found the one she wanted and took it over to her couch. Suddenly the heat in her small space felt oppressive. She shed her robe and the sweatshirt under it and turned the thermostat down to a reasonable seventy-two. But once she spread the familiar book open on her lap, with her father in full pilot's gear smiling jauntily up at her, she sat back abruptly with the realization that he must have been younger than she was now when this picture was taken. She turned the page and a handful of un-mounted photos spilled out.

Ariel picked up a tiny black-and-white. It was bent back at one corner and its white border was smeared with something that looked like dried chocolate. The good-looking young couple that stared back at her from an earlier time were standing so close together that it looked like they would have burrowed right inside of each other if they could. Their two faces were split with identical ecstatic grins. She didn't remember ever seeing this photograph before. She couldn't recall ever seeing her mother and father so obviously and undeniably in love.

She brought the picture closer to her face and squinted. Her mom's face was thinner, but the contours of her jaw, temple, and cheeks were just like her own. She wondered how she could have been so blind to how much she resembled her mother. Before she knew it, tears were coursing down her face and dropping onto the diminutive photograph in her hand. She let herself cry full tilt, and rocked a little back and forth as she gently rubbed teardrops from the photo with the tip of her finger. Jezzie appeared at her side and nuzzled her face. Ariel found herself humming a song from her childhood, telling herself she was singing "You Are My Sunshine" to comfort Jezebel.

After a while the crying wound down, and she felt oddly relieved. She got up, walked slowly into the kitchen, uncorked the bottle of pricey Kathryn Hall Cabernet Sauvignon she'd bought to celebrate Ben's opening night, blew her nose a couple of times on a paper towel, and sipped the wine as she stood by her kitchen table. It tasted unusually full and rich, and she could feel a warmth spread through her limbs.

She pulled a cut-out newspaper item from under a pile of unopened bills and scraped a chair across the floor to sit and stare at it. She smiled ruefully. The three columns of text were superimposed with a series of coffee cup rings. She'd read this particular article scores of times in the past few weeks. She wondered how long it would be before the UCLA researchers would finish with Eve and ship her bones back to Africa. Ariel picked up both the wine glass and the bottle and walked to the window. Setting the bottle precariously on top of her microwave, she nursed her drink as she stood there, looking out at the starless sky.

Twenty

THE SANTA ANAS were blowing so intensely that Ben had a hard time lighting his cigarette in the alley behind the Gracias Madre. At heart a rural boy, he was one of the few smokers he knew who didn't mind the law that banned smoking in the workplace, since it gave him an excuse to get out-of-doors more often. But today, he cursed the lawmakers. After the full blast of air-conditioning inside the restaurant, this heat was suffocating. He could feel his dry lips crack as he took a deep drag on his Marlboro.

His obsessing about the weather was less a holdover from growing up in the Midwest than a brief distraction from the one thought that wanted to dominate his mind, waking and dreaming, these days. He corrected himself. It was more a feeling than a thought—a feeling of disbelief that Ariel could let a brief misunderstanding come between them. She had to know he was in love with her. How could he feel so powerfully connected to her without her realizing it? He shook his head at the irony—moving all the way to Hollywood to find a woman who made him feel like he'd finally come home.

How could she be threatened by someone like Cindy Simmons, who looked like every model grinning vapidly from a magazine cover? He'd assured Ariel over and over again that Cindy didn't do a damn thing for him. He'd pretty much begged her to believe him, though he couldn't see what he'd done wrong.

Oh, she said that she would try—after he left about a million messages on her phone and banged on her door several nights running until she finally caved in and opened it; after he absorbed a host of cynical comments spewing out of her mouth like that vomiting kid in *The Exorcist*; after he painstakingly walked her through what had really been behind his passionate kiss of Cindy. Oh yeah, she'd said she would try to let it go, but she hadn't.

The night afterwards, when he'd arrived to take her to the movies, she'd opened her door to him like he was a bill collector. She wore a pair of stained slacks and a wrinkled cotton blouse, and it looked like she hadn't even brushed her hair, which cobwebbed her forehead with limp tangles. Her eyes barely met his, and when they did, it felt almost like she didn't recognize him. And when they sat together in the flickering dark of the IPIC Westwood, she flinched when his fingers touched hers as they reached simultaneously into their shared bag of popcorn. He hadn't even been able to get a laugh out of her when they passed the Mad Skater on the way home.

He'd asked her then, and he asked her yet again in several subsequent phone conversations—she'd declined going out with him after that one crummy movie date. Tried his utmost to coax an answer out of her. "Ariel, what's the matter? It's not the Cindy thing still, is it? Don't you think we should talk?" But no matter how hard he tried, all he'd gotten back was "Fine" or "Nothing's wrong" or "I don't know what you're talking about." He even considered trying the words he knew he probably should have said long ago, but he was damned if he'd make a fool of himself now. It was clear she was through with him. Shit, she'd probably met a more interesting man. Maybe the episode with Cindy was just an excuse; maybe she'd been cooling toward him anyway and he'd been too blind to see it. It just couldn't be possible that he'd lost her over something as stupid as stage-kissing Cindy Simmons, somebody he clearly didn't give a flying fuck about.

Something was hurting him. It took him a moment to realize that it was a bare stub of the burning cigarette that he clenched between his lips.

He spat the red-hot butt out onto the sizzling asphalt. *Screw it.* It was time to think about leaving L.A. The play had been canceled after only a few performances. The energy had just gone out of him, and Cindy's acting had strangely suffered, too. He might as well face it. He wasn't going to have any luck in this town.

He looked at his watch, the one that he'd belatedly noticed was marked with the letters "Ro ex," that some fast-talking guy outside a Massive Attack concert had conned him into buying, insinuating that he was getting a stolen Rolex for next to nothing. Ben had figured later that he'd gotten what he deserved for being so willing to get a deal for himself off of somebody else's pain. Didn't thieves sometimes kill people for their Rolexes?

He had to get back to his station or the pasty-faced new chef manager would get on his case again. It would give him great satisfaction to quit on the guy, though he'd better wait until he was packed up and ready to go. But in the meantime, there was no way he was going to jump to his clock-watching tune. In spite of the heat, he decided to shoot the breeze for a few minutes with Cesar and Jesus, who'd be taking a break between their lunch and dinner valet shifts just about now. They were good guys. *Salt of the earth*, as his sister would say. And he liked their sly sense of humor, which came from seeing this part of the city from the bottom up, so to speak.

It was the fuck-you slowness of Ben's stride that caused him to just miss seeing Ariel's dusty Corolla cruise past the entrance to Gracias Madre at such a snail's pace that she was nearly rear-ended by a good-looking guy driving a hunter green Jaguar, Van Morrison's "Into the Mystic" wafting into the sultry air from its wide-open windows.

If Ariel's attempts to strike a mature pose over her estrangement from Ben were belied by her adolescent attempt to get a surreptitious peek at him, Terry's methods of coping with Matt's no-show were hardly more evolved. In the week following their evening at the theater, Terry had spent a series of insomniac nights sprawled on her bed. As time progressed, her rumpled white duvet accumulated an eclectic pile of litter: empty cans of Diet Coke; a fake-leather album containing a collection of photos of her and Matt with their hands all over each other on the Santa Monica Pier, up the coast at Will Rogers State Beach, and even a few at Big Sur (though, now that she thought about it, she had no idea what he'd told Bonnie to warrant spending several nights away from home). She's also managed to dig up an overflowing, sombrero-shaped ashtray she'd brought home from a weekend trip with him to

Ensenada (ditto for how he'd pulled that one off); a dog-eared paperback copy of the *I Ching*; and three tarnished pennies, which she kept tossing and tossing in hopes of getting a hexagram that would somehow make the pain go away.

She'd tried repeatedly to get in touch with Ariel, telling herself that she was being a good friend, ready to offer some consolation for her misery over Ben and Cindy. But, in reality, she longed for company and commiseration and felt increasingly annoyed that Ariel refused to take or even return any of her calls.

Tonight was a little different. She'd foregone the Diet Coke for wine, figuring that if she didn't get some decent sleep soon she'd be fired from her temp job for zombie-itis. But, so far, it hadn't worked. Three-quarters of a bottle of Chablis had rendered her maudlin, rather than sleepy. She'd spent the better part of the early morning hours crying on her messy bed, holding a make-up mirror up to her face every now and then to see how swollen and pathetic her eyes and nose were and to re-pump the melancholic well. It was the kind of orgy of misery that she used to indulge in as a teenager, but she decided it had outlived its glamor. Her mouth tasted like dog shit and her whole body had a zoned-out chemical feel.

Scratching her sweaty scalp, she addressed the face in the mirror. "This is no good. An' it's all Ariel's fault. If she'd picked up her damned phone, she'd have talked some sense into me 'steada crawling into the woodwork, feeling sorry for herself."

Terry had the decency to laugh at herself, but she knew that she was right about Ariel, who had a bad habit of X-ing you out of her life when she was hurt. She'd first seen it in action in middle school, whenever Ariel got it into her head that she and Jasmine didn't want her around. Ariel was one of the most solid friends in the world, loyal and devoted as all get-out, except when she fell through the frayed netting of her self-esteem.

Terry hiccupped, grabbed the *I Ching*, and clasped it to her chest as she lay back on her bed. Her eyelids fluttered and within seconds she fell, at last, into the deep sleep she'd longed for. The book slid to her side, its pages splayed open to the hexagram, "Work on What Has Been Spoiled."

Not too many blocks away nor many hours later, Dr. David Nussbaum shared a typically interminable wait for one of four Cedars-Sinai Medical Towers' elevators with an impatient group of people—sour-faced patients, pert receptionists dressed to the nines in hopes of snagging their own boss or a rich patient for a husband, and doctors and nurses identifiable by their white coats and green operating-room gowns. They all gambled on which elevator car would land at the third-floor lobby first by where they positioned themselves.

David nodded as one of the emergency room nurses caught his eye. She mouthed a question across the heads of the crowd. Are you coming or going? Laughing a little as he repressed the obvious corny response, he began to mime back that he'd just finished his lunch in the building's deli and would see her later in their common quarters in the ER.

His reply was truncated by two simultaneous events. As was frequently the case, three elevator cars arrived at the same time, and the crowd acted like ants before an earthquake as they scurried to get inside one of the closing doors. At the same time, a cream-scarfed woman with a long, floral skirt dancing around her ankles tried to negotiate a trio of children through the heavy outer doors into the lobby, while also pushing a younger child in a stroller whose handles were loaded down by what looked like a couple of hefty diaper bags. David rushed to hold the door open for her.

"My God, Edith," he said, "I don't know how you do it."

She looked up at him with dark-lashed, doe eyes. "Why, David. Thank you, but it's not so bad. You get used to it." A shy smile played at the corners of her mouth as she looked down and passed a hand over her belly, which he realized was slightly rounded.

He shook his head in mock disbelief that she could be pregnant again. "No." Then seeing her nod in confirmation, "Yes?" He stared at her appreciatively, hesitated, then emboldened by the safe presence of the children, let rip the thought that crossed his mind. "That lucky Max, he's making the most out of a good thing."

Arms akimbo, she made a face at him. "Now don't you get fresh with me, Dr. David Nussbaum." She playfully wagged her finger as three pairs of dark eyes looked up at them. "Don't you forget I knew you when." She looked down at her children and said, "Do you know I used to babysit for the doctor here?"

While the oldest of the children articulated for all the kids their amazement that a grown man, and a doctor at that, would need babysitting, David's face went beet red.

He scratched his head, realized he'd almost knocked his yarmulke off and re-pinned it hastily, then asked how Edith's mother was.

He regretted the question immediately. Edith's face fell and she moved closer to whisper hastily. "She's so lonely with Papa gone and most of their old friends, too. About the only person she talks about is the girl who delivers her mail. Oh, David, she's getting so frail, I don't know what we're going to do when ..." Her eyes flicked in the children's direction. But, looking down at the kids, he thought she needn't worry. Little Aaron in the stroller was fast asleep, and Deborah and Rebekka were busy pinching and taunting each other. He noticed that Jacob, the older boy, was assiduously digging his finger into his nose and spreading the proceeds onto an elevator call button, while an older woman in a thick white sweater—her painfully swollen feet stuffed into baby blue bedroom slippers—looked down in disgust.

"Really? Last time I talked to Fred Samovitz, he mentioned that he'd hospitalized your mom for observation after a bout of probable postural vertigo, but that he thought she was as strong as an ox."

Edith's face lit up, and for a moment she looked just like the teenager who'd stimulated his first wet dreams. "Really? He said that? Why, that's wonderful." She paused. Aaron had woken to the foul-mouthed bickering of two pimply-faced boys dressed in cargo pants baggy enough that they looked like they'd crapped into them, making David wonder if that ridiculous saggy look was actually coming back into fashion. Picking up the outraged-sounding Aaron and guiding the rest of her brood a few steps away from the teenagers, Edith pressed her lips to Aaron's downy cheek.

David felt a flare of heat leap from his belly to his groin and moved closer, pretending interest in the child. *What kind of a slime bag am I?* he wondered, as he smiled benevolently at Aaron.

But Edith's mind was clearly still on her mother and alive with guilt. She spoke almost inaudibly. "Max is lobbying pretty heavily to put her in a home. You know, there's a great place out in the valley—

kosher, clean, great medical care, lots of field trips, arts and crafts." Her porcelain skin reddened. "It sounds like a nursery school, doesn't it?" She frowned, then assumed an earnest tone. "But, honestly, we Jews do seem to know how to take care of our own." She looked at him, as if he had it in his power to offer her some kind of reassurance.

Her moods come and go like clouds on a breezy day, David thought. Fascinated, he watched her graceful hands dance in the air as she spoke.

"And heaven knows,"—she shifted Aaron to one arm and put a hand on her tiny mound of a belly— "Mama's house on Martel is a lot to take care of. It's not as if she can afford full-time help." She looked worried.

Deborah called out to her. "Mama, Jacob's smearing boogers on the wall." Edith leaned over and smacked the child's hand. The boy gave his sister the evil eye, while his mother looked her question at David. "I just don't know," she said.

David sighed. It really was beyond him. Parents, children. He'd be grateful if he could just get laid.

Just a few blocks away, but far beyond the reaches of modern medicine, Danny was having a hard time breathing. He knew it was getting close to the end. Curled into a ball near the storage shed at West Hollywood Park, he forced his mind to focus. He had to figure out what to do about Jane.

She was all he had left, and somehow he felt that if he could set her up to survive well enough after he died, he'd get his own version of immortality.

Sadie was gone, God knew where. He had a paranoid fantasy that some animal rights person had lured her away while he nodded off on Little Santa Monica. Which was actually far better than somebody stealing her for one of those labs where they test cleaning agents on animals. Or worse yet, some psycho street person mistaking her for food. One thing he knew for sure, she wouldn't have left him voluntarily. She hadn't wanted to leave his side for a minute since he'd rescued her—a cringing, starving little bundle of fur he could just about fit in two hands.

Sarah was gone, too, having taken up with a Russian pimp, a burly guy with a sneering face who had a soft spot for skinny redheads. Must have, since all of his women looked like that. Danny had to give it to her though. She'd hung in there with him until he refused to go to the hospital. Said she couldn't stand to see him die on the streets, not understanding that the street was the only place he *could* die, the only place where he could trust that nobody would try to tell him what to do. Only these past few days, as his chest had gone nuclear on him, filling him with such pain each time he breathed that it was nearly impossible to sit or stand, he wished somebody would tell him what to do about Jane.

He figured it was her protectiveness toward him that kept her going. That's what she was doing right now, begging up change for some ice cream and ginger ale to mix up an old-fashioned ice-cream soda for him. That was all he could get down anymore. Besides, the bubbles gave him a hit that was a little like drawing cigarette smoke into his lungs. With his difficulty breathing and all, that was a pleasure that had had to go, too.

Danny's mouth moved into something approximating a smile. There was something about a woman who liked to put food into a man. Most of the time, his own mother had been too much of a junkie and whore to even remember there was somebody at home to feed. But he'd had the good luck to be born looking like something most women wanted to give to. Running his hand over his scarred face, he winced. Even that one piece of good luck, the devil that had dogged most of his life had finally wrested from him.

He pushed the thought away, reminding himself proudly that Jane was only one of a whole line of females who'd wanted to take care of him. Hell, even Sadie would wait until he'd eaten a few bites of his food before she'd start begging for scraps. And that old lady in front of Canter's who'd dropped her whole wad of groceries by his feet before taking off in a taxi? He could still taste the smoked fish from her Bloomingdale's bag. Delicious. He laughed. He could tell by how she'd set her groceries down that she'd thought he'd been asleep and her gift anonymous. Little did she know he'd discovered where she lived the day after the Canter's windfall. Walking from Plummer Park to the Farmer's Market to scrounge some change, he'd seen her unlocking the door of a graceful, two-story Spanish house on Martel.

It came to him then. It was brilliant. That old lady had a kind heart. If she'd drop her whole day's shopping at the feet of a scary guy like him, what wouldn't she do for an innocent like Jane?

He just had to figure out how to get the girl over to Martel without giving away what his plans for her were. She wouldn't want to think that she was a burden on anyone. Danny sighed, and his sigh turned quickly into hacking. That was the thing about Jane. She was already getting too damned familiar with having nobody to depend on.

Twenty-one

ACROSS TOWN, Theosophus Kelly was just settling his weary backside down onto the steps to Haines Hall.

It had been a hell of a long hike to Westwood from West Hollywood, too far to achieve in a single day for feet swollen so bad they nearly popped out of his shoes, now crudely held together with masking tape foraged from a Staples trash bin. Speaking of bins, he'd had to spend the night sleeping behind a couple of them in a residential alley near Century City. Not so bad, he thought wryly, since it put him close to breakfast. He shook his head over the waste of it. What rich folks threw out as garbage could feed a nation of street people. Which—now that he thought of it—was exactly what was going on.

He knew for a fact that you couldn't survive solely by panhandling. In most parts of the city, you could barely get yourself a few beers from what you could beg off of people, and if you were one of those schizos, you were shit out of luck. Almost nobody wanted to lay a quarter in the hand of a crazy person. They were scared the madness might be catchy.

Theosophus wasn't a stranger to people's fear of the unknown. Before he'd ever been to school, he'd gotten his earliest race education in how white people's eyes darted away whenever he looked at them with his insatiable curiosity. And later, as a teenager, especially in the nighttime, how white women, and sometimes even white men, would pretend to just have to cross over to the other side of the street when they saw him coming. His brother Gwayne used to joke, "If I was some nigger with evil on my mind and a gun in my pocket, do they think I couldn't just as easily cross the street right after them and mug their white asses?"

As a street person, Theosophus was aware that he didn't seem to carry that kind of threat anymore. Now he was just invisible. He got to the point where he actually began to miss the days when people acted like he was dangerous.

The sun finally stopped teasing and broke through its cloud cover. Sweat beading his forehead and upper lip, Theosophus stood up. Most of the students wouldn't even notice him on their campus, but the Unicops would. He was thirsty. Gambling that he could get himself a drink in the men's room in Haines Hall before some staff person reported him to the university police, he hurried inside.

If this were a couple of days ago, he'd be figuring out how to get himself some Old Taylor to slake his thirst, but he'd made up his mind to sober up after his last conversation with young Jane. He'd been warning her about the danger of the drugs he knew the people she was hanging with used. After some hemming and hawing and reassuring him that she wasn't even a little inclined in that direction, she'd challenged him—her voice timid but her gray eyes frankly confrontational—about his drinking. Looking at her tiny hands writhing together like they held snakes, he knew what speaking up to him cost her. She was returning his gift of a blanket and food with the only thing she had, her awareness of him. And he was wise enough to recognize it for what it was.

As Theosophus cupped his hands to drink from one of the bathroom sinks he saw that they were beginning to shake. He frowned. He was going to kick his habit, get healthy, and get himself a job, but he didn't have any illusions that it was going to be easy. And he'd be a fool to put himself through the misery of drying out in plain sight. Which was why he was here. His hand strayed to his pocket, and he jangled the keys inside reassuringly. His supervisor thought he'd turned them all in when he'd fired him, but Theosophus had been a man full of survivalist precaution in the old days and had made himself copies of every key he'd gotten his hands on. Not to steal anything or vandalize, as the spoiled, rich frat boys did from time to time, especially near Mardi Gras, but because you never knew.

Theosophus considered the face in the mirror. He looked bad. His hair had pieces of grass sticking out of it. As he struggled to pull them out, then despaired at the finickiness of the task, he could almost hear his mama yelling at him to clean that mess out of his hair. His eyes were bloodshot, their expression pleading, and his brows knitted into a permanent frown. He looked a little like Gwayne before he got himself shot over a dime bag. I'll never make it, he thought. If I try doing this cold turkey, I'm gonna die.

Then he heard his granny's voice. "Now that ain't like you, boy, giving up so quick, before you even begin. Remember what I told you about that underground railroad? Think on it—how did those people survive? Why, they took the memory of their grannies and great-grannies with them, that never left them, no matter what. You don't need nothing else. You've got me with you, don't you?" Theosophus nodded, thinking of the folded-up photo of Granny that he kept in the only safe place he had, worn down to softness inside the ankle of his threadbare sock. The Granny who walked with him was old, with a grin that was toothless, but, Lord, was it ever wide. She had horizontal lines of laughter etched all up and down her dark brown face, even though her life had been mighty hard.

He bowed to the face in the mirror, acknowledging the wisdom of copying those keys and keeping them safe in even the most drunken nights and days. Because you never knew, he thought, when you'd want to go down and hide out in the underground tunnels of UCLA while you got yourself free.

That freedom ended up taking a little longer than Theosophus had anticipated. It was nearly a week later that he woke from his nightmare with a terrible crick in his neck. He sat up, wincing as he massaged the stiff, painful knot, and slowly looked around. His dark eyes squinted as he sought to orient himself in the dimly lit warren of pipes and utility lines where he'd fashioned his makeshift bed. He couldn't figure out why his neck hurt so. He was used to sleeping like this, with just a few thin blankets between him and hard concrete. Little did he know that he'd been sleeping in an unusually skewed position, his body curling itself into a tight fetal ball in defense against the tremors that had rocked him, like some crazy mama on speed, as he sweated the poisons out of his system.

He licked his parched lips and reached hesitantly for one of the fat jugs of Arrowhead water he'd lugged down here in preparation for his miseries. He was wary of inviting another bout of the dry heaves. His throat felt so raw and his mouth tasted so nasty, he didn't think he could take any more. He leaned the jug over and poured just a little liquid onto the wadded-up T-shirt he'd used as a pillow, stuck the damp part into his mouth like a nipple and sucked it. He felt fuzzy and weak, but he noticed his hand was pretty steady. Lifting himself up from the ground with a groan, he slowly stood. At least, he tried to stand before his head banged on the low ceiling of this particular part of the tunnel.

His surprised wail echoed along the narrow walls. "Gawd-dammit," the tunnel said back to him. It sounded like somebody he knew—maybe his mama, maybe Gwayne. He hunched his shoulders and put a finger up to his lips. "Shhh," he whispered, looking around nervously, worried that the walls would give him away.

He didn't like being closed up like this. It gave him the jimmy-jams, like he was cooped up with ghosts or something. That's right, he told himself, you're used to living outside now. Probably can't go back to living inside again.

It was a depressing thought. His thumb reached up to work inside his nose with the ritual movements of his childhood. He caught himself at it, remembering Mama warning him she'd put some glue on his thumb if he didn't cut that out, then what would his friends say when he showed up at school with his thumb stuck up inside his nose all day?

Then he recalled that, in most houses, you could stand up tall and walk around. Realizing that he had to get to a roomier part of the tunnel system, and realizing, too, that he must be getting better to even care, he began to gather his things together. Muttering "tsk, tsk," he kicked a blanket with dried vomit on it over toward a corner next to a faded pinkish-painted metal tank, then undid his zipper and relieved himself against it. He wrinkled his nose as some of his urine hit the tank and steamed. He hadn't realized that this particular container was so hot and was glad he hadn't touched it during the worst of his DT's. The pungent odor reminded him of the urinals at Venice Beach.

It would take some thinking to make sure nobody caught him as he made the several trips it would require to move all of his stuff. But the fact that he could contemplate this move at all gave him heart. He'd beaten the worst of his tyrant. He just had to stay strong and stay the course, like his granny used to say.

Twenty-two

THE VAGARIES OF life in the City of Angels were no less arbitrary than anywhere else. As a grim-faced Theosophus crawled through a cramped passageway of the UCLA tunnel system, his old mentor Matt Hayes was riding an invigorating set of waves at Manhattan Beach under a morning sky that was so clear, it looked like it went on forever.

He knew he had an audience for his audacious moves, and he played it for all he was worth. It's not for nothing they call me Wild Man, he thought, his board sweeping smoothly across a wave, unconsciously leaving out the word "Old," with which the younger surfers prefaced his nickname. But the fact was, as his pliant body seduced the Southern California waters like a seasoned don Juan, a line of pre-teens sat on the shore, saucer-eyed, *oohing* and *aahing* over his masterful moves. At least from that distance, Matt looked not much more than sixteen or seventeen.

It was only when he'd exhausted himself more than he cared to admit that he was reminded of what he'd come out here today to forget. Carrying his now five-hundred-pound board past the young kids noisily rushing the shoreline with their boogie boards, he silently argued with himself. He tried convincing himself it was only pity he was feeling for Terry, that and a little guilt for having let her down at the last minute.

Once he'd passed the kids, moving from the silken mud that made sucking noises as he walked through it to hot mounds of dry sand, he slowed his pace as his board got heavier still. Somewhere a horn honked. It got louder as he approached the parking lot.

He frowned. A voice was calling out. It sounded familiar. "Daddy, Daddy!" Someone was standing next to the Volvo station wagon, waving frantically. It had to be Holly. She was the only one in the family who knew he came here. Just a few years ago, he'd brought her here to teach her some basic surfing moves.

He broke into a run. What in the world was she doing here now? Something terrible must have happened.

His daughter was clad in a canary yellow halter top and denim short shorts. The two garments parted company in the middle to show off the gold ring that pierced her pooched-out belly button. She was waving a piece of paper that the sea breeze played this way and that. When he dropped his board, grabbed her arm, and made her spit out the news, his eyes locked onto the words on the page. He'd been right to be afraid.

"I had to tell you. I knew you'd appreciate what this means for me, and I just couldn't wait. Oh, Daddy, I got into Brown! Do you believe it? I mean, it was one of my biggest reaches. I was surprised when I even got wait-listed. And now—oh, my God, I can't believe I got in."

Matt held his breath as he watched her dance on the hot concrete. He was reminded of her first ballet recital. She'd been so little, dressed in a pink-net tutu that kept falling down around her ankles as she pirouetted in dizzying circles, her pudgy arms flung up to the sky.

And now—oh, God—she was going to move away. His hand moved toward his stomach as he felt the acid surge. He forced out the obligatory words. "Hey, that's terrific, baby. I'm so proud of you."

When she saw the tears in his eyes, Holly grabbed him tightly, her navel ring uncomfortably tickling his groin.

She was crying now, too, still hanging tightly onto him. Her hot tears mingled with the dried ocean salt on his neck.

"Oh, Daddy, you're so sweet. I knew you'd be thrilled. You're the best father in the whole world and the kindest, wisest man I know."

Selma Goldberg was worried, and whenever she worried, her thoughts invariably turned to her husband Chaim, whose wisdom had been such a comfort to her throughout their years together. She lay quietly under soft white sheets in her darkened bedroom, her hands trembling as she clutched the lacy bodice of her nightie.

She'd never gotten over her gratitude that such a learned man had chosen her for his bride, nor her resentment over the unfairness of his fate. A descendant of a long line of Talmudic scholars, coming from the Old Country to this land of opportunity on a three-week boat trip you wouldn't wish on a Cossack, only to get stuck having to earn a living for his family as a shopkeeper. He, who'd staged Shakespeare plays in Yiddish as a teenager, reduced to selling women's undergarments!

Selma reached across to her bedside table for a tissue, blew her nose loudly, and laughed at herself. Chaim used to tease her that she was more dramatic than any of Shakespeare's heroines. Her eyes sparkled as she recalled how he'd loved to come home, have a little brisket and maybe one small glass of *schnapps*, go through his *semitchke* ritual, and then settle with her into this very bed and read to her from his favorite philosophers and poets. He should have been a university professor. He would have been, if life were fair.

Not that he hadn't done well by her and Edith with the silks and the satins, devoting his good mind to the intricacies of doing business, saving every extra penny to buy a shop of his own in Boyle Heights, then expanding into a small chain of what they used to call "better clothing."

Selma became aware of the reassuringly familiar tick of the grandfather clock in the hall. Chaim was out of the realm of time now, and she was nearly out of time herself. She wasn't so afraid of death, at least she didn't think so. Though she dreaded becoming sick and helpless, dependent on a daughter who would only find her a burden.

But she had a more immediate worry. Not so much about Edith. Her daughter was too busy, overworked even, but Max was a good provider. Selma had no doubt that he loved her daughter in his own way, and Edith had all those children to keep her company.

Selma passed wind, giggled a little at the faint whiff of pot roast in it, then frowned. It was Ariel who was worrying her. It had been nearly two o'clock before she'd delivered the mail yesterday. Selma had waited for her at the front window for ages, shifting her body from side to side on achy feet, while a dish of pot roast made with the girl in mind grew cold on the dining room table. She'd finally seen Ariel appear on her walkway, moving uncommonly slowly, almost as slow as that fat-bottomed Denise who used to deliver the mail. Ariel's face had been even paler than usual, and she actually looked gaunt. Selma had been riddled with guilt that she'd missed her young friend's transition from a healthy figure of a woman to this *skinny marinky dink* who didn't even look toward the window as she stuffed the mail into its slot.

To make matters worse, Ariel had accepted her invitation to a little lunch with a listless air, barely listening to Selma's recitation of her most recent conversation with Max and Edith at Canter's Deli and her sense of impotence as Max continued to build his case for the attractions of the Eden Rose Retirement Home in Encino, with Edith pretending to be fully occupied with reapplying her lipstick.

How different Ariel was from her own daughter. Even with her belly bulging with her fifth child, Edith was still a very pretty woman. And she knew it. Selma could see that in the way she pouted her lips at the mirror in her little red Chinese-fabric-covered lipstick case. She saw it in the way she dressed for a simple meal at Canter's—with what Chaim used to call "understated elegance."

Ariel, with a natural beauty of her own, certainly didn't have the sense of style that her daughter did. How could she hold onto a man when she seemed so unaware of her own charms? But, Selma thought, I can't be objective. How can I know what a *goyishe* man such as her Ben likes? She shuddered. She would hate to see Ariel throw herself away for a *no-goodnik*.

What did they say about youth being wasted on the young? Her skin felt sticky. The bedroom drapes shut out the light, but she guessed it was already a hot day. She flung the covers off her legs and fretfully traced her fingertips along the varicose veins that stood out on them. These legs had been smooth once. She had to admit that she used to look pretty good in the delicate underthings Chaim would bring home from his shop. She recalled with satisfaction that his goods were quality, most of them imported from France or Italy, not coarse like the gaudy panties and brassieres they sold these days in stores like Victoria's Secret. She touched the simple brassiere that enclosed her large breasts. She'd had to wear one to bed ever since Edith was born, she'd gotten so big with the milk. But now they sagged, almost down to her belly button.

Selma was swept by a tide of melancholy. She remembered the

sensation of breast-feeding Edith, the near-orgasmic pleasure of it, the joy of having a little girl. Scenes of Edith's first year came to her in a rush: witnessing her first earth-stopping smile; watching her eyes grow big and her lips purse like an old woman's with her first spoonful of baby cereal; bathing her, running a washcloth tenderly over her silken olive skin—softer by far than any of Chaim's finest lingerie. And not so much later—so fast she grew up, where did the time go?—walking into the startled girl's bedroom and, before Edith shyly grabbed her blouse up to her chest, seeing that what she used to think of as her tiny fleabites had blossomed into voluptuous orbs. Her Edith, following in her own footsteps, a buxom woman, too. She remembered the pleasure of seeing her daughter breastfeed her first grandchild.

Inexplicably, a thought of Ariel's Eve crossed her mind. To think of it: a black woman the mother of them all. Chaim, egalitarian that he was, would have appreciated that. She smiled.

Was Ariel still taken up with those old bones? They hadn't really had time to talk since the girl had started seeing her Ben more seriously. Maybe she should cook her a dinner tonight. A nice meal, something special. A brisket. *Lattkes.* Homemade applesauce.

Selma cursed her rotten memory. What was she thinking of? Things weren't normal with Ariel right now. Something terrible was going on, to make her so indifferent, so thin.

Selma's hand went to her heart. "Unless she's gotten sick," she whispered. "Oh, Chaim." She cried out to the empty room. "Her mother died early from cancer. She told me. What if Ariel ..."

She didn't wait to finish her sentence. In seconds, she was out of bed and exerting herself to sweep back the heavy curtains from her bedroom windows, late morning sun springing into the room like a tiger. Soon, steam poured from her bathroom, and Selma lathered her enlivened body with ruthless efficiency. She had to be ready for Ariel when she brought the mail. Rain or sleet or snow, she was going to get the girl in to see Fred Samovitz this very day or she wasn't Selma Goldberg. Nothing would stand in her way.

––––––––––––––

By ten a.m., the heat had evaporated the early morning dew on Selma's rose bushes, and the Saltillo-tiled path to her door was littered with black curlicues of earthworms seared by the sun.

As Selma made a late breakfast for herself, spreading cream cheese liberally on a water bagel and pouring hot tea into a thick glass (as her Russian ancestors had done before her), two young people stood on her walkway. Unseen by Selma, they looked down at the dried worms as if they were hieroglyphics just waiting to be deciphered.

Both Jane and Danny were young, but their expressions were full of old pain. Their speech was halting, filled with ellipses on both sides, as if they were unfamiliar with the effort of putting their feelings into words.

Danny was trying the hardest. He had a case to make and so little time. He leaned heavily on the cane Jane had scrounged for him. He couldn't believe he'd made the walk all the way here. His chest was on fire. "It's good." His voice gurgled. He took in as deep a breath as his congested lungs would allow. "My dream last night ... A sign."

Jane sighed. A lot of street people put credence in their dreams. She didn't know what they were talking about. She hadn't dreamed for years.

"She'll be good to you." Danny's face grew purplish and he started to slump downwards. She leapt forward and eased him to the ground. She brushed a few dead worms away so that she could sit beside him, stroking his clammy forehead and shushing him. Her heart was beating fast. She was afraid he was close to the end. She'd promised him she wouldn't send him to the hospital, but if it came down to it, if he couldn't breathe anymore, what was she supposed to do?

Selma set her purse down on the polished mahogany table that faced her front door. She made a wry face at herself in the beveled mirror that hung above it, sweeping a stray coil of silver hair off her forehead. Getting Ariel to the doctor today wasn't going to be easy. For one thing, she wouldn't put it past some of her neighbors to call and report her if they didn't get their mail.

She certainly didn't want to get Ariel fired. God knew, from the state of her apartment, she needed the money. Maybe she should call Samovitz's office and see if she could come in at the end of the day. Or maybe they should just go to the Cedars emergency room.

Selma was so startled by the doorbell that she saw herself jump back from her mirror. The bell didn't stop, but chimed over and over again. It must be Ariel! She flung open the door.

She stared. It wasn't Ariel who stood on her doorstep, but a little blond wisp of a teenager. Her tiny hands beseeched the air and her eyes shouted alarm, while her mouth worked open and shut.

An unnatural calm swept over Selma. She put a hand on the girl's heaving shoulder. "Relax. I'm not going anywhere. Tell me what you need."

Still speechless, the girl gestured to the walkway. A form that looked as small as a child lay curled at the border of the pink and yellow roses, its sneakered feet pointing towards her. Something about the mismatched shoes looked familiar.

Gripping the girl's elbow, she hastened down the path. As she got closer and saw that it was an adult—or very nearly one—who lay there, she breathed with relief. She couldn't bear anything bad happening to a child. This, she could deal with.

As the girl slid down beside the young man, Selma lowered herself onto arthritic knees at his other side. She blinked, recognizing the beggar she'd seen at Canter's a few weeks ago. His eyes were closed. His wretched face shamed God, but she could tell that he still breathed by the slow popping of spittle at the corner of his mouth.

The girl reached her trembling hand toward his brow, but then held it out mid-air as something in the young man's throat gurgled and a thin trickle of bright red blood slipped out of his lips. Instinctually, Selma grabbed the girl's hand away from the boy and squeezed it. He wouldn't need it now. At this age, Selma had been around the death block more times than she could count. He was gone.

She straightened and summoned the girl to follow her into the house, throwing hurried words behind her. "I'm going to call nine-one-one. They'll help. That's the best thing to do."

She pushed the hesitant girl down onto a dining room chair and planted herself next to her like a sentry before speaking quickly into the cordless telephone that Edith had given her for her last birthday. It was the first time she'd ever used it, relying instead on the stationary unit in her bedroom. Cell phones for her were always going to be out of the question.

She felt a momentary panic when the harried-sounding emergency operator actually put her on hold. When the woman came back onto the line, Selma spilled out her address in hasty syllables. "Drug overdose? I don't know." She raised her eyebrows quizzically, then said, "No," into the phone as the girl shook her head.

The first word out of the girl's mouth was so faint she had to ask her to say it again. "Of course," she mumbled to herself before repeating it to the operator. "AIDS." In her mind, she anxiously replayed those few moments out on the walkway with the young man. No, she thought, I didn't touch him. Ashamed of her selfishness, she nonetheless snuck a quick look at her hands and those of the girl and was reassured that neither of them bore any traces of his blood.

The operator had hung up before she had time to say anything more. She hoped they'd hurry. She couldn't help it: she desperately wanted to wash her hands. And what, in God's name, was she going to do with this poor girl?

———————————

As Selma determinedly set about trying to prove that a good meal could improve virtually any piece of misery short of a pogrom, Jane lay on Selma's bed in wordless misery. Two shafts of sunlight from the bedroom windows bisected the red and black afghan that covered her, but her goose-fleshed skin trembled anyway. She could hear the clatter of pots and pans in Selma's kitchen, but the sounds seemed to come from very far away.

At the best of times, Jane had a limited palette of choices with which to step back and color her experience. She functioned too much on minute-to-minute survival to have much left over for perspective and overview. If she'd had as many lost Uncle Harry dollars as she'd had shocks and disappointments, she would be a millionaire.

But the fact that Jane lay there without a thought in her head didn't mean that she felt nothing. If anything, she felt so much that she couldn't even have told you what she felt like, except maybe "a blob." She barely knew that she was crying as she repetitively wrapped and unwrapped a loose thread on Selma's afghan around her finger. Each time she wound the soft black worm of wool around her skin, she pulled it so tight that it hurt.

Selma, hard at it in her gleaming kitchen, was full of thought. In fact, she juggled the layers of reflections going on inside her like a seasoned circus performer. On one level, she was preoccupied with getting the proportions of ingredients for her *kugel* just right, as if making the perfect noodle pudding would sweeten the existence of Jane sufficiently to put some life into her blank stare.

Selma shuddered. Jane had said nothing when the paramedics pronounced her unfortunate friend dead. Only her eyes looked more hollow as she squeezed her thin arms with her hands and kicked distractedly at the dried worms on the ground.

Selma kept adding more balls to her juggling act: one for her cooking; a second to spare a moment's fervent gratitude for the paramedic's confirmation that she had nothing to fear from the dead boy's disease, since she hadn't touched him, nor had the girl made contact with that last ominous spurt of blood; another for wondering what monstrous fate made a girl so thin in body and spirit; and now—thinking of thinness—Selma's mind threw another ball into the air. Ariel. Where was she? Yesterday, she'd come two hours late. What time would she show up today?

Selma looked over at the oven clock. Nearly two o'clock. If she arrived soon—Selma craned her neck down the hallway trying to discern a sound, but none came—how was she going to persuade Ariel to go to the doctor with the other one lying there in her bedroom?

She was a *shikseh*, too, most certainly. You could tell by her looks. Ball number five. And six flung itself immediately up after it: what would Edith say when she heard her mother had watched a homeless boy with AIDS die on her doorstep and that she'd invited his girlfriend, a stranger with maybe a gun hidden in her underwear, in for *kugel*?

Selma wasn't worried about a gun. This one who lay in her bed was like paper, skin and bones, she wasn't going to do any violence to anyone. She looked already like she'd half gone over to the other side.

That did it. The cooking ball recycled into the mix. The *kugel* would do the girl good, but she'd better get something into her right away, or she'd have another death on her hands today. Selma shuddered. She hadn't even let her mind go near the image of the poor boy in front of her house, his surprised-looking eyes staring unblinkingly at the sun until the burly paramedic had the wits to close them with a tender pass of his gloved hand.

Selma grabbed two fistfuls of eggs from the refrigerator, cracked them handily into a large bowl, and whipped them to make *matzoh brei*. The familiar action began to calm her. She ran squares of *matzoh* under the cold water tap before breaking them into pieces that she tossed into the soggy egg mix. As she prepared to heat some butter in the pan, ball number six bounced back into the picture, and she engaged in an imaginary dialogue with her daughter.

"The girl in my bedroom? She's so skinny and her clothes so worn and thin, there's no place she could hide a gun. Besides, you haven't seen her like I have. She wouldn't hurt a fly, except maybe herself."

Selma's eyes widened as her hand jerked to her mouth. "Oh, my God!" she cried. "What if she wants to hurt herself? What a *putz* I am, not thinking to check on her, and her so quiet and her friend only a few hours dead."

Wooden spoon in hand, she rushed from the room and stumbled down the hall toward her bedroom.

When she reached the threshold to the room, Selma caught her breath, then smiled. The girl was sprawled on her back on the bed, fast asleep. Selma was reassured to see the afghan rise and fall rhythmically above her little mound of a form. Selma looked up at the ceiling, mouthed a silent *thank you*, then tiptoed to the side of the bed. The girl's thumb was in her mouth. Selma stifled a motherly temptation to remove it, then gently pulled the afghan over her stockinged feet. They looked heartbreakingly small.

She sniffed the air. What was that smell?

Then it came to her. She cursed herself as she sped back to the kitchen.

"*Oy*, my rotten memory!"

Flames shot up from the stove, where melting butter had staged a blackening revolt in its pan. The kitchen was as hot as a sauna, and wallpaper was already peeling down from the ceiling toward the floor.

Selma panicked. She forgot everything she'd ever known about grease fires. She rushed to the sink, grabbed the large bowlful of egg-sodden *matzoh*, drowned it with water from the kitchen tap and ran back to the stove to fling the contents onto the flaming pan.

The whole thing went up with a fearsome bang and whoosh. A sensation of intense heat shocked Selma's face.

She felt hands pushing her away from the stove and then someone said, "There," as a kitchen towel was flung over the fire. She was seized by a spasm of coughing. The fire was out, but there was smoke everywhere.

The air was rent with a cacophony of smoke alarms. She didn't know what to think when the blond girl reached toward her and swept the hair from her hot forehead. The fearsome screech of smoke alarms drowned out all other noise, but she could tell the girl was laughing by the way her lips curled away from her teeth. She allowed Jane to take her hand and lead her down the hall to the bathroom, where the girl positioned her in front of the vanity mirror.

Selma stared at herself in shock. She looked like a circus clown. Her grizzled hair stood up electrically from her scalp, the whites were visible all the way around her dark eyes, and fire had singed her eyebrows right off.

Twenty-three

HALF THE NEIGHBORHOOD could hear the music blaring from Ben's apartment on that sizzling July afternoon. The front door was wide open, as were his two bedroom windows at the back, in the delusion that cross-ventilation could bring some relief in this kind of heat. It was a husky male voice, a voice that you just knew had suffered like crazy, that begged his baby to rock him all night long.

Usually, he couldn't get enough of the blues, but the CD that Ben had chosen to play for the woman who lounged on his vintage 1950s orange sofa was grating on him. He'd thought his favorite R&B compilation would fit the bill in the sexiness department, but it only served to highlight how empty he felt as he stroked the woman's naturally carrot-colored hair. He had the errant thought that he might have chosen her because she went so well with his furniture. But he hadn't.

The woman's eyes were closed as she purred with pleasure. He studied her face. Contrary to Ariel's fantasies about the desirability of Cindy Simmons, this woman was the real deal: an Irish beauty, imposingly tall—just about as tall as he was, but with plenty more curves. The wide apart setting of her limpid green eyes was perfectly proportionate to her high, naturally rouged cheekbones and her full, sensuous mouth.

He'd met Mary O'Reilly in his acting class six months ago, and he'd been startled then by her hint of availability when she'd playfully draped her abundant tresses over his shoulder during a break between scenes. It was hard to believe that such a confident beauty would be even faintly interested in him. That was before he'd come to realize how many actors in this city were off-puttingly narcissistic. And whatever his own flaws and failings, he knew that most women found him a decent enough guy.

Right this minute, though, he wasn't so pleased about that decency. Because as sure as he was that the luscious Mary was primed to surrender to him, he was just as certain that he'd never be able to follow through on B.B. King's suggestive lyrics.

He could kick himself. Mary was much more of a trophy woman than Ariel would ever be, and it wasn't just that. She seemed like a good person—caring, interested. He had a hunch she was pretty bright, too. But it was Ariel's honest brown eyes he wanted to be looking into right now, the thighs that she despaired of he ached to be stroking, her loopy humor that would be his most reliable aphrodisiac, and her shy grin when he kissed her that made him want to rock *her* all night long.

Clearly sensing that he was miles away, Mary sat up and tapped him on the chest.

"Where'd you go?" She cast her eyelashes downwards and flung her luxuriant mane to one side. Her voice was pure Blanche du Bois. "I thought you wanted to play." She wasn't normally so actressy. He realized she felt hurt.

He couldn't have been more apologetic. "Oh, God, what a creep you must think I am. With a woman like you and all. I just ... it's just that I can't ... I thought I wanted ..."

Mary dropped her nervous posturing. She fished into her voluminous handbag and pulled out a baggie-wrapped spliff, let him light it, then leaned back, taking a long toke. "I can't pretend I'm not feeling rejected, but I'll live." She paused, shooting him a crooked grin. "So who is she?" When he stared at her blankly, she laughed. "Oh, come on, I wasn't born yesterday. I know you're not gay and,"—she tossed her head confidently—"most straight men who aren't in love with someone else don't say 'no' to fooling around with me."

He shook his head and laughed. "That transparent, huh?" Then he gently touched her shoulder. "You're right, you know. Under any other circumstances ..."

She spoke dryly. "So tell me about Miss Circumstances. Why isn't she here, instead of me?"

———————————

The woman whose identity had piqued Mary O'Reilly's interest had just parked her mail truck on Third Street. The smoke that issued from Selma's house was still hovering over the one hundred block when Ariel turned onto Martel. Gawkers lined the street—a democratic mix of old people in their bedroom slippers; scarf-headed Orthodox housewives in aprons with small children in tow; unemployed actors and musicians out walking their dogs; cigarette-smoking, fuck-you-blue-haired truants from Fairfax High sauntering coolly down from Melrose. For a brief moment, they forgot who they were supposed to be and actually talked to each other, speculating about what had taken place to merit the two L.A. Fire Department trucks and one Paramedic truck currently blocking the street, and wondering if anybody had gotten hurt. Selma's next-door neighbor repeated gleefully to anyone who'd listen that this was the second time today that an ambulance had been summoned to this particular house, pointing shamelessly and describing in gruesome—and false—detail how the dead body of a vicious criminal had lain just there with such a mean expression on his face that God Himself must have struck him dead for his evil intentions.

Ariel ran up just in time to hear the fifth repetition of the story. She used her mail pouch to shove aside the talkative neighbor, and she hurried through the open doorway, nearly tripping on the neighbor's cat, who was at that moment digging his claws into Selma's plush living-room carpet. She sent him hissing toward the front door with a nudge of her toe and stumbled toward the voices emanating from the dining room.

The tableau that greeted her stopped her dead in her tracks. Seemingly impervious to the acrid smell that pervaded the house, men in bunker gear and fire hats stood around Selma's dining room table, laughing and talking and eating what looked like *kugel* from blue and white paper plates that had something printed on them. Ariel squinted and craned her neck forward to read the Hebraically-stylized letters spelling out the words *"HAPPY HANUKKAH."*

A young, good-looking guy in a paramedic's uniform was sitting next to a skinny blond girl, who bared her teeth in a painful imitation of a smile as the guy flirted with her.

Ariel glanced anxiously around the room, past the wall where Mrs. G's *bubbe* and *zayde* presided with unconcerned dignity over the improbable group. She pounded her forehead in frustration. What in the world were all these people doing here, what had happened, and where the hell was Mrs. G?

She didn't have long to wonder. Selma, her face streaked with soot, emerged from the direction of the kitchen bearing a steaming casserole dish of *kugel*, chirping, "I warmed up some more in the microwave." Ariel's mouth began to water in Pavlovian response to her memory of the sweet satisfaction of Selma's noodle pudding, even as she tried to figure out what was wrong with Selma's appearance. As Selma leaned over to place the serving dish on the table, and just as the noisy crowd of strangers moved avidly forward to refill their paper plates, Ariel got it. Her eyebrows! Mrs. G's eyebrows were all gone.

Ariel forgot to support her mail bag, and it landed heavily on the floor. The room fell silent, and all eyes were on her. Before she knew it, Selma had rushed to her side.

"*Oy*, thanks be to God, it's Ariel." Selma grabbed her arm and held her fiercely as she addressed the assembled group. "This is my dear friend Ariel." Then Selma turned quickly and whispered urgently into her ear. "The mail, it's too heavy for you all of a sudden? Maybe you should see a doctor."

As Ariel looked at her incredulously, Selma backed up a few paces and hunched her shoulders. "I know, I know, it's none of my business, but you've been behaving a little unusual lately; I only thought ..."

Ariel started to titter, and a few of the firefighters closest to her studied her with unabashed curiosity. Selma looked around in bewilderment, spreading her hands. "A joke, I made?"

Ariel couldn't take it anymore. She was bent over double, tears of mingled hilarity and relief coursing down her cheeks. "Unusual, Mrs. G? Me? And what about you?" She swept her hand before the group of firefighters. "I feel like I've stumbled onto the set of *I Love Lucy*. What in the world is going on?" She ran a finger along Selma's grimy forehead, and then held it up and waved it back and forth before Selma's guilty eyes so that she could see the smudge on it. "What's this? Ash? What's happened to you?"

The firefighters cast startled looks at each other. Mumbling embarrassed thanks, they laid their half-finished plates of *kugel* onto the dining room table and began shamefacedly filing out the front door. It was as if Ariel's words had broken some spell that Selma's cooking genie had worked on them, like some bizarre Jewish twist on a familiar fairy tale.

Out of the corner of her eye, she saw the blond girl pick up a couple of dirty paper plates and hastily exit the room.

Selma looked away from Ariel, reached for a stack of unused napkins on the table, and began to sidle toward the doorway. Ariel put a firm hand on her shoulder. "Oh no you don't, Mrs. G. Not so fast. You're going to stay right here until I know exactly what's been going on. Those fire trucks out there and your ghoul of a neighbor talking about somebody dying in front of your house nearly gave me a heart attack."

Selma paled and leaned her weight heavily against the dining room table. "A heart attack? It's your heart, then, that's been bothering you? There's something the matter with your heart?"

Ariel groaned. She took a deep breath. "Selma." She sat down and motioned Selma to sit beside her. She enunciated her words carefully. "Let me spell it out for you. I'm fine. I'm okay. There's nothing the matter with me." She paused to let the words sink in. Selma stared back at her in disbelief. "Honest." The doubt remained palpable on Selma's face. "Well, if you must know, I've stopped seeing Ben. I've been a little bummed out."

Selma began hurling Yiddish epithets toward the ceiling, flinging her hands in the air as she called Ben names like *momser* and *putz*. Ariel didn't know what the words meant, but they sounded awful.

"Wait. It's not what you think. The problem wasn't him. It was me. I mean, it was me who broke up with him. And not,"—she held up her palm and hastened to add as Selma opened her mouth to interrupt her— "and not because he did anything terrible." Ariel squirmed. "Well, at least he doesn't think so." Her face reddened, and she bit her lip. "But listen, we can talk about that later." She pointed to Selma's missing eyebrows. "Right now, I want to know about you."

It took Selma a good twenty minutes to describe the day's events. When she marveled at the coincidence of the boy she'd given her groceries to dying on her own doorstep, Ariel snorted.

"What?" Selma said. "You think they came here on purpose?" She patted Ariel's shoulder. "Excuse me for saying it, but it doesn't make any sense. That poor boy, he wouldn't know me from Adam. He was fast asleep when I came out of Canter's that day, and besides, how would he know where I live?"

Ariel stood abruptly. Leaning over the litter of dirty paper plates to get hold of what looked like a clean plastic spoon, she helped herself to a bite of the noodle pudding. She almost reached the spoon back in for another helping, then caught herself as she noticed Selma watching her. "Sorry," she muttered. "Bad habit. I know double dipping's unsanitary." As she brushed the back of her hand across her lips, she felt her stomach start to rumble. She spoke quickly and loudly to cover up the imminent gurgle that ran the risk of throwing Selma into one of her cooking fits.

"I don't know, Mrs. G, but there's something just a little too coincidental about a guy you gave a whole bag of groceries to on Fairfax dropping dead on your front porch here on Martel." Her eyes bright, she looked around. "Where's the kid? Jane, you said her name was? Speaking of *I Love Lucy*, I think she has a little 'splaining to do, don't you?"

Twenty-four

BEN AND A very relaxed and barefooted Mary O'Reilly clinked wine glasses for the third time in his tiny kitchen. They pointed at each other and laughed as rivulets of sweat ran down their faces.

"I must be crazy to be cooking in this heat," Ben said. He turned on his oven light, and the two of them knocked heads as they leaned forward to peer at the homemade pizza beginning to brown and bubble inside.

Rubbing her head, Mary made a rueful face. "I swear, I can't tell what's got me higher, the spliff, the wine, or that smell. It's heavenly." She patted her belly and rolled her eyes dramatically. "And I'm starving."

Ben wove over to a cupboard, extracted a plate of cheese and crackers he'd prepared earlier with seduction in mind, and passed it to her.

She didn't even bother to pretend embarrassment as cracker crumbs littered the shelf of her ample breast as she talked. "Where did you learn how to make pizza, anyway?"

He messily spread some Brie on his cracker, then answered before stuffing it into his mouth. "If you'd grown up with the kind of down-home American cooking I did, you'd have learned how to cook a few pizzazzy dishes, too."

She burst into laughter, cracker crumbs flying. "Pizzazzy? Is that a word?" Then she looked up sharply. "Is Ariel 'pizzazzy,' too?"

He felt like she'd slapped him. He shook his head resentfully. He didn't want to think about Ariel.

"Stop." Before he knew it, tears were coursing down his face and Mary's arms were around him, wine from her glass spilling down his back. That wasn't the only thing that got spilled. He found himself blurting out a lengthy description of the whole miserable affair. Mary finally removed one of her arms from his back and put her hand over his mouth.

"Shut up," she said, putting her arm back around him once she'd gotten his attention. "I want to say something now." Her words were slightly slurred, but he realized that even in her tippsiness she'd probably have more insight into what had gone wrong than he had. Ariel had once told him she thought women were wiser about relationships because of the human race spending its formative years hunting and gathering—the females wandering together in intimate groups with their babies on their backs, picking fruits and vegetables and gabbing about themselves and their lovers, while their spear-toting men just had to grunt a few, quick commands back and forth to each other as they circled their prey.

"You've got to go and get her. She wants you; I can feel it. She's just very insecure. You've got to hold her and hold her and tell her you're never going to go away." Her wine glass dropped onto the rug without breaking and lay on its side like a wounded soldier.

Ben's mouth flew open. It was that simple? How blind he'd been. Through hiccups and sobs, he babbled his gratitude. But Mary couldn't hear him; her body was now dead weight in his arms. He'd never seen anything like it. Perpendicular, she'd passed out on him, right there in the middle of the kitchen. It was all he could do to remember to turn off the oven before helping her back into the living room and laying her unceremoniously onto the sofa.

He lurched over to the screen door, pressed his face right up against it so hard it almost hurt, and watched the shadows lengthen on the balcony as Mary O'Reilly softly snored. She was sweet, but he didn't dare let her spend the night. How in the world was he going to get her home?

————————

As darkness descended on that long day, the occupants of Selma

Goldberg's house were wide awake. Ariel rolled to the side of Selma's queen-sized bed to turn on the bedside table lamp. She couldn't believe that she'd been talking with Selma and Jane for so long that it was already evening. It had taken that much time to extract all of Jane's story from her.

Ariel had been so angry that Selma had been subjected to the double calamities of Danny's death and the kitchen fire that she'd badgered the frightened, tongue-tied girl until Jane ended up unloading the whole history of her flight from Ohio. As her stammered words became a torrent, the teenager's sense of herself as something soiled and worthless made Ariel's skin go clammy. That son of a bitch, she thought, wishing she could strangle Jane's stepfather.

It was clear to Ariel that the poor child had herself convinced that she was crazy. What she'd actually said was, "I don't know what all got into me. I had my own queen-sized bed, just like this one, except mine had a canopy with yellow and white flowers. Everything matched—the canopy, my chenille bedspread, even the wallpaper." She went on wonderingly. "Had my own TV, too, and CD player, and a white push-button princess phone." The expression in her gray eyes hardened. "Gave all that up for life on the street."

Ariel broke in. "Oh, give me a break. Do you hear yourself? Wasn't it on that same pretty yellow and white bedspread that your stepfather violated you?" Her eyes sparked with anger. "What were you supposed to do, just endure the misery? It might look nuts to other people, but you had the courage to go with your gut and take action. Don't you think you deserve a little credit? Christ, some people stew in their own misery for a lifetime." She fell silent. The room felt suddenly small and confining.

The doorbell rang.

"That was quick." Surely it hadn't been more than ten minutes since they'd called Domino's to order a pizza. It was a miracle that Mrs. G had consented to it, and that, Ariel knew, was only because Selma's oven was off-limits and there was no more food to heat up in the microwave. Selma was convinced that she and Jane were at risk of starving to death.

———————————

Selma was only too relieved to slide off the bed. "I'll get it," she said.

She hurried down the hall, her mind swirling. That poor boy's death, a fire in her own house, and now, *Gott in Himmel*, this terrible story of the man—he should rot in hell—doing all those unspeakable things to his stepdaughter. It was no wonder she'd allowed herself to be talked into ordering take-out. Still, she was ashamed. A pizza, yet. She extracted a few bills from her purse as the bell pealed again.

"Alright already." She swung open the door.

But it wasn't the man from Domino's. It was her next-door neighbor, who had a suspiciously nasty smirk on her face. Her hooligan of a tom ran into the living room and surveyed the carpet briefly before commencing to drag his claws through it.

Mrs. Brillstein spoke with unctuous charm. "My dear Mrs. Goldberg, so *nu*, what a day it's been? I'm sure it's all been too much for you. I hope you don't mind, but I knew you'd be too proud to call your daughter Edith. She gave me her phone number when you were hospitalized a few weeks ago. She said I should call her if you had any problems, so I took the liberty. I hope you don't mind." She smiled triumphantly. "I finally got hold of her, and she said to tell you that she and her husband will be here soon. They just have to collect the children first from their play dates." She paused for effect. "Did you know they've reserved a spot for you at the Eden Rose Home?"

Selma reddened. So, she'd been right. She quietly closed the door on her neighbor, then jerked it back open to let out the woman's suddenly panicky, howling cat.

This time, Selma slammed the door shut. Bullies, she thought bitterly. They're all the same.

———————

Ariel knew something was wrong as soon as she saw Selma's face. She rushed to her side. "Selma, what is it?"

Selma wrung her hands. "Oh, Ariel, don't let them put me in a home."

"Who, the pizza man?" Selma shook her head. "Selma, help me out here. What's going on?"

In anguished spurts, Selma explained.

"Oh, shit. They wouldn't really ..."

"I'm telling you, my neighbor knew all about it. You don't know Max. I'll bet he was so excited when Mrs. Brillstein called, he'll probably break the speed limit to get here." Her voice caught. "If they put me in that home, it'll kill me."

"Do you want to go to my place?"

"No! Edith knows your name. She'll come and find me. I have to hide somewhere she wouldn't think of. Somewhere far away."

Ariel felt for Selma, but the old woman wasn't making any sense. She wasn't going to be able to avoid her daughter forever. Besides, from the little she'd heard about Max, if he was hell-bent on finding her, Selma would have to go all the way to Africa to evade his clutches.

Ariel blinked. And then she blinked again. No, she couldn't. She really couldn't. She glanced at Selma, who was staring at her piteously. Ariel bit her lip. Maybe she could.

"Selma, excuse me, but I need to make a call."

She was so nervous, she misdialed the first time. She paced in a circle until the call was picked up. "Terry? God, I'd hardly know it was you. You sound like shit. Ha, ha. I'm at Mrs. G's. Yeah, well, listen. I've got to talk fast. You know how you told me you and your friends used to sneak into the UCLA tunnels? C'mon, just humor me for a second—did you say the tunnels ran right from the Powell Library to Haines Hall?"

When she got back to the bedroom, Selma was sitting on the edge of the bed, her head in her hands. Ariel knelt in front of her. "Selma, do you remember me telling you about Eve?"

Selma looked at her quizzically. "The African?"

Ariel laughed. "Yup, the African. What if I said I know a way to get to her?" Her voice rose. She felt more energized than she had in years. "I don't know about you, but I'd sure love to take a peek at those bones. I've got this gut feeling they're calling me. What if we paid her a little visit?" Observing Selma and Jane's expressions, her voice grew faint. "Well, you know, I was thinking it'd give Edith and her husband a little time to cool down. I mean, once they have a chance to think about it, they'd realize it'd be too cruel to take you away from your own home." She flushed. "God, you're right. Forget it. I'm just your basic lunatic. Who am I kidding? I'm not a teenager anymore, and you certainly aren't. How could I even think of subjecting you to those dirty tunnels? And walking that kind of distance—God, what an idiot I am."

Selma's laugh was scornful. "You, too? I'm so old, better put me out to pasture? I'll have you know I can walk from here to the Farmer's Market and back without even a pain in my knees or a cramp in my side." She poked a finger at Ariel's rib cage. "So what's this about tunnels?"

Ariel hesitated, but Selma stared at her unflinchingly. Ariel took a deep breath. "There's a whole system of them crisscrossing the UCLA campus below ground level. Since the building where they must be keeping Eve is locked up at night—they call it Haines Hall—about the only way to get to her right now would be through those tunnels. And Terry knows exactly how to get down into them, from the Powell Library. We could enter the tunnels from the library, walk across to the stairs up to Haines Hall, and then bingo, we say hello to Eve's bones."

Jane frowned. "Who's Eve?"

"Only our first female ancestor. I mean, it's amazing. They found her bones in Africa, and now they've brought her here to do some research." Jane's wide eyes gave her pause. "Well, to be fair, it might not exactly be her. But someone who lived during her time and had to have been pretty damned close, genetically speaking. An ancestress of all people alive today." Ariel ran a hand through her hair. "But, forget it. It's too crazy."

Selma interrupted. "No, no, it's not such a bad idea. Edith wouldn't think of it in a million years. It's a little unusual, but why not? A day like this, everything's upside down. Better a tunnel than a prison."

Ariel hesitated, but Selma got that look on her face again. "Well, if you really ... God forgive me, but maybe if we took it nice and slow ... Oh, Selma, are you sure?"

"If I wait to feel sure, I'll still be debating it in some nursing home in Encino."

But Ariel was having second thoughts. "You know, this might not be such a great idea. Your daughter'll be worried sick to arrive here after what your neighbor told her and not find you home."

"Let her worry. Her and that evil Brillstein. Who asked for such a babysitter?"

"Maybe we could leave her a note or something. Not telling her where you are or anything, but reassuring—"

"No note." Selma squared her shoulders. "No more treating me like I'm an infant. A little worry will give her a chance to reconsider. Besides,"—Selma laughed weakly— "when she finds out I wasn't too old to go on such an adventure, she won't be so quick to put me in a nursing home." She shrugged. "Anyway, we'll be back in no time."

Ariel felt a vague disquiet, but Selma put a hand on her shoulder and gave her a persuasive smile. "So, *nu*, what are we waiting for? If I'm going to make like a fugitive, what do I have to do?"

Ariel convinced Selma to grab something warm and to dig a flashlight out of one of her drawers before taking her by the elbow and leading her to the front door. She peered cautiously through the peephole before flinging it open. "Here we go, then. We really do need to hurry. I think Powell Library closes at ten, and we still need to round up Terry. My mail truck's around the corner." She turned to Selma. "There's still time to change your mind."

Selma shook her head.

Jane coughed. "Oh God," said Ariel. "Forgive me, it's just that we're in emergency mode here. Listen, we can give you whatever money we have, or you can come with us. It's up to you."

Jane pushed a hand through her hair. She took a deep breath. "Danny—" she paused, frowning, then gave a little shake of her head. "Danny said everybody comes to L.A. to find themselves. I reckon finding your Eve might be just as good."

Part Two

Well, that's all right mama
That's all right for you
That's all right, mama
Just anyway you do.

—Arthur "Big Boy" Crudup, "That's All Right Mama"

Twenty-five

BY THE TIME Max and Edith's SUV pulled up in front of the darkened house on Martel, their children's cranky voices were clamoring for attention from the rear seats and a reddish haze had begun to tint the evening sky. One of the regrettable verities of life in the City of Angels was that arsonists tended to be as excited by Santa Ana winds as fabled werewolves by a full moon. Tonight, both conditions prevailed and, not too far north and west, in the Malibu hills, a raging brush fire telegraphed its fiendish glow across the miles.

Max had barely turned off the ignition switch before Edith was out of the car, hurtling with frantic urgency up the same pathway where Danny's spirit had quietly slipped out of its tortured shell that morning.

"Mama, Mama," Edith cried, struggling to fit the key into the lock and bang on Selma's imposing front door at the same time. When it became apparent that no one was responding, she put all of her attention to the key and shoved open the door, just as a baby-toting Max and the rest of the children reached the porch.

Heedless of his mother's distress, Jacob danced around crazily, one hand between his thighs, and whined.

"*Eema*, I have to make pee-pee."

He looked up in alarm as his father grabbed him by the elbow and exhorted him to be quiet. Jacob had become accustomed to his mother speaking in a worried tone—it was so common, in fact, that it had become synonymous with his bodily sense of her. But the unease he saw in his father's features was new to him. He forgot that he had to urinate and looked at his sisters, who were holding hands. They stared back at him with unaccustomed sympathy.

He could hear his mother's high heels click against his grandmother's kitchen floor as he followed in the footsteps of his father, who walked through one room after another, flicking on the lights. And all the while, he could hear his mother anxiously calling out, "Mama! Mama?"

The dining room felt unusually stuffy. It smelled terrible, as if *Savta* had cooked something she wasn't supposed to. He hoped it wasn't pork, which he knew was forbidden food. He worried that God would be mad at him if he let even the smell of it get inside his body. He held his breath until he couldn't stand it anymore. Even then, he tried to breathe as shallowly as possible, taking little goldfish gulps of air so that he wouldn't swallow the invisible thing that made the bad smell.

Abba came back into the room, cradling in one arm the still sleeping baby Aaron, his other arm flung over the shoulder of the somehow shrunken form of his mother. *Eema* was crying noisily, repeating over and over again how the kitchen looked like a disaster zone. She didn't even bother to wipe the snot from her face, which looked puffy and red.

He wondered where *Savta* was, why she hadn't come running when they arrived, wrapping each of his siblings in turn in her stoutly comforting arms, and lifting them onto her dining room chairs that she'd stack with bed cushions so they could reach their plates. He loved how *Savta*'s cheeks would go pink with pleasure when they came to visit, her eyes sparkling as she watched them eat, having tucked festive paper napkins under their chins. He understood that she sat on the edge of her chair so that she could quickly fetch more food from the kitchen if they emptied their plates. Only when they ate so much that their tummies felt like watermelons did she let herself relax.

But Jacob didn't have much time to think about how it was when his grandmother was there; so many things happened so fast that he couldn't even keep them straight. His mother sat with him and his sisters in *Savta*'s living room, picking at her fingernails and staring straight in front of her as if Jacob and his sisters weren't even there, while his father went next door with Aaron to talk to the neighbor lady. Then, as all of them waited for the police to come, his mother and father threw words at each other across the living room as if they were spears—sharp words, nasty words, words that his mother would have washed out of his own mouth with soap if he had said them himself. And then there were two policemen at the door, looking nothing like the guards he saw sometimes at the bank or outside his synagogue on the High Holy Days. These men were skinny and they talked in quiet voices to his mother and father in the other room before they took their flashlights all around the house, making pitying smiles at him and his sisters before they left.

For the first time in his life, he didn't want to be in *Savta*'s house. Not even to pee. He only let himself breathe normally once his father had turned off all the lights and led them down the rose-edged walkway. He wanted to ask, but somehow sensed that he shouldn't. He didn't know what had happened to *Savta*, but he moved his lips silently in prayer to God to bring her back soon and to make sure she was okay.

———————————

As Jacob sat in the back of his parents' SUV, silently praying to God to forgive his grandmother and not to punish her too harshly for cooking what had surely been *treif*, the woman shepherding his grandmother through the streets of Los Angeles in a dusty U.S. Postal Service van had some worries of her own.

One of them was the mail she hadn't finished delivering. There was going to be hell to pay for failing to complete her route.

Another—and, truth be told, it was bugging her a lot more than the security of her job— was Jezebel. Although she attempted to console herself with the thought that Jezzie was probably plump enough to go for days without eating, she couldn't believe she'd forgotten to stop off at her apartment to feed the cat before setting off for Terry's place in Mar Vista. She hoped to Christ she'd left the bathroom door open in case Jezebel finished off the water she'd put in her little blue and white bowl.

She turned onto Inglewood Boulevard, passing clusters of brown-faced people milling around in front of small storefronts marked by neon signage in Spanish only, or Spanish and English, but none in English alone. She marveled how fast this city was being reclaimed by its Mexican ancestry, as if its Anglo settlers had cut off the limbs of a vast tree, forgetting about the roots stretching invisibly underground. Anyone who called these people "illegal immigrants" had conveniently forgotten who'd been the actual intruders on this soil.

She wondered if she could really pull off her plan. More likely, she was about to make a whacking great fool of herself. *And* break the law, she reminded herself, flicking a guilty glance over her shoulder at Selma. She peered up at the darkening sky, which was strewn with gorgeous crimson streaks. Was this just a glorious sunset or was there a wildfire nearby?

"Look," she cried, sharing her enthusiasm with Selma and Jane. As they exclaimed over the unusual vista, she realized she'd almost overshot Terry's apartment. Calling out, "Hold onto your hats," she abruptly pulled over to the curb.

Terry was a mess when she opened the door, her hair unbrushed and her nightie chocolate-stained. She didn't bother apologizing for how she looked.

Ariel sized her up with a quick glance. "Oh hell. I could kill that bastard. But we can't let him win. And he will if you let him take you down a second time. So here's the deal. You feel like shit, and so do I. You've been asking me where my crazy spirit went, and I suppose you could say I've just found it. I've got Mrs. G and a teenage runaway from the Midwest named Jane out in my van, raring to go. Well, anyway, I'm raring and they're willing. You're the best one to lead us through the tunnels to Eve, and, anyway, it wouldn't be the same without you there. Just like old times, eh? Besides, it'll sure as shit get your mind off of you-know-who."

Terry's eyes grew wide with confusion, but she let herself be led down the hall and into her disordered bedroom. The flat screen TV, perched at an angle on her pine dresser, was going full-blast. Ariel glanced up to see the credits scrolling for "The Bachelor" and flicked off the set. "Yuck! I don't know how you can watch that crap." Ariel dove into Terry's jam-packed closet and fished around for a pair of jeans and a T-shirt. "Here," she said in a muffled voice, flinging the clothes backwards at an open-mouthed Terry, who dressed hurriedly. Thrusting a plump pillow from Terry's bed into her friend's hands and taking one herself, Ariel said, "We've got to hurry. I don't want to get there after they close the library doors."

Twenty-six

JANE SCOOTED OVER to make room for the attractive stranger who ducked her head to enter the postal van. As Ariel introduced the two of them, Jane saw Terry frown, and she felt a surge of shame. In her perfectly fitted jeans and periwinkle T-shirt, Terry looked like a model in one of the fashion magazines Jane used to go through like popcorn, flopped on her chenille bedspread back home.

She looked down at herself: her own jeans were torn more than was fashionable; her shirt was stained; and her scuffed tennies had incipient holes at the toes. She pulled her knees up to her chest and hugged them, pressing her back harder against Ariel's mailbag and taking a weird pleasure in the fact that it hurt.

She was prepared to dislike this Terry, with her inquisitive, big dark eyes.

As if sensing her thoughts, Terry looked away, responding to Selma's delighted greeting.

The conversation between Terry and Selma was polite. You could tell, Jane thought, that they didn't know each other that well. But they sounded like they were genuinely happy to see each other. Back home in Ohio, when acquaintances bumped into each other, their smiles often looked like they were plastered on, like the heavy make-up that some of the young hookers on Hollywood Boulevard wore when their skin was badly broken-out. You just knew when you looked at them that there was something ugly under the seamless surface. At least, that was how it had seemed to her once Creepo started messing with her. After that, she'd developed some kind of radar for anything fake. It was as if, in removing her pajama bottoms, Vern had also stripped curtains from her eyes that most people preferred to keep closed.

In spite of her initial mistrust of Terry, Jane couldn't help but feel mesmerized by the resonance of her voice and Selma's as the two of them talked. She let her grip around her knees relax and closed her eyes with the beginnings of a familiar ecstatic sensation. A wave of tiny pleasurable goose bumps was washing over her scalp. She hoped that the women wouldn't stop talking. She didn't want this feeling to go away.

Terry wasn't quite as engaged in her conversation with Selma as Jane was imagining. Old memories rose up in her like unwelcome ghosts as Ariel drove through the intersection of National and Sawtelle. The megalithic new Ralph's shopping complex sprawled on what was once the undeveloped lot behind Webster's baseball field, where she and Jasmine used to sit on the freshly-mown grass, leaning back on their hands like *Elle Girl* models until their wrists fell asleep. They flirted industriously with peach-fuzz-faced boys who teased and joked nervously as if they had no idea what to do with these girls who, prior to sprouting tits and asses, had been invisible to them.

She remembered how aggravated she used to feel sitting on that field—having spent half the lunch break making up her face to *Elle*-specified heights of glamor and sophistication, only to be subjected to the spectacle of boys from her class vying for the girls' attention with desperate physical antics like circus clowns. The guys didn't get much better in high school, thinking that competing with each other in the macho department was appealing to the opposite sex.

She guessed that was at least partly why she'd been so ripe for Matt Hayes when he'd made his move on her on the Santa Monica Pier. Handsome as hell, with the finesse of an experienced man and the natural self-confidence of an athlete, he'd certainly known what to do with her. Looking back, it would definitely qualify her for membership in the "Me Too" movement, but she had to be honest with herself: she'd loved every minute of it.

Because she'd loved him. God, what was it going to take to get him out of her mind?

———————————

How could Terry have known that the object of her obsession was barely a mile away? As he took a toke of his spliff in one of the rear storage rooms of Fowler Museum, Matt took wry pleasure in the stillness that surrounded him. He was all-too-conscious of the irony of enjoying this silence, since he was filled with dread of a house soon-to-be empty of Holly and her incessant chatter. He was also aware that he was taking a risk by smoking weed here. It might be legal these days, but it was still banned on campus, and Biggs would fire him in a heartbeat if he learned about it.

He could no longer sustain his denial about Holly's imminent departure for Brown. His daughter's only regret seemed to be that she and her boyfriend would be parting company, since the "amazingly brilliant" Greg had ended up with an "amazingly unfair" GPA, along with— according to Holly—equally unfair low SAT scores, consigning Greg to community college for the next two years.

When Holly had first been waitlisted at Brown back in the spring, Matt had been lulled into a false sense of security that, like her older sister, she would attend UCLA and, worst case scenario, live in a sorority house during the school year, returning to the perks and comforts of home several nights a week.

Silly me, he thought, taking a hit so deep he burst into coughing. How Bonnie would be smirking at him right now if she knew what he was doing. He could almost hear her familiar taunt, "See, that's God punishing you for pretending you're not a grownup. What man of your age uses cannabis anymore—except for bums and losers?" *Only about half of them, Bonnie, but how would you know?* He ventured into the men's room to take a piss. Looking into the mirror, he groaned. Something about the prospect of his youngest child about to leave for college seemed to have made him age overnight. Why had he never noticed the prominence of the frown lines etched between his eyes, the incipient double chin threatening the sculptural integrity of his jaw? How in the world had he ever imagined that Terry would be interested in him for anything but a one-night stand for old times' sake?

He flared his nostrils, bared his teeth, and growled. Then he put his face up close to the glass, looking so piercingly into his own eyes that gooseflesh crawled over his arms. "I guess it's just gonna be Bonnie and me," he told himself, and, for the first time since his father walked out on the family all those years ago, he felt real despair.

———————————

Selma Goldberg's mind was about as far away from affairs of the heart as it could be. She was thinking aching bones. The girls, bless them, had tried to cushion her *tuchus* and back with a few of Terry's pillows, and she wouldn't dream of complaining, but they weren't helping much in this spartan vehicle.

Gott im Himmel, half of her mind pled, as she nodded at Terry's comments on the quixotic nature of their current venture. She prayed that their trip wouldn't take much longer. If they went over one more big bump, she was going to have a bruise the size of Poland on her backside.

Indeed, some of the streets between Mar Vista and Westwood were pot-holed and knotty. Ever since the citizens of the Golden State had voted for Prop Thirteen in 1978, an initiative sponsored by conservative lobbyist Al Jarvis designed to lower property taxes to a fraction of what they used to be, the City of Angels' revenue base for street repairs and other services had dwindled to next to nothing. Nobody squawked though, at least not in an organized way.

In the state she was in, Selma Goldberg wouldn't hesitate one second to vote to repeal such a measure. Her hand sneaking down to rub her lower back, she silently cursed Al Jarvis in English, Yiddish, and the little bit of Spanish she'd picked up from Cecilia, her Salvadoran cleaning lady.

Ariel took a curve way too fast and yelled "Asshole!" as her tires squealed ominously. Selma instinctively braced her feet against the floor of the van. Ariel shouted, "That son of a bitch was leaning on my ass the whole time I made that turn. Sorry about that, guys. Are you okay, Mrs. G?"

"Sure, sure. I'm fine," Selma shouted back disingenuously. "It's a little like riding in a train, isn't it?" She smiled brightly at Terry and Jane, who were white-faced, their hands pressed hard to the floor of the mail truck.

Suddenly, Selma was awash with guilt over what her fear of facing Edith was putting these nice young girls through.

As soon as Ariel pulled into the parking lot for the Ackerman Student Union, she slid out of her seat and rushed around to liberate Selma from the rear of the mail truck.

Selma was thankful to be freed from that torture chamber at last, noticing how carefully Ariel finessed her through the van's shallow doorway, with a hand on top of her cream-scarfed head to prevent her from banging it.

"*Oy.*" Selma struggled to straighten her knees and panted once her feet met the ground. With trembling hands, she ironed her wrinkled skirt and blouse, which were damp with perspiration. Attempting a little stretch, she stumbled, then smiled gratefully as Ariel steadied her. Her brown eyes twinkled. "It's like unfolding a spare table that you use maybe once or twice a year, for the holidays. A little WD-40 never hurts, my Chaim used to say."

Ariel eyed her doubtfully. "It's a ways up the hill to the library. Do you think you can make it? Maybe I should drive you up there and come back and park."

Selma shuddered at the thought of re-entering the van. "No, no, please. It'll take me a minute, then I'll be fit as a fiddle." She smiled at Ariel and Terry, peripherally registering that Jane stood away from the other two, looking like she'd just missed a plane. Selma raised her voice. "I come from strong peasant stock, you know. All I need is a healthy young girl to maybe hold my hand in case I lose my footing."

Jane hastened to her side, avoiding Terry's curious gaze.

Selma squeezed Jane's hand as the two of them followed Ariel and Terry up Bruin Walk. She felt more heartened than she dared to express when the girl squeezed back.

Twenty-seven

TERRY STIFLED A laugh when she heard Ariel hiss through her teeth, "Hey, Terry." Even though there were still plenty of students hurtling down Bruin Walk from the library, wearing stuffed backpacks like pack mules and some of them picking their way carefully in the gathering darkness in impractical platform shoes, Ariel was whispering and skulking like one of the girls in the *Baby-Sitters Club*.

Now Ariel was poking her in the ribs. "Remember those crumb doughnuts we used to buy from vending machines in Ackerman? They came two in a package and tasted like white sugar heaven." Terry's eyes crinkled in recognition. Ariel continued, "Cheap thrills, baby, stretching the concept of junk food to its nadir, but the best thing in the world when you didn't have a man. Come to think of it, I got so fat on those babies that a man couldn't get next to me without burrowing a Santa Monica Tunnel's length through my belly first."

Terry gave her a mock punch in the arm. "Do you think I left a perfectly good, self-indulgent, nobody-loves-me fest to go on this wild goose chase with you, just to hear you put yourself down? Shit, girl, we could've stayed home and gotten drunk together for that."

"Do you really think it's a wild goose chase?"

Before Terry could respond, Selma's panting voice broke in. Her breath a wheezy rasp, she was obviously working hard to sound cheerful. "Thanks be to God, it looks like we won't be going up much longer. I don't want to be a pill, but are we almost there?"

When Ariel quickly ushered Selma to a concrete bench next to

Powell Library, Terry winced to hear Selma grunt as Ariel eased her down. What the hell had Ariel been thinking, dragging Selma out here?

Selma seemed to read her mind. "Don't. When I said it was a good idea, I meant it. So don't remind me of what a burden I am by turning back now." Ariel opened her mouth to respond, but Selma raised a silencing finger. "All the way up the hill I'm thinking about your African. Don't cheat me. This is my adventure, too." She gestured toward her sensibly-shod feet, planted solidly under the bench. "How often do I get a chance to see bones older than my own?" Selma retrieved a handkerchief from inside the sleeve of her sweater and reached forward to dab the solitary tear sliding down Ariel's cheek.

Jane startled Terry by actually speaking. "I wonder what Eve was like. I mean, I know it won't be like seeing her alive, but still ... It's got to be like going back in a time machine, having a chance to be with your great-great-granny's great-great granny, even if it is just her bones. Nobody I know's ever done anything like that." They all stared at her in wonder.

Terry broke the silence in a businesslike tone. "Okay, it sounds like we're still on. But now that we're actually here, I'm thinking what a bitch it may be—sorry, Selma—to get into the storage closet. Why don't I go in first and check it out? If it looks do-able, I'll come back out and get you guys with the excuse that Selma has to use the restroom. Then we can sneak into the storage closet before they lock up for the night. Once they do, the basement's ours."

She was as good as her word. A mere fifteen minutes later, she'd managed to beckon her little group into the library and to lead Ariel, Selma, and Jane from the restroom to the storage closet. Only when Terry gently shut the door behind them, pulling it slowly until they heard the little click of the latch, did someone—she couldn't tell who—whisper a relieved "Thank God." As they huddled in the dark, her fingers itched to grab Selma's flashlight from Ariel, but she knew it wouldn't be wise to turn it on until the library was locked up for the night.

Terry's pulse was beating loudly in her ears. God shmod, she thought, beginning to devise fiendish plans for how she'd make Ariel pay for this. She'd actually had to flirt with creepy Fred Phipps, of all people, to get them this far. But creep or not, it had been helpful to find an old familiar face still working here. And—if she did say so herself—it had been an inspiration to hit on the idea of Selma needing to use the restroom, since it was just two doors down from the storage closet.

But this was only the beginning. They'd be locking up the library any minute, the campus emptying out like a stadium after a rock concert, and then would come the real test of finding their way through the tunnels to Haines. She heard a whispered, "Sorry," as someone trod on her foot, then nearly gasped at the childlike smallness of the hand she grasped in acknowledgment. The hand knotted into a near-fist at her touch, then seemed to relax as she squeezed it gently, reassuringly, a few times. She sensed Jane's fear, but couldn't divine its source, not having heard her story. She just knew somehow that, in the dark like this, it was important not to let go.

––––––––––––––

Somewhere in that vast warren beneath the four women and certainly unbeknownst to them, Theosophus Kelly was getting antsy. As the poisons slowly vacated his system, he'd become increasingly aware of the need to get his stuff out of the tunnels, clean up, get his hands on some healthier food than the junk he'd liberated from some of the still-existing campus food vending machines, and actually take steps toward getting himself a job.

He sat with his legs stretched in front of him in one of the larger boiler rooms, a creased photograph in his hand. He knew it was nighttime because he'd ventured outside half an hour ago to sneak a piss on the neatly-manicured lawn in front of Haines Hall, his nostrils twitching at the blend of eucalyptus and ash whipped up by the Santa Anas. Hadn't it been Matt Hayes who'd once told him that something like eighty per cent of men admitted to taking a leak on the grass at least once a week? Theosophus guessed it was because they were all dogs at heart, but what territory had he given himself to mark, living off the streets for so long? The corners of public elevators in city parking structures? The alleys behind other people's homes?

Theosophus looked more closely at his picture of Granny. He ached with the memory of her arms around him in her big old bed, how good she smelled with her old lady smell, like the whole of a lifetime had blended inside her to make a musky perfume of her skin. He figured he must be more of a dog than he'd realized, remembering his granny through her smell. And then the gooseflesh started to crawl up on him, because it was like Granny's smell started talking to him, telling him that if he was a dog, then he had to trust his instincts that he'd come to claim his territory—that he belonged on this campus, and that he should just go on up to Matt Hayes's office and tell him he should give him one more chance to be the best janitor the state's money could buy.

Theosophus started to tremble and worried for a moment that the DTs were kicking up all over again. He hardly felt like the best anything. But now his granny's expression looked like he was letting her down, thinking wrong thoughts like that.

"But, Granny, what would Matt Hayes want with the likes of me? I let him down bad after he gave me my good job and all, getting lost in the drink like I did. Like as not, he wouldn't remember me, anyway. Think I was nuts, showing up at his office like somebody important."

But Granny just snorted. "Before you got yourself carried away by that false friend, Mister Old Taylor, did you or did you not do a good job at this school?"

His eyes brightened. It was true. He'd learned the ins and outs of this campus and what it took to keep it going like he'd learned his lessons back in grade school. With his warm sociability, he'd brokered a spirit of friendship among many of the blacks, whites, Asians, and Latinos who serviced the campus infrastructure. And, over the years, he'd become such a crackerjack at small repairs that he used to reckon he'd saved the university trouble and money many times over by doing the work some campus plumber or carpenter would rack up days of high union wages for.

Granny piped up again. "And I do think you're just about finished with learning how to live with the derelicts and the hoboes."

"Aw, Granny, I never meant to let the drink get out of hand. It just kind of snuck up on me."

"Snuck up, nothing. You thought you were a big shot, with your women, weed, and wine. You was looking for the easy way, and that's the truth." She relented a little. "Now, I can't see as I blame you entirely. It's not a world that makes it easy for anybody, and most definitely not a black man. But I reckon there isn't one of us wasn't born on this planet for good reason. The question is, son, just because you're scared, are you going to throw away your good reason?"

Theosophus reverently inserted Granny's photo back inside his shoe and stood up like a Marine called to attention. Just as quickly, he banged his forehead on a yellow horizontal condenser pipe.

Little stars tickled at the periphery of his vision. The most he could get out was a whimper. He raced frantically three times around the circumference of the boiler room, retaining enough of his wits to keep his head low, until the sensation dissolved from its bolt-out-of-hell sharpness to more of a throbbing ache.

He could hear a scuttling from somewhere out in the tunnels, and prayed fervently that it was rats, and not roaches. Rats he could deal with.

He rifled through his pile of belongings till his fist found a Sprite, still cool from the vending machine. Holding it against his forehead, he addressed his granny plaintively. "Alright, all right, I know it can't always be easy, but does it always have to be so hard?"

Twenty-eight

THE DOOR WAS unlocked! Ariel's hand began to tremble as soon as her brain registered that it wasn't encountering any resistance. The portal to UCLA's subterranean passageways swung silently open, letting a dank mushroomy smell into the green-linoleumed hallway where the four women stood breathless.

Ariel passed a hand over her sweaty brow. She had a fantasy of Eve's spirit secretly moving obstacles out of their way.

Casting an exultant look back at the others before pointing Selma's flashlight toward the wooden stairs beyond the threshold, she took a few jaunty steps forward. Then her toe met some kind of soft, clumpy resistance, and she was catapulted helplessly down the rest of the stairs, somehow managing to hold onto the rail and keep her head up as gravity sped her down. She wondered almost idly whether the shrieks she heard were her own or belonged to the three women she'd left behind in that safer, upper world only moments before. She realized that such a loud racket just had to be a group endeavor.

With dusty hands she explored the multiple screaming sites on her body for broken bones. She'd landed on her bottom; now she stood up with a groan and scanned the stairs with the flashlight, zeroing in on the hapless creature that looked like he'd expired seeking a way out.

She was embarrassed to detect an incipient whimper worming into her voice. "I thought you guys would be right behind me. As it is, you missed the Welcome Rat. I guess you ought to watch your step." All three spoke at once. Ariel interjected hastily, "Listen up. Thank you all so much, and yes, I hurt a little, but I'll definitely live. The question is, how do I move Ratty without catching the bubonic plague or something? And he should be moved. I don't want Mrs. G leaping down the steps like I just did."

It was Terry, of course, who rose to the occasion. "Hold on a sec, I'll be right back." Ariel was terrified to see her disappear from the range of the flashlight, but she reappeared at the doorway only moments later with a tall broom lined up at her side like a scared-stiff bridegroom. "I was right next to this baby in the storage closet. It wouldn't hurt to bring it with us, anyway. You never know what else we might want to clear out of our path."

Ariel watched Terry tiptoe gingerly down the first few steps. "I've got to hand it to you, you looked just like Glinda the Good Witch up there. Now, here's a question for you, was the bad one the Wicked Witch of the East or the West?"

Ariel felt rather than saw Terry shoot her a withering look. Realizing she'd better quit the corny humor, she pressed anxious fingers into the sorest places on her limbs, just as her tongue, with some curious life of its own, used to test the limits of a loose tooth when she was a kid, waggling it back and forth from its frail anchor until it bled. Wondering what kind of witchery had landed her here, she recalled sitting in her peaceful kitchen not that many months ago, her skin prickling as she read that first *L.A. Times* article about Eve.

But Terry was coming down now. With a quick flick of her broom and a loud "Yuck!" she dispensed with the rat and went back up to escort Selma down the stairs with a firm grip on her elbow. Jane bounded down behind them with surprising speed and agility. I forget that she's just a kid, Ariel thought, noticing that Jane's gray eyes looked brighter, almost blue, down here.

Once her own eyes had made the necessary adjustment, Ariel realized that she could turn off Selma's flashlight. The basement space they were in was lit by muted overhead lighting.

Selma and Jane slowly picked their way around blue and yellow piping that thrust down toward the cement floor like a cartoon version of stalactites.

Ariel made a half-turn to face Terry, who was whispering out of the side of her mouth in the direction of Ariel's left ear. "That was a hell of a dive. It's a good thing I was partially blocking Mrs. Goldberg's view, or she'd be having shit fits. I thought you were going to do a somersault before you hit bottom. I can't believe you're up and walking. Are you really okay?"

Ariel grinned lopsidedly and scanned the surreal scene before them. "Actually, I think every inch of me hurts at least a little, but then, what's a little pain when you're on your way home?"

Terry stared at her. "It really means a lot to you, doesn't it—going to find this Eve?" As Ariel nodded helplessly, Terry went on. "I just hope you realize that it's just bones we're going to find. It's not like she's going to knit herself together for us and do a dance of the seven veils."

Ariel waved her hands in front of her as if she were trying to erase Terry's cynicism. "You just don't get it, do you? Stop for a minute and think about it. Skin or no skin, this could be the mother of our species."

"Maybe, Ariel, but she was probably just another woman alive at around that time."

Ariel knew Terry could be right, probably *was* right, but still she pled her case. "Even the fact that they might have been contemporaries is enough to—"

She was caught up short by the sound of Selma's voice. It was only a brief "*Vey is mir*" that she'd uttered, but it was enough to fill Ariel with guilt at having forgotten the woman's welfare in the aftermath of her fall. She rushed to Selma's side.

"What is it, Mrs. G? Are you okay?"

The pressured pace of Selma's breathing belied her words. "It was nothing. Only, for a minute the floor felt unsteady. You didn't feel it?" As the other three shook their heads and exchanged worried glances, she sighed. "It's my age," she mumbled apologetically, "half the time forgetting what is, the other half imagining what isn't." She put on a brave smile for them. "So *nu*, I think we're here for a purpose. Which way do we go?"

To Ariel's surprise, it was Jane who ended up leading the way. The girl had listened intently, a deep frown line intersecting her pale brows, as Ariel and Terry held a brief powwow to reorient themselves in this subterranean world.

Jane took off like a shot once they settled on their direction. Ariel watched her lithe frame move through the tunnels as if she were a natural denizen of this dim terrain. Struggling to keep up with her, she looked back to make sure that she wasn't losing Terry, who had a stoic-faced Selma securely gripped on one side of her and the rat-vanquishing broom on the other. Christ, what had she been thinking of? This wasn't some teenaged joyride.

Ariel nearly bumped into Jane before she realized that the girl was standing still. The rattling noise in this part of the tunnel was something awful, and she only knew Jane was speaking by seeing her lips flap open and shut. Perspiration pearled Jane's upper lip. This part of the tunnel system must be about twenty degrees hotter than where they'd started. As she looked around, she saw steam escaping from dark green pipes, some rectangular and some cylindrical, that sprouted up from the cement floor like weird vegetation. Worse still—and with this realization Ariel had to stifle an impulse to panic—the walls were closer together here, making the air feel especially dense.

Jane's eyebrows flicked up and down as she mouthed words and gesticulated wildly. Maybe she's seen something up ahead, Ariel thought, leaning forward and cupping her palm around her ear to signify that she couldn't hear. Out of the periphery of her vision, she saw Selma, Terry, and the broom lined up behind her.

Jane pressed her lips against Ariel's ear. "Did you feel it?" Ariel cocked her head in confusion. Jane raised her voice. "The shaking."

Ariel looked at her with dawning comprehension and pointed to the busy pipes.

Jane shook her head vehemently. "No. It wasn't that. More from the ground. It was something else."

The hair on Ariel's arms prickled. She looked back at Selma. Hadn't she said something earlier about feeling the ground move?

Selma was far too vigilant to miss the horrified expression on Ariel's face. She strained to hear what she and Jane were saying, but with the pipes making such a racket, she couldn't hear a word.

Selma was no small-time worrier. Life's predilection for disaster, torment, and mayhem had hardly been lost on her. And even though she'd stopped keeping kosher after one too many first-person stories of

Holocaust-surviving relatives and neighbors, she was still a profoundly spiritual woman, with no question in her mind that whatever inspired hope and meaning was precious. A cynic she could never be. Which was why, she supposed, she didn't regret joining Ariel on her undeniably quixotic quest and why she didn't resent being ushered through these murky tunnels. Never mind the fact that, as they proceeded farther along the underground system, she had to dig her fingernails into her palms to stop herself from thinking about the increasing shallowness of the ceiling and how much closer the walls were.

But this shaking was something else. What if it was a symptom of some nerve disease? What Edith and Max would do with that possibility didn't bear thinking about. But she could, in fact, imagine it all too well: evicted by the betrayal of her body from the bed she and Chaim had slept in together like a couple of *rugelach* for fifty years; barred from the stove where she followed her *bubbe's* recipes like her mother before her, right up to this very day, when her rotten memory made her blow up her own kitchen; stuck in some kosher board and care facility, marinating in her own urine and fed by some brown-skinned stranger who'd probably season the brisket with Mexican hot sauce; abandoned by her new young friends because she was too far away and too depressed for them to want to visit.

Selma silently bargained with the God of her nervous system. *Keep still,* she vowed, *and I'll be a better person.* She failed to notice that the deity she pictured bore more than a passing resemblance to her deceased husband Chaim. *I'll be more open-minded. Maybe hire a woman to help care for me at home. What's a little extra seasoning on a brisket? So* nu, *it's forbidden in the Torah to add something new to* bubbe's *recipe? If you keep me healthy a little longer, I'll even make a little experiment with it myself.*

But now she noticed that Terry had halted and was peering into her face with concern.

"What'd you say, Selma? Is this getting to be too much for you? Do you want to sit down for a while?"

———————————

Jane had never felt the earth tremble before—at least, not when she was awake. But when Vern first came into her life, she had a recurring dream of standing in the middle of her street with the asphalt cracking under her feet, exposing dark holes that belched smelly gasses. Each time, she'd flap her arms at her sides in vain hope that enough speed would propel her into flight. She'd scream for help at the top of her lungs, but nobody ever came.

Somewhere in the midst of this awful day, beginning with watching Danny die in Selma's front yard, Jane realized that she didn't want to feel so alone anymore. It had felt good to lie down on a mattress again, with clean sheets and a blanket perfumed sweetly like the old woman herself. Selma didn't seem to mind that her clothes were dirty or that she probably didn't smell so good after living on the streets.

Jane frowned. She'd depended on Danny, but what Selma seemed to offer was different. Danny had been like a life raft that she'd clung to in a terrible storm. The old lady felt more like the land you longed to reach when there was nothing but heaving, churning water around you.

That was why she'd kind of understood what Ariel was after in wanting to track down her Eve. As soon as she'd seen Ariel rush hell-bent into Selma's dining room that afternoon, Jane had recognized that her brown eyes had the drowning look. And if she thought that touching those old bones was going to situate her on dry land, Jane wasn't inclined to contradict her. As for Jane herself, she wasn't about to volunteer to part from Selma's side for one instant. When the old lady had agreed to this journey, it hadn't even been a question in her mind whether she'd come along, too.

As she moved through the consistently narrowing passageways, Jane couldn't help but notice that they were, at uneven intervals, marked with odd objects, obviously discarded by previous trespassers. She nearly tripped on a single dusty-brown suede boot intersecting her path at an awkward angle, reminding her of the many times she'd noticed a single sneaker—usually a kid's-sized one—in the middle of the highway. Inevitably, the sight of such a lonely shoe in the middle of the road would provoke in her a restless worry about whether its young owner had gotten a whipping for arriving home without a full set.

Jane was fully practiced in the art of shifting her awareness away from sources of pain. As Ariel, looking more than a little panicky, started describing her terrifying experiences in the last big earthquake, Jane bit at her cuticle, wondering what had happened to the owner of that old boot.

Twenty-nine

THE NORTHRIDGE QUAKE of 1994 had generated as many aftershocks as the Bible boasted begats, and, as was typical for the area, there had been numerous temblors of minimal to moderate size since then. Angelenos uneasily awaited the predicted apocalyptic Big One, but their anxious anticipation usually remained buried beneath everyday concerns. Most members of the burgeoning population of the City of Angels kept their eyes not on the ground, but at windshield level, seeking safe lane changes amidst increasingly dense traffic, trying to make it from home to office and back again with barely a moment to spare for unpleasant thoughts of what Mother Nature might have in store for them.

Rich and poor alike were preoccupied with maintaining their livelihoods, the latter much like the poor everywhere and the former to maintain the accoutrements that at least made it look like they were having the time of their lives (and made them feel guilty if they weren't). Unlike its stereotypical image in the national mind as a land of milk and honey, about the only ones with free time to regularly soak in the sweet rays of the famed California sun were the outcasts from its bustling economy. It was most often the unemployed and homeless who loitered on park lawns and beaches on weekdays, contemplating with something more akin to despair than leisure the clear California skies.

Just as the increasingly discordant rhythms of its residents' lives were so much more complicated than its weather, so too was the life underground more bumptious than its mostly flat vistas. After a period of relative seismic quiet, the earth that supported the City of Angels was on the move again.

It took noticing somebody's old 7-Eleven coffee cup jumping down off a baby-blue horizontal pipe to convince Theosophus Kelly that the bouts of mild shaking he kept feeling weren't evidence of a second wave of the DTs.

"Aw, shit," he mumbled, "just when I start to get myself together, ol' Mother Nature starts jumping and jiving again." He shook a fist at the ground beneath him. "Now, don't you go spoiling my re-entry into the labor force." He started to laugh, then caught himself up short as he noticed that someone had scrawled something with a red pen on the side of the pipe from which the cup had fallen. He knelt down on one knee and squinted to decipher the ragged lettering, then looked around him with wide eyes. The message read, "HERE LIES THE BEAST."

The faint flutters that spooked the current illicit crop of UCLA tunnel visitors were still too weak to be felt by most Angelenos above ground. But that didn't mean that no one else had been alerted to these latest signals from the earth's shifting crust. Scores of needles measuring seismic activity began to zig and zag on monitors at Caltech in Pasadena and at various research labs throughout the county. The sweet slumber of scores of scientists, government officials, and city and county service administrators was broken by late night phone calls alerting them to the escalation of activity. Since the current tremors were unusually frequent but still small, and since such flurries occurred with some regularity in the state, most of those called asked their informants to continue to monitor the situation closely and to call again if there were more ominous signs. They hung up their phones and rolled over to resume their innocent dreaming.

No such luck for Matt Hayes. Chancellor Biggs, the coup of a lifetime plastering a shit-eating grin across his face, had boarded a plane that afternoon for his son's wedding to the daughter of a prominent Southern senator. Which left Matt in charge for the rest of the week. Which meant he got the call when a monitor in the bowels of the campus signaled a computer somewhere above ground to set off an all-purpose emergency-response sequence.

Having smoked more than his usual small spliff before bedtime—and that on the heels of his early evening toke at the Fowler Museum—he hadn't wanted to pick up the phone at all. But, even in his mellow state, he realized that if he let it ring any longer, Bonnie would come into his bedroom and smell the telltale pungent odor of high-quality weed that no amount of patchouli room spray could cover up. He definitely didn't want to deal with her predictably snide remarks if she busted him yet again.

Once he picked up the phone and heard campus utilities honcho Burt Weston speak in an unaccustomedly nervous tone, he resigned himself to at least a fifty percent wake up. He took the cordless landline with him into the bathroom and listened with a drooping heart to Burt's unwelcome words as he peed.

Shit, he thought. Wouldn't it be this night, with Biggs away and me still high as a kite, that the utilities would act up? Matt scratched his balls compulsively until they started to hurt. Burt was telling him that something had triggered an automatic shut down mode, though he wasn't yet sure of the source of the problem.

Matt wondered aloud what could do that. "Maybe age?" he said to Burt.

Burt squawked a vehement denial, as if he himself would be held responsible for the ravages of time.

––––––––––––––

It didn't take a phone call to alert Ariel and her friends to the problem. The automatic safety shut-off had visited an eerie quiet upon what had been a noisily steaming Hades. Though the warm and dry Santa Anas turned the landscape above ground into an arsonist's wet dream, the still-moist air in the tunnel began to cool, and at some point Ariel registered that it was starting to feel downright chilly. Realizing that Selma and Terry would catch up with them soon, she hurriedly whispered to Jane how, on that God-awful day in ninety-four, she and her mother had clung to each other in terror as the contents of the kitchen cupboards flung themselves with suicidal force onto the linoleum.

"I know I was theoretically not supposed to remember it, being that young and all, but I swear I do." She noticed, not for the first time, that once she got going in the tale of her Northridge Quake terror, she had to compulsively go on to the end, no matter how bored her listener might be. And with her eyes focused somewhere over Ariel's right shoulder, Jane didn't exactly look fully engaged.

It was at this moment that Selma and Terry caught up with them. "Jeeze, is it getting cold or what?" Ariel said. "I guess they just shut the whole thing down at a certain hour." She looked anxiously at Selma. "Are you okay, Mrs. G?"

"*Oy*. It's not me you should be worrying about, with my cozy sweater and my kerchief. It's you, walking around with nothing on." Her face fell. "It's my fault. If it wouldn't have been for your hurry to get me out of the house I set fire to, you would have thought to bring warm clothes."

Ariel shook her head. "Oh, Selma, Selma, what are we going to do with you? If it weren't for me, none of you would be in this mess at all."

Terry's eyes twinkled as she walked over to Jane, whose bare arms were sprouting goosebumps. She began rubbing the girl's arms up and down with quick hands, talking all the while, as if she were trying to distract Jane from what she was doing. "You know what Ariel and I used to do when we were kids? We'd twist each other's arms with a wringing motion until it made a burning sensation." Responding to the look of alarm in Jane's eyes, she said, "Don't worry, I won't do that. We used to call them 'Indian burns.' I know, racist as hell, but that's what everybody called them back then." She shot Jane a surprisingly tender look. "Did you ever do that, whatever they call them now?"

The girl shook her head in the negative, but Ariel took note that she didn't move away. Nor did Terry stop.

Ariel wondered why she'd never realized how kind her friend could be. Was this unusual situation calling forth something new in Terry, or had she herself been blind to someone she'd known half her life? And what, Ariel asked herself, does that say about me?

Thirty

DR. DAVID NUSSBAUM had just finished scrubbing his hands in the
ER men's room, the stench of his last patient's diarrhea still lingering in
his nostrils, when he heard a familiar voice out in the hall.

Hastily wiping his hands on a paper towel, he emerged to a scene
of minor mayhem. Just as he'd thought, it was Edith who was speaking,
her swelling belly pooching out ahead of her. But at this moment she
wasn't exactly a picture of pregnant serenity. Her usually melodic voice
was hostage to a gathering hysteria and her hands chopped the air like
Jackie Chan as she tried to describe her mother's appearance to an
exasperated-looking night shift nurse. A straggling band of tired and
cranky-looking children was lined up behind her long blue skirt.

"Ma'am, ma'am," nurse Stella Reeves shouted over Edith's
pleading. "You need to go back out to the waiting room. We can't have
you inspecting every bed here to see if your mother's in one of them."
Stella tore at the abundance of copper hair piled on top of her head, and
just as her locks broke free and fell luxuriantly over her shoulders, the
rubber band that had bound them flew like a slingshot across the hall to
the delighted cries of the children.

"But I've got to find her," Edith wailed. "And I was hoping, I
mean, not hoping, you must know what I mean, God forbid I don't
want her to be ill, but if she's not here, I don't know where else to look
for her." Edith looked around unseeingly, her voice dropping to a near-
whisper. "Selma Goldberg. She's my mother."

Just then, a uniformed guard came barreling down the hall with a hand inching down toward his imitation LAPD nightstick. David sucked in his breath. The mostly-Jewish staff doctors at Cedars called the unfortunately-named Herman Himmler "the Night Shift Nazi" behind his back. They joked that his name alone was nearly enough to send shivers down your spine, but for David the man's Hitler Youth good looks and buff physical condition were the clinchers.

Right now, the guard looked frustrated. His voice echoed along the walls. "Hey, lady, we've got procedures here, and you're trespassing where you don't belong. I don't care who your mother is. I told you already, you've got to follow the rules and take your turn like everybody else. You come back with me to the admitting desk right now."

As he attempted to grab her arm, the children began to cry and Edith jerked away, looking up at him with undisguised fury.

Uh oh, thought David. The last time he'd seen that expression he'd been ten years old, and Edith the babysitter had overruled his wish to watch a *Dennis the Menace* special in favor of *Soul Train*. He'd called her a *fart-faced maroni*, and she'd shot him a look just like this one before slapping him smartly across the face. He didn't know which had been worse, the pain or the sting of her shaming eyes.

But Edith had no idea what she was up against in Herman Himmler. He was a godsend when the staff had to contend with out-of-control gang bangers escorting one of their knifed or shot-up homies into the ER, but he was liable to go into authoritarian overdrive when dealing with gentler souls.

David cleared his throat, stuck out his chest, and straightened into his full sixty-eight inches of authority. He looked up at an astonished Herman and tried to sound persuasive. "Why don't you let me sort this one out? I know this woman." He was embarrassed that his lips broke into a placating chimpanzee grin as soon as he saw Herman's jaw tense and his eyes narrow.

But there was nothing the security guard could do, not without risking his job, and he knew it. With a flick of his shiny blond hair, he strutted down the hall without a word.

David turned back to face Edith and raised a quizzical eyebrow. She began to describe her alarming phone call from Selma's neighbor and her family's frantic rush to Martel, only to discover that her mother was mysteriously absent from her fire-damaged home. Only half of

David's mind was registering Edith's words. The other half was occupied with noticing how expressive her wide, moist eyes were, and how vivid and dramatic her thick, wing-like black brows. The only thing that stopped him from getting a full hard-on was Edith's announcement that Max should've been here by now. She looked around wildly. "Where is he anyway? He was only parking the car. The outdoor lots were full, so he dropped us off before heading to the Saperstein Tower parking structure. Maybe he got lost?"

It was then that a sound began to filter into David's awareness, at first nearly imperceptible, then quickly amping up into a loud rumbling that seemed to gather momentum as it moved toward them, as if George Lucas's "The Audience is Listening" synthesized crescendo of sound had finally taken over the world and was moving south from the Hollywood Hills. "Earthquake!" somebody shouted, and Edith's mouth snapped shut as the floor beneath them began to sway. Suddenly, the whole ER went black.

Edith began to shriek in a repetitive sequence. "Rebekka, Deborah, Jacob, Aaron! Rebekka, Deborah, Jacob, Aaron!"

"Mama, Mama!" her frantic children cried.

Heedless of Edith's pregnant state, David pushed her to the ground and tried covering as much of her and her children's bodies as he could with his own meager frame. Wordlessly, he counted off the seconds, knowing that if the lights stayed off for ten seconds, the emergency generator system should kick in. But it didn't. He was uncomfortably aware that most earthquakes in his memory, including the nasty one in ninety-four, would have subsided by now. This one, if anything, seemed to be gathering in intensity, bouncing his body like a rubber ball. His teeth clicked together with every bounce.

Punctuating the frantic cries that filled the darkness was a host of jarring sounds as a kind of caustic musical accompaniment, as if Philip Glass had composed a score for the end of the world. Hospital instruments clanked like brassy cymbals; heavy objects rolling across the floor suggested a badly out-of-tune organ; shattering glass shrieked like some hysterical xylophone. More ominous still, mysterious sounds issued from the very walls that enclosed them, high-pitched squeaks and low groans that sent bolts of panic through David as he registered the unthinkable possibility that the building itself might collapse. He gritted his teeth and held tightly onto the little hand that was clutching his own. He didn't know if it was Rebekka, Deborah, Jacob, or Aaron, but whoever it was, until the damned shaking stopped, he would not let go.

In Ariel's humble apartment on Poinsettia, just a few miles southwest of the Hollywood sign, the cat Jezebel padded agitatedly from room to room. On Ariel's workdays—following the most meager of pettings and chin scratchings begged off her groggy mistress before she stumbled out the door—Jezebel only came alive again when Ariel returned home. Until then, she typically spent most of her time curled into a black ball under Ariel's bed. In the summer, it was cooler there. But this evening, with the Santa Anas in full eerie blast, it was too warm even in that dust-bunny-carpeted cave. The stifling heat and a sudden thirst had wakened her, and she was puppet to the restlessness that overtook her when her mistress should by all rights be home. She meowed indignantly as she headed for the bathroom.

She was leaning her head into the toilet for a good long drink when her fur started to stand crazily away from her body. She backed away from the toilet as if a snake lay coiled inside. A low primeval howl erupted from her throat. She leapt backwards and slammed against the wall as if she'd lost her bearings and misread where she was. She hissed, then awkwardly scaled the slippery side of the bathtub and crouched inside, heart beating fast. She was scaring the shit out of herself. She was spooked.

Only then did the serious shaking start. The movements were sharp and sudden, rocking her porcelain cradle with a relentless vengeance. As if she'd heedlessly ventured into a jungle populated by giant creatures, her ears were filled with a tremendous roar. Her trembling body flinched but did not move away, as one end of the shower curtain rod above her was wrenched free from the wall and speared the bathtub floor right next to her. She didn't even lift a paw to brush away from her eyes the moldy yellowed-plastic curtain, as it was flung like a hasty shroud over her body.

When the shaking finally stopped and the noisy world went strangely quiet, Jezebel was herself very still. It was almost as if she weren't even there.

When the tunnel went black—the darkness bringing with it a familiar gathering rumble, like some prehistoric monster awakening from a deep sleep—Ariel knew that she and her companions were in Big Trouble. She wanted to warn them, even got so far as opening her mouth, but before she could utter a single word, the monster came and stole her mind.

The women under the UCLA campus were flung roughly from side to side like rag dolls, their four screaming voices amplified into a mob scene by the reverberating tunnel walls. The world became nothing more than sensation and sound: the roar of thousands of tons of shifting earth; the grunt of moving concrete; plaster cracking and shredding; the rattle and crash of glass and metal; and pain—in all its demonic gradations and variations, pain. This new Ariel-without-a-mind became nothing but a register of what her body felt: abrading, pinching, slapping, banging; and a heart that pounded so hard and fast she became a supernova of anxiety about to explode, until, with one last searing stab in her forehead, all the battering sensation and sound dissolved like granules of sugar in black coffee.

Wrapped in the black gauze of unconsciousness, nothing in her was present to hear the other three women calling out to each other, their voices feeble and tremulous.

"*Oy, gottinyu.*"

"I want my ma."

"Oh, Jesus, I don't believe it. Selma, Jane, Ariel? Are you with me? Is everyone okay?"

Thirty-one

IT WASN'T JUST in the UCLA tunnels and Cedars' ER that the impact of Big Mama's move was being felt. And it wasn't solely the quake that was cramping the city's style. Two endemic threats to the region had partnered up this time, with only Flood absent to complete the classic trio. Throughout the city, pet dogs and cats ran off from their suddenly unstable homes, and the wildlife in the foothills dividing the city from the valley fled their own familiar haunts. Out west, where fire licked vegetation like a hungry beast, scores of coyotes and squirrels and opossums found momentary safety in urban backyards, while others were forced to navigate the treachery of Pacific Coast Highway as they scurried and leapt from the red monster at their backs. The flames were fanned and tensions heightened by the hyped-up Santa Anas, which moaned like a cross between a crying baby and a cat in heat and spread luxury ash from Malibu and the Pacific Palisades over lawns and cars as far as Ventura to the north, the beaches of Hermosa and Redondo to the south, and the gritty, Spanish-speaking reaches of East L.A.

Some people hunkered down with guns and vigilance in homes whose walls ranged in damage from merely cracked to collapsed. Prepared for marauding packs of coyotes or human looters—they didn't give a shit which—they were ready with the human equivalent of fang and claw to defend their own. Here and there, some poor soul continued to cower under a table or bed long after the worst tremor, all thought banished, paralyzed like a deer before the grisly, shiny face of an oncoming car. That was how it was in nature: the surge of adrenaline serving either fight or flight.

The instinct for survival was impersonal. Old Darwin had that one right, though what he hadn't reckoned on was love, which had a larger-than-life inexorability of its own.

It was David's love—and some kind of lucky hunch about where the proverbial shit was about to happen—that had him scoop Edith's young daughter Deborah safely to the right, just a second before one of the ominously-creaky fluorescent lights came crashing down onto the ER floor.

It was love that zipped Matt's mouth shut as he acceded to Bonnie's lunatic plea—their three-million-dollar home, reinforced to modern earthquake specifications, still trembling like a bowl of jello—to help her gather all of her best jewelry into a Gelson's bag and lock it in his trunk, as if every potential looter in the city were just waiting for the earth to stop moving before making a bee-line for this very house in Westwood.

It was certainly love that made Ben drive like a blindfolded rat in a maze through dark intersections, desperately hoping to intuit his way back to the apartment building on Poinsettia from a bar on Sunset Boulevard, where—after tucking an endearingly semi-conscious Mary O'Reilly into her own bed—he'd been trying to drink his way into courage to declare himself fully to Ariel.

Love, as well as survival, compelled the women under the ground at UCLA to reach toward each other like human magnets. So it was that, in the mercifully still tunnel, Terry's frantic fingers probed Ariel's body, feeling for a pulse, for breath, for blood. Ariel had been hit by something. They'd heard her cry out in the dark, and now she was out cold.

"Ariel's breathing, at least. I just wish she'd wake up." Terry cringed at the unnatural loudness of her own voice, and she wondered if this is what they meant by the blind having more acute hearing. Why in the world hadn't she brought her cell phone with her? Ariel had been in such a damned hurry to get here. Nor could she find Ariel's phone in her friend's pocket, which was where it should have been. It wasn't as though any of them had brought a purse with her on this crazy expedition. And where the hell was that flashlight? She asked the other two if they knew where it was. No response.

Terry was having to exert all of her will not to panic at the utter darkness, and her body hurt; it felt like the rough tunnel walls had scraped her exposed arms everywhere. But at this point it was for Ariel's sake that her heart was pounding a mile a minute. When they'd done their informal roll call, the absence of Ariel's voice was like a punch in the gut.

One of the other women coughed, and Terry choked a little herself. She could feel and taste the thick dust swirling around them, making their respiration labored. She hoped to Christ it wasn't asbestos they were breathing in. Leaning her head close to Ariel's body and circling her wrist with her hand, she continued reporting to Selma and Jane. "Her pulse is pretty regular. A little faint, but regular. And I can't feel any wetness anywhere, so I guess she's not bleeding. Let's see if we can wake her up without actually moving her. I don't want to jiggle any potentially broken bones." She pushed out of her mind an image of Ariel, lying paralyzed in some hospital bed from a spinal cord injury.

She could sense Selma rocking back and forth next to her, utterly unresponsive to what she was saying. Selma kept moaning a melancholy chant that sounded a thousand years old. "*Ayiyi, little babeleh, ayiyi, little mommeleh ... ah, ah, babeleh.*"

As she stroked Ariel's face, Terry wished she had children. She wished she'd had them with Matt. Her heart skipped a beat as she remembered her mother's achingly-familiar, gravelly smoker's voice uttering the familiar phrase, "If wishes were kisses," before lavishing quick pecks all over her young face, as if that were the closest she could come to granting her daughter's desires.

Without thinking, Terry gently pressed her lips against Ariel's soft cheek. She was surprised at how good her aim was, as if her body had its own radar that kicked into gear now that the darkness was so absolute. She caught her breath as she sensed Ariel begin to stir. Ariel's hands reached up to grasp her shoulders. Terry offered a silent prayer of thanks.

For a long moment, their bodies gently swayed together. Then Ariel, moaning, let go of her neck and pushed away from her, struggling to sit up.

Terry ran her hands up and down her arms and shivered. She couldn't remember the last time she'd felt so cold. She wondered how

Jane was doing. The girl had fallen silent. Little did Terry know that Jane wasn't bothered at all—her mind knew just what to do, blotting out her pain and fear, along with Terry's attempts to wake Ariel. Yes, that clever mind of hers had taken her to a golden place in the sky, where Ariel sat on a cloud, touching the face of Eve. But Eve's face quickly became her ma's in her best sunshine mood, and Ma was taking Jane home to be with her and Bobby. No Vern. Vern was dead. But that thought threatened to open the door to Danny's blind stare on the pavement this morning. Jane squeezed her eyes shut even more tightly to make that picture go away.

As for Selma, Terry was having a hard time getting through to her that Ariel was okay, even able to sit up on her own steam. Despite Terry's best efforts to point this out to her, the old woman kept mumbling that she'd let down all the young ones: Ariel, who, God forbid, might be fatally injured, and her own precious Edith and her family, whom she prayed had survived the terrible shaking. Selma sounded like she thought God was punishing her personally for distrusting her own daughter. She pled her case piteously. "How could I know? A wise woman, I've never been. It wasn't Edith I was running from. It was my own aging. Who am I kidding? I thought maybe I would live forever?"

Another voice piped up, and Terry had to laugh in spite of herself. The first words that issued groggily from the lips of her stunned friend were classic Ariel. "Jesus Christ. What the fuck? Either I've gone blind, or someone turned all the lights off. And my head feels like somebody used it as a football. Is this some asshole's idea of a joke?"

———————

Theosophus paused as the women's voices traveled through the tunnel toward him. *Well, I'll be,* he thought.

He'd just about convinced himself that he'd hallucinated the sounds when he heard them resolve into actual words. "Bleeding," a woman was saying. A disconnected phrase wafted toward him. "... try to wake her up."

He kept moving through the pitch-black passageway toward the voices. Lord knew why there were women down there—white women, from the sound of it—but after all that shake, rattle and roll, he worried that they might be in trouble. He could hear his pulse pound in his ears, along with Granny's voice telling him, "Hurry up, boy." He tried to pick up speed, but it was hard going. Hard enough, he thought, when you're a man. Even harder when you're a dog. His palms were stinging, and his knees ached from how tightly he'd wrapped them around a low horizontal pipe to save himself when the shaking had been going on. He was crawling clumsily on all fours through a low stretch of tunnel, trying to avoid pools of water where steam pipes had obviously burst and emptied themselves. Every time one of his hands met up with anything but hard concrete—a piece of dispossessed wiring shaken free by the quake or some loose scrap of hardware once holding one of the surreal structures of the energy system together—he recoiled back onto his knees so fast that he lost count of the times he bumped his head. He shuddered to think it might be roaches he was touching, scared up out of the earth by all the action. You never knew what was going to get stirred up in one of these earthquakes. He'd heard that after the Northridge Quake, some nasty prehistoric germs had been let loose all over the San Fernando Valley. Theosophus grimaced in revulsion as he reluctantly crept forward along the cracked concrete floor.

It finally penetrated Selma's awareness that Ariel was more or less okay, that fact having been established by Ariel's grumpy comment that if Selma was planning on dying anytime soon, who else would listen to her *kvetch* about how much her head hurt? Only Ariel pronounced it "ka-vetch," which made the old woman start to titter. Before she knew it, she was swept into a full-out fit of nervous giggling, gripping her hand between her thighs for fear that she might wet herself. She couldn't help it, the juxtaposition of near-disaster and Ariel's hopelessly *goyish* mispronunciation, flung into this waking nightmare of darkness, was just too ridiculous.

Worse yet, the other three females pitched in with nervous shrieks of hilarity. We could have died and then who would be laughing? thought Selma confusedly, when another high-pitched whoop from Terry set her off all over again.

So complete was the women's joint hysteria that they jumped as if one when a man's voice flung itself at them, its cadence right off the streets of South Central.

"I thought y'all might be in trouble, but now I reckon not."

Somehow, in the dark, they found each other instantly and clasped arms and legs together like some dry-skinned octopus. The sudden silence was palpable. Selma could feel a hand trembling. She wasn't sure if it was someone else's or her own.

"Ain't this a bitch?" The man's voice sounded disgusted. "We just survived what might have been the Big One, and you all act like the cat got your tongue when you hear my voice." His next words were faint, as he muttered to himself. "Even when he's invisible, a black man is the most dread thing. I've been scraping my way here like a crab, thinking somebody might need my help." He grunted harshly. "I'm a dang fool, and that's the truth." Selma could sense that he'd turned away.

"Wait." Ariel's voice was still wobbly. "Please. Don't go. It's just that we didn't know anybody else was down here."

No answer.

This time, Ariel sounded even more tentative. "Are you okay?" When he still failed to respond, she laughed ruefully. "Actually," she said, "we're the fools, or at least I am. We came here tonight to try to find some bones."

———————————

For a moment, Theosophus worried that he'd actually died in the earthquake and landed in some white ghoul limbo, but then, dead or alive, his curiosity got the better of him. "What kind of bones?"

It was weird to hear her disembodied words in the darkness. "The fossil remains of a woman. She could be the ancestress of us all."

"Say what?"

The woman coughed in embarrassment. "The remains of a woman who lived thousands and thousands of years ago. I know it sounds like an exaggeration, but they're calling her 'Eve.' She's like our great-great-great-great grandmother." She added brightly, "She's from Africa." He heard her clap her hand to her mouth. "Oh, I'm sorry. I didn't mean ... I just thought you might like to know." Her voice trailed off.

Theosophus grinned and decided to stay put for the moment. He'd obviously come across a group of nuts, but maybe they were interesting nuts. And what if she actually knew what she was talking about? Over the years, he'd seen some of the African folk objects stored in Haines Hall, before everything had been moved to Fowler Museum. He supposed that the professors just might want to add some actual bones to their collection. Besides, the way the woman used the word *grandmother*, with a kind of hushed respect, felt just right to Granny, who smiled with satisfaction and kept nodding like she knew something he didn't right inside his own head.

The fact that a strange man—even one who sounded like he meant them no harm—had now joined them in the dark did little to allay Terry's fears. She'd lived through enough earthquakes to suspect that, at the very least, they could count on some nasty aftershocks. At nightmarish worst, what they'd just survived was but a foreshock of an even larger temblor. With a sense of urgency, she fished around Ariel's body for the missing flashlight. Ariel objected loudly. "What the hell do you think you're doing? Get your hands off me."

When Terry explained what she was looking for, Ariel replied gruffly, "Ugh. So that's what it is. I think I've been sitting on the goddamned thing."

Terry could hear a soft rustling, then the flashlight was roughly thrust into her hand, as if Ariel resented the fact that she herself was in no shape to be in charge.

With a faintly audible click, light entered and transformed their world. Terry anxiously peered at her companions, all of whom blinked and squinted. All but Jane, who seemed too scared to open her eyes.

Terry saw Ariel wince, press her palm tentatively against her forehead, then lay back onto the cold concrete, curling up into a ball with both hands cradled between her thighs.

"Are you okay? Your poor head—first the Welcome Rat and now this."

But Ariel merely muttered. "The damned rat was probably trying to tell us something. As in, 'Welcome to Hell.'"

Now that she could see with her own eyes that her friends were more or less intact, Terry pointed the light at the stranger who crouched a few feet away from them, then pulled it away as she saw the expression of alarm on his face. Agitated by the unknown quantity he represented, she played the flashlight shakily over the contours of the tunnel.

They gasped. The introduction of visibility was a mixed blessing, lifting them out of the anxious void of blindness, but reinforcing the magnitude of the upheaval.

As always with earthquakes, the damage was eerily uneven. Some parts of the subterranean passageway looked virtually untouched, while signs of raw wounding to other sections made them wonder how in the world they could possibly get out of here. Segments of some of the walls had cracked into thick slabs and were collapsed inward at awkward angles. Not too far from where they sat, the floor had buckled like an accordion, and they could actually see harsh clumps of dirt pushing up through the broken concrete. The ceiling looked mostly intact, though scores of wires dangled crazily from little fissures, still swinging from the earth's movement. Several bright yellow pipes had split open, and some had clearly punctured their neighbors as they'd broken apart. In the lower-ceilinged part of the passageway, clear liquid pooled the ground. The dust that had been kicked up seemed reluctant to settle, giving the whole spectacle a gray, grainy look.

Terry sniffed the air. She was surprised when the stranger, who didn't even appear to have looked at her, seemed to divine her fear. His voice was soothing, like velvet. "Don't you worry 'bout that. I used to work here. Know these tunnels and what's in 'em like the back of my hand. Ain't nothing going to poison us down here."

Terry nodded curtly. This guy hardly looked like an expert; why should she trust him? "Damn it, Ariel," she said, as she continued to sweep the light in a wide arc over the tunnel contours, "I love you dearly, and I know I said I was up for this, but I sure wish we'd gotten drunk tonight at my apartment instead."

Theosophus knew exactly how she felt, but he'd maneuvered his way through mean streets too long and he'd traveled these tunnels' corridors too often in the past to doubt that he could navigate an exit.

He took advantage of the women's need to orient themselves in their fractured surroundings to eyeball each one of them. He nearly jumped back when he spied a familiar face, her eyes still tightly shut, like a kid blocking out a gory scene in a horror movie. Well, I'll be damned, he thought, if it ain't little blondie from West Hollywood Park. He shook his head at the irony of finding the one who'd inspired his sobering-up in the very place he'd come to face his devil.

She looked pretty messed up, the gray dust-streaks on her skinny arms crisscrossed with a latticework of angry red abrasions—no doubt from being thrown against the tunnel walls. An old lady was holding onto her like she was some valuable jewel she'd brought with her into a crowd of pickpockets.

He laughed bitterly, speculating that the lady thought he was the big bad black bogeyman come to cart away Miss Jane's pretty white ass. Then he shut up real fast as Granny gave him a swipe inside his head for thinking so disrespectfully about the one person who'd bothered to talk some sense into him.

But he hadn't stopped laughing soon enough to prevent the old lady from turning around. She was clearly reluctant to stare, but for one brief moment her gaze lit directly on him. Seeing her full face, he nearly jumped back in terror. Her wary brown eyes widened at his reaction, little guessing how startling a picture she herself presented, with her kerchief twisted around on her head like some Ku Klux Klan hood and the eyebrows gone eerily missing from her forehead.

Theosophus told himself he didn't even want to know what was wrong with her, though he couldn't help but worry that these were ghosts after all.

It took his first long, lingering look at the wielder of the flashlight to persuade him that he couldn't be dead. Standing up now and picking her way over the cracked concrete to get a closer view of the damage, she looked like the star of some disaster movie, her current state of dishevelment only emphasizing her good looks. Her honeydew melon tits were too high and the glint in her dark chocolate eyes too vibrant for her to be dead. The fact that his dick was beginning to rise like the summer sun convinced him he couldn't be, either. But then, remembering what he must look and smell like and how he'd been living lately, his face burned with shame and he looked down.

Which was where his eyes found the fourth woman. He figured she'd gotten pretty hurt by the earth's jumping and jiving. She lay curled up now on the concrete floor, a plum-sized bruise protruding from her forehead. She had the lazy, sensuous grace of a big cat, her rounded hip thrust seductively upward and her sexily unkempt light brown curls swept away from a face whose expression was open and unabashedly curious. He realized with a start that she'd been watching him the whole time. When she beamed him a smile, he wanted to cover his face in embarrassment, but instead found himself grinning back. His insides felt as warm as if he'd taken a generous swig of Old Taylor.

She tentatively rubbed at the blue knob on her forehead, then gestured toward the assortment of rips and smudges on her clothing. "We're a hell of a harem, aren't we? I'm surprised we haven't scared you away." Her laughter gurgled like a rushing brook, but then she groaned. "Jesus, I know it's a cliché, but it really does hurt the worst when I laugh."

She made an odd noise in her throat, and he worried that, with her head injury, she was getting ready to pass out. But instead she apologized. "Excuse me. So disgusting, but it's this damned dust. I know it's gross, but my nose keeps running." With effort, she lifted herself up and sat facing him, legs crossed, her fingers continuing to cautiously probe her bruised brow. "Did you ever see such a mess? I should've known this mission was ill-fated when we first got here. First thing I did was fall down a full flight of stairs. Tripped on a dead rat."

He nodded. He'd seen plenty of the nasty creatures down here in his days on the payroll. No matter how many he trapped and swept up, there'd be double the number of replacements the next day.

"Never should have wanted to go after Eve in the first place. What was I thinking, anyway—that I had some personal entitlement to those bones? Only reason I had us sneaking down here was that I knew I had no business messing with them." Shooting a furtive look at her companions, she leaned toward him, lowering her voice to a near-whisper so only he could hear. "I feel terrible for bringing them here. What if the exits are caved in and we can't get out? Damn it, this is all my fault."

He found himself whispering back. "Naw, don't say that. You can't take the blame. It's nature and all. You couldn't have known what was going to come. Besides, what about me? All alone in here when it was shaking so strong and all, like to be whupped up one side the head and back down the other. I count myself lucky that you chose to come after your bones on this night, so's I don't have to face it out entirely alone." He paused. In her remarkably open-book eyes, self-doubt and hope were an even match. "Don't you worry, I know this place. I'll get us out of here." He laughed. "But if I'd known it was gonna be a party, I'd have spruced myself up. Worn my best suit. Yes indeed, I would."

Terry carefully paced the scarred tunnel floor and shot her beam of light over the newly pock-marked tunnel walls, searching in vain for Ariel's cell phone despite her near-certainty that, even if she found it, they'd get no signal down here. She was intensely aware of Ariel talking quietly with the funky-looking stranger. She couldn't believe Ariel—laughing and flirting at a time like this. Was she nuts?

It took Jane's cry of surprise to bring her back to the group. Finally daring to open her eyes, Jane had called out, "Theosophus! What are you doing down here?"

Terry looked on curiously as Jane, her pale cheeks actually sprouting a little pinkish color, crawled over and sat on her knees at the man's side, looking up at him expectantly.

Terry moved back to the group, propping the flashlight on its end so that a diffuse glow arched over their heads like a vast penumbra.

Jane made the introductions. The man seemed embarrassed with all this attention. He hemmed and hawed, keeping his gaze zeroed in on the girl's face. Terry had the uncomfortable suspicion that he was taking particular pains to avoid eye-contact with her.

He spoke like he'd been tumbled in some strong waves and had come up spitting out sand. "Pleased to meet you. As for what I'm doing here, well I ... I just ... Like you said, I—" He glanced at Ariel, who gave him an encouraging nod, then he turned back to Jane. "I decided that you was right. Time to take myself in hand. Haven't had a drink in days now." His eyes shone. "Truth be told, even with this whole shebang here, I don't believe I miss it."

Terry watched Jane open her mouth, then shut it just as quickly. Twisting her fingers together, the teenager smiled up at him beatifically.

"Hell's bells," said Ariel. As much as she felt drawn to Theosophus in this insane moment, she was uncomfortably aware that she would have gone to some trouble to avoid him if she'd met him on the street; in her own chicken-shit way, she was a snob.

Unlike Ben. She remembered how impressed she'd been when he'd talked to the pathetic-looking beggar outside Il Fornaio like he was just some ordinary kid, not somebody with a face screaming of the AIDS infection that made her want to ignore him. There wasn't even a whiff of that typical Mr. Cool bullshit to Ben, no drawing a line between who really mattered and who was the equivalent of an extra in the movie he and his friends were starring in. She shook her head. With an egalitarian attitude like that, he'd never make it big. Not here, not in L.A.

Her eyes filled with tears. What if he'd gotten killed in the quake? Their building was one of the worst kind—cheap post-war construction. Her stomach felt like someone had poured lead into it. She pictured Ben's third floor apartment, perched over the parking area like a stork's belly, with nothing but a few posts holding it up.

If this damned quake has taken him out, she thought, just shoot me.

And then it dawned on her, and she began to hyperventilate. "Oh, God. Jezzie! Oh, my poor baby! Even if she's alive, she must be terrified. And what if she's gotten loose? She'll be hit by a car for sure! She can barely see!"

Thirty-two

THE MONOLITH THAT was Cedars-Sinai Medical Center was actually comprised of a number of buildings, including the twin towers on Third Street that housed hundreds of doctors' offices. Just north of them, on the improbably-named Gracie Allen Road between (what else?) George Burns Road and San Vicente, two main hospital buildings serviced the more seriously sick. The ER resided below the Plaza Level of the northernmost of those two.

In the best of times, Cedars' emergency room was a hectic hive, attracting everything from wounded homies to car wreck victims to people who put off going to the doctor for a cough or stomach ache because they were scared or poor or in denial, until pain presented its implacable demand for balance due. At the worst of times, the ER staff was hard-pressed to keep the demanding, whining human chaos at bay.

The current crisis superseded all previous challenges to both procedural guidelines for dealing with mass emergencies and individual resourcefulness born of hard precedent. This time, it was Cedars itself that was injured. Saperstein Critical Care Tower had partially collapsed, and some of its lethal concrete detritus had collapsed onto its adjacent parking garage, crushing cars and hapless souls entering or exiting them at the time. This very same structure contained one of the generators designed to return light to the hospital in case of a power outage, and it took the Center's capable team of engineers fifteen extra, precious minutes to get the auxiliary back-up system up and running.

Light hit the ER like the flash of an atom bomb, revealing such a scene of disheartening devastation that David nearly succumbed to panic. Instead, he took a deep breath, gently lifted a whimpering, trembling young Deborah to a sitting position, and forced his unwilling eyes to roam the room. Nothing was in the place it had occupied before the lights went out. Everything had moved downward. The emptied screens of dismembered EKG and ultrasound machines, whose glass fragments now pebbled the floor like a European beach, recalled the open-mawed horror of Edvard Munch's *The Scream*. Beds had hurtled beyond the reaches of their curtained cubicles. One was actually standing on its side against a wall; its hapless previous occupant, an elderly Latina with a bandaged forehead, stared up at it in utter disbelief from the floor onto which she'd slid. The bodies of both patients and ER staff littered the floor like roaches after a Raid attack. Those who moved made heavy sounds that were more animal than human, but it was the number of unmoving silent bodies that made the hairs on David's arms stand on end.

A few of the staff—identifiable only by their hospital whites and greens, their bewildered expressions more like those of patients than professionals—began raising their heads and looking around, struggling up from the wreckage-strewn floor onto their knees and then their feet like zombies coming up out of a graveyard. The whole thing looked like a horror film played in slow motion.

David felt a stab of anxiety in his chest. They needed to speed it up, get moving. There were lives that needed saving here. He didn't want to think of the probable damage to the rest of the city, whose wounded would soon be moving toward this very ER like it was Mecca, but even the faintest whiff of that awareness had the helpful effect of pushing his adrenals into high gear.

Though it had felt like hours since the quake had hit, David's observations had taken place in a matter of seconds. Now he quickly counted off the heads of Edith's four children, who maintained a terrified silence but appeared to be physically uninjured. He looked hastily around for Edith herself. It took a moment to locate her. She lay on her back in a corner, eyes closed and face as white as a rice-paper-powdered geisha. One hand flung over her forehead as if to ward off a blow and the other curled over her groin, she looked like a woman preparing for rape. David cursed his God as he saw that blood had pooled under Edith's torso, staining her rucked-up skirt and continuing to ooze an ever-widening crimson arc on the floor beneath her.

He wanted to reach toward her, but his own body wouldn't move. He couldn't seem to get the requisite muscles and bones working together to break the sudden paralysis. How had he ever managed to sit, stand, walk before now? His mind locked. This couldn't be real. Surely it was all just a bad dream.

Stella Reeves suddenly materialized at his side. Her prompting tone as she said, "Dr. Nussbaum?" broke the spell. He was a doctor. He could do this. Suddenly aware of young Deborah and her siblings looking on, he signed to the nurse and whipped into action.

David's focus now was absolute. He was blind to the other injured souls in the ER, as Nurse Reeves occupied Edith's children and he gathered tools from odd corners of the room to do what he needed to do.

If Selma was feeling torn apart by a host of conflicting emotions, she was determined not to show it. While bitter bile so filled her stomach that she was unsure how long she could hold off the impulse to throw up, she worked at keeping what she hoped was a pleasant, encouraging expression on her face. In the current crisis, she figured that her young friends needed the burden of an old lady's worries like a hole in the head. She daren't even mention how desperately worried she was about Edith and the children.

How many times had she chided Edith for having all those kids? If only she could just fly out of the tunnel and over the city to Edith's house in Beverlywood and make sure her daughter was okay. She spat. So *nu*, she thought, you think you're some bride in a Chagall painting, floating over the city with the cows and violins?

The fact that the tunnel's exits might all be collapsed or blocked with debris wasn't far from Selma's awareness, either. Now that their initial hysteria had passed and they'd begun to discuss the best strategy for getting out of there, the group's mood had taken a nosedive. Ariel was speaking in a monotone and not wisecracking at all now, which Selma knew was a bad sign; Terry looked confused and frightened; and Jane was scratching at herself like she had head lice, which, Selma thought, God forbid, after where she'd been sleeping, she actually might.

The black man was the only one who looked like he wasn't daunted by what lay ahead. His eyes shone and he gestured expansively as he explained which exits were closest.

She suspected that this unlikely candidate with swollen feet, smelly clothes, and—God and Chaim forgive her, but it was true—lint in his hair might be their salvation. Selma cursed her rotten memory for forgetting his name. The whole idea of salvation had always struck her as a little too philosophical. She went through a list of the famous thinkers Chaim used to read. She'd never told him how she used to invent stories for her own private amusement about what they were like at home: Kierkegaard a moper, inhabiting some one-room apartment, eating his solitary meals with his bare hands; Sartre someone who secretly broke into silly songs; Marx suffering from bloating and gas and a longing for his mother. How funny it would be if this black man's name were Kant, or Hegel, or even Henry David Thoreau.

Theosophus saw Selma grin and was encouraged. He'd been worrying that the old girl was a racist, especially when she'd suddenly leaned to the side and spat. Actually, the spitting had been a shock. He hadn't seen a woman spit since Granny's tobacco-chewing friend Esther passed on. He thought now that if this old bird had half the spirit of Esther Beauchamps—a wide-hipped, high-assed Creole woman with cafe-au-lots-of-lait skin and a throaty laugh that jiggled her pillowy chest—then their journey out of the tunnel could be mighty entertaining. But as he saw Selma's face crumple again into a worried mask, he set his shoulders.

"Look here," he said, "I got an idea. If Miss Jane don't mind, me and her could inspect the tunnel together, see if we can't find the best way out. Once we've found it, we come back and get the rest of you." He held up a hand as Ariel opened her mouth. "Don't make sense for us all to go up some blind alleys together. Bound to get uncomfortable. I myself had to crawl part of the way to get here to you. Some parts of these old tunnels are buckled."

But Ariel wasn't about to be shut up. "You don't think we could just aim for the closest exit first? Go back the way we came? Maybe it's free and clear. If it is, we could be out of here in no time. Then we wouldn't have to split up, which, God knows …"

Theosophus rolled his eyes meaningfully a couple of times in Selma's direction, but Ariel just stared back at him with a stubborn expression. "Well, now," he said, "you want to give that a try, I'm open."

Theosophus grabbed the flashlight and led the way. The flashlight's illumination was barely enough to help them navigate the uneven, concrete floor. They ducked and sidestepped to avoid broken pipes and dangling wires, but Theosophus was reassured by the relative ease of their passage. Just an occasional "Ouch" or "Watch it" broke their silence. As they approached a particularly narrow part of the tunnel, forced into a single file and touching the rough walls for support, Ariel exclaimed delightedly, "Yes, yes. Remember this? We must be nearly there."

But when they rounded the next bend, Theosophus abruptly halted. He shot up a warning hand, but the women, talking excitedly to each other as they anticipated their freedom, piled up right behind him. Someone gasped, then they all went dead silent.

In front of them, the walls of the tunnel were completely caved in. Eerily, about halfway up the crush of broken concrete, a dusty boot dangled by a single lace, its end grasped in the fearsome jaws of two intersecting hunks of dismembered wall.

Theosophus whipped the flashlight away from the scene of devastation. Rivulets of sweat ran down his face and his voice was shakier than he wanted it to be. "Now I know it don't look good, but no cause to panic. There's more than one way out of here, and you're lucky—I do believe I know them all." He flashed them a wide, forced grin. He realized he wasn't doing much good when he noticed that Ariel's teeth were chattering. It didn't help that the ground jumped a few abrupt times just then.

"Go! Go back!"

His own way was blocked by Ariel, who just stood there, paralyzed. It took a shove from him to get her feet moving, and even then she ran blindly.

The shaking stopped. They were all breathing hard. Theosophus realized he needed to talk and move fast or he'd have four hysterical females on his hands. He hadn't liked what he'd seen just now, but he wasn't about to give up.

"Awright, plan number one didn't turn out so good, but that don't mean we ain't got a plan number two." He turned to face Jane. "What do you think, girl? Are you up for a little expedition?" Except he pronounced it, "Ex-petition," and she looked a little puzzled for a second until she figured it out. She hesitated. "C'mon," he said, "can't be much worse than Hollywood Boulevard on a Saturday night."

She smiled bleakly. "Sure."

"No!" Ariel stepped forward and put a restraining hand on her arm. "I think Jane should stay here. I'm the one who started this. Let me go with you."

"Honey, I like some meat on my bones as much as the next man, and you got what it takes, but our little skinny-assed chicken-wing over here is a lot more likely to get through if we hit some real tight spaces."

Ariel's face flushed. Terry moved quickly to her side. She spoke to Ariel out of the side of her mouth, but he could hear her anyway. "He's not being insulting, just practical. He's right, you know. She could squeeze through some crevices you and I could barely see through." Ariel, arms crossed, shot her a betrayed look, but Terry shook her gently and hissed through her teeth. "For Christ's sake, do you want to die in here?"

Ariel reluctantly capitulated. "I guess you're right. But, Jane, listen to me." She pressed her fingertips so deeply into the girl's arm that Jane flinched. "Oh hell, I'm sorry. But this is important. I want you to promise me you'll be really careful. I won't be able to live with myself if anything happens to you."

Jane nodded. Ariel turned to Theosophus and put her nose about an inch away from his, so close that his eyes began to cross. "If anything happens to her ..." she warned. She stepped back hastily, then gathered herself up and pointed an imperious finger at him. "I'm holding you personally responsible."

Theosophus nearly saluted. She had no idea how good those words sounded to him. He felt like a human being again.

Thirty-three

AS THEOSOPHUS AND Jane moved off, Ariel could see them crouch down, then actually get onto their hands and knees and crawl. Light disappeared with them. Ariel shuddered, then turned in the direction of Terry's voice, which floated in the darkness like a vapor.

"She's a brave kid," Terry said.

"You don't know how brave," said Ariel, who commenced to fill her in.

Just as she was finishing her own version of Jane's abuse—peppering the tale with far angrier expletives than the docile Jane would herself have uttered—Selma's voice broke in.

"And to think," Selma was saying, "it was only this morning that she watched her friend, God rest his soul, drop dead. Right next to the Mr. Lincoln rose bush. Planted by my Chaim more than twenty years ago." Her voice cracked. "Forgive me. Always a burden. It's just that ... Edith. The children. I'm so afraid for them. What if—"

Ariel scooted toward her. She didn't know whether it was her own touch that got it started or whether she'd grabbed hold of her just in time. Either way, the floodgates opened. Selma wailed. Ariel had never before heard a human being sound so much like a wild animal.

When the deluge finally subsided, Selma stuttered softly, "Thank you, my dear." She patted Ariel on the cheek, just missing her eye in the darkness. Ariel stifled an incipient giggle. "You're such a nice girl. Chaim always said that crying was our gift from God, a little mercy to sweeten the salt of our sorrow." Ariel could sense her twisting around.

"God forgive me," Selma said helplessly, "but now I need to urinate. I don't know how long I can hold it."

"Mrs. G, you're a peach. I was just waiting for somebody else to say that they needed to pee, too." Wishing there were just a little light in the tunnel, Ariel awkwardly helped Selma up and carefully inched her to what she hoped was a corner, stifling a curse as she banged her already sore head into what felt like a wall. She helped the old woman squat and do her business. As she sensed her pulling up her panties, she said, "Hang on a mo'," and sighed pleasurably as she relieved herself.

After they'd clumsily groped their way back to their original spot and lowered themselves to the ground, Selma whispered apologetically that she'd like to lie down. Ariel felt that it was no longer blood that ran through her own veins but pure guilt. Enlisting Terry's help, she suggested that they lay Selma's sweater under her trunk for at least a little cushioning, and she situated herself so that Selma could rest her head in her lap. Selma sank down with a loud, "Oomph." Without thinking, Ariel gently removed Selma's kerchief and began to tease her fingers through her stubbornly wiry hair. She could hear Terry re-settle herself across from her. For the first time in hours, and in spite of the darkness, Ariel was able to take a few normal breaths.

The silence was interrupted by a strange sound. It took her a moment to identify what it was. Selma was snoring. A burst of Terry's giggling rent the air.

"Shh," Ariel hissed angrily, but Selma was clearly dead to the world, her lips continuing to burble their rude sounds. Sighing, Ariel put a hand up to her forehead and winced as she fingered her bruise. Between Ratty tripping her and Mother Earth battering her, she figured she hurt everywhere. "God," she said quietly, "I sure could use a smoke."

"Better not," Terry said. "I don't know if I believe Theosophus about there being no gas down here."

"I guess you're right."

They fell silent again, which made the rustling somewhere off to Ariel's right sound even more distinct. "Jesus Christ," Ariel cried, her muscles tensing, "what the hell was that?"

Terry grunted. "Remember Ratty? Must be one of his relatives. We need a mouser down here."

Ariel moaned. Oh God, she thought, please let Jezzie be alive. I'll do anything you want ... I'll quit smoking. It'll kill me, but I'll do it if you only get us out of here and let Jezzie not be dead.

Unaware of the terror she'd unleashed in her friend, Terry spoke wonderingly. "You know, it's funny, all I can think about wanting to do if we get out of here is see Matt."

"You just don't give up, do you?"

Terry's riposte was quick and surprisingly abrasive. "Unlike you. You don't even try."

"What do you mean?"

"I mean you actually have a man in your life at last, and you piss it away. Just like that." The snap of her fingers made Selma stir for a second, but she settled down again as Ariel stroked her forehead, murmuring, "Shhhh."

Terry continued, her voice filled with awe. "I think he really loves you."

"Doubt it. Even if he did, it's the old cliché. Wouldn't want to belong to a club that would have me as a member. Let's face it, I'm not exactly up to the standard of the Cindy Simmonses of this world."

"What are you talking about?"

"Oh, I forgot, you wouldn't know. You were always the one the guys went for, and why not? You're gorgeous."

"Thanks a lot. Is that supposed to be a compliment? Like my looks are all I have to offer? Easy to pass it off to that. You're just scared. Scared and lazy."

"Lazy? What the hell do you mean?"

"I mean, what are you doing working for the Postal Service, anyway? You were always the smartest one of the three of us. What happened to you?" Terry stopped. The ground had started to sway a little, rocking gently back and forth. As Ariel's heart beat so hard she thought it would jump out of her chest, she instinctively bent forward over Selma's head and cradled her protectively. She waited with clenched fists and tensed shoulders for the rolling motion to shift into the jarring thrusts of the earlier quake. Instead, the swaying simply subsided. She couldn't believe her ears when Terry just went on as if nothing had happened. "I feel sorry for Ben. I don't think you take anything seriously."

"You just don't get it," Ariel hissed. "I take the big things seriously.

You never would have realized the importance of something like Eve."

"And look where that got us."

"That was a low blow."

"No, really. Think about it, Ariel. That's how you've always been. Disdaining what you've got because there was always something bigger that you didn't have. Now it's Eve, but how about when your mom was dying? Acting like you didn't care? Or pretending you weren't into any of the guys in middle school because you preferred to tend to that overblown shrine to your dad over your desk? You've still got his pictures all over your house. I guess a mere human like Ben couldn't hold a candle to a saint like that. Except that saint deserted you. He was so great he couldn't even stick around to watch his own daughter grow up."

Ariel, with uncanny aim, slapped Terry so hard that her hand stung. Terry cried out.

Selma stirred. "*Vus is dus?*"

"Shh, don't worry, Mrs. G, go back to sleep, everything's okay."

This was all too surreal. Ariel kept waiting for someone to wake her.

"I guess I deserved that." Terry sounded teary. "I just got carried away." When Ariel failed to reply, she ceded, in a tiny voice, "Well, I guess more than a little. I should have said something before now. Respectfully. I just hate it when you get down on yourself." Her voice got smaller still. She sounded like a little girl. "I'm sorry I said that about your father. Can you forgive me?"

It was almost as if Ariel hadn't heard her. "You might be right about Ben, I don't know, but I just can't get over that fucking kiss. I don't care what he says, it was too intense to be just acting. Oh Christ, I know it sounds crazy, but I'll never get the picture of it out of my mind."

"Oh, come on. You're bigger than that. He told you he was imagining he was kissing *you*. Besides, I personally think Cindy looks a little…"—her voice took on a catty edge—"pinched."

Ariel snorted.

"But really, all nastiness aside, Ariel, you're the woman who utterly adores an old half-blind cat. You don't give a shit what she looks like. It's her personality, her essence, that you love."

"You saying I look like shit but have a heart of gold?"

"Cut it out! I'm saying there's a whole lot more to either one of us than how we look, for Christ's sake. A hundred years of the women's movement, and you're fixated on not being beautiful enough to be loved? Besides, you may not be Kate Moss, but you've got your own look. Don't you get that a guy like Ben wouldn't fall for a dog?"

Ariel laughed at the irony of it. "You realize you've just simultaneously told me that looks don't count and that I'm attractive enough for Ben."

Terry laughed. Then she grabbed her friend's hand. "But that's just part of it. Don't think I didn't notice that Magna Cum Laude after your name at graduation. You're sharp as a tack, even if you are inclined to loony adventures."

Ariel pulled away, muttering, "Not funny," but she didn't feel combative anymore, just tired and scared and confused.

"No, really, with some actual stimulation, you could really take off."

Ariel snickered derisively, but she was also touched by Terry's concern. She'd never told her about her flying lessons. She did now.

"And there I was; I'd saved up all that money for a million years, just so I could become a pilot, and once I actually went up in the air, I totally lost it."

Terry found her way to Ariel's side. "I didn't know. Oh baby, I'm so sorry."

"The thing is, Ter, pilots use the word *angel* as slang for each thousand miles of altitude. But for me, terror became a devil that dogged me during every millisecond of ascent. It broke my heart, but I could not wait to get back down."

"What is it?" Selma said groggily. "How long have I been asleep? Have Jane and ... *Oy*, my rotten memory, what is his name? Have they come back for us?"

With an anxious start, Ariel realized that Jane and Theosophus were taking an awfully long time.

––––––––––––––––

Theosophus was beginning to doubt that he and Jane would make it through. He'd aimed for Royce Hall, the closest building to Haines, but so much water had spilled into this part of the tunnel from broken pipes, and the pass-through area was so low and tight, that they had to push themselves to keep going despite the twin terrors of suffocation and drowning. Theosophus kept Jane talking to him, as much for his own sake as hers.

The kid was a champ. He knew lots of guys who would have panicked before now. She just kept inching along in front of him, while he kept the flashlight poised over her head, his hand cramping, to light her way. If they could just make it to the next bend, they could be home free. Royce Hall had been reinforced after the Northridge Quake, and he was banking on it holding up this time around.

He hadn't reckoned, though, on the aftershock that hit right then. It rose up quickly, roaring, and heaved them back and forth like a distracted parent pushing her hapless children on the swings.

He stretched his arms and torso over Jane's body like a Halloween ghost, inadvertently dropping his flashlight in his rush to shield her from falling debris. He cursed as he heard the glass break. Their small beacon of light went out. The tunnel continued to rock and moan for a few more unbearable seconds, and even after the temblor died down, Jane kept squealing like a stuck pig. "Holy Jesus! Ma! Theosophus, please don't let me die."

Small chunks of concrete rained onto his back. He couldn't hold out much longer. His lifted his head upwards in a last-ditch appeal to Granny to save them.

Theosophus gasped. A glimmer of light showed through a small crack in the tunnel ceiling. The sound that came out of him was like a peacock's scream. Jane echoed him with her own screeching. It was only when the two of them paused to gather fresh breath that they heard a third and then fourth voice join the fray. Except that the latter two made words with their sounds. He felt confused. In the state he was in, he'd lost his capacity to understand language. But the strangers' intonations meant something to him; authoritative, reassuring, the sound of their voices seemed to signify that help was at hand.

Thirty-four

BEN JUMPED IN his seat as a siren blared suddenly behind him. He swung his car frantically to the right until the red cross on the ambulance's side blurred passed. With the city's electric grid down and piles of rubble here and there, the streets of L.A. had been rendered a barely visible obstacle course. He wiped a trembling hand across his forehead. Sweat was oozing from every pore of his body. He cursed the Santa Anas for this heat, as well as the wildfire whose proliferating ash forced him to keep his car windows closed.

Making a turn, he slowed to a crawl until his lights picked out a group of people huddled on the sidewalk. "Yes!" he crowed, as he recognized a few familiar faces. He left the Jeep, lights on and parked at an awkward angle to the curb, and ran toward his apartment building. His hand slammed his chest as he saw a sheet of what looked like roofing shingles on the sidewalk.

Ben's eyes raked the small crowd of neighbors sharing war stories on the front lawn. A few held candles, and another couple of candles had been set down on the grass. He approached the group, asking if anyone had seen Ariel. As they shook their heads and commiserated at the loss of cell phone service, he flew to the door of Apartment 204, relying on the faint light from his car to help him navigate. He rang the bell. No answer. "Shit." He pounded at the door and cried her name repeatedly. Still no reply.

He tried the knob, then kicked the door viciously, but it wouldn't budge. He shrugged, moved back from the door and ran at it like a crazed bull. With pain searing through his shoulder and the sound of splintering wood still echoing in his ears, he stood inside Ariel's living room.

Without the benefit of his headlights, the world was black again. Shouting Ariel's name, he stumbled from room to room.

He couldn't find her anywhere. Only the bathroom was left. Reaching around blindly, his hand hit a pipe-like object almost as high as his chest, and he slid his fingers along it. It took him a minute to realize that the shower rod had fallen into the tub, one end of it projecting over the toilet tank like a flagpole. Just in case, he felt around gingerly underneath the shower curtain and sprung back hastily as he encountered something soft. The room suddenly felt very cold. "Ariel?" he whispered. He reached forward gently. When his fingertips once again met their object, he experienced a momentary disorientation before he realized that what they were touching was Jezebel's fur.

As he exited Ariel's apartment, propping the broken door closed as best he could, Ben tried to talk himself down from a gathering hysteria. *Okay, okay. Think this through. The quake hit long after she would have finished her mail route. Where could she have gone after work?*

He was so preoccupied that he failed to notice that the front of the building was now extremely well-lit, his own car's headlights having inspired several of the neighbors to position their cars so that they faced the building with their own headlights on. One of Ben's neighbors, a tattooed man who was hauling a couple of large Arrowhead bottles out of his trunk, set down his burden and walked toward him. He said, "Hey, man, you okay?"

Ben looked up blindly.

"I said, are you in trouble? Need some help? We did a door-to-door check already, you know. It looks like there's not too much damage. I'm pretty sure everybody rode it out just fine."

Ben walked past him blindly. *Selma's,* he thought. *I'll bet that's where she is. It'll be faster on foot.* He leaned into the Jeep and turned off the lights, then broke into a run.

Close to an hour later and gasping for breath, Ben neared the intersection of La Cienega and Third Street. His heart sank. While few cars save emergency vehicles roamed the streets, a huge crowd of people on foot were moving like refugees toward Cedars, where he himself was heading. Having learned from Mrs. G's garrulous next-door neighbor that there'd been a death and a fire at Selma's home that day, and having satisfied himself that neither Selma nor Ariel were there, he was making his way to what he hoped was the logical next step, praying that the images that tormented him—the two of them mummified in white gauze in some Burn Unit, skin charred down to the bone—weren't true. His own chest felt like it was on fire.

As if they were playing the old childhood game "Freeze," the crowd stopped still for a brief moment as a huge bank of lights, obviously the product of emergency generators, lit up the area. Some wise-ass behind him shouted, "Local government is ... once again ... your friend." A few others laughed and cheered, but then the crowd quickly resumed its pushing and shoving. Ben shouldered his way toward a scene that suggested some mainstream contemporary version of Woodstock, with all races and religions gathered here, as if the City of Angels were truly the diverse melting pot the mayor touted it to be (though with the proliferation of ash, almost everyone looked pretty gray).

A winded Ben sat abruptly down on the northwest corner of Third Street and San Vicente, next to an exhausted-looking firefighter. He nearly laughed when the guy reached into his pocket and pulled out a pack of Marlboros and a well-creased matchbook.

Without a word, the fireman held out his pack to Ben. The man smiled as Ben pointed to his rising and falling chest. The guy raised an eyebrow as he lit up. It was all Ben could do to try to calm his breathing. Still, the smoke that wafted from the man's cigarette smelled tempting. Ben learned that the firefighter was a captain and that his name was Jeff Levine. When the quake hit, Jeff had already been pulling overtime on the Malibu fire assignment. Then the reports of damage to Cedars had come in. He'd been reassigned here to help coordinate the movement of the injured from Cedars to other hospitals. Their five minutes of smoking together on the curb of San Vicente and Third—Ben had finally given in—was the only break Jeff had gotten in about twelve hours and the only one he was likely to get for some time. They'd sat together just long enough to share their personal worries: Jeff about his wife and two young kids in Sherman Oaks, Ben about Ariel.

By the time Jeff stood up and began to gather his gear together—

his cigarettes, his ash-smudged yellow helmet, a mobile dispatch radio—Ben had enough time to scan the huge wave of people now lapping at the beleaguered Cedars. How would he ever get inside to look for Ariel? Already, frantic hospital administrators were announcing through bullhorns that the hospital was full beyond capacity, though they promised that National Guard personnel were on their way with staff and equipment to deal with genuine emergencies.

Ben glanced at Jeff, who was bent over tying the heavy laces of his dusty boot. "Hey, man, I wonder if there's any way you could get me inside there?"

Jeff shook his head. "Believe me, if there was any way I could, I would." He gestured at the multitudes that continued to pour around them. "You can see what I've got to deal with here." He reached out a sooty hand to shake Ben's. "But, hey, I sure hope they're okay. Don't give up hope."

Hope. How could he maintain that with his head full of gruesome pictures and his body as heavy as lead?

Jeff's radio crackled into life. Ben couldn't help but lean forward in curiosity as Jeff did, so quickly that the two of them knocked foreheads, then broke into slightly forced laughter to hide their embarrassment. They stopped, puzzled, when it seemed like the radio was laughing with them. But no, Ben thought, in a surreal moment, they can't see or hear us.

But there really was laughter barking out from the radio. The dispatcher's words were sputtering between hysterical gusts. He and Jeff struggled to make out the gravel-voiced female dispatcher's words amid the laughter and the inevitable static.

"A little comic relief here, guys. You never know what's gonna crawl out of the woodwork when disaster hits. This time, we've got a report coming in from the Unicops at UCLA. They were checking for damage to a few of the older buildings there. Now they say a couple of homeless people just emerged from the utility tunnel system, mumbling a cock-and-bull story about some women looking for Adam and Eve's bones buried under there."

Before the radio went silent, Ben was gone.

Nearing his apartment building, he felt vainly in his jeans pockets for his keys. Nothing. He realized he must have left them in the car. He prayed that no one had stolen it. He was going to need it to get to UCLA. Turning onto Poinsettia, he looked heavenward in gratitude. The Jeep was still there. But he ran right past the vehicle and up the concrete walkway to Apartment 204. There was just one thing he had to do.

Thirty-five

BEN WASN'T THE only one making his way toward the sprawling UCLA campus. Matt Hayes had far less ground to cover as he navigated his BMW through the winding avenues of residential Westwood, but he took almost as much time, stopping at almost every block to try to improve the reception of the squawking cell phone pressed to his ear.

When the first temblor hit, he'd had his hands full making sure that his wife and daughters were okay, and then humoring an irrational Bonnie by stowing her jewels in his trunk before he left for UCLA. He had to contend with a series of acerbic calls from Chancellor Biggs, still back East for his son's wedding, demanding that he get the fuck over to the campus and cover both of their asses. It took a creatively-inspired pretense of another major aftershock, with a thoroughly fed up Matt yelling devilishly, "Oh, my God, the humanity," to shame Biggs off the line once and for all.

After a few botched attempts, Matt had managed to reach Burt Weston and to carry on a series of fragmented conversations with him, cursing the primitive crudeness of cell phone technology every time they lost their connection. Only later would he learn that it wasn't so much the lousy technology as the overloading of circuits that was getting in the way. In call number three Weston informed him that some of the tunnels seemed to have collapsed, and then in number four, Burt reported agitatedly that some people, including an old woman who might be unable to walk, were trapped down there. Weston said that their rescuers reported that two of an original group of five had been freed, adding, "Thank God, they're not students or faculty or even university staff. Just a couple of homeless people."

Just, thought Matt, but he didn't want to offend Burt right then by saying anything. Burt's being Johnny-on-the-spot was the only thing standing between Matt and certain unemployment if anybody died down there, especially after Matt had lazily left it up to Burt to check out the utilities shut-down. He realized now that it was undoubtedly some initial shifting of the ground that had put the system on the fritz, then he cursed as the connection went yet again.

He was just about to punch in re-dial when the cell phone signaled a new call from Burt, an excited one. It turned out that one of the rescued duo was a previous employee, a janitor who apparently knew exactly where the still-trapped women were and had some ideas about how they could be extricated.

When Burt told him that the man's name was Theosophus Kelly, Matt nearly dropped the phone. His forehead wrinkled in perplexity. Theo? Previous employee? Matt felt terrible. He'd been good enough to buy weed from and bar-hop with in the old days, but not good enough, evidently, to keep in touch with as his own fortunes had continued to climb. *Shit.*

Matt had to stop himself from lighting the roach in his center console cup holder as he remembered watching the eager little boy take his first triumphant lap across the public pool too many summers ago to count.

———————————

As Matt's BMW swerved around a downed tree into one of the easternmost entrances to the campus, Ben abandoned his Jeep in front of the Student Union. He willed his protesting calf muscles to propel him up Bruin Walk toward the Quad that anchored the older part of the campus.

When he crested the rise, he saw a crowd—some in uniforms, some holding shovels, others obviously from the media—gathered around an excavation site surrounded by ugly piles of broken concrete, dirt, and turned-up grass. He ran toward them.

Two still figures stood in their midst, their eyes locked on what was happening at the center of the restless gathering. But their postures were tentative, as if they really didn't belong. They were covered from head to toe with chalky dust. One was a compelling-looking black man with eyes that turned down at the corners. He had his arm around a wide-eyed teenaged girl whose arms looked like she'd run a thorny gauntlet. Ben edged his way toward the front of the tense group of bystanders. From the edge of the chasm, a red-faced laborer called down to his co-workers below. "Take it slow now. We want 'em out alive."

Matt had reached the Quad just seconds after Ben. Catching sight of Theo, he flew to his side and began peppering him with questions. "Are you okay? Do you know who's down there? Are they alive?"

Theo nodded without looking at him, his eyes glued on the laboring men. "There's three of 'em, and so far's I know, they're still alive. Don't know their last names. Ariel, Selma, and Terry's how I know 'em."

Matt's face went white. "Holy Jesus."

Theosophus nodded. "You can say that again." His voice shook slightly. "You better pray Holy Jesus is looking out for them. That earth is unsteady as a woman full of the Holy Spirit, weavin' and fallin' in a crowded church."

Ben had broken out in a cold sweat. For God's sake, what was taking them so long? At last, somebody called out, "Here goes nothin'," and a line of grunting men pulled hard on their rope. Ben's eyes bulged as he watched a worn-looking Ariel slowly rise from the dark confines of the earth. Her hair was like a nest of writhing snakes. Worry lines streaked her filthy forehead, which had a purple knob the size of a plum on one side of it.

Ariel stumbled up to ground level, gasping with relief. Two of the diggers awkwardly struggled to untie the rope that circled her under her armpits. A fresh-faced younger version of Katie Couric eagerly thrust a mike up to her face.

"Jesus Fucking H. Christ." Ariel waved the blanching young reporter away. She turned back toward the chasm. "Mrs. G, Mrs. G!" Ariel gesticulated anxiously to the rescue team. "Oh, God, now we know it's safe, get her up." Her voice was surprisingly commanding. "Hurry!"

Two paramedics appeared on the periphery of the crowd, carrying a stretcher, but then one of the men standing at the edge of the pit waved widely, and Ben saw Ariel move back a few paces as two men lifted another figure from the earth. A tightly-packed bundle of an old woman pushed away the proffered arm of a Unicop, as if to demonstrate that she could stand on her own two feet, thank you very much. Ben couldn't help but grin.

And then a respectful hush broke over the rescue team as Terry was pulled up and out of the tunnel, her good looks undiminished by the dirty confines of that stricken underworld. Her big brown eyes flashed as the assembled group of men broke into loud applause

Ben saw Ariel look around wildly, then grin as she caught sight of the grubby-looking couple at the edge of the crowd. Effusively burbling her thanks to the assembled dirt-smudged rescuers, she began to edge toward the first two who'd been rescued. Ben hurried toward her, and when she saw him she stopped dead in her tracks. He knew he would never forget seeing her eyes moisten and her hand clutch her heart in relief. He came right up to her and further unzipped the slightly-open backpack he'd been carrying.

Shooting him a mingled look of disbelief and gratitude, she took what he'd brought her and dropped to her knees, laughing crazily as tears forged dirt tracks down her cheeks. "Oh, Jezzie, you're alive, you're alive," she cried, as she buried her face in the purring animal's dark fur. She looked up at Ben and soundlessly mouthed the words, "And you are, too. Thank God. And thank you."

Ben and Matt weren't the only ones vibrating with anxiety at that rescue scene. As soon as she and Theosophus had scrambled up from their living grave, Jane Deare had been battling the familiar sensation of unreality that crept over her when her system went on overload.

When she was trapped in the tunnel with Theosophus piled on top of her and debris falling around them like a demonic hailstorm, her body had a life of its own that made her limbs flail under her protector's weight, like a fish caught in rocks close to the shore. But once above ground, her world switched to slo-mo: Theosophus shouting suggestions to the rescue workers, the way their shovels teased and finally penetrated the ground, other people appearing on the scene, yelling, gesticulating. She barely noticed when a well-dressed blond man appeared at Theosophus's other side.

Only when Ariel emerged from the ragged earth did time start to speed up. Jane put her hand to her forehead, overtaken by dizziness.

Suddenly voices got loud and arms were thrust around her. She looked up into the relieved faces of Ariel and Terry and burst into tears. She didn't know why she was crying, but she couldn't stop. If anything, the more the two women looked at her with such palpable concern, the more out-of-control she felt.

She sagged to her knees. She looked up at them and tore at her hair. As the two of them struggled to grab hold of her agitated hands and lift her up again, she slapped at their arms and shouted with the full horror of her realization. "Danny! Danny's dead. He stopped breathing. I couldn't help him. I saw him die."

Selma insinuated her body past Ariel and Terry's helpless hands and wrapped the sobbing girl in her arms, murmuring and making soft clucking noises of comfort. "Of course, you did. You poor *bubbeleh*. You were his angel, his Godsend. He chose you for it. It was a *mitzvah*. So he didn't have to die alone."

Thirty-six

FROM A DISTANCE of fifty feet, Matt couldn't tell what the hell the women were doing. Like Jane, he'd barely been able to breathe as first Ariel and then Selma were hauled out of the dark earth like a couple of twins torn from their mother by C-section, and when Terry's tousled head had finally risen above the top of the gaping hole, a wild cry had escaped his lips.

It took a nudge from Theosophus to call his attention at that moment to his ringing cell phone. Matt's eyes had been riveted on Terry, who was scanning the crowd. Spotting Matt, she'd straightened and flashed him a warm smile.

He tried to send her an equally enthusiastic message with his eyes as he took the call and tersely answered, "Matt Hayes," about ready to tell Biggs to fuck off. But it was Holly, sounding excited. "Daddy? Oh, Daddy. I can't believe it. We've been listening to the radio, and the reporter's been giving us a blow-by-blow on the rescue. Are the people really okay? Mommy says to tell you to be careful. It's a little scary here, with the aftershocks and all. Oh, Daddy, I can't wait until you come home."

He mumbled a few reassuring words into the phone and ended the call, glaring down at the torn-up earth as if it were jinxing him. Fighting the suffocating lump that had risen in his throat, he watched the ritual of the crying girl and her comforters. From his left, he noticed that Burt Weston was approaching him. The zealous young reporter followed fast on Burt's heels. As Matt began to speak into her microphone, he managed to catch Terry's eye. She flicked him a hurt look, then offered her arm to Selma.

Matt had his charm routine down so pat that a good part of his mind could actually travel free while he gave the excited cub reporter what she'd come to him for: dramatic phrases and clever quips to throw at her network's dogged appetite for ever higher ratings. On tiptoes as she held the mike up toward his face, she looked barely older than Holly and just as unworldly. Matt felt terribly ancient himself. He stole a glance at his old friend Theo. He'd obviously been through some kind of hell.

The reporter finished with him at last and, like a bloodhound, zeroed in on Theo and his harem of rescued women. Matt tried to make eye-contact with Terry again, but he'd lost her. She was gabbing a mile a minute with her companions. He turned away from the crowd and looked northward, where the sky was lit with a gorgeous orange-reddish hue as if it were heralding the Second Coming.

He tried to pull himself together. He had Bonnie, didn't he? Wholesome, decent Bonnie. He sighed. Something about Bonnie just poured right through him without making a dent, like the time as an undergrad that he'd taken LSD and was thirsty, but no amount of water could slake his thirst. He wanted a spliff. He looked at Theosophus, at the cluster of women grabbing him, hugging him. How long, Matt wondered, have I felt so dead and so alone?

As it turned out, Matt didn't have much time to philosophize. As the reporter and her crew packed up their gear, Biggs finally managed to get through to him, barking out commands. Like Holly, he'd heard the live interview and was cackling with the possibilities for milking the rescue drama for a bonanza of future fund-raising. By the time Matt had made the necessary calls to get the publicity mill churning, he was disgusted, depressed, and ready to go home.

He tried to catch Terry's eye before she and the other women moved toward a Jeep that had pulled up in front of Haines Hall. But she was avoiding his gaze, and he had to admit that he didn't blame her.

Only Theosophus remained, sprawled on the ground with his swollen feet stretched out in front of him. Matt had signaled Theosophus earlier to wait for him and had just as promptly forgotten about him as he made his round of calls. As Matt registered how worn out the man looked, he felt deeply ashamed. He shoved the cell phone into his pocket and strode toward his old friend.

Theosophus looked up, his sad-dog eyes lifting at the corners. Matt fished in his pants pocket as his belly started churning acid. Putting a hand on Theosophus's shoulder, he suggested that he come home with him, unaware of the chalky white Tums residue spidering the creases of his lips.

Although Theosophus simply said, "Thanks, man," the relief on his weary face said it all.

But as they approached Matt's ash-covered BMW, Theosophus turned to Matt in a panic. He gestured expressively at his torn and filthy clothing. "You got some newspaper or a blanket or something in your trunk? I can't get in your car like this."

"Jesus, Theo, will you just get in? What kind of a pussy do you take me for?"

Now that the sun had come up, it took no time at all for Matt to dodge downed signs and navigate around the debris-littered side streets of residential Westwood back to the house. Bonnie and the girls rushed out as soon as he pulled the Beamer up the sloping driveway. It didn't take much to notice that Bonnie's relief at his safe return was leavened by dismay at his choice of houseguest. Matt prayed that Theo hadn't noticed Bonnie's frown.

It was a good couple of hours before he could lead Theosophus out back to the converted pool house that he called his studio and actually get him alone.

Matt locked the French doors of the studio and drew the cotton-duck curtains closed. Noting that Theo—who now wore one of Matt's thick Turkish towel robes and a pair of his pristine white socks—looked like a different man after his bath, he motioned for him to take a seat on one of the two cheap rattan chairs in the cluttered room.

With a sly smile, he pulled out a spliff.

Theo's sad face was suddenly transformed and he shook his head wonderingly. "My man," he said.

Matt held out the spliff, and Theo started to reach for it, but then he pulled back. "Wait a minute. Before we go pretending nothing's happened, there's some things I got to say. I let you down, man, that's the truth of it. Lost my job and my self-respect in one move, no better than a drunken hobo. You went to bat for me two times—when I was a kid, and then when you got me my job at UCLA." Theo hung his head. "And I screwed it all up with the liquor. I don't know what happened. Thought I could hold it as good as the next man, then it kind of crept up on me, sometime after my brother Gwayne died." He shrugged. "I know that's no excuse. It's just that it kind of took me sideways. The last of my flesh and blood I was still in touch with. My sisters'd just up and disappeared on me a couple of years before. Suddenly I was wanting to drink all the time. It got so's I was reaching for the bottle earlier and earlier in the day till my foreman caught me passed out in Ackerman with a fifth of Old Taylor still in my hand." He started to laugh, then caught himself. "How's a thing like that happen, man?" Matt just stared back at him. "Well, I guess it don't matter, since it ain't for damn sure gonna happen again. I won't let it. I just hate to think how I let you down."

Matt snapped, "Don't talk to me about letting people down. I'm the king of it."

Theosophus eyed him cautiously, but when Matt failed to amplify, he rushed on. "Any chance I could get my old job back, I would surely appreciate it. I swear I wouldn't let you down again." His fists clenched and unclenched at his sides. "I just gotta get back on my feet again, and I don't know any other way than going back to work for you."

Slumped in his chair like a teenager, Matt took a couple of deep tokes. "Work for me?" His heavy-lidded eyes scanned the messy room. "Hmm, now that's an idea. Work for me." He thrust the spliff at Theo, leaned his head back, and gazed at him with stoned languor.

Theo stared down at the spliff as if he'd never seen one before.

Suddenly, Matt sat up straight. "Hey, man, I've got a great idea. You know, Bonnie's been bugging me to get a full-time handyman for ages, and there's a nanny flat over the garage that we've never used." He reached under his shirt and scratched his flat belly.

Theo's dark eyes narrowed and he shoved the spliff back at Matt. "I don't want no handouts."

"Whoa, man. Wait a minute. Don't get paranoid on me. I mean it. It'd be cool. It's the perfect solution. I could get Burt to hire you back, easy, after how you helped those women get rescued ..." He winced, remembering Terry's delighted smile at him when she emerged from that living grave. He forced himself to go on. "But you still need a place to stay until you get enough bread together to rent your own place. Sure, if you wanted, I could lend you the money to get an apartment—"

"Look here, that's just what I don't want. I been begging too much already."

"But that's the beauty of it, see? Nobody would be giving you anything. You'd be working for your lodgings, earning it with your labor on the weekends and stuff. Come on, man, you know it's perfect. Shake on it with me." He smiled disarmingly.

Theo just stared at his outstretched hand. Matt was high enough by then to interpret his wary grin as agreement.

Matt got up, nearly stumbling over a pile of old high school yearbooks. He went behind a ripped nautical-blue chaise lounge and, as he disappeared from view, said in a muffled voice, "Hey, there's something I gotta show you ..." He re-emerged, breathing heavily, with a dusty old-fashioned record player gripped awkwardly in his arms. "Glad I never threw this baby away." He set the machine down on a tall cardboard box, and began dusting it off with the bottom of his shirt. "And I do believe I've got some old LP's around here somewhere."

As Bobby "Blue" Bland sang balefully about having to use his imagination to keep on keeping on, Matt scooted his rattan chair closer to his friend and re-lit his spliff. He passed it to Theo, who still refused to take a toke.

Matt felt the rebuff as if it were personal, but then the silky darkness of Bobby Bland's voice enveloped him. It was true, he didn't have the guts to leave Bonnie and he'd probably never see Terry again. But swaying to Wayne Bennett's crying guitar, he thought hazily, I guess when all else fails, I'll still have the Blues.

Thirty-seven

THEOSOPHUS AWOKE WITH a start. His heart beating erratically, he looked around, wondering where he was. Reaching down to his dick for a primitive kind of reassurance, he realized he was naked. He'd slept curled up in a fetal ball, and now, as his legs broke free into a full-out stretch, he was surprised at the silky feel of the material that covered him. His eyes slowly adjusted to the faint light that was just beginning to penetrate through the expensive curtains of Matt and Bonnie's guest bedroom. A delicate silver alarm clock on the bedside table told him it wasn't quite five o'clock.

Eyes wide open, he lay still as a stone, the events of the past day crowding his mind. He wondered how his tunnel companions were doing and realized that he'd probably never see them again.

Somewhere, a mockingbird began to sing, sweet and clear. He marveled at the infinite variety of its calls, then laughed when a chorus of sparrows and a couple of haranguing crows joined in. He felt relieved. If another big aftershock were coming, the birds wouldn't be singing; they'd be laying low. He heard a door slam and sat up hastily, holding the pale-green silk bedclothes against his thickly-matted chest. A loud fart let itself out without warning, and he cringed, worrying that Matt's wife was close enough outside his door to hear him. He suddenly recalled something that his mind had half-registered yesterday—Bonnie, betrayed through a revealing ornamental hall mirror, holding his clothes like they had the cooties on them as she snuck down the hall.

He leapt out of bed. There was no way in hell that he could imagine living here, even if it meant sleeping under sheets that almost gave you a hard-on with the feel of them, even if it meant a quick end to sleeping rough.

He tiptoed into the adjacent bathroom, shaking his head at the sight of the Jacuzzi bathtub in the corner. Though his holey brown socks seemed to have gone missing, he was relieved that his scruffy Oxfords were parked discretely on the black-and-turquoise tile floor with his black and white photo of Granny carefully spread inside the right one; a pair of better and newer socks tucked into the left; and that his clothes, washed and pressed—probably by Bonnie—and even stitched up neatly where they'd gotten torn, were folded into a neat pile next to the sink. He did a quick double-take before rushing to the toilet to relieve himself. The sink was actually adorned with an exotic scene of riotously-colored flowers and butterflies.

Minutes later, Theosophus slipped out the front door, a cleaner man but a guilty one— hyper-aware of Matt's expensively cushioned socks on his feet.

He was amazed at how unscathed most of these houses of the privileged looked, though a few had lost their chimneys to the quake. He wondered whether Mother Nature had been as kind to his brothers and sisters in the 'hood. But as he turned a corner and walked up a hill lined with sorority houses, he saw signs of significantly more damage. Walls and walkways bore large spidery cracks, and several big jacaranda branches were downed, making the sidewalk into a purple hazard course. Though he spied a few cats skulking around as if they were still spooked by the shaking and weren't too happy with the ashy air quality either, there were no signs of human life anywhere. It was as if the city were sleeping off the quake like a bad hangover.

The campus was just as quiet, and the first buildings he passed— including the Admin. Building where he'd been hired—looked untouched. Walking past a barely recognizable Schoenberg Hall, home to the Music Department, where he used to polish rows of exquisite ebony pianos, he realized that here, too, some of the buildings looked like they'd been shaken by a mother under too much pressure, venting her rage on some of her kids and sparing the others.

He approached the gaping chasm where he'd directed the rescuers to dig. Even in the gathering morning light, he could see nothing, only that it was dark down there, a place darker and tighter than he'd ever want to be again.

As if out of nowhere, a voice whispered into his ear.

"They say it's hard not to come back to the scene of the crime."

He spun around. "Well, I'll be. What got you up so early, Miss Terry Mae?"

She grinned wryly. "Same as you, maybe. When I woke up, I wasn't sure it hadn't all been a dream, so I had to come and check it out." She arched an eyebrow. "You're looking good. Seems like you got all cleaned up. Where've you been?"

He motioned her toward the steps of the Powell Library and settled down beside her. "I got lucky, saw a man I'd been about to go looking for anyway. My old boss." He hesitated. "I guess you could call him an old friend, too. Leastwise, someone I knew from back when I was a boy. He's Vice-Chancellor here. Name's Matt Hayes."

He could sense Terry stiffen beside him. Aw nuts, he thought. She thought he was making it up. "I know it's hard to believe. It's a long story, but I swear on the memory of my granny I'm not lying to you." Terry didn't say a thing. "Hey, now, I'm telling you the truth; don't do me like that." Still, she averted her head. He was getting angry now. He put a hand on her shoulder and pulled her around to face him. He was stunned to see silent tears streaming down her face. "Holy Jesus, what'd I say?"

She shook her tangled mane of hair and wiped her face with the back of her hand. "You must think I'm an absolute nut case. Matt Hayes was my boyfriend. A long time ago. We reconnected recently." She lowered her face and fished around in her purse for a cigarette. She let him light it for her and took a couple of quick drags. "I thought ... I mean, he arranged to meet me." Her face flushed. "At a hotel, for God's sake." She looked away in embarrassment. "Shameless. And a fool. He never showed up. I guess you know that he's married." She shrugged. "I don't know what I was thinking."

It was the fact that Matt had stood Terry up that dumbfounded him. Matt Hayes had a chance to be with this woman and had chosen that ice queen of a wife instead? No wonder he was popping Tums like candy and smoking weed every day. The man was sick.

"Shoot, girl, that woman don't hold a candle to you. She could be the wife of a Kleagle of the KKK for the way she looked at me. Now, I know that Matt's not like that himself. It's almost like he's white, but don't want to be. If anything, he's so hungry for soul you can almost taste it. But that Bonnie of his, she's like some version of anti-soul." But Terry looked more and more down-at-the-mouth as he talked. "I ain't making it no better, am I, Miss Terry Mae?"

She frowned. "If she's so bad, then what's wrong with me?"

"Well now, he does have a couple of kids. Maybe he loves you more than her, but he figures he's got to do the right thing. Those girls of his are grown and to my mind it'd be no sin at all to split from their mama. But with some folks, you never know what they believe."

He felt like he was digging a hole as deep as the one in the middle of the Quad.

"But, wait," he said consideringly, "maybe we're looking at this whole thing the wrong side around. He's from the past, see? Maybe you ain't supposed to go back. Maybe that ain't the way to move on."

He scanned the nearby buildings. He didn't even have to think how to do his old job; he could go through the motions of it like some sleepwalker. But there was a down side to that. One thing he'd actually relished about his life on the rough was that it had kept him on his toes all the time, forced him to do what he used to call his "thinkin' in between the drinkin'" just to stay alive.

He turned to Terry and spoke with a surprising urgency. "Miss Terry Mae, I do believe I owe you something." She eyed him quizzically. "What if neither one of us was meant to go backward? Not you, with that fool of a Matt Hayes, and not me, either? I was so fixed on trying to get me back my old job, but maybe I need to be doing something else now."

———————————

For Terry, comprehension dawned suddenly and it came with a secondary kick. She hadn't known what in the world he'd been talking about. Going on and on about not moving backwards. But then he'd finally explained himself, and his smile had so transformed his face that he looked ten years younger and so suddenly handsome that she ached inside. She leaned back and tried to consider him objectively. No, she wasn't wrong, how could she have missed it before? He was such a sweet-faced man, but with the touch of an impish light in his eyes. She couldn't believe that yesterday she was so untrusting of him just because he looked and smelled like a bum. She flinched as her conscience kicked into high gear. Admit it to yourself, Terry, she thought, he also made you nervous because he was lower-class and black.

"Look," she said, "Did you eat anything this morning?" He shook his head. "Me neither. How about coming back to my apartment for some pancakes and bacon?" She laughed. "Unless you're a vegetarian." She stood up and gestured with her head. "My car's down the hill near Ackerman." Dusting herself off and grabbing her purse, she said, "I mean, if you'd like to continue the conversation—"

They had to go through what felt like some ritual of him asking several times, "Are you sure?" and her responding increasingly emphatically, "Yes, of course I am." But once that had been settled, she was surprised how comfortable she felt driving him back to her place, the two of them not talking much, except to point out signs of damage along the way and to comment on the citywide disaster reports being obsessively re-capped by a deep-voiced announcer on her car radio.

She left him sitting in her living room, while she went into a storm of activity in the kitchen. They ate quietly, companionably. Terry noticed that he used his utensils in the European style and that he smothered his bacon in syrup, along with his pancakes. When she teased him about it, he looked so sheepish that she skewered a piece of bacon from her own plate and swirled it around in the thick sea of syrup on his dish, lifting it to her lips with a wink.

As he leaned back in his chair, she got up to refill their coffee mugs. He told her it was the best he'd had in a long, long time: black and strong. She didn't know why, but it made her feel happy that he liked it the way she made it.

They talked about what it would mean for him to find another kind of job. He looked upset, said he didn't know how to do anything else, and besides, who would hire him after having been out of work for more than a year?

Terry had worked in what she thought of as the *mondo bizarro* stratospheres of motion picture publicity for too long to be daunted by the constraints of objective reality. She knew how much the world they lived in was crafted out of a combination of desperation, will, and the evident limitlessness of the human imagination. She urged him, "Forget about what you think you're qualified for. What would you like to do?"

"I've been concentrating on just getting myself through the day, talking folks out of their spare change, enough to buy me some Old Taylor and a little food now and then—though nuthin'," he said, smiling charmingly, "like this meal here, fit for a king. And that ain't all. Finding me a place to shit in private. Excuse me for saying it, Miss Terry Mae, but that's one of the hard realities of living on the street, and it ain't so easy. Sometimes takes half a day to scope it out. And then there's avoiding Mr. Police Man. And crackheads and bullies and mean sonsabitches who like to set fire to men like me, black and homeless and, I'm shamed to say, drunk as a hoot owl, while we sleep." He raised his hands beseechingly. "Now who'd have time in there to even consider what I'd like to do?"

Terry lit a cigarette, exhaling a couple of perfect smoke circles and then poking a finger through one of them. "Well, Mr. Theosophus Kelly Mae, you've got the time now." He laughed, but then she sat up straighter, her expression intent. "Let me ask you something. When you were younger, before living on the street, before working at UCLA, what did you used to like to do? Any hobbies?"

He snorted. "Girl, don't you know hobbies is a word white people made up? Only hobbies I ever had was go to clubs, hear me some good R&B, dance with the hottest women I could find, get high. And get laid."

Terry refused to dignify that last comment with a response. She massaged a knot in her shoulder. "God, I wish I could have a swim, work these kinks out. That tunnel was a monster. Maybe I'll take a bath instead. Would you mind? I'll be right back out; I think we should keep talking about this." She held his eyes for a moment. "Seriously. But right this second, my body's killing me." She clasped her hands behind her and tried to crack her back, but her spine was too tight for even that. "Besides, I probably stink to high heaven. I don't know how you could stand sitting in the same room with me." She grinned.

As she walked toward her bathroom, he said, "Swim?"

She glanced back at him for a moment. "What?"

"You like to swim?"

"Mm," she said, as she disappeared into the tiny hallway.

Rummaging in her linen closet for a couple of clean towels, she kept talking, raising her voice so he could hear her. "Yeah, it's my favorite thing to relax my muscles and my mind. Almost like a meditation. I usually go every other morning before work to the Culver City Y." She appeared at the doorway for a moment with a couple of dusty-rose towels in her hands. "I used to be a camp counselor there, way back when I was in high school. They were like a second family to me." She bent over suddenly to scratch her ankle, mumbling distractedly that they must have fleas in the tunnels. She straightened. "As a matter of fact, the same director of the swim program is still there. He's a good buddy of mine. A sweet old guy. They've got a great indoor pool. After school hours, the kids come for their lessons and free swimming, but it's all adults—nice and quiet—in the morning."

Terry walked over to the table to retrieve her half-full mug of coffee and saw that, though Theosophus was staring in her direction, his eyes were glassy, as if he were looking right through her. She turned on her heels and entered her cramped bathroom, flicking on the light switch with her elbow. She lay the towels down on the side of the tub, yanked hard at the two resistant knobs, and gulped down the last of her coffee as she stared at herself in the quickly-misting vanity mirror. She leaned over to turn off the tub taps, then automatically pulled her periwinkle T-shirt over her head.

Suddenly her arms broke out in gooseflesh. She had the feeling that she was being watched and realized with a pang that she'd been living alone so long she'd forgotten to shut the door. She stood stock-still and stared fixedly at her barely visible torso in the steamy mirror. Then, just as suddenly as it had arisen, her apprehension left her, as ephemeral and insignificant as a soap bubble. Slowly, without once looking toward the open doorway, she continued to undress, removing first her bra, then her dusty jeans, and finally her orange-and-white-striped bikini panties, turning just slightly, this way and that, to give the man she knew was staring at her a full view. Strangely, it didn't feel seductive or dangerous or cheesy. More like an act of mercy. He'd saved her life, for Christ sake. If he liked to look, why shouldn't she let him see?

———————————

As he watched her strip to the bare bones of her matchless body, something else besides lust stirred inside Theosophus. What was it she'd said, that children came to swim at the pool after school?

He called out loudly, "Do they have lifeguards?"

"What?"

"At the Y. Do they have lifeguards for the children at the pool?"

"Of course they do," she said lazily. "I'm not usually there when the children are, but when I've popped over there on the odd afternoon, I've seen them. Most of them look barely older than the swimmers, but that might just be my warped perception. Probably high school kids from the local privates, accumulating extracurricular hours for their college applications." She sounded distracted. "Listen, will you do me a favor? I think I left the coffee maker on and there's no more coffee in the pot. Could you just turn off the switch? It's right on the front."

He started toward the kitchen counter, then stopped in his tracks and shouted back to her. "But even if you're young, I guess you got to be specially trained to teach kids to swim. Get certified or something. They must not hire just anybody."

He could hear water sloshing around heavily. He figured she must not have heard him. And then he froze.

She was standing in the hallway with one pink towel covering her body and the other wrapped around her head like a turban, though the towels weren't doing her much good. She was dripping water from head to toe, but she didn't seem to notice. Her eyes grabbed him. "Theosophus, do you want to become a lifeguard? Or a swimming teacher?"

He backed up, raising his hands like he was under arrest. "Okay, okay, I know it's crazy." He strode back over to the coffee maker and switched it off. With his head still turned away from her, he mumbled. "It's just that I remembered how, when I was a kid, once Matt Hayes showed me the moves, the one thing I liked to do was swim. Come summertime, you could hardly get me out of that pool."

She was at his side in an instant. He could feel the water dripping off her body onto him as she pulled him around to face her. Oddly, he didn't even get hard having her near-naked body up so close. She was frowning, and he worried she was angry with him.

"Do you like kids?" she said.

"I can't say I've had much to do with any for some time now.

Closest I've come to a kid is young Miss Jane. I was crazy 'bout my sisters' kids. Used to buy them clothes and stuff, my sisters being poor and all, living off Assistance. Lived right across the hall from each other, in the projects. Over to Compton way. But one day I went 'round to see them, and the both of 'em had just picked up and left, with no word at all for me. All I could get out of their neighbors was they thought Joylene had fallen in with a man whose auntie had some kind of housekeeping service in Sacramento, promised both her and Araytha a job." He shook his head. "You'd think, wouldn't you, they might have taken the trouble to let me know? So mad at them now, don't care if I never see their skinny black asses again. But I sure do miss those kids. One of them was named after me; everybody called him Little Theo so's not to mix us up. They must've forgotten about me by now." He turned his head away. "Aw, shoot." His eyes were wet.

"Theosophus. This may be it."

He couldn't look at her.

"What do you think? You wouldn't get rich on it, but it'd be a living."

He turned around suddenly and banged his fist on the kitchen counter. "What are you trying to do to me?" He was shouting now and pointing his thumbs dramatically at himself. "Look at me. I can't afford to live on the same cloud as you. My body's a wreck, probably pissed out more than half my brain cells by now along with the Old Taylor. Don't have me a place to live. No change of clothes ..." He pointed down to his worn right shoe, wagging it at her violently and hopping on his other foot. "Or a car or even no driver's license anymore since some damned fool of a teenaged junkie took it from me, thinking he could buy some liquor by passing off his white ass as me. No more than a high school diploma and I don't even talk right for most jobs." He laughed. "Get rich? Man like me, I'll be lucky to just keep my black self from doing something stupid like pick up the bottle again." Tears streamed down his cheeks. "What's the point? What's the point? I ain't got nobody. It's hardly worth it trying to stay alive for just me."

Later, Theosophus was to marvel at how far he'd let himself go in the direction of feeling sorry for himself that he hadn't even considered putting the move on Terry when she wrapped her arms around him, letting the two pink towels fall to her feet as she rocked him back and forth like a baby. But at that moment, he just knew that it felt good.

As his sobs subsided, she held him at arms' length and spoke haltingly, as if she were thinking something through out loud. "Kids from all over West L.A., Culver City, Palms, even Westchester come to the Culver Y." She grinned. "It's a regular hotbed of diversity. I'll bet it would make good PR and good sense for them to have a black swim teacher who can relate to the kids of color. A true mentor." She let go of him, reached down, retrieved one of her towels from the floor and wrapped it around herself again—tucking in the end of the towel at the cleft between her luscious breasts, as if her momentary nakedness had been the most normal thing in the world. "I'll make you a deal. If you go swimming with me every day and get yourself in shape, and you promise me you'll stay off the booze for good, you can stay here for a little while—" Seeing his expression, she laughed. "On the couch, if you please." She arched an eyebrow. "Let's not make this more complicated than it has to be. This was the closest you'll ever get to my beautiful body." He pretended to look affronted, then, just a little disappointed for real, he nodded earnestly. She continued. "And I'll see what I can do to get you a job at the Y."

His smile vanished. Was she nuts or something? "They ain't going to want to hire the likes of me."

"Not with that attitude. But if they get used to you around there, and if you schmooze them up just a little, and I give you a major glowing reference, you never know." Then she burst into high-pitched laughter.

"Why're you laughing?"

"Oh, nothing," she replied, her voice just a little shaky. "The irony of it. That it was Matt Hayes who taught you to swim."

Thirty-eight

THE WEEKS THAT followed the 6.7 Cheviot Hills blind thrust quake, its numerous aftershocks, and the Malibu Hills Fire were marked by the uncovering of striking instances of tragedy and heroism. Surprisingly, while over two thousand people were injured, only fifty-seven people were counted as having died, though the victims' families railed bitterly at the use of the word "only," and those familiar with the subterranean life of the city figured you could probably realistically add a third again to the body count in the ranks of the homeless and undocumented who never made it into official statistics anyway.

For one brief cosmic moment, the City of Angels lived up to its name. The crime rate went down, good neighborliness was passed around as generously as a joint in the sixties, and with the help of armies of governmental agencies and charitable organizations, the city struggled back onto its feet like a onetime movie star making a poignant comeback. Anglos and Hispanics, blacks and Asians smiled at each other as they passed on the street. Even the habitually cool hipsters of Melrose Avenue, just north of Selma Goldberg's staid Jewish neighborhood, couldn't stop themselves from nodding warmly at each other as they passed on the crowded sidewalk.

This being L.A., the young and daring immediately converted their experience into a fashion statement. More than a few musicians adopted a screaming red hair tint laced with streaks of ashy grey. Homies from East L.A. to Venice emblazoned their already well-decorated arms with tattoos of dramatically stylized flames.

A razor-thin twosome with nine small hoop earrings and one nose ring between them walked a pair of pit bull puppies down Martel Avenue after a late breakfast at the trendy Kings Road Café. They halted their animated speculation over whether it was safer to live in L.A. or New York—the female of the two having been mugged in broad daylight during a photo shoot in Manhattan just a month ago—when a white-aproned Selma came out of her front door with a broom clutched determinedly in her plump fists. They slowed as they passed her, smiling wryly and nodding, a sympathetic witness to her efforts to clear her front walk of ash.

Selma automatically smiled back, but her amiability seemed forced, her forehead creased with anxious lines. "The ash, it doesn't want to clear away. I tried it already yesterday. Really, I'm just moving it from one place to another, then the winds move it right back again. But what with this water shortage, what else can I do?" She shrugged haplessly.

They made consoling noises while the two puppies sniffed at Selma's ankles. As her eyes widened, they yanked the dogs back and moved hastily on. Undaunted, Selma continued to mutter to their disappearing backs. "Thanks God, the house is standing anyway. What's a little ash when that *momser* of an earthquake made some homes into a graveyard?" She looked up at the sky, where innocent clouds scudded across the first really blue expanse the city had seen for days. She continued to speak out loud, as if the heavens themselves were listening. "And, God help us, not just houses. Poor, poor Max, crushed to nothing in that parking lot." She shuddered and prayed for the thousandth time for God to forgive her for every mean thought she'd ever had about her son-in-law. "And my poor little girl."

Selma's home had fared much better than most. Only three bricks had fallen onto the driveway from the chimney, and a few new cracks had appeared in her front tiles and around her front door.

That was nothing compared to what had happened to Edith's home in Beverlywood. Its roof and walls had collapsed and splintered as if the whole thing had been made of balsa wood.

It was clear that anyone inside would have been killed. When Ben had driven Selma there straight from UCLA, that was exactly what she and the rest of the Jeep's occupants had assumed. Selma had to be held back from throwing herself onto the ugly pile of rubble. And when the world went black on her, Ben and Terry and Ariel had lifted her back into the Jeep for the drive to Martel.

They'd found David Nussbaum sitting on the porch with her grandchildren, bearing the news that Edith—if not her husband, nor the baby she'd carried inside her—was alive. Only then had Selma re-entered the world of space and light and time.

Selma forcibly pushed that day out of her mind. She opened the door and crept inside, peering with guilty satisfaction through two open archways into a visible corner of her kitchen. She'd used the time while Edith was recovering at the astonishingly intact Olympia Medical Center to hire a handyman to re-paper the denuded sooty walls. But as she rubbed her hands in pleased appraisal of her new floral wallpaper, she reminded herself that neither that accomplishment, nor replacing her grandchildren's wardrobes and providing them with some toys from Kmart, could have been accomplished without the assistance of her angels from heaven: Ariel (a bit worse for wear, thanks to her mild concussion), Terry, and, especially, young Jane.

Selma leaned her broom against the entry wall and tiptoed down the hall. She poked her head into the room where Jane sat cross-legged on the edge of the bed, with Deborah, Rebekka, and Jacob clustered close around her. Baby Aaron slept peacefully in his portable playpen, one arm curled over his favorite teddy and the other grasping the afghan crocheted by Selma's *bubbe* nearly a century ago. Jane was reading to the children from *Goodnight Moon*, her tone more assured and containing than Selma would ever have thought possible. Selma shook her head. She'd give anything to bring back the unborn child who'd been lost. "What kind of a monster am I?" she berated herself. "And who elected me the Sage of Martel Avenue, judging my own daughter for getting pregnant again?"

From where she stood, she could see the children's eyes shine with wonder. These little ones were four good reasons why Edith still had something to live for. And to live up to. A mother and a father she'd have to be. Selma leaned against the wall outside the doorway as she felt her legs about to give way. If only she hadn't fled the consequences of setting her house on fire, Max and Edith wouldn't have gone to Cedars that night.

Selma had to remind herself again that, if they hadn't gone looking for her, the whole family would have perished.

She looked up at the picture of Chaim on the wall. "All right, all right, already. Maybe *you're* the Sage of Martel Avenue. I don't understand it, but somehow, by being such a coward, I helped save our daughter's life."

———————————

Her young friends would hardly concur with Selma's self-assessment as a coward, but they were well aware of the stress the woman was under. Which was why Ariel had parked her dusty Toyota at the corner of Martel and Beverly the next day, rather than directly in front of Selma's house, to wait for Jane. Ariel kept looking at her watch, worried that they'd gotten their signals crossed. She and Terry had arranged this meeting in a series of secretive phone calls, Jane whispering on her end like some conspirator. The plan was for Jane to plead the need for a break from the children (an out-and-out lie—the teenager couldn't seem to get enough of Edith's kids) so she could go off to see some movie at the Grove.

Their actual mission was to release Danny's ashes in Franklin Canyon.

After what felt like a million commercials, the "Jack FM" DJ played another oldies hit. As they heard Tommy Tutone ask Jenny, Jenny who he could turn to, she and Terry exchanged grins, then joined in boisterously at the end of the refrain: "Five-three-oh-nine."

Throwing her head back in laughter, Ariel caught a glimpse of Jane hurrying toward the car. Panting, the girl slid into the back seat. Ariel turned off the radio. No one spoke as she inched the Toyota through the usual traffic congestion around the Beverly Center and picked up speed once she turned onto Crescent Drive.

Finally, Jane broke the silence. "Do you have them?"

Terry nodded and passed her the polished cedar box. It was she, ever the practical one, who'd tracked down Danny's remains and wheedled their release by the county coroner, though it had taken the pooled resources of Ariel, Terry, and an insistent Ben to pay the astonishingly expensive cremation fees. They'd lied to Jane about that part and told her the city had covered the costs, since Danny was an indigent.

As Ariel drove past the Beverly Hills Hotel, Terry excitedly pointed out the site of the famous Polo Lounge to Jane, who stared blankly at the hotel's manicured grounds.

They fell silent again. From time to time, Ariel snuck a look at Jane in the rearview mirror. The girl was stroking the box tenderly and mouthing words with no sound.

Ariel wished somebody would say something, anything, to keep her mind off Ben and the time he'd brought her here. The mountainside, in these hot summer days, was still dotted with hardy orange and yellow wildflowers, and the sweet smells of wild sage and eucalyptus permeated the air.

Ariel found a fairly shady place to park and, relying on her memory of her day in the canyon with Ben, she led the other two over the low brick wall to a spot that afforded a good view of the reservoir. The brush here was dry, but even the scraggly foliage and dusty earth were a welcome change from the harsh geometric shapes of the urban landscape just a few miles below. Luckily, this being a weekday, there were barely any other people around. Neither Terry nor Jane had ever been here before and Ariel felt some satisfaction in sharing such natural splendor with them.

But Jane wasn't disposed to waste much time on sightseeing. As if drawing from some secret reserve of authority, she directed Ariel and Terry to form a little circle with her and launched immediately into her eulogy.

Jane squinted at the sky, her hand curled tightly around the cedar box. "Dear Lord, we're standing here with all that's left of Danny Bales. He died too young, so I sure do hope you had some need of him, to call him back to you so soon. I know some people would think he wasn't worth much. He took drugs, and he had sex for money. He stole food sometimes, too, but he didn't mean any harm by it. He didn't know any other way to be. He lived on the street and didn't have too many friends, 'cept me and Sarah—till she got fed up—and his dog Sadie. You took them both away from him before he died." She hesitated, then pushed on. "Anyway, he was as good as could be to me. He made sure I got somewhere that was gonna be safe before he passed on." Jane paused, looking around sightlessly, then mumbled to Ariel and Terry with profound agitation, "It was the walk to Selma's house that did him in. If he didn't worry so much about me, he might have been okay."

"Don't even go there." Ariel's expression was stern. "Danny was on his last legs, and you know it. If anything, his concern for you probably kept him going an extra couple of weeks. He may have been a victim of a piece-of-shit disease, but he died a hero. Don't take that away from him."

Jane stared at her, then nodded. "Okay, but where was I?"

Terry piped up. "He found you a safe place."

"Thank you. Well, I'm here to pay my respects and say, 'Take good care of him, please, 'cause he took good care of me.' And please tell him he found me the best new home. I think he'd rest in peace if you could just let him know that."

She fumbled with the lock to the cedar box. Terry stepped up to help her. Ariel craned her neck to look at its contents. The ashes looked grittier than she would have imagined.

Jane stared down blankly at Danny's remains, as if she couldn't believe that this was all it boiled down to. Ariel knew all too well how that felt.

Jane looked around, as if trying to decide exactly where to pour the contents of the box. And then suddenly, from out of nowhere, a not-quite-full-sized, gorgeous golden lab—with big paws and enough zany exuberance to signal it was still a puppy—broke into their circle, its jaws snapping as it chased a huge white butterfly that wafted just a little too tantalizingly high for its reach. Before they knew it, the dog had knocked against a gasping Jane's hands, and the little cedar box went flying, releasing Danny's ashes in a graceful arc through the air. As the dog's owner called, "Phoebe, Phoebe," the dog turned back, its tongue hanging out of its mouth, some of Danny's ashes freckling its nose and some more making a smudgy crown above its eyes.

Ariel and Terry looked over at Jane, holding their breath. For a moment it was touch and go, but then—God bless her—Jane just shrugged. "Well, anyway, he did love dogs."

Ariel was afraid Terry was going to make her lose it, but Jane broke into a song that cut through their silent hysteria. Her wobbly soprano sounded so innocent that Ariel and Terry felt obliged to join in.

Mercifully, Phoebe the dog had the amazing grace to hold off her accompaniment until they'd nearly finished, launching into a fit of soulful howling only when they reached the last verse, "Was blind but now I see."

Thirty-nine

IT WAS NEARLY a month later when Ariel leaned over the waist-high, red-velvet rope in front of Grauman's Chinese Theater like a shameless gawker at a premiere. But unlike the rest of the noisy crowd that surrounded her, it was Terry and Theosophus she was cheering for.

In this L.A. version of the traditional gathering to honor local heroes that follows any natural disaster in any American city, the mayor had invited, not just the expected local dignitaries, but a mini-Who's Who of Hollywood to pin medals of momentary celebrity onto the chests of the simple people who'd surprised themselves and their neighbors by coming through in a crunch, big time. And he'd chosen as the site of this well-televised ceremony nothing so prosaic as City Hall, but the entrance to the recently-restored Grauman's (now known as TCL), famous for its concrete walkway covered with handprints of the stars. The mayor was a man of few words, but he was also no political fool. Lest the world fall into the sin of thinking of L.A. as just one more urban center with its share of shit to contend with, global audiences needed to be reminded which city ruled their collective imagination and how quickly it would be prepared to receive again its tithe of tourist dollars.

Ariel was too busy scanning the two groups spread out on risers on either side of the mayor to wonder why the affair had been pulled together in such an unusual fashion. To the left of the mayor posed a gaggle of casual-chic-clad celebrities. To his right stood a group of blinking and blushing honorees decked out touchingly in brand new polyester slacks and crisp shirts and blouses, probably ironed with their own hands. Ariel couldn't help but notice that the former group was just about all white, while the second was composed of a good many dark-skinned faces.

With her right leg bent and her foot aimed backwards, poised threateningly at potential encroachers on her desirable position at the front of the crowd, Ariel located Theosophus, standing between a guy in a black-and-gold dashiki and an older man whose broad features and diminutive height proclaimed his Salvadoran origins. Terry's face was partially obscured by the mayor. She stood just behind him, and each time he bent forward to shake someone's hand, Ariel could see her looking down at the pages he held, which she knew contained the speech Terry had written for him.

Ariel did manage to at least catch Theosophus's eye. He waved so enthusiastically back at her that the people next to her looked at her curiously to see who she was. Once they determined she was a nobody just like them, they resumed ogling the mayor's VIP assemblage, and so did Ariel. She had to admit it was the biggest concentration of recognizable superstars she'd ever seen. Once the ceremonies were finally underway, Ariel was surprised to find herself listening with rapt attention to the mayor. Nothing was as boring as a politician's patent phoniness, but reading the speech Terry had written for him made him sound almost profound. He certainly was glowing.

She had to remind herself that the man was only basking in other peoples' honest hero-glow. Though the city's police were much vaunted as "L.A.'s Finest," these humble citizens who treated their neighbors as worth saving were the ones she'd bet on as the finest of all. She knew that she herself wouldn't have half the guts to do what some of them had done.

And now her old friend Terry, Miss Meese-ka, Moose-ka, Mouseketeer herself, was being introduced by the mayor to make her big pitch and bat her long eyelashes at the world. This catastrophe had transformed her. It was as if Theosophus's need were a circumstantial "slipper" that finally fit and she was emerging as what she'd always been meant to be, but no one had seen: a kind of moral Cinderella. Ariel couldn't believe how Terry's practical imagination had parlayed her plan for getting Theosophus a new job into a major new citywide project.

She called it "the Post-Quake Revival Plan." Reporters who'd seen the advance press releases were already calling her "Mahatma Terry." It was a groundbreaking and ambitious plan to rehabilitate and retrain the homeless, what Ariel privately thought of as a sort of Head Start for fucked-up adults. Terry had organized a gala fundraiser for the Plan later this evening, which was how the mayor had landed so many big names for his civic hors d'oeuvre.

And the crowd is going wild, Ariel thought, as she watched a lecherous-looking mayor grab Terry's hand and raise it aloft with his own, the mayor's wife giving the two of them a resigned, plastic smile. Flashbulbs popped all around them, and everybody cheered.

It took Ariel nearly twenty minutes to get close enough to actually see Terry in earnest conversation with Liam Neeson, their two heads bent together like a couple of old friends. She shook her head in amazement.

She finally found Theosophus, looking like he was trying to stuff several dainty sandwiches into his mouth at one time. Approaching the long buffet table, she said, "You gonna save some for the rest of us?" He looked around shamefacedly, a daub of cream cheese on his cheek. She dabbed at his face with a napkin. "You've got a man overboard there." She made him show off his ribbon and embarrassed him by thanking him once again for saving her life. As he occupied himself with trying to flick a gob of smoked salmon off his new white shirt, Ariel noted that he was already fitter and more vital-looking from his daily swimming regimen and was undeniably handsome in the stylishly-cut, charcoal gray Men's Warehouse suit Terry had insisted on buying him.

Ariel glimpsed Terry inching through the crowd toward them. She ran to meet her. "Hey, baby, you're God. I want to kneel down before you."

"Oh, please. Just get me out of here. My Spanx are creeping up my ass and these spike heels are killing me."

With a proud "Hey, hey, hey," Theosophus wrapped Terry in a warm bear hug.

But now, all three of them froze. The mayor was barreling towards them with a host of political toadies at his heels. Terry turned to Ariel. "Save me." Ariel took her by the elbow and began pulling her away.

Terry turned her head, flung her hands into the air, and smiled apologetically at the mayor. "Sorry. Important meeting." Then, ever the PR pro, she shouted, "Will you sit next to me tonight?" and offered him what Ariel later described as her "little me" expression, a charming pout that somehow managed to heighten her appeal. He grinned, hopelessly smitten.

Terry whispered in Ariel's ear. "He's letting me duck out now because he knows the amount of press coverage we'll get tonight at the Four Seaons. The gowns and jewels and gossip over who's fucking who will guarantee that."

"Honey, you're shameless," Ariel said. As the three of them burst out of the VIP area and pushed through the throng still craning for a look at the stars, Ariel asked, "How about some lunch? All this bullshit makes me hungry."

As they rounded the busy corner of Hollywood and Highland, Ariel heard Theosophus mumble to himself, "Don't know why we got to pay for lunch, when they had such tasty fixings back there."

As a couple of cameramen with press badges buzzed past in animated conversation, Terry hissed, "That's why, Mr. Theosophus Mae. I'm so sick of all this glad-handing, I could spit. I know it's for a great cause and all, but I've got to preserve my resources for tonight."

In the end—and against some initial objections from Ariel—they ended up at Gracias Madre. It was Terry who'd pushed for it, and Ariel didn't have the heart to object on what was, after all, her big day.

Once they'd been seated in the outdoor patio by a good-looking hostess who Ariel could have sworn was a twin of one of the actresses back at the awards ceremony, she spent more time than she wished darting glances around the patio. She was unusually subdued throughout their meal, but Terry made up for her silence, revved up by the enthusiastic reception for her Plan.

After the waitress had cleared their dessert plates, Terry threw her lipstick-smeared napkin onto the table and turned to Theosophus. "You know, I've tried to convince Ariel to come and work for me, but getting her to make a change is like trying to move God."

Only then did a little light reappear in Ariel's eyes. She stretched her arms into the air. "Well, you know what they say about God. She moves in mysterious ways."

————————————

Ariel managed to get out of the apartment bright and early the next morning, tip-toing to her car and praying it would start before Ben could come out to ask what she was up to. As the motor blessedly turned over on the first try, she chewed her lip. What a fool she'd made of herself over the Cindy Simmons affair. *Or, rather, my own personal hallucination of an affair.* Ben—who had to be one of the sanest and most honest people she knew—had to think she was the most insecure person on the planet. She turned on the radio to block any further meditation on her vanity and pettiness. If Terry had any doubts about why she couldn't get back with Ben, she need look no further. Every time she saw him, she actually felt physically ill, cringing in mortification.

Finally finding a parking spot in an already jammed lot off of Westwood Boulevard, she ascended Bruin Walk and approached the Quad with trepidation, but she needn't have worried on that score. Considerable repair work had already occurred. The pile of dirt excavated in her rescue was gone, and in its place new sod had been laid.

She rehearsed her words as she mounted the concrete steps to Haines Hall, but once inside, she felt lost. Hadn't the anthropology department offices been located just to the left of the main entrance? She clutched the manila envelope bearing her transcripts more tightly as she looked around like a middle school kid on her first day of school. Worse still, as several students entered the echoing pale-green hallway, she noticed that they looked like they were fifteen or sixteen years old. What were they all doing here, anyway? Then she caught herself. *That's what happens when you get old. Everybody else looks like a baby to you.*

————————————

When Terry came over a few nights later to join Ariel for a rare home-cooked pasta in her tiny kitchen, she found her friend unusually subdued. Which was a particular surprise given that Jezzie had just made it through cataract surgery, proving its success by unerringly leaping like a cat half her age onto the table and stretching her paw with perfect aim toward what was left of a triangle of blue cheese atop the remains of Terry's salad. Terry, her original optimism having been revived by post-quake events, couldn't help but reflect yet again how good things can come from awful events. The only way this cat was able to see this well was that a UCLA-educated veterinary surgeon had been moved enough by the televised rescue of what journalists were calling "the UCLA Tunnel Five" to volunteer her services.

Gently nudging Jezebel off the table, Terry looked over at an obviously tipsy Ariel. "I thought you'd be over the moon about the results of her surgery."

Ariel gave a bleary smile, grabbed her cat from the floor, and held her right up to her face, smooching her noisily on the nose. "Oh I am, aren't I, little girl?" Jezzie leapt out of her arms and landed right in front of the refrigerator. Ariel laughed, and said, "And you are, too, I know. You've already had your dinner, but here." She leaned across the table, swiped the blue cheese off Terry's plate with her finger and offered it to the cat, who happily licked it off while Terry objected, "Hey! I wasn't done with that."

Ariel put a hand to her mouth, made a guilty face, then hiccupped. "Well I guess you are now."

Before the distraction, Terry had been describing several stars' agreement to donate sizable sums from their latest films to the Revival Plan. She resumed now, but Ariel seemed almost bored with the topic. Finally, Terry just shut up and poured the last of the bottle into a couple of mismatched wine glasses.

"It's raining," she said unnecessarily.

"Mm." Ariel's pupils looked unnaturally large, and her usually pale face was flushed. She opened her mouth as if she were about to say something, then closed it again with a little catch in her throat.

Terry was beginning to feel a little dizzy. She started to laugh.

"What's so funny?" Ariel said reluctantly.

"This is a hell of a party. I feel like we've just come from a funeral."

"Sometimes changes feel a little like death."

"That's cryptic. Did you get high or something before I came over?"

Ariel shook her head violently.

"Okay, I'll bite. This business about changes. You talking about anything in particular?"

Ariel stood up and stretched. "Well, I guess I didn't realize how stale things were getting."

Terry's voice was wry. "I can well imagine you'd want something different." She looked away carefully. "Have you seen Ben?"

"Yeah, I've bumped into him here and there, around the building. Actually, he asked about you. Calls for bulletins sometimes about Mrs. G."

"Maybe calling about Selma is just an excuse to talk to you."

"Yeah, well. Whatever."

Terry studied her wine glass as she swirled its golden contents around. "Don't you get lonely?"

Ariel looked up, as if Terry's question surprised her. "Oh shit, I'm used to it." She leaned down and bent to pick up Jezzie, who'd been busy licking her genitals noisily on the cracked linoleum floor. "Besides, I've got this little honey." She looked piercingly at Terry. "Do you? Get lonely, I mean."

"What do you think?" She wanted to stop herself, she knew she'd get nothing but grief for it, but she couldn't hold back the tide. "I can't believe that he's right there, downstairs, and you ..."

"Don't you get on my case again. Not now. Not tonight." Ariel bit her lip. "You won't believe what I've done." Taking a deep breath, she described her visit to UCLA.

Terry's eyes widened. She leapt up, nearly knocking over her chair, and grabbed Ariel. They did a crazy polka around the cramped kitchen, the two of them just drunk enough to manage to bump, consecutively, into the fridge, the stove, the table, and both chairs. They ended up next to the tomato-sauce-splattered sink, holding hands like a couple of five-year-olds. "Oh baby, baby, I'm so proud of you. When do they let you know if you've been admitted?"

Ariel explained what she'd been told by the head of the anthro Department.

Terry felt like she could have stood that way all night. That is, until Jezzie—a bubble of blue cheese at the corner of her mouth—started to make sickening lurching grunts.

"Oh, shit," Ariel cried, leaping across the room. She managed to time her grabbing of the cat with the first of Jezzie's projectile spurts of putrid bluish-white spume, so that a cloudy line of the stuff dripped across her T-shirted chest, making her look like the victim of some drunken skywriter. Simultaneously, the rain beat more forcefully at the windows. The two friends threw back their heads and laughed so loud that the neighbor on the other side of the wall yelled at them to shut the fuck up.

Forty

THEOSOPHUS KELLY TOOK his time walking past the dilapidated apartment building where he'd spent most of his childhood. Straining his ears, he could almost hear Mama and Granny laughing together in the kitchen and the shouting, teasing voices of Gwayne, Araytha, and Joylene in front of the TV.

The lawn in front was scraggly and dry, and so much paint had peeled off the window frames that you could see the bare, termite-eaten wood. But the building had survived all the shaking. Some weird cosmic law had allowed something of such obviously substandard construction to prevail when more glorious structures had fallen like pick up sticks.

Somebody's door opened, releasing a blast of heavy rap, and a young boy slid furtively out. Theosophus could smell the pungent scent of weed from where he stood. The child's coffee arms were mottled with bruises, green snot bubbled from his nostrils, and his torn trousers revealed knees that looked like they'd been scraped, scabbed, and scratched at in an endless cycle. Catching sight of Theosophus, he halted and eyed him warily.

Theosophus, yawning and stretching casually, nodded. "S'up, my man? Out to have some fun?"

The child only stared at him.

"'Scuse my manners." Theosophus walked slowly toward him and knelt down to shake his hand. "Sorry. My name's Theosophus Kelly. Did I say I used to live here? Number seven." He laughed. "They say it's a lucky number, know what I mean?"

Still, the child didn't speak.

Theosophus reached into his pocket, and the boy began to back up, keeping his eyes on him.

Theosophus raised his voice just a little. "These days, I'm gettin' ready to teach swimming at the Y. Got a card here somewhere. Wanna see? Thought I had some chewing gum, too, if I can find it."

Somebody leaned out of a window and yelled. "Diondre, who you talking to, boy?"

But the child was obviously torn as Theosophus continued to hold the card and—undoubtedly more importantly—the stick of Wrigley's Doublemint out to him.

"You better go. Didn't mean to get you in no trouble." He whispered urgently. "Take 'em. You got a phone in your house? You call me whenever you want to. Hear me? Any time at all. I been where you are, and I promise you there's something better out there just waiting for you."

"Diondre!"

The child turned around and ran, stuffing both objects in his pocket.

Theosophus sighed. He'd never call. Why did the heaviest burdens fall on the most innocent shoulders? The boy must be about the age of Little Theo when he last saw him. Theosophus's jaw worked. He hadn't been able to get hold of his sisters' whereabouts, but he wouldn't stop trying. He'd learned that sometimes you could do the impossible. It just took a little time.

With one last glance back, he boarded the bus that would take him to the small studio apartment in Venice he'd rented with his stipend from the Plan. At every stop, people of color got on. He couldn't afford a car yet himself, but he promised himself that someday he would.

The next-door neighbor's mutt yapped nastily as he approached his apartment. It was hot and stuffy inside. He opened a window onto the alley and left the front door open. It was the only way to capture a little breeze.

Furnished with mismatched hand-me-downs from Plan contributors, the place sure enough wasn't the Ritz. An old leak in the apartment above had made a mess of the drywall in the tiny bathroom, the oven didn't work (though the stove top did), the television only got a few channels, and he was fighting a losing battle with roaches, which had at least so far confined themselves to the kitchen. But it was home and he had a few new possessions of his very own—a comb and toothbrush, fancy shaving gear Terry had bought him from Crabtree and Evelyn, a nail kit, even some cologne signaling he was back to the land of the living. He'd actually had sex last night on his sofa bed with a big-hipped honey he'd met at an AA meeting.

He'd also managed to put up a few impromptu decorations. His medal from the mayor was propped proudly on the shelf, next to his picture of Granny and a Day-Glo tangerine bullhorn that he took with him each day to the Y.

He sighed. He still had a long way to go. He thought about the little boy he'd met this morning and wished he'd asked him for his number. Then he laughed at himself. Who was he kidding? The kid's family would think he was a child molester or some meddler from the Department of Children and Family Services.

He aimed for the kitchen, bumping his shoulder on his way back on the cheap hat stand next to the wall mirror. Only two objects were suspended from its wrought-iron arm—he'd vowed to never get rid of them. His dusty old shoes hung by their fraying laces, retired from active duty, their worn soles sporting a couple of gaping holes. Theosophus saluted them, then sunk down onto his sofa and took a nice long draft of root beer.

————————————

A mere fifteen miles east, Ariel sat much less comfortably in the back seat of Ben's Jeep, listening uneasily as Terry caught Ben up on how well Theosophus was doing. Ben had been pushing for a month for the three of them to visit Selma, and Ariel had managed until now to put him off until he'd gotten downright insistent.

Terry laughed. "I keep telling Theosophus he doesn't have to keep thanking me all the time. I'm the one who should be thanking him for waking me up to what life is really about."

Ben looked thoughtful. "Yeah, but think about what it must mean for him to have a place of his own again. I'll bet that apartment feels like a mansion to him after the grief of living on the streets."

As they approached Selma's neatly-swept walkway, Ariel wondered if shared grief had helped Selma and Edith make some kind of truce. She'd barely spent time with Selma herself except for delivering her mail. Understandably, Selma's family was consuming most of her attention.

A small voice cried, "Who is it?" after Ariel rang the bell. Little Deborah, her dark eyes as round as marbles, opened the door. She still wore a butterfly bandage bisecting her right eyebrow to show that she'd survived the quake's nasty transit through the ER. Ariel said a silent prayer of thanks that the gash requiring seven stitches hadn't actually extended to the eye itself.

Her Shirley Temple curls bouncing, Deborah marched self-importantly ahead of them into the dining room, where, under the gaze of Selma's *bubbe* and *zayde*, three adult heads were bent together over what looked like a photo album. Across the table Rebekka and Jacob were hard at work on their coloring books.

Jane looked up as they entered, but Selma seemed oblivious to them, as if she were so consumed with what she was telling Edith that nothing else existed. "You see," she was saying, "I told you so. I just didn't remember that I actually had a picture of your father with his *semitchke*s. Believe me, the way he went at those seeds, with his tongue darting in and out, he was just like a lizard with glasses."

Oh, Selma, you heartless woman, Ariel thought. But then Selma looked up at them with a welcoming smile and introduced them.

Ariel eyed Edith curiously. Especially in the early days after the quake, Selma had described her daughter's condition in sepulchral tones whenever she caught Ariel delivering the mail.

Ariel had to admit that Edith didn't look great. She had dark circles under her eyes, her olive skin had a sallow tinge to it, and the sleeveless housecoat she wore over her still-pooched-out stomach emphasized the stick-like thinness of her arms.

No one referred to either of her tragedies, but the specter of the missing Max and the harsh irony of Edith's belly sat heavily on the room. Ariel saw Selma steal a worried glance in her daughter's direction, then slide her arm over Edith's shoulder. Edith looked up at her mother with such easy affection that Ariel had to look away.

Ariel and her friends pulled chairs up to the table, and they felt their way into conversation that was so polite it was almost surreal. How fucking L.A., she thought. After what they'd been through, they were talking about what TV shows they liked. She noticed Ben pulling nervously at his eyelid, and Terry was obviously swallowing a series of yawns.

They all looked relieved when Edith got up and brought her youngest from another room. Ariel watched, fascinated, as Edith set down a jar of baby food onto Selma's polished table and began urging spoonfuls of the revolting, dark green mush at his determinedly pursed little lips. Ariel figured she knew exactly how he felt. As the rest of the group dove with suspiciously enthusiastic gusto into the topic of how cute Aaron was, Ariel couldn't help but notice that every time Edith aimed the spoon at her child's mouth, she opened her own eyes and mouth as wide as Jonah's whale. Noticing that Jane unconsciously mimicked Edith in this bizarre ritual, Ariel stifled the impulse to laugh aloud.

Still more small talk. Ariel thought she was going to explode. She could have kissed Selma when, after a painfully prolonged pause in the conversation, she turned to Terry and asked how Theosophus was doing, adding with a meaningful rolling of her eyes and an apologetic tone that she wanted to thank him with a meal, just as soon as she caught up with herself, for saving her life.

Selma went on to speculate what she should cook for him. "A roast chicken is filling, but maybe not special enough to fit the occasion."

Edith put a restraining hand on Selma's arm. "For heaven's sake, Ma, don't go on so much." Ariel could have killed her.

But Terry hastily interrupted. "It's just amazing. He's like a new man. Sometimes I stop by the Y just to sneak a peek at him at the pool. He's so vital and animated when he's with those kids, and they're all crazy about him. It's like he was born to do this." She paused, looking over their heads, then grinned around the table. "And frankly, swimming every day has done him no end of good. He's tons more confident, and he's in great shape physically. Really buff. He's a good-looking man, you know."

Ariel frowned. What Terry wasn't telling them was that the last afternoon Terry had stopped by the Y—not just to see Theosophus, but to arrange some training for other beneficiaries of the Plan—she'd bumped into Matt Hayes, who'd evidently come by to touch base with

Theosophus. Terry's description of standing across the pool from Matt had been painful to listen to. Ariel could just see it: the two of them awkwardly registering each other's presence, Matt starting to walk around the pool toward Terry until her barely perceptible shake of her head stopped him dead in his tracks. Ariel had only been able to relax again when Terry assured her that she was determined to keep a greater than pool's width distance from Matt Hayes. The way Terry had put it, "There's got to be some poor guy like me out there somewhere, a little flawed but essentially sound, who just fell through some crack in the cosmic mating ground."

Ariel's attention was called back to the conversation when Jane spoke up. "But he's not really a swimming teacher yet, is he?"

Terry shook her head. "Well, actually, no. Not yet, anyway. My friends at the Y are generous, but they're a little nervous about who they put in charge of the kids. We managed to come to a compromise, a sort of probationary period where he volunteers time when one of the paid lifeguards is on duty. The important thing is to let them see what a great guy Theosophus is and what an inspiration he can be for the kids. And I think it's working."

Selma frowned and cocked her head inquisitively. "But what does he do for money? Does he live with you, still? He's such a good man — he shouldn't have to live on the streets like an animal."

"Oh, Selma," Ariel said, "he saved all of our lives. You know we wouldn't let that happen."

Terry jumped in before she'd even finished. "Better still, *he* won't let it happen." She looked around the table. "I tell you, he's a new man. An inspiration to me, for sure." She turned back to Selma. "But, don't you worry, Selma. He's earning his own wages from the Plan. We underwrite internships like his. That's just what we're for."

But Selma looked confused. "And he's staying with you?"

"Well, no, actually. The Plan provides temporary housing, too. He's got his own apartment in Venice. But we stay in pretty close touch." She grinned. "He makes sure that I make good on my offer to cook him a pancake breakfast every Sunday. It's a kind of ritual with us. Actually, it started the day after the quake." A mysterious smile played at her lips.

Jane, holding Rebekka on her lap, spoke over the child's head. "I think it's wonderful what you're doing. I mean, people like Theosophus, well, you know. There're a lot of good people living on the streets, and before this, nobody bothered doing anything about it."

Selma added enthusiastically, "She's right, you know. You're making a real contribution. I read in the Times that you're the queen of City Hall."

Terry snorted and wagged her finger. "Selma, you're an intelligent woman. You must know that you can't believe everything you read in the paper." She sighed. "The reality is that nobody in politics wants to put their money where their mouths are. Our mayor has the attention span of a three-year-old, so it'll be up to me to make sure the whole thing doesn't die a slow death for lack of visibility." She shrugged. "I figure if I accomplish a tenth of what I've set out to do, turn at least some lives around, I'll die happy."

Selma put a hand on her heart. "Death? Who's talking about death?" She reached across the table to pat Terry's hand, though she couldn't prevent her eyes from sliding over to her daughter as she spoke. "The important thing is to keep trying. Not to give up hope."

"Hope." Ariel nearly jumped when Ben spoke. She'd been trying so hard to let him blend into the background. "Wasn't that the last ingredient at the bottom of Pandora's box? Sometimes I think that's all we've got left."

Selma looked at him with such surprise that you'd think he was a gorilla who'd suddenly cracked the code of human language. Ariel knew that Selma couldn't bring herself to forgive the man who she was convinced had broken Ariel's heart.

Ben pointed proudly at Ariel. "Actually, we can all be hopeful about this one. She's going to be saying bye-bye soon to the U.S. Postal Service. Look out Leakey. Or whoever's the shining star in anthropology these days."

Jane gave a nervous cough, then chimed in, "Maybe you'll actually get to study your Eve bones some day." She paused, and her next words were so kind that Ariel teared up. "I was sorry they took her back to Africa before you could even see her. I mean, after all that."

Her words lingered in the air.

Ariel shrugged as nonchalantly as she could muster. "What'd John Lennon say? Something like life being the thing that happens when you're busy making other plans?"

Ben shot her a penetrating look. "Well, that's the truth. But I won't be surprised if you end up digging up your own famous find one day."

Ariel blushed, though she was secretly pleased by all the attention. "Whoa, wait a minute. I've got to complete my undergrad prerequisites before they'll even let me into grad school. By the time I'm ready, I'll probably be so old they won't want me anyway."

Terry muttered, none too softly, "Oh, please, give us a break." She turned to Ben. "Speaking of breaks, heard you landed a part on *Star Trek*."

Ben made a wry face. "Not really a part. A walk-on. Not exactly what you'd call career momentum." He threw a quick glance in Ariel's direction. "Hard to know whether to keep trying or just give it up."

The doorbell rang. Deborah slid excitedly off her chair to get the door. She came back with her pudgy hand tenderly grasped in David Nussbaum's slim pale one. Under his arm, he clasped what Deborah was quick to point out were a couple of Curious George Blu-ray discs.

Selma thanked him with what sounded to Ariel like an excess of enthusiasm, and Ariel noticed that his face went beet red. Ariel looked David up and down. You wouldn't think he had much on the ball: short and skinny, with a diffident manner, his yarmulke pinned on crookedly with a bobby pin, for God's sake. His complexion was pasty and his sharp brown eyes almost disappeared behind Coke-bottle-thick glasses. But accompanied now by a surprisingly bouncy Jane, David confidently led the suddenly noisy gaggle of children out of the room to pop one of the Blu-rays into the player in the den.

Selma whispered conspiratorially that, with David's help, she'd found a tutor who would prepare Jane to take her high school equivalency exams. As she talked, her voice kept rising in volume, until they were all listening. "She told David that she'd like to work with children later. But he's trying to convince her that she'll make more of a living if she goes to college first. They have a two-year course they offer at Los Angeles Community College. They call it ..." Looking around blankly, she clapped her forehead. "*Oy*, my rotten memory."

Edith was quick to rescue her. "It's called Early Childhood Development, Ma."

Selma shot her a look of gratitude and patted her cheek tenderly. "Thank you, *tatteleh*."

Ariel gave a strained smile. She could hear gales of giggles coming from the den. Selma was still talking, oblivious that Jane had re-joined them. "Just think of it—Jane could follow in Ariel's footsteps, both of them college girls." Ariel's face felt hot as she and Jane exchanged a quick look. Selma went on. "Who knows, with four children already living here happily, maybe—if I can *strudel* the *yente telebente* next door into submission, and the other neighbors don't complain—we can make a little daycare center in the backyard. Such a big yard. When we bought it we used to think of building a pool, but I was afraid. You never know, some child might drown. But a little play group? I can think of worse uses to put it to now."

Ariel studied Jane's face as the girl sat there, her arms folded as if she didn't know what to do with her hands. Could the pale and scrawny, inarticulate runaway she'd first met in this house not that long ago actually be college-bound? Ariel looked up at Selma's chandeliered ceiling, and then she looked back at Jane. Why not? A girl with the survival skills to escape a creepy stepfather, get loose of a miserable excuse for a mother, and survive on the streets without turning to either drugs or hooking had to have some remarkable hidden reserves. Ancient reserves. Never before was Ariel as aware of the strength of spirit Eve had bequeathed to virtually everyone alive today.

Ariel had taken some pride in having convinced Selma, Terry, and Jane herself that the teenager couldn't possibly make contact with her family again until she had some kind of plan. But she'd gladly left it up to the persuasive Terry to actually make the call to Jane's mom. That pathetic woman hadn't taken too much persuading—she'd been only too glad to protect her psycho relationship with Jane's stepfather Vern by signing over guardianship of her daughter to Selma.

Looking at Jane now, Ariel realized her instinct had been right on target. The fact that Selma and Edith had needed her so desperately had given the girl a new confidence, as if she'd gone from being some paper-thin facsimile of a person to someone with dimensionality and weight. She'd actually literally put on five pounds or so. Probably thanks to Selma's cooking, Ariel realized enviously.

The conversation at the table ground to a halt. Edith and David were whispering together under the hall archway now, and Ariel noticed two splotches of color on Edith's wan cheeks as she hefted a sleepy-looking Aaron from one shoulder to the other. Ben stood up and said that they probably ought to be moving along. Ariel was about to protest that they'd just gotten there when she noticed that, though Selma was objecting to their departure, she also looked a little relieved.

Ben walked slowly behind Ariel and Terry to his car. Terry reached the Jeep first and settled who would sit where by sliding into the back seat. Ben was uncomfortably aware that his hands trembled visibly as he held the passenger door open for Ariel. But she didn't seem to notice. As he pulled away from the curb, she sighed and bit at her cuticle. "Anybody got any ciggies?" she said.

He flashed her a sideways glance. "I'm done. I thought you were trying to quit, too."

She crossed her arms and cleared her throat, as if she were about to give him an argument, but then she let her head fall back against the headrest, and her arms fell limply to her sides. "Well, if I'm not going to smoke, I've got to eat. I think it's the first time I've visited Selma and she hasn't offered me any food." She laughed ruefully. "I hate to say it, but I think I'm a little jealous. It looks like Selma and Edith have made up for good."

"No doubt about it." Terry leaned forward in her seat, caught Ben's eye in the rear-view mirror, then said chirpily, "You know what, guys? I'm so bushed, I couldn't eat a thing. I spent the whole damned morning trying to put some order back into my files. I think every one of them spilled out after the quake, and I need to find some of my old stuff for the Plan." She yawned theatrically, patting her hand against her mouth a few times.

Jesus, Ben thought, she's about the shittiest actress I've ever seen.

Terry went on. "Can you just drop me off and then get a bite? I hate to flake on you, but I'm pooped."

Out of the corner of his eye, Ben saw Ariel skew around in her seat to throw Terry a dirty look.

As soon as they pulled up to her Mar Vista apartment, Terry grabbed her sweater and handbag. She yelled back at Ariel, "Call me," as she rushed away from the car.

Okay, this was it. Ben knew he couldn't afford to hold back a minute longer. One hand still on the steering wheel, he turned toward Ariel with a startling suddenness. She looked so apprehensive that he could hardly bear it. But he didn't dare let this moment pass.

"So what is it to be then, Ariel? Back to your apartment so you and Jezzie can chow down together in front of the idiot box? You know it well. You've done it a million times. Or is the woman who went to hell and back trying to touch Eve's bones willing to take her chance on a fool like me?"

Her face went blank, as if she were determined to stay blind to where he was leading the conversation. "What do you mean?"

"I mean, I can't keep my life on hold forever. What I'm trying to achieve out here, well, it's just too damned hard to do it alone. I can go back to Iowa, teach drama to high school kids and grow old and fat on my memories. Or I can do what I really want—take you to dinner, bring you home, fuck your brains out, and be with you as long as you'll let me." He could hear his voice quaver as she regarded him with obvious disbelief, but still he went on. "It's never been over for me, Ariel. You're not an easy woman." He paused. "Actually, you're the most difficult woman I've ever met. But this time apart has nearly killed me. I'm in love with you. You've got to know that."

She just sat there, gaping at him, and his hands were still shaking embarrassingly, but he wasn't going anywhere till he had an answer.

She started to speak, but then seemed to choke on her own spit. She coughed for what felt like an eternity, rolled her eyes and started again. "As always," she said, "Miss Elegance itself."

He waited, refusing to drop his gaze. He was aware of the pulse beat, loud in his ears.

She sighed, and then—like someone waking up muzzily in the morning to the all-consuming need to stretch her limbs—she reached her arms over her head as far as the car roof would permit, walking her fingertips along its beige cloth ceiling. Slowly, she turned to face him.

"You mean it?" she said helplessly, her hands pressed to her cheeks. "I thought we—I was such an idiot. I don't believe you can just forgive my stupidity. I've been so ashamed." She flushed. "Oh, hell, this is too weird."

He almost burst into laughter, but asserted control over himself.

"Well, if you really mean it." She shot him an accusing look. "Do you realize you never said it?" She met his staring eyes. "You're right. I didn't either." She made an anxious grimace and sighed, adding almost reluctantly, "I love you, too."

As he pulled her to him, she murmured gruffly into his hair. "But I'm still starving. Where do you want to eat?"

"Shut up," he said, pressing his lips against hers.

They forgot about food and rushed back to Ariel's apartment instead, shutting a surprisingly compliant Jezzie out of the bedroom.

———————

When Ben lay down next to her, stroking her torso with silken tenderness, Ariel felt something inside just open up and let go.

She trembled as he traced the contours and hollows of her limbs, her nipples hardening with a sweet ache as he teased them with the tip of his tongue. Only when he moved his hand from her breasts down toward her thighs did she halt the momentum. She had her period and felt embarrassed to go any further. He didn't care.

After he'd conquered every folded recess of her with his determined urgency, after she'd experienced an orgasm with him inside her, something so intense that she was shocked over what she'd been missing all these years, he'd taken his finger and playfully run a horizontal line of her own menstrual blood across her forehead. She was overtaken by a torrent of tears. And he just held her. It was as if a lifetime's cargo load was landing, as if his heart were an expandable runway that kept opening up more and more ground beneath her as long as she needed it, until her sorely grieving spirit could come to rest.

Finally, with a few trembling hiccups of sound, she was silent. Ben plucked a tissue from a floral box on the side table. She accepted it from him without a word and blew her nose with comfortable gusto. She knew her face probably looked red and swollen, but Ben kept looking at her as if he'd discovered the Holy Grail.

Just then, a plaintive cry punctuated the silence from the other side of the bedroom door. Ariel raised a quizzical eyebrow and Ben nodded, an expression of mock-resignation on his face. She rose up from the bed to let Jezzie into the room.

It took her love-slowed mind a few seconds to catch up with itself. For one startling moment, she had the sense of another female's presence beside her, a woman whose sumptuous curves swayed as she strode with a primal swagger toward the door. Naked as a jay, big-assed and even bigger-breasted, with a generously curved belly that looked like it could expand readily to carry untold generations. Her face fit her body; it looked like somebody lived there, with the beginnings of finely-etched laugh creases at the outer corners of her honest brown eyes, and a streak of dried blood like a ritual marking on her forehead, emphasizing the vertical line of deep thought beginning to bisect her brows. This was no stranger. She'd been here all along. Ariel had just a moment to recognize her own lips curve upwards in a surprised but delighted grin—reflected back to her in the full-length mirror mounted on the bedroom door—before she turned the knob to let Jezzie in.

Jezebel jumped onto the bed right after Ariel. The cat stretched out shamelessly on her back between her and Ben, purring like a house afire as the two of them stroked her chin, her ears, her luxuriantly soft white belly.

Ariel stopped and considered Ben with frankly curious eyes. Yes, she decided, there was no doubt about it. He'd shaken her world when it had needed some serious shaking. Was it possible they could move through a lifetime of changes together? She knew she'd betray herself if she didn't at least try. When he met her gaze, she held it. Reveled in it. It didn't even occur to her to look away.

Acknowledgements

My kids and grandchildren Chris, Claire, Tray, Tahlia, and Braden are as essential to me as the air that I breathe; each of them, my dear friends, and my extended family on both sides of the pond have helped keep this writer's spirit engaged and alive.

On its way to publication, a book goes through many incarnations. My publisher Melinda Clayton has continued to be an absolute godsend of know-how, patience, and support, and I owe a particular debt of gratitude to my son Chris for going over every word with a fine-toothed comb. The artist Holly Heath, whom I befriended on Facebook because I was convinced she was a relative, became soul kin as she created the striking image for the book's cover.

In the 1980s, Janine Sieja—at that time UCLA Public Information Officer serving under the late Randy Cook, Chief Engineer and Utilities Manager—gave me a private tour of the hidden arteries of UCLA's infrastructure. Much of what I saw in that dark and magical world I've recorded in this story, and I'm deeply grateful to Randy and Janine for generously affording me that subterranean adventure.

Flight instructor Marc Grillo gave me a taste of what it takes for humans to master what birds know by instinct, and he filled me with great respect for the sorts of flying conditions that make piloting a courageous calling, a science, and an art.

I have the Anthropology Department of UCLA, host of my first college major, to thank for introducing me to what fossil remains can teach us, not only about those who went before us, but what makes us who we are today. The Eve bones in this novel are fictional—an amalgam of finds over the past forty-five years, amplified by the fantasies of Ariel Thompkins and myself. For the purposes of fiction, I've played rather freely with the theory of the Mitochondrial Eve that arose from the early work of Allan Wilson, Mark Stoneking, and Rebecca L. Dann on molecular approaches to human evolution. But the basic premise of an unbroken line of matrilineal descent still holds.

If there was ever a time when we as a species needed to acknowledge our kinship with one another, it's now. In this book, I've hoped to convey how the lives of strangers intersect with our own in ways both known and unknown to us. Characters are often a novelist's greatest teachers; Ariel and her companions have reminded me that, while we're each solo acts in so many ways, we're deeply connected at the root and down to the bone.

About the Author

Sharon Heath writes fiction and non-fiction exploring the interplay of science and spirit, politics and pop culture. A certified Jungian Analyst in private practice and faculty member of the C.G. Jung Institute of Los Angeles, she served as Guest Editor of the special issue of *Psychological Perspectives,* "The Child Within/The Child Without." Her chapter "The Church of Her Body" appears in the anthology *Marked by Fire: Stories of the Jungian Way,* and her chapter "A Jungian Alice in Social Media Land: Some Reflections on Solastalgia, Kinship Libido, and Tribes Formed on Facebook" is included in *Depth Psychology and the Digital Age.* She has blogged for *The Huffington Post* and *TerraSpheres* and has given talks in the United States and Canada on topics ranging from the place of soul in social media to gossip, envy, secrecy, and belonging. She maintains her own blog at www.sharonheath.com.

More Novels from Sharon Heath

The History of My Body
The Fleur Trilogy Book 1

Tizita
The Fleur Trilogy Book 2

Return of the Butterfly
The Fleur Trilogy Book 3